Book III of the Clan Elves of the Bitterroot

The Elf Mage

Lyndi Alexander

Fantasy Novel Published by
Dragonfly Publishing, Inc.

THE ELF MAGE

Clan Elves of the Bitterroot (Book III)
Urban Fantasy

Paperback Edition
EAN 978-1-936381-35-7
ISBN 1-936381-35-4

Story Text Copyright ©2011 Barbara Mountjoy
Cover Art Copyright ©2011 Dragonfly Publishing, Inc.
Dragonfly Logo Copyright ©2001 Terri L. Branson

Published in the United States of America by
Dragonfly Publishing, Inc.
Website: www.dragonflypubs.com

For my favorite geek, who made this book possible.

Acknowledgements

With deepest thanks to my Pennwriters critique group. You are the best! It would be hard to keep producing stories without your support and sincere work and comments.

A special thank you to my critique partner Jean, whose purple pen gave its lifeblood to comment on this volume. You make me a better writer, and I appreciate it. [And, yes, I'll buy you another purple pen.]

Thanks, too, to my beta readers, Debbie, Pam and especially former Zooville resident Linda Caler, who proofed us for all the local references, even the zombies!

I also appreciate the comments and letters of those who are reading the series. Your support really inspires me to keep it going!

Thank you to Terri Branson, who is more than just my publisher, but also a fan of these stories and their motley crew of characters. Thanks for sharing my vision and letting me share it with the world.

Most of all, I want to thank my husband Eric for all his work in collaborating, critiquing, mapping, charting, planning, reading and rereading these chapters, especially without stabbing me when I keep asking all those questions. It's better that way.

Clan Elves of the Bitterroot Series:

The Elf Queen
[Book I]

The Elf Child
[Book II]

The Elf Mage
[Book III]

Special Terms

ELVISH DICTIONARY:
Denami: *Beloved*
Elder: *Elves alive during the schism*
Idan: *Magical Element*
Idellan: *Balance of the six mages/powers*
Intalus: *Elven Mage*
Lelan: *The Clan, the People*
Nian: *Male elf*
Neris: *Female elf*
Santwarja: *Realm where mages train*
Younger: *Elves born after the schism*

ONLINE GAMER TERMS:
BSOD: *Blue Screen of Death*
DoTs: *Damage over Time*
PvP: *Player versus Player*
Toon: *Game Avatar*
MMORPG: *Massive Multiplayer Online Role Playing Game*

CHAPTER 1

DAVEN Talvi awoke to blackness.

His head hurt. His cheek lay against the cool soil floor. The air was still and silent. Too silent.

As he pushed himself upright, his left foot kicked a chair. The screech of wood on wood echoed in the darkness.

"*Daggaha*," he whispered.

Lights powered by elven enchantment flared into existence. He was inside the queen's tree house, the place he had built for her with his own magic.

The last moments before unconsciousness filtered into his mind. His son Astan had been there. Elf Queen Jelani stood by the table, tearful, angry, and accusatory. Astan and Jelani's child was missing. Jelani blamed Daven. Astan attacked Daven with a chair. Daven struggled to remember more.

It wasn't my fault.

Leaning on Jelani's handcrafted bentwood rocking chair, Daven got to his feet. The change in altitude from the floor made his head throb. He took a drink of spring water from the hollowed gourd on the side bench. Laying a hand at the base of his skull, he marshaled his healing powers to control the pain enough to allow him to think.

Astan, it wasn't my fault.

At the time the child was taken, Daven had been with the Circle, the ruling body of their elf clan hidden away in a forest glade of the Bitterroot Mountains in the land the humans called Montana. Daven had assured the matriarchs of the Circle that, though Jelani's behavior might seem somewhat erratic and overly possessive of her son Elliun, such actions were reasonable in a new mother, particularly one who was half-human. The infusion of human blood into the clan rattled many traditions and expectations, bringing effects both good and bad. The old *neris*, wise females of the clan, agreed not to remove Elliun from the queen's care.

I did everything I could to help you.

Astan had followed Daven to the meeting of the Elders, leaving Jelani at the tree house with her human friends. The queen and her child had been easy targets.

Grigor seemed the most likely culprit. Since the queen had come to live in the forest with the clan, Astan had often voiced concern that the banished Grigor would return to avenge his dead master, Bartolomey. Daven counseled his son not to take action, but to wait and watch. Although Astan had disagreed, he had obeyed his father as duty required.

And look what that has brought me.

Had Daven underestimated the evil Grigor held within him? A sense of blackness still pervaded the atmosphere inside the queen's home. As a full-blood elf well trained in the ways of divination, Daven perceived several mental voices lingering, several personas who left behind the barest impression of menace and ill will.

Something about that felt familiar to Daven. Something he had not felt for many years. Something so vague he could not put a name to it. Yet. But he would.

At one time Jelani and Astan had asked him to set a protective spell on the door, something to keep out uninvited guests. But he had refused. The Circle worried that Jelani would use the spell to keep them from the elf child. Instead, Daven's omission may have enabled someone to take the infant who was so dear to them all.

I failed you, Jelani. I failed you.

He had lost so many who were close to him in his service to the elf clan. Friends and family. Astan's mother, Veraena. Each loss carved a small chink from his determination to persevere for the greater good. The chinks added up. Knowing this tragedy could be laid at his door broke Daven's strong heart.

The hearth fire was cold in more ways than one. It was too late to join the search for the elf child now. Daven's fate lay on a different path.

He took a small sack of runes from his pocket. "Lady of the Forest, show me the way. I need your guidance."

For several reverent moments, he held the woven brown bag in his hands. Then he plucked five runes from it. Shoving aside balls of yellow yarn and the remains of cake, he laid the small colored stones on the table and assessed the import of each singly and in combination with the others.

The first stone, *kala*, foretold betrayal.

The next, *pag*, division, separation.

The third, *daka*, the Outcast.

The fourth, *les*, the Great Battle.

And the last, *gran*, a champion, but a champion with a shadow on him, one who did not know fate had chosen him.

Daven stared at the sinister forecast for several long seconds before he picked up the runes and returned them to the bag. Dark times awaited the clan. He must retreat to clear his mind and set his path straight once again.

Somehow he had lost his way, failed to choose the true lines of responsibility. He saw this now. A deep breath cleared his system and drove him toward the door. His duty was to correct the mistakes he made.

"My pride, my mistakes, my fault, Astan. I will make it up to you. I will bring your son home. I swear it."

Daven opened the door. As he stepped outside, snow blew in his face and wind whipped through the trees around him.

He hesitated, wanting to tell the others he was leaving. Jelani's human friend Iris, the pretty blonde social worker, awaited him back in his tree dwelling. But he could not stop to bid her goodbye. That would only create complications. She would find out about his actions soon enough. Perhaps she would not forgive him for the hurt he brought to Jelani. She would find her way back to the city. She did not need him for that. Perhaps none of them needed him. Better to begin.

Daven broke into a run, passing lightly over the snow and headed north, away from the clan grounds and everything he knew, praying he would find a path to redemption.

CHAPTER 2

OUT of breath, her ribs aching, Jelani dug in her coat pocket to make sure she still had the deed her father had left her. The paper transferring ownership of the old cabin to her was still there.

The wind rustled the pine branches overhead, the moonlight creating ghostly shadows around them. Astan stood behind her in shin-deep snow, half turned away with his gaze on the forest.

"Hurry," Astan scolded. "I want to make sure we're safe before...."

"Before what?" Jelani growled, five-foot and three-inches of furious elf queen. "Before you just leave me here to get yourself killed? We just ran, what, twelve miles, to get here from the famous secret home of the wretched Bitterroot elves? After they've taken our son?" She paused to catch her breath. "And the best plan you can come up with is 'I have to save Elliun because I'm the man'. Really?"

"Open the damned door," Astan snapped. He stamped his feet to knock snow off his boots. "I'm not going to discuss this out here. I'd unlock it, but you've got the enchanted paper."

"Fine!" Jelani reached for the lock that held the door closed. It shook loose easily in her grasp.

She stepped inside, allowing Astan to follow, and then closed the door behind them. They shrugged off coats, boots, and other wet gear, dropping them on the floor. The cabin's single fifteen-foot square room was lit by a shaft of moonlight raining in through one dusty window.

Shivering, Jelani dug a flashlight out of a chest of drawers and flicked its button. As she moved the beam around the room, their breaths appeared as frosty vapor.

"Crispy was the last one up here," Jelani said. "He must have used the space heater. I wonder where he put it?"

"How should I know?" Astan took the sting out of his words with a raised hand of apology and started looking behind furniture for the gas-powered heater.

Jelani bit back the hateful retort. It wasn't Astan she was angry with. She went to the small counter that served as a kitchen and dug a propane camp stove from under the sink. The whiff of gas as she struck the match nauseated her. The day seemed overly long. Usually she was asleep at this hour. But she wasn't sleepy. Would she ever sleep again?

"Here it is," Astan said. He pulled the dome-like heater into the middle of the room and knelt down to click the self-starter. After three attempts, it finally caught.

Reaching into the same cabinet where she found the stove, she pulled out a gallon of bottled water. Cracking open the seal, she poured enough in a small saucepan for two cups of tea. Then silence set in. So much to say, but she didn't dare start.

Astan paced. He said nothing.

They had escaped the doomed tree house carrying only what they needed and leaving Astan's father crumpled on the floor like last week's garbage. The one thing they both wanted most in the world was no longer there, their three-week-old son Elliun.

In their search for the kidnappers, the only tracks they had found were those of Lane and Crispy heading back to Lane's old truck. Since elves in motion left almost no trail, Astan had followed a disturbance in the top layer of the snow for several minutes. The only result had been tripping a couple of booby traps that dropped several bushels of heavy white snow on Jelani, knocking her to the ground.

"I can't keep you safe and hunt at the same time," Astan had muttered with a defeated look.

Changing direction, they had arrived at her cabin.

The journey had been long through the dark of night, filled with tears, self-recrimination, and angry words. Sometimes the words were directed toward each other, sometimes at the evil ones, and sometimes at the cruelty of fate. The last plan Astan had suggested was for Jelani to remain safely hidden. Since no one could enter the cabin without her express invitation, that would leave Astan to track Grigor and his fellow criminals.

But Jelani Marsh had no intention of being left behind.

Jelani had only known Astan a matter of months, a tempestuous span during which each discovered a hidden past and mysteries concealed by well-meaning families. Jelani, revealed as the love child of the previous elf queen Linnea and Vincent Marsh, accepted her place as the new clan leader, but not without experiencing a few large bumps in the road.

Astan had learned he was no orphan, as his father Daven Talvi returned from an enchanted sleep to help save the old elf queen and then to serve the new one. Astan understood Jelani's tenacity and her love for their son, despite the odd circumstances of his conception and birth. She would fight for Elliun to the death.

But how would they find him?

Jelani puzzled over that question. Holding cold hands near the edge of the cook stove's blue flame, she stared at the water. Bubbles churned the surface in the small pan, and steam rose above it. Behind her, the hiss of the heater preceded a gradual feeling of warmth. Her arms ached to hold Elliun. Eyes filling with tears, she turned off the burner and poured water into the cups. She sensed Astan behind her just before his arms encircled her waist, pulling her close to him.

"We'll find him, *denami*," Astan said.

The emotions that swirled in Jelani's gut lay far from his comforting reassurances. Her instincts cried out for violence. "And we'll find Grigor. Just long enough to destroy him for real this time."

"Grigor will die for this." Astan's voice in her ear held an edge of cold ice. He held her close for a brief moment and then released her. Opening a drawer, he pulled out prepackaged tea bags and dropped one into each cup. "I should have taken action when I realized Fontine was still his mate and was still helping him. I shouldn't have listened to my father."

Jelani's breath caught. "Neither of us should have. Who knows what other damage he has caused on behalf of the damned Circle?" She handed one cup to him, and took the other for herself, wrapping her fingers around it for warmth. "Fontine, though. Do you know where to find her?"

"Now that Grigor and his companions have acted, they are likely hiding somewhere they believe cannot be detected. I doubt she would have the courage to face any in the clan again once they realized her complicity in this."

Jelani searched her memory. "Who among the clan has the gift of finding other elves? There must be someone!"

He stared into his steaming cup. "Perhaps Daven. Or the midwife who birthed Elliun might still have some connection."

"Daven's out." She frowned. A shadow outside the cabin's single dusty window caught her attention, and she hurried over to see what moved. It was only a deer nibbling on the sparse greenery of a nearby pine. "But the midwife? Would Rashia be able to sense where he might be?"

Alerted by her attention, Astan moved aside where he could keep watch out the window. "Elliun's different, *denami*. From the moment he came into existence, nothing about him has been normal. I can't say."

She was already shaking her head. "I'm not going back to the Circle for help, not unless we have no other choice. Those witches got me pregnant—"

"We did that, Jelani. They may have interfered with the conception, but Elliun is all ours. We have responsibility for him. Not Daven. Not the Circle. No one else except us." His dark eyes shone with emotion. "And we will find him."

Astan's voice was full of conviction and Jelani believed him with all her heart. Their bond was such that each could often read the other's thoughts, as was often true with elven pairings. She trusted him like no one else she knew. Of course, she trusted Lane, Crispy, and Iris. But when it came to elves, there was only one she trusted. Astan.

"We should find dry clothes," Jelani murmured. She drained her already-cooling cup of tea, before she began rummaging through the drawers of the tall oak chest that once belonged to her father. None of the pants would fit either of them. Her father had been a larger man. But she found two plaid flannel shirts and some dry socks. That would have to do.

It took a few minutes to change in the now-lukewarm air of the cabin. Then they put on their coats and boots again and headed out into the woods.

* * *

HOURS later, the sun now up over the horizon, they were cold and soaked through again.

Astan had picked up something with what Jelani called his flash-sense. His elven gift constituted the ability to take bits of any situation, even those seemingly unrelated, and construct the true nature of it. The revelations came to him in flashes, pictures, insights, combined with gut instinct that let him understand the whole image. They had just crossed a small creek when Astan held up his hand to stop.

"Wait," he said. He stared down at a pattern in the wet rocks under a layer of ice. Several pairs of feet crossed there. As light as elf steps were, they could still disturb the ground beneath them. He closed his eyes a moment, thinking of Grigor and Fontine and Yadin and the others. *Flick*. Running, carrying a small bundle, something. *Flick*. Running. But to where?

Toward the deep part of the woods. The same direction Fontine had taken the day Daven confessed that she was going to meet Grigor and that he knew of her actions all along.

"This way," he said, grabbing Jelani's hand. "They went this way!"

He felt her fatigue through the woolen gloves she wore, read it on her face. As of yet, she was not recovered from the contrived pregnancy. Her human side not completely adapted to the elven ways. But her determination shone bright in her eyes. She would not give up.

They ran, Astan stopping periodically to regain his bearings on Grigor's trail. The path led from the elf clan's forest home to the northeast, away from the city of Missoula into the Mission Mountains. They traveled another mile or more before a sudden change in the wind brought them to a halt.

"Something happened here," Astan said.

He pointed out several sets of footprints. Someone had paused there long enough to make a permanent mark in passing. He hunkered down, studying the scene.

"This way," Jelani said, pointing out a light trail that led to the west into the trees.

Astan shook his head. "This way, too." He showed her another trail that went north.

She chewed her chapped lip, rocking a little from foot to foot. "Do you think one's a fake? Intended to throw us off?"

"No. Something else is going on." Astan walked a little way down each of the two paths, sensing elf presence on both. Surely, Grigor had taken one of these trails, but which one?

If only I possessed Daven's skills, Astan thought. *Damn him for betraying us.*

"What then? We can't just stand here! Elliun is getting farther and farther away." She stamped her foot.

He cleared his mind and tried to sense an answer, but nothing came. Two trails, no truths. He chose the one that seemed to lead away from the original destination. Something happened here to change the path. Whatever it was, it would give them an answer.

"Come on, *denami*. It won't be long now," he promised, praying to the wind he wasn't just speaking empty words.

She stayed close behind him, dodging trees and piles of snow.

Astan scanned for any sign their child or his captor had passed this way. Nothing for the first few minutes. Then he saw a drop of red on the white snow, followed by another and another.

Jelani gasped. "Is that blood?" She stumbled into a tree, banging her shoulder on the trunk.

He helped her upright, his throat closing at their shared thought. Blood. Was it their child's?

Astan and Jelani followed a short trail through the snow. It ended at a bloodied body. But it wasn't their son. Grigor Biren lay tangled in a bear trap, pale, and dead.

Stunned, Astan and Jelani stared for several minutes. This had been their one hope. That they would find their child *with* Grigor. But though they searched all around, they found no trace of Elliun, no indication he had ever been there.

"This is wrong." Jelani stared down at the elf who betrayed them more than once. "This doesn't feel like an accident."

Astan nodded in agreement. "Grigor was smarter than this. Even weakened from living apart from the clan, he would have stepped much more lightly than this. His steps would not have set off the trap. This was murder."

"Was he alone?" Jelani whispered.

"I can't see. No other trails lead from here." Astan looked back they way they had come. Their passage along the trail was already snow-covered. It was too late.

"A dead end," she said. Her voice broke. Choked with tears, she threw herself into his arms. "A dead end."

"If we return to the cabin, Daven may lead the Circle there." Astan's heart filled with emotion, but he could not seem to release it. Instead it grew cold and hard.

They had found all the answers they could here. He glanced down at Grigor's body, knowing it would be proper to return it to the soil. But would the soil reject it?

Jelani nodded against his shoulder. "I want to go home."

"Back to the clan? Why?"

"Not to the clan," she said, her tone dripping hatred. "Home. To Missoula. Lane will know what to do."

"Lane?" Astan sighed. He did not want to depend on Jelani's human friends, but Lane Donatelli had proven himself to be an honest man who could be trusted. With some luck, and the good graces of the soil, Jelani would be safe there. Putting all their heads together, they should be able to figure out what to do next.

Stay safe, little Elliun. We will come for you.

Hoping his small thought reached his infant son, hoping it would bring him comfort, Astan took his mate by the hand and began the long journey back to Missoula.

CHAPTER 3

IN the five years he and his roommate Ron "Crispy" Mendell lived in their second floor apartment, Lane Donatelli had never found the place too small.

In fact he built the Cave, his getaway, four computers ensconced in a space enclosed by walls constructed from an assortment of cardboard boxes, crates and storage bins, to have an even smaller and more secure space to feel 'at home' in. But suddenly the whole apartment seemed practically microscopic. Or at least not soundproof enough. He couldn't get a thing done, and his head hurt.

"Oy. And this seemed like such a good idea." The pudgy computer geek shoved himself out of his wheeled office chair, and left the Cave in search of the bottle of ibuprofen. Again. "What's the matter this time, Crispy?"

"I'm handling it." Crispy's thin fingers tapped out a nervous rhythm on the kitchen countertop. His bangs hung in his face, hiding his dark eyes from view. Two old T-shirts, layered, both black and long sleeved, served to keep him warm, and his jeans had seen better days back before the turn of the century. Crispy slouched in front of the old electric stove, staring at the saucepan on the front left burner.

"Yeah, I can hear that." Lane groaned and popped open the lid of the childproof bottle with his thumb. He dumped four pills into his hand and then into his mouth, grabbing a bottle of juice from the refrigerator to wash them down.

Crispy didn't turn around. "You can't put that bottle back now that you drank out of it."

"Of course I can. After all the time we've lived together, we can't possibly have a germ that the other one doesn't have. I mean, seriously, Crisp? Seriously?" Lane polished his glasses with the hem of his worn Serenity T-shirt.

"We have to be extra careful about germs now."

Lane groaned again. "Crisp, I swear to God—"

His roommate and former foster brother was saved from any further threat by a knock at the door. "Coming!" Lane called. He ignored Crispy's mild protest that the knock was not a proper signal and went down the short hall to answer it.

Outside he found Kevin Briscoll, owner of the computer store on the first floor of the building and fellow online gamer. The young, black Afghanistan veteran, a large box cradled in his left arm, paused with his hand still up, ready to knock again. Kevin wore his leg brace over denim jeans so stiff they looked new. He must be having a bad day, Lane thought, what with the erratic temperatures forecast for the early February thaw.

"Hey, Lane."

"Kev! Come in! Man, you should have called. I woulda come down and saved you the steps." He stepped aside so Kevin could skinny past him. Fortunately, Kevin kept himself in military trim. On the other hand, Lane's longstanding love affair with Creamy Cupcakes kept him mostly round.

Kevin continued into the kitchen. "What's that noise? I thought you took that hawk back to the forest?"

Lane swallowed hard. "Oh, the hawk. Yeah. Yeah, we did." He wandered back into the small living room where Crispy sat curled into the corner of the brown Salvation-Army couch.

"That's a—" Kevin blinked as he leaned on the counter.

"Yep. That's a baby." Lane smiled at little Elliun.

He was snuggled into Crispy's arms, both hands grasping the bottle just warmed for him. Elliun's blue fleece sleeper was zipped all the way to his chin, but Crispy still insisted on wrapping him in a knit blanket, too. Just in case.

Kevin put down the box he was holding and walked into the living room, staring. "Where did you get a baby?" Each word dropped like heavy stones of accusation. He glanced first at the door, then to the webcam at the edge of the Cave. "Are we going to have police on the doorstep?"

"Not likely." Lane sighed. "We're just babysitting."

"Babysitting." Kevin's dry tone was laced with skepticism. "Really?"

"At least I hope so."

Satisfied Crispy was meeting the child's needs, Lane leaned against the doorframe into the kitchen. Satisfied Crispy was meeting the child's needs, Lane leaned against the doorframe to the kitchen. *Babysitting* wasn't really the right word. *Kidnapping*, now that was more accurate, in a legal sense. For the baby's sake, he had to take him, before something bad happened.

Lane had not gone to Jelani's tree house with the intention of kidnapping Elliun. Really, the thought never crossed his mind. Then Jelani had gone crazy with that gun. Watching her wave it around, even shooting the ceiling, made Lane flash back to the frightening days of his childhood. When his angry drunken mother yelled "Delano Marco Donatelli, get your ass in here," he wondered if she had the belt with the buckle that left such ragged marks or a loaded gun. Either way, he knew to get as far away as he could as quickly as possible.

His mother never actually shot anyone, as far as he knew, but the walls and ceiling were peppered with holes from all the near misses. He never knew who reported her to the authorities. It wasn't him. He was never courageous enough to stand against her. After the foster care worker removed him, the court ordered her to rehab, but she told them to screw themselves. So Lane never went home again.

He had gone into the nursery to retrieve his computer bag, but the sight of Elliun brought on the powerful flashback. He did not stop to think. Instead he acted. It was up to him to save the baby. He wrapped the sleeping child up warm and tucked him inside his computer bag. Then he said goodbye to Jelani, as if everything was fine, even though it wasn't.

Crispy suspected, but said nothing until they got in the truck. Then he turned into the perfect little mother, tending to Elliun's every need. But that did not keep the little one from crying. It had been less than a week, but the noise and need of the baby grated on Lane's nerves.

More ibuprofen, please.

"Seriously, Lane. Isn't that your friend's baby? How long are you keeping it?"

Crispy looked up, a Madonna-like smile on his face. "Until he's safe. Everyone needs to be safe. You know that. You were a soldier."

A furrow developed between Kevin's thin brows. "Well, I can't argue with you, Crisp. Everyone sure does need to be safe. It's just really peculiar." He inched closer to the couch. "He's a handsome little guy."

"Takes after his Uncle Lane." Lane grinned. "So, what's in the box?"

"Couple of things I was going to throw out, but I thought you might like them." Kevin grabbed the box and hauled it into the living room. "This laptop wouldn't boot. Guess you could use it for parts. I tore up this router when the Wolf overloaded." He tossed a few small parts to Lane. "A flash drive someone left at the shop. I'm not responsible for what's on it. And I think there's some memory chips in there too. Oh, and a PDA someone traded in last week."

"Oh, great! I left mine when I bailed at Jelani's." Lane pawed through the contents with a smile on his face. "Just like Christmas!"

"It's too late for Christmas. Maybe Valentine's Day," Crispy scolded. "Maybe Kevin loves you."

Kevin whirled around. "I what?"

"Don't mind him." Lane closed the box lid. "I'll take it all, thanks. You want something to drink? Tea? Juice?"

"No, thanks." Kevin took a seat at the opposite end of the couch from Crispy, who was burping the baby. "You look like you know what you're doing."

"Ehow.com," Lane said. "They also have a page on how to change a diaper and how to mix formula."

Kevin laughed. "I guess I never looked it up. I had plenty of brothers, aunts, uncles and cousins. We did it all by watching. You want to know how to put a baby to sleep?"

"We learned that on WikiHow," Crispy said. "They even have a video."

"Unbelievable." Kevin shook his head. "Do you think I could hold him?"

Crispy looked suspiciously at Kevin. "Do you have baby credentials?"

"Probably more than you do, Crisp," Lane said. "Go ahead. It'll be fine."

Elliun went to Kevin without a peep, studying his dark face curiously. He reached out to touch Kevin's skin and then broke into a smile.

"He's so focused, it's weird," Kevin said.

"He's way ahead of all the milestones, according to the online charts," Crispy said.

"Probably magic," Lane interjected. "All that elf blood mixed with caffeine. Who the hell knows?"

A knock at the door sent them all into shocked silence. Crispy hid his head behind a green sofa pillow. "The government's here! Your camera told them we're criminals!"

"It can't do that, Crisp," Lane said. He glanced at the Cave, unsure for a moment. Had Astan whammied the webcam for real? Would Jelani report him? Could he go to jail? He broke out in a sweat.

Another more urgent knock echoed.

Kevin, holding the baby, eyed Lane. "Are you going to answer that?"

Lane looked over his shoulder at the door. "Do I have to?"

Suddenly, the door opened. Lane remembered belatedly he hadn't used the chain lock. He turned to face the door, blocking those in the living room from the view of the intruder. But it wasn't the police. It was Iris Pallaton.

Iris looked terrible. Her blonde hair was uncombed and wild, her face dirt-streaked. Her clothing, usually immaculate and color-coordinated, was disheveled. She took several steps inside the door and started to cry.

"Iris, honey, what's the matter?" Lane lumbered over to put his arms around her.

"Oh, my God, the world's come to an end. The elf clan is destroyed. Grigor took the baby. Daven's gone. And Jelani's missing, too."

"Jelly Bean's missing?" Lane stepped back, holding Iris by her shoulders. "What do you mean, Jelly's missing? Where did she go?"

Iris sniffed and wiped her face with the back of her mismatched glove. "I don't know. I waited a couple of days to see if they'd come back. They're gone. All of them."

The pain in her voice struck at Lane's heart like a stiletto.

"Not all," Lane said, his voice cracking.

Keeping his arm around Iris' shoulder, he locked the door and then led her into the living room. When she saw the baby, she actually screamed.

Crispy covered his ears and hunched into the corner of the couch.

Kevin nearly dropped the baby.

Lane shushed Iris. *Please, by all that's holy, by Grapthar's Hammer even, don't let that child start crying again.*

"Is t-that Elliun?" Iris' knees buckled. "You h-have Elliun?"

Lane caught Iris before she hit the ground. Kevin jumped up and Lane helped her onto the couch.

"We have no smelling salts," Crispy observed.

"Is he all right?" Iris whispered, her eyes filling with tears again. "He's not dead? He's safe? Sweet Goddess, thank you."

"He's fine," Kevin said, holding the baby out to her. "See for yourself."

Iris took the baby and squeezed him close to her, cuddling him. "Thank you, thank you, thank you." She kissed Elliun's round cheeks and smoothed his hair. "What a blessing."

Lane pulled a chair over from their small dining table and sat next to her. "So wait, now. Who did you say had the baby?"

"Grigor Biren. He took—well, they thought he took the baby for revenge against Jelani."

"One of old Black Bart's guys? I thought they were all outcast."

"He was. But apparently several of the Youngers conspired with him to take Elliun and bring down the new elf queen." Iris could not take her eyes off the baby.

"And here I thought the witches would be the culprits." Lane leaned back in his chair until it creaked in protest. "Astan was more worried about them, I think."

"Where is Jelani?" Crispy whispered.

Iris must have realized that she had alarmed them, because she took a deep breath and pulled herself together. "No one knows. I woke up alone at Daven's. When I went looking for him, I found Djana and the others of the Circle, all confused as hell. The tree house was trashed inside. Someone had heard Daven and Astan arguing. Astan blamed Grigor for attacking Jelani and taking the baby. But they were all gone."

"Someone attacked Jelani?" Lane asked. "Is she all right?"

"No one knew. Or where this little guy was." She cuddled the baby close again. "I was so sick worrying about him. You have no idea. Did Jelani ask you to take him?"

"Um, not exactly." Lane fidgeted, the chair squealing again.

Her face registered surprise for a moment, before she nodded emphatically. "It's a blessing. I think you did the right thing."

Lane became aware of Kevin's expression of horror, as he took in all the drama.

"Come on, son," Lane scolded. "Put your tongue back in your mouth and take a chair. This is normal around here."

Kevin shook himself a little. "Normal? Missing people? Stolen babies? Pregnancy potions? Wizards, spells, elves? You've got to be kidding."

"Does sound a bit like the game, doesn't it?" Lane forced a smile. "Crisp, why don't you make some chai? We need some sustenance and energy. And maybe a cupcake."

Crispy nodded and slipped out to the kitchen.

"And Daven?" Lane asked. "Just gone? He didn't even say goodbye?"

Iris shook her head, her eyes filling with unshed tears. "I don't know if he went after them. Everything was scattered in the tree house, as if there was some sort of fight. And there was blood on the floor." She bit her lips, as if to stop any more words from coming out.

"Blood." Crispy came to the pass-through, his eyes huge and

hands shaking.

A cold emptiness formed inside Lane. He felt disoriented. Everything was going wrong. Even Iris, usually the quiet strength of their little band, was headed toward a slow disintegration.

But maybe Iris was right. Maybe Lane had saved Jelani's son, even if he had not saved Jelani. Wait. What was he thinking? That Jelani was dead? Astan would never have let that happen. Never. Even slimy used-car salesman Daven would have protected the queen with his own life. So whose blood was it? And what were they going to do about it?

"You know, Lane, I would be glad to go out and take a look," Kevin offered. "You could come with me, while Crispy and Iris stay here with the baby."

Another knock at the door brought the room silent again. They turned as one to look down the hallway.

"I locked the door," Lane said. "They can't get in."

"Are you expecting anyone?" Iris asked.

"No."

They stared a few more seconds.

"It could be someone with news," Kevin said. "We should open it." When none of them moved, he took the first steps toward the door. "I'll open it." He inched down the hallway, visibly steeling himself before he turned the door handle.

Lane stood and placed himself between the door and Iris, who was still holding Elliun. Any bad guys would have to come through both Kevin and Lane to get the elf child. He caught sight of Crispy in the kitchen, who had hidden behind the edge of the refrigerator with a heavy skillet in his hand. Oh yeah, this was a mighty fighting force.

"Lane!" Astan Hawk called in a gritty voice. "Lane, are you there? We need your help."

"Astan?" Lane moved toward the door.

It had been some time since he had moved that fast. Unfastening the locks, he pulled open the door. Astan stood on the stoop, holding an unconscious Jelani in his arms. Both were wet and dirt-streaked.

"Come in, come in," Lane urged.

Lane and Kevin took Jelani from Astan, the two of them half-tripping over each other as they carried her into the living room. Iris vacated the couch seconds before Jelani was laid on it.

"Iris?" Astan asked in bewilderment.

"Oh, honey, here's your baby. He's safe. He's safe." Iris handed the baby to his father, who stumbled, mouth gaping in shock.

"But how?" Astan asked.

"Germs," groaned Crispy, still hiding in the kitchen. "They're filthy."

Elliun let out a wail.

Jelani stirred and then her eyes opened. "Is that Elliun? Lane? Oh, my God." She burst into tears.

A roll of paper towels flew in from the kitchen. "Wet wipes," Crispy muttered.

Lane surveyed the scene before him, as explanations began to fly among the participants. He noted that no one had killed him yet. This, too, was good. "Crisp, forget the chai. Bring whatever we've got that's alcoholic. All of it. I think we'll need it."

CHAPTER 4

THE march through the forest might have seemed endless to those companions who did not know where they were going. To Vez, who had finally taken the first steps to his own ascension to power, the time passed in a flash.

He held no regrets about leaving Grigor Biren to die. His mother Veraena always taught him to look out for himself. "No one else will assure your success," she had said. "They'll watch for the clan, for the queen, for the horizon. They'll leave you to drown in sorrow or in pain. Only you will pursue the course your heart lays before you. You must count on yourself."

Thank you, Mother.

Now they were reunited, mother and son, their common purpose to restore the power of the forest mages, the *Intalus*. Both hurried along in the snow as the sun rose over the eastern mountaintops, tinting the world a pale golden-orange. A pair of hawks floated in the crisp air above them, resting on an updraft. The elves that accompanied heavy-set Vez and the delicate, silver-haired Veraena lost some of their earlier haste, the farther they traveled from the Bitterroot. Blonde Fontine was near the end of her strength. Vez could see that.

"Not much farther, Love," he said softly.

Pride glowed hot inside him, as he considered the second reward. Not only did he strike a blow at the elf clan to honor the *Intalus* Bartolomey, he stole the *neris* who once was Grigor's sworn lover.

A smirk played across Vez's lips as he recollected Grigor's veiled promise one day to pass on Fontine to him. Of course, that would have been after he won the mysterious Firefly as his own. Not once did the arrogant elf realize the Firefly was indeed Vez's own dear mother, Veraena. And never would she find the weak Grigor fulfilling, not when she held the power and the love of the forest mage.

A short while later as the sun fully cleared the horizon, Veraena lifted her hand to halt their progress. Dark-haired Terzon and non-descript Hidal pulled up short, breathing hard. Fontine sat on a fallen tree trunk near them, brown cloak draping to the ground, hands on her knees. Exhausted, she bent forward to lay her head on her arms. Yadin, once the childhood friend of Astan Hawk, now his tall, muscular enemy, spoke with the other Youngers who had abandoned the clan with Vez and Fontine. Terzon's gray eyes studied Vez. Did Terzon suspect Vez's treachery in Grigor's death? Would he care once he learned the truth?

Veraena stepped forward, lifting her arms toward them. The wind swirled around her, tousling her silver strands of hair, filling the air with the scent of warm spices and fresh-cut cedar.

"You have done well, children," Veraena said, her eyes flashing almost violet. "We have traveled a great distance, and you are now safe. Welcome to the land protected by the *Intalus* of the forest."

Vez inhaled deeply, the fresh woodland aromas filling his lungs, chasing away his fatigue. His admiration for his mother filled him as well. In recent days they had separated, while Veraena went about Bartolomey's business, but their bond was deep.

"Mages? Truly there are mages in the wood?" Yadin asked, shrugging back his hood, revealing a sharp-cut visage, a sculptured nose and thin lips. "Grigor spoke of them often. He said that Master Bartolomey survived. This is true?"

Veraena exchanged a glance with Vez. "This is true, my dear friend. The power of Bartolomey is strong, stronger than any in the Circle, or in the clan itself. Though Lorenz and the humans tried to destroy him, they could not." She smiled, and the warmth that radiated from her seemed to melt the snow around them. "You serve a noble cause, my children."

Terzon growled, stepping forward, stiff in a pose of challenge. "You are not my mother. I have left her, my father, and brothers behind, everything I know. I trusted Grigor, but now he is dead, so where do I stand now?"

At first Vez bristled in defense of Veraena, but he knew better than to interfere. She could handle Terzon. Instead, he sat down next to Fontine on the log, rubbing her back gently. She shifted slightly, responding to the touch of his hand. He concentrated on the effort to relieve her pain, hoping in the process to help the memory of Grigor Biren fade from her mind.

"Where do you stand, my fine *nian*?" Veraena's dark eyes fairly snapped with flirtatious intrigue. "Where would you like to stand? When we have achieved our goal, you will be able to stand where you wish. Those you left behind will serve you, not use you as their slave."

Terzon scowled. "Talk, more talk. What I want to see is action. Something real behind your promises, not just more empty words."

"You will see action soon enough." Veraena's tone changed. No longer the siren, she was now the soldier. Rather a sudden switch, to Vez's mind, but surely she knew what she was doing. "Now you need to eat and take your rest."

She stepped away from the group, bent down and took a handful of soft snow, and tossed it in the air. It blew in the direction the wind carried it, and formed into a doorway. As they watched, an elven bower came into existence before them, previously invisible to their eyes. "None shall find you here. Inside there is warmth and food and drink and beds for your slumber. Go now, take your ease, as long as you need. I shall return when you are ready to continue."

Terzon looked for a moment as if he would argue, but as he stared at Veraena, his resistance faded. The others, too, went meekly into the bower, the exhaustion of the many miles' travel sucking away any protest. For now.

Vez waited until last. He saw Fontine inside and paused on the threshold. "Is the Master pleased, Mother?" he asked.

Veraena stared into the woods. "He will be. We have much to discuss, Bartolomey and I." She turned toward the bower and studied her son. "We must decide what place you will hold in his kingdom."

"Then I shall have a place there?" Vez smiled, the promise warming him even in the cold mountain air.

"You shall. I will see to it." Veraena crossed her arms and stared at the ground.

Vez noticed the look of sadness as it crossed her face and did not understand. What did she know about Bartolomey that caused such expression?

"Is Bartolomey my father?" Vez asked. For many years he had desired the answer to this question. After the Sleepers went into hibernation, his mother had wandered free of the clan. Vez knew Veraena was the mother to the accursed Astan Hawk whose sire was Daven Talvi of the beloved Circle. But once Daven slept, Veraena was left to fend for herself. She knew very well the lessons in self-reliance for she had taught them to Vez.

"You are weary, my son. Take your rest. We will speak of this later."

Veraena pulled the front edges of her dark green cloak close about her and turned from him. Before he could push her for more information, she walked away, quickening her step until she faded from view.

"Vez?" Fontine called to him from inside. "Are you coming?"

His questions would have to wait. He headed for the bower and the lonely Fontine. For now there were other things to occupy his time. "I'm coming. Don't worry. Everything's going to be much better from this day on."

CHAPTER 5

THE cave was not exactly where Daven remembered.

He had traveled many hours north to locate the dark opening. Overgrown with skeletons of strong root-vines and thick saplings, he almost did not see it. He pulled aside what he could, before squeezing himself inside and leaning against the rocky wall.

What did he expect? He had not been there in nearly twenty-five years.

Over the years the terrain changed.

But so had the world which he knew.

But even so, he realized his mistake. He was not changed.

He lightly tapped his head several times against the wall behind him, as if it would jar his churning thoughts into cohesion. His breaths slowed and became deeper. He focused on the information he could glean from the scents of the cave. The scent of animals. Bears had used this space for a winter home, but not for years. The most recent scent was that of a pair of foxes. But he could not detect any animals in residence now. This portion of the cave was too exposed to the cold for fresh water, but he could smell water running free farther inside.

He needed water.

Daven pushed himself upright, his head starting a drumming ache now that his desperate escape was over. He shut out the pain, all thought, all rumination. No time for recriminations when he was on the move. Just focus. One thing at a time. Travel. Survive.

He inched deeper into the cave, allowing his eyes to gradually adjust to the darkness. Water dripped ahead, the sound guiding him. When the light from the cave's opening no longer showed his way, Daven reached into his pocket for some elven flash powder. Placing just a few granules on his palm, his feet firmly planted on the soil, he wished light into being.

And it obeyed.

He stared at the small glow in the palm of his hand. It provided light and even a little warmth. A given, a gift he could conjure since he was a lad under the tutelage of Djana and the other Elders. Magic, it was part of the very fiber of his being. Since those early days, he believed magic was the key to life.

Under the rule of the elf queen Ele and her consort Lorenz, the clan lived many prosperous years. Not years as the humans reckoned them, in measured and fixed numbers divided and fractured into months, days, hours, minutes, and seconds. Elven time passed in seasons, in flowing moments that spanned perhaps a flicker, perhaps a whole event. The young elves grew strong and secure in the warmth of the elven enclave in the mountains.

They had been so young back then, Daven and the rest of his generation. Linnea, Ele's daughter, had been the brightest and most beautiful of the *neris*, the one every male aspired to win. How Daven had loved her. Their future together was not foretold, but was at least expected. Under the rules and traditions of the clan, Daven had wanted to be Linnea's consort. Her king.

Daven might have succeeded, if the human naturalist Vincent Marsh had not arrived in the forests of the Bitterroot. Linnea had fallen in love with the outsider. The break with tradition had fractured the royal family.

Nearly murdered by her brother Bartolomey's treachery, Linnea's essence was placed in an old tree to wait for healing when the civil war had passed. As Bartolomey rallied his rebels in the forests, Vincent left Montana with Jelani, the infant child he and Linnea shared. Daven's mother Djana, and the others who clung to tradition, escaped to the human cities or into other forests. Then the chosen warriors, Daven among them, vanished into enchanted Sleep, so they could be awakened to protect Linnea when she was restored to the throne.

Veraena, the mate Daven had chosen in lieu of his lost Linnea, took their son Astan to the city with Djana. But Veraena soon disappeared into the larger world, leaving Djana to raise

Astan by herself.

Pondering all the years he had lost, Daven continued into the cave. He remembered an area, a small round room, a dry place where he could wait, rest, and think. After all this time, the layout could have changed, of course. But for him, the memory was as fresh as yesterday, before he had spent the years of Jelani's youth in the elven hibernation commanded by the Elders to give them a chance to save Linnea's essence.

So many years lost.

When he had emerged from Sleep, he was still a young and strong warrior. One fixed on his task. Again, human influences changed the rules and Linnea could not be saved. When Jelani, the child of Linnea and Vincent, aged out of the elven protection bestowed on her by her birth, the clan took matters into their own control.

Magic again re-established the balance of things. Released from the prison of the Douglas fir where she had been trapped, Linnea was reunited in spirit form with the soul of her beloved Vincent. Per tradition, Linnea's daughter ascended to the ruling seat of the clan. Jelani had become queen.

But this time magic was not enough.

Daven proceeded into the cave until he reached the spot where he expected to find a dry haven. An influx of broken rock the height of an average male elf blocked the entrance.

"I have not yet been humbled enough, is that it?" Daven sighed. Exhausted, he wanted only to rest and heal, but he would have to earn even those moments with hard penance. "Then let it be as you command, Lady. Let me be open to your lesson."

He grabbed the top rock and tossed it aside, and reached for the next. When he had finished, he crawled into the dry space on hands and knees. Then he collapsed with his face in the dirt, exhausted.

He slept.

* * *

DAVEN awoke. The smell of damp earth and the cool darkness and the rustling of some small animal nearby filled his senses. He drank in the natural world.

This is where his life would begin again.

Breathe. In. Out.

Listen.

Hear the water trickling under the soil, the wind whistling through the main cave, the scratching of the tiny claws of some small animal taking shelter from the snow.

Feel the texture of the soil under fingertips.

Sense the dampness of the air, the ice that waited just outside. He could sense his body healing. Its muscles and organs were superior to humans, but not so different from theirs as Jelani's friend Lane Donatelli hypothesized.

He was elf.

He was alone.

Daven lay there for an indeterminate time, bonding once again with the soil that nourished the elves. When his strength returned, he sat up and scooped a shallow bowl in the earth. Then he created a small fire in the depression. With his encouragement, flames soon burned a foot high, creating enough light and heat to illuminate the chamber he would use for his home until he could face the outside world again.

Leaving the fire to warm his space, Daven walked into the main cave, his shadow huge on the opposite wall, a distorted image of his weary body. He found the water he heard dripping earlier and drank until his third was slaked.

He listened to the sounds all around him. Elves perceived much more than humans. He had taught Jelani many things when she first came to the forest, giving her the gifts of elf heritage, lessons missed in her youth spent among humans.

No.

He stopped on the threshold of his tiny rock chamber. Pride in his own accomplishments threatened to devour him again. His desire to become indispensable and perhaps king. These things were what bent him to the will of the Elders, to the Circle, bringing disaster to the clan regardless of the motives behind them. He had neglected his ultimate duty to serve the queen.

When Jelani had asked him to secure her residence, he should have done so. Plain and simple. Instead, he put his judgment ahead of hers. Even if she was young, half-human, and unpredictable with her new-mother demands, she saw more clearly than he.

Had his mother, Djana, clouded his vision to serve her own needs and the needs of the Circle?

Daven returned to the fire, hunkering near it and feeling the need to be ready for action. He should not allow himself to be comfortable. Not yet. He would find those responsible for the abduction of Jelani and Astan's child. He would make sure Jelani and Astan only found support and devotion in their future. He would purge himself of this failure and prepare himself once again to serve the queen as she deserved.

CHAPTER 6

ONE day after her arrival at Lane and Crispy's apartment in the city, Jelani felt like her old self, thanks to a real shower with hot water and the use of some fruity shampoo and body wash that Iris brought to Lane's and Crispy's apartment.

She put on some clean clothes that belonged to Iris as well. The low-cut turquoise pullover and soft polyester slacks were not Jelani's usual style, but she was not about to complain.

Nothing to complain about, whatsoever. That in itself was an unusual circumstance for her.

She was curled up on Lane's couch with a warm blanket on her lap. Elliun slept safely in her arms. Astan was within her reach. Her world was complete.

Their impromptu arrival occasioned a round of hasty introductions, after which Iris made a quick trip home to clean up and get clothes for herself and Jelani. Astan took his turn with a shower, before shrugging awkwardly into some of Crispy's jeans and an oversized flannel shirt. At Lane's suggestion, they ate and drank until the world seemed a little less like it was spinning on a new axis.

In the afterglow, she and Iris sat together, fussing over the baby until he drifted off for a nap. Iris offered to take him into the other room to sleep, but Jelani was quick to nix that. She did not intend to let the child out of her arms any time soon. Maybe until he was twelve or thirteen. She savored the smooth softness of his skin, his long eyelashes, and every little noise he made. She had received a gift, one she might not deserve, but she intended to be grateful for every bit of it.

While Elliun slept, Crispy insisted on telling her everything he did to care for the child since his arrival at their apartment, showing her the spiral notebook in which he kept detailed notes on the baby's every burp, bottle, and diaper change. Jelani listened in disbelief.

Iris watched, thoughtful. "Who would have thought our Crispy had so much innate parenting skill?"

Crispy looked up at Iris through a curtain of brown bangs. "You mean because my mother was a total loss? I didn't need her to teach me." He pointed to Lane's laptop on the kitchen counter, where Lane, Astan and Kevin hunched over it, studying something. "It's all there, on the Internet. Lane helped me find all the answers I could ask."

"I'm not saying it was wrong, Ron. I think you did a wonderful job," Iris quickly assured her former client.

"You bet he did," Lane interjected from the kitchen, where he tapped on the keyboard. "He may have found his new calling."

Jelani eyed the three men framed by the pass-through, noting their grim expressions and furrowed brows. "What are you conspiring about in there? If this is about us, I want to be in on the discussion. Because we're not making the same mistakes again."

Astan frowned. "Jelani."

Her anger grew when she heard his tone, one that said 'you're wrong and messing with something that is not your concern'. "No," Jelani said. "No and no. After what they did…."

Iris spoke with a tart edge to her voice as well. "What who did? Don't you think you better determine who the bad guys are before you just cut out the clan altogether?"

Lane growled. "You mean it's not obvious that the witches are out to run everything in the world themselves?"

Kevin cleared his throat and raised a hand. "It's not obvious to me. I know you've all been involved with this for a while, and it might be obvious to you, but I'd sure like some cheater notes. Or a program."

In the silence that followed, Jelani felt regret wrap around her like a damp blanket. Iris could be right. The clan was not an individual. Only some of those in the clan were likely responsible. The rest were committed to see Jelani lead as their queen. She glanced over to see Astan watching her with a knowing eye. She gave him a little nod, and he relaxed a little.

Jelani smiled at Kevin. "It's a crazy story. Something out of a fairy tale. Are you really sure you want to get into it?"

Lane straightened and stretched his shoulders, stepping back from the laptop. "You know, maybe he should, if there is going to be a war here."

Crispy shot to his feet, poised to run. "A war? War? Here?" He snatched his notebook off the cheap coffee table.

Lane grimaced. "Not here, Crisp. I mean, in the clan."

"But he may have something, Lane." Iris tapped her chin with her forefinger, her head cocked and her eyes narrowed. "If Jelani and Astan are here, whatever element is after them, or Elliun anyway, will they not come here?"

"Nah," Lane said, patting himself on the shoulder. "No one without a user account is getting in my domain."

Crispy hurried toward the kitchen, pausing at the doorway, before turning and retreating to the bedroom. Shortly afterward, the scent of a clove cigarette wafted out to the living room.

Astan sniffed and frowned again. "That cannot be good for Elliun."

"I'll handle it." Iris followed Crispy into the bedroom and a discussion in soft but distressed tones ensued.

Astan left the crowded kitchen and sat next to Jelani. "As kind as your friends have been, we cannot place them in danger," he said. "We should return to the forest."

"But that's where the hostiles are, right?" Kevin said. "You shouldn't leave the Green Zone." They all stared at him a minute.

"He means you don't go where it's unsafe until the scene's secured," Lane said. "Right, Kev?"

Kevin nodded. "Now, do we have a map of the clan lands? Where you all have clear reign?"

Lane paused at the refrigerator door, a glass in his hand. "A map? Sure. I've got the U.S. Forestry Services map bookmarked on my...." Lane trailed off as he stared at his laptop. He looked down at his hand and then at the screen. "Huh. There it is."

"Good," Kevin said, not missing a beat. He leaned on the

counter to study the map. "Now where are we talking? What's the terrain like?"

Astan returned to the kitchen to give them a tour, indicating the extent of the clan lands. The pride in his voice tore at Jelani's heart. Her beloved clearly wanted to return to his cherished forests. She, on the other hand, wondered if she could ever feel safe there again.

The thought of losing her son made Jelani's fingers twitch possessively on his soft body. Elliun stirred, opening his brown eyes to study her a long moment before a smile fleetingly appeared on his rosebud mouth. He snuggled his shoulders a little deeper into his thick blanket and went to sleep again, apparently satisfied all was well.

Would it be fair to keep this child from the clan that made him unique? She was secreted away as a baby. She knew nothing of her very special beginnings until it was almost too late to recover her real family. No. They would go back to the clan, but not until it was safe.

* * *

ASTAN did not know this new man, Kevin Briscoll.

Lane seemed easy around him. Even Crispy did not seem to mind him, so he was probably all right. Lane's introduction included information about Kevin's recent service in the country's military operations, which probably meant he had expertise in firearms and other human weapons, as well as the conduct of combat operations. Astan could not be sure if that was a benefit for himself or the clan, no matter how much Kevin might want to help.

Since they were eight or nine years old, Astan and the other Youngers had trained to take on Bartolomey, the one who called himself king in violation of all the traditions. They each learned to use their elven talents to the best effect, preparing for a woodland battle that would likely be fought one-on-one as the Youngers and the Circle worked together to take back their land. But Jelani's return, the drama of Linnea's release and the belatedly found magic vessel of the departed Lorenz and Vincent changed the playing field. When Bartolomey was trapped in the vessel and sent away, the clan moved into the forest believing they were safe.

But they were betrayed by their own.

All the firepower in the world, human or elf, could not cure betrayal.

He shared what he could about the boundaries of the lands he knew to be secure. "I've got to admit, I'm not sure what I can tell you about the traitors. Where they are, what they're doing. Even how many there arc." He turned to Iris. "Who left the protection of the clan since the baby was taken?"

Iris walked through the living room and then stopped in the kitchen archway. "The ones Jelly said. Vez and Hidal. Fontine, too. And several others I didn't know. Maybe ten or twenty altogether."

"And Grigor," Jelani added, hate lining her voice.

Iris nodded. "Fontine and the others reported Grigor as strong and healthy. None of them could explain it."

"Grigor is no longer an issue," Astan said. He caught Jelani's wince from the corner of his eye, and knew she remembered the elf's bloody remains as well as he did. It was an image he would not likely forget for many seasons. The others were horrified when Astan shared earlier details, but observing such a thing personally seared it into one's memory.

He could only imagine what went through Grigor's mind, lying there, trapped, frozen, bleeding. The humans might call it karma. Astan thought of it as justice. Even if Grigor did not steal their child, he certainly intended to. He would have harmed Jelani, or allowed his companions to. He obviously considered himself beyond traditions that bound their elf clan. If he survived without their protection, then he certainly fell without their forgiveness as well.

Lane dug in the cupboard. "He's not the only one. Don't forget Daven."

"Daven's not a traitor!" Iris snapped.

Lane leaned back against the kitchen counter, a box of Creamy Cupcakes in hand. "Funny how he disappears just when all this happens, isn't it?" He took one cellophane wrapped cake out of the box, and set the open box next to his laptop. "Cake anyone?"

Astan wondered how Lane could eat during a period of such stress. He, himself, had no appetite. His mind wandered a moment, during which he felt the tug of a flick at his thoughts, distracting him from Iris' spirited defense of Daven. Something was trying to pull itself together. Some clue. Something he had missed.

He turned away from the others and closed his eyes. *Come on, message. Tell me what I need to know.* His thoughts spiraled. Kevin. Army. Woodland warfare. Magic. Betrayal. Bartolomey.

Flick.

Bartolomey in the glade, angry and defiant, shouting at his father, Lorenz. Lorenz calm and strong, the magical vessel glowing red in his hand before it swallowed Bartolomey whole, trapping him inside where he could do no more harm.

Flick.

Where did Bartolomey go? The vessel seemed to disappear into thin air. But Astan knew that energy did not vanish, whether by science or magic. Energy only translated into another form.

Flick.

The memory of standing with Daven, watching Fontine walk into the forest to meet Grigor. As an outcast elf, Grigor should not have survived alone.

Flick.

Who kept Grigor alive? Who?

"Bartolomey," Astan whispered, before he thought better of it. But it was too late.

Lane, who was busy poking at his laptop, looked up. "Bartolomey?"

"Bartolomey!" Jelani's voice, choked with shock.

The baby started to cry.

Kevin looked at Astan, lost. "Maybe more alcohol?"

Shaking head, Astan stepped out of the kitchen and scooped Elliun out of Jelani's arms. "Hush, my son," he said, holding the boy close, rocking him. He should have been more careful.

"What do you mean, Bartolomey?" Jelani demanded. On her feet now, Astan could see she was working up to a full upset blow-out. "Bartolomey is dead!"

"Yeah, dude," Lane said. "Thought that was a given. Even the Circle ladies all seemed to think that was a done deal."

"So I believed as well," Astan replied. "Grigor appears to have thrived alone. This is not possible. In all our history, even before the humans populated this land, an average elf alone could not live. We need the energy of the others to sustain us. The fewer elves that surround us, the less energy we share. An extended period of low energy drains us of our abilities, of our life force. We lose our access to magic."

"So you become human," Lane said with a broad grin.

Crispy peeked out of the bedroom. "Is that where humans came from? They were elves that got booted from the clan?"

"But we saw Bartolomey disappear," Jelani insisted, jaw set. "The old king put him in that vessel." Her gaze fixed on Elliun, who had calmed in his father's arms.

Astan knew if he returned the child to her at this moment, her agitation would set the baby off again. Human emotions broadcast so strongly.

"I was there with you, *denami*. I understand." Astan shrugged. "Yet this remains unexplained."

Kevin cleared his throat. "So Bartolomey is a hostile, that's what you're saying. And you suspect he might be living in the forest. Even though he's dead?" His frown penetrated all the way to his dark eyes. "How many more hostiles are there? Can we pinpoint their location? Do we have eyes on the ground there?"

Astan considered the phrase, knew the army man did not mean the literal rendition of the expression, but he wanted to be clear of his meaning. "On the ground?"

"Anyone still in the clan location you can count on for valid intelligence."

Lane snorted. "Intelligence isn't something you really look for up there."

"Lane!" Iris didn't hold back her anger and frustration. "You're always complaining how the elves make you feel inferior.

Dumping on them doesn't make you superior, either."

Astan squeezed Jelani's hand, while cradling Elliun in his other arm.

"Where do you think Daven went?" she asked. "Could he be with Bartolomey?"

That thought had never occurred to Astan for one simple reason: he knew better. "Never," he said. "My father may be many things, but he would always serve the tradition of the clan."

Iris nodded, her eyes filling with tears. "Daven loved everything about the clan. He would do nothing he knew would harm it." As Jelani opened her mouth to protest, Iris raised a hand. "He didn't mean you any harm, Jelani. He thought he was doing what was best for everyone. He loved you, almost as if you were his own daughter. He told me so."

Like a daughter, she said? Astan stiffened, knowing what he read in his father's mind. Perhaps that is the story he told a naïve Iris about his intentions and feelings. Astan knew the truth. Daven wanted to be king, whether it was at the side of Linnea or her daughter.

But that is my place, Astan thought, *and I do not intend to give it up.*

"But back to the human thing, man." Lane poked at the laptop some more. "So it's possible that humans descended from fallen elves?"

Astan shook his head. "This knowledge is beyond me. It would seem that an elf without his abilities would be like a human. That much is true."

"Let's see," Lane said. "Four hundred years ago, there were no human outposts, no access to protection. I imagine a lone elf would perish. But today, people camp all across the region. I mean, look what you all did when old Bart took over in the first place. You all bailed for the city. You passed for human. So it would be a different situation now."

"That could be." The discussion mildly disturbed Astan. He did not want to think about fallen elves, alive or dead. He turned to Kevin. "I will not allow Jelani to return to the clan lands while we are in danger. We will have to find another means to get information."

He felt Jelani fidget by his side when he issued his edict, but her attention was on their son. She had calmed enough that he felt comfortable handing the baby back to her. Once Elliun was in her arms, she walked out of reach.

Lane's laptop uttered a sharp "For the Horde!" that startled them all. He tapped the keys. "Email," he explained with a sheepish grin.

Crispy came out of the bedroom, crossing the living room to where he could stand next to Jelani and interact with the baby. Iris poked through the refrigerator, muttering about pomegranate juice. Kevin just looked uncomfortable.

Astan took a deep breath. They could not stay here. His nerves were already crawling, being inside four walls again. They needed direction, but in all likelihood Kevin Briscoll was right. First, they needed to know what was going on with the clan.

"Well, I'll be damned," Lane murmured.

"What?" Kevin peered over his shoulder.

"I have an email," Lane informed. "From Max."

"Max?" Astan felt a vibration crawl up his spine. "From the forest? How could he send you such a communication?"

"Beats the hell out of me. But here's your full news report. I'll get everyone a copy." Lane tapped the keys. The printer whirred and groaned back in the Cave. "Get ready to have your socks blown off."

CHAPTER 7

LANE knew something was definitely screwy.

First, the laptop automatically had brought up the map he wanted without touching the keyboard. But this was way out there. An email from Max? How was that even possible? DSL in the woods? The elves didn't even have electricity.

Yet here it was.

Granted, Astan said the fragile white-haired Max carried an unusual predilection for technology, but conjuring up lines of electronic communication ought to be beyond magic.

Lane handed copies of Max's email to his curious companions, and the next several minutes were spent poring over its contents.

The email read: "I know this is a far-sender, but I fear you are far, very far. And I only hope I have the skill to set this message before your eyes. Time is short and even one as powerful as you may not be able to help. A great tragedy has come to the clan. We believe the queen and her son are dead. Astan Hawk is missing, as is his father and several of the Youngers. Blood has spilled on the soil of the clan which, as you know, dooms the future of our people until the balance can be restored. You were there when the old queen was briefly resurrected, when the new one came to us, and you know the secrets of our people. The queen finds you a trusted counselor. I can do no less. Djana and the Circle entrusted their truths to you, so we have faith that you understand our ways and our needs. Please find the power within yourself to help us uncover our way in this troubled future. Come to see us. But be careful. We will be waiting."

Lane, reading, wandered into the Cave and plopped into his chair. He called up his email program on the second of his four computers. The first was compiling a new set of 'mods' for his

WoW games. The third and fourth were defragging. Searching through his daily mail receipt list did not reveal the message from Max. He checked three times.

He heaved his bulk out of the chair and walked back to the kitchen counter, where the laptop waited. The message sat there clearly on the screen. But there were no server tags, no IP address, no trail showing how it passed through the Internet system. The email had come from nowhere.

Max, you little albino minx. More of an imp, really. Yeah. An imp.

Lane grinned, recalling the role of imps in the online game that was such a large part of his life. "Hey, I could stand having a few minions."

"Minions?" Kevin asked. "What the hell are you talking about? Where are you going to find minions?" He waved the email. "Where did this come from?"

Iris perched on the arm of the sofa, her brow scrunched with thought. "Max was lurking outside the tree house after Djana left. He went inside. I'm not sure what he was looking for, but he spent a lot of time in the baby's room."

"Ah, ha!" Lane wagged a finger in Iris' direction.

The picture was coming together now. When he had saved Elliun from 'Crazy Momma', he needed more space in his computer case. As big as it was, he ended up leaving a whole pile of bits and pieces at the tree house, including his PDA—Portable Digital Assistant. That piece of equipment had email capability. That's what Max must have picked up.

But even so, how had he managed to make it send a message?

Lane eyed the message again. Max called the PDA a 'far-sender', hoping it carried the skill to reach Lane. Not power. Skill. The last time Lane visited the tree house, Max literally grounded the laptop by grinding some of the clan's soil into it and laying it open on the dirt. The process apparently made the laptop part of the elf clan. Or so Max said.

At the time, Lane dismissed the statement as another one of those murky *elfy-feely* things they all tolerated because of Jelani. But had Max actually made the machine magical?

Lane snorted. *Nonsense. Non. Sense.* A laptop computer was a machine. It did not get happy or sad. It did not pull rabbits out of its USB port.

Still puzzled, Lane set the matter on his mental back burner to concentrate on the chaos in his living room. All of them talking at once, more people than this apartment usually saw in a month, created an overload for Lane. If he was overwhelmed, then Crisp was likely about to short out.

"Crisp?" Lane asked, looking around.

His thin roommate was nowhere in sight.

Leaving Astan and Kevin in the midst of a conversation about troop strength, Lane made his way down the short hall to the room on the right, the bedroom where he guessed Crispy would be hiding. He tapped lightly on the closed door. Without waiting for a response, he entered.

"Crisp? You in here?"

Lane surveyed the small room with its worn brown braided carpet. Two twin beds wore matching superhero spreads. The walls were plastered with movie and gaming posters. A couple of second-hand, or more likely third-hand, wooden boxy dressers were piled high with clothing neither of them put in their ill-fitting drawers. What sat on top of the dresser was clean. What lay on the folding chairs were worn at least one time, but passed the 'stink' test. If it was on the floor, it should have gone in the hamper. But then they didn't have one of those anymore, not after Crispy's pet hawk had done a number on it. Who knew hawks disliked the color red?

Immediately behind the door stood the closet, a protruding rectangle that was an obvious last-minute addition to the room. Next to the closet, in a small three-foot square, was a beat-up old blue beanbag chair. Crispy was curled up in the beanbag with a multi-colored afghan over his head.

"Hey," Lane said, his voice as soft as the years-old shaded yarn of the afghan. He sat on the end of the bed nearest to the lump under the blanket. "You okay, bro?"

Crispy murmured something unintelligible.

Lane rubbed his forehead, chasing away a dull throb threatening to break free. "I know we're crowded, son. Funny, huh? I can work in this kind of noise but one baby crying sets me right off. For you, it's just people in our space." He rolled his ample backside a bit farther back on the bed, trying to find a more comfortable place on the aging mattress. "We want to help Jelly Bean and Astan, right?"

"And Elliun," Crispy muttered from beneath the afghan.

"Right. And Elliun." Lane sighed. Of course he wanted to help them, but what could he do? There was Bertha, the big old gun he had hauled out to the woods the day they rescued Jelani from the Big Bad. But he had never shot the damned thing at a living person. Even if he was so inclined, whom would he shoot? Grigor was dead. Astan's telling of the tale seemed to exonerate Grigor's followers as weak and unable to form such conspiracies on their own.

Bartolomey?

Was it possible he was still alive? If so, Lane's money was betting the Big Bad was mighty pissed off. But what the hell good would an old human gun do against a gifted elf or a wizard? What did Lane have among his few possessions that could make a dent in the kind of magic Bartolomey could conjure?

Crispy peeked out from beneath the blanket. "Are they staying here?"

"Here?" Lane blinked in surprise. "I guess. We didn't get that far yet. I'm still in the 'glad everyone's not dead' mode."

"Iris can go home." Crispy nodded.

"Right. Iris can go home. Jelly Bean could go home, too, if those meddling old women wouldn't have talked her into giving up her apartment. I knew nothing good would come out of that. You gotta look out for yourself." He grumbled on about the old witches of the Elf Circle, ranting quietly, since Crispy was already upset. "And now where's she going to take that baby?"

"Cabin?"

"Cabin." Lane raised a finger in concurrence and realization. "The one her dad left her. Exactly. Come on. Let's see if she remembered." He held out a beefy hand and pulled Crispy upright, blanket and all.

Back in the living room, they found Astan and Kevin in hot

conversation on the couch. Iris was hunkered down across from them, leaning on the coffee table. The three of them were engaged in a debate over the virtues of some sort of reconnaissance mission into the mountains.

A soft murmur from the kitchen drew Lane's attention. He stepped to the left about twelve inches and caught a glimpse of Jelani in her borrowed clothing, her hair awry. She held Elliun close, wrapped in a knitted coverlet, and looked down at the child with a gentle expression Lane found it hard to define, surely one he never seen on her face. The baby reached up with one of his tiny fingers for his mother's cheek. Both smiled at the exact moment contact took place.

Lane watched, mesmerized. The scene could have been cut from the front of any Christmas card of Madonna and Son. His rough, awkward, self-centered friend stopped just short of a halo, but she and this child obviously loved each other in a way he never experienced. At that moment he realized how much things had changed for her. Perhaps for them all.

Wishing for another cupcake but not wanting to disturb that perfect moment in the kitchen, he joined Crispy and the others, snagging chairs from the small dining table. He gave Iris one of them and Crispy took the other. Lane ducked into the Cave for his large office chair and dragged it over.

"So you got your input," Lane interjected into the conversation. "Everything's gone to hell and taken the hand basket along for the ride. Guess someone's going to have to go out and confab with the witches, hmm?"

Kevin eyed him. "Seems they want you."

"Me? What the hell am I going to do? Toss some DoTs at them?"

Iris looked baffled. "Polka dots? Candy dots?"

"Damage over Time," Kevin interjected. "Spells that start slow and then ramp up."

She scowled. "You're going to damage them? Really? What for? Which ones will you punish for doing nothing at all? Lane, that's not like you!"

Astan sighed and sat up straighter on the sofa. "I wish I knew what was right. I do not believe it is safe for Jelani and our son to return to the clan soil."

"Damn right," Lane interrupted.

Astan gave him a quelling look. "At the same time, I wonder, considering the current state of affairs, if it is not advisable to let the Circle believe as it does, at least for now."

Iris put a hand to her chest, along with a sharp intake of breath. "Lie to them? They are genuinely worried for the welfare of Jelani and Elliun!"

Everyone spoke at once.

Astan's raised voice finally conquered the others. "So they say. So they say!"

"I agree with Astan." Jelani left the kitchen to join them, her baby sucking happily on a bottle. "I don't want to give them any advantage. The sooner we let them know we're out here, the sooner they'll send someone after us."

Kevin shrugged. "No sense in me going. They don't know me from Adam."

"Max asked you," Crispy said to Lane in a voice barely above a whisper.

Lane felt his throat close up. They were right. They were all right. "Guess I'm the one. Who's got the red paint to draw the target on my front?"

CHAPTER 8

EVEN as his growing number of companions, some eighty or ninety now, settled into the new bower plied with luxuries they had not enjoyed at the Bitterroot clan's gathering places, Vez felt restlessness bubble up through his soul. He was meant for more than bits of fresh fish and conjured sweets and games in the snow.

Walking alone in the woods, he breathed in cold air, clean and fresh, untainted by the poisons of human cities. His booted feet crunched through the very top layer of snow, crusted with a thin coat of ice after a brief warm-up and a day when the sun shone from dawn to dusk, the sky bright blue like his own eyes. Mid-winter had passed. Soon the time would come for new fawns and the swelling of the creeks and streams with melting ice. Soon the time would come for action.

He did not intend to make Grigor's mistake. Power in and of itself was a deadly draw, an addiction that fed upon itself until it consumed the seeker or made him stupid. Grigor fell into the latter. It was all too easy to prey upon his vulnerability. The stories told by the clan said Bartolomey was swallowed by the magical vessel of the long dead old king in a confrontation caused by the arrival of the false queen, that half-breed Jelani Marsh.

But Veraena said Bartolomey lived.

Both she and Grigor claimed to have seen him. Both stated an increase in his powers, even while his small section of the clan began to fade. Perhaps he studied in the magic corridors of the mountain energy fields. Perhaps he ascended to *Intalus* status.

If Bartolomey was *Intalus*, his powers were superior to all but other mages, those who trained and mastered the majority of magic skills. Lorenz was a mage, if what the clan whispers said were true. Others existed, but Vez did not know their identities.

The Youngers, too, were taught their share of magic, each to his or her abilities. Vez found over the years that he excelled at nothing in particular, but possessed minor propensities for several skills. He could move extremely fast over short distances. He could heal himself almost instantly. There was one skill where he excelled, the art of invisibility. He could vanish and remain unseen by anyone passing by him. Around elves he could not stay so long, but around humans he could sustain for substantial length of time. He practiced for hours. Hunting down the humans who camped in their forest, stalking them, remaining in their camps, their cabins, even their beds while they slept, completely undetected.

The skill came in handy when they stormed the false queen's tree house. Unfortunately, the child was already gone. He wanted to know what happened to the baby. Why was it not there? He wanted to know the answer so badly that it was like a physical pain in his belly. Why could he not have the gift of far-seeing? Then he could search out the truth.

If he were *Intalus*?

He considered the possibility. He was taught that mages were more powerful than an individual elf of the clan. But this was not taught by the Circle. Those old dried up witches believed they controlled their little elven world. They controlled nothing. This, his mother Veraena told him. She said several powerful mages existed in and about the mountains. Elves that evolved past ordinary magic and elven skills, and they were the reason the elves still lived.

"Long ago, Vez, very special *nians* and *neris* studied the traditions of the clan and learned the deepest secrets the Lady of the Forest had to share."

In the reflected firelight, her face lit with excitement as she shared the tales. During the years as he grew up, they often met late at night, away from his foster father and the soil of the clan. She could not come there, she said. She would be unwelcome.

"When they learned all the Elders could teach them, they went to the soil. The earth itself taught new lessons. Lessons in clearing the mind and the heart, and becoming one with the essence of natural things. This opened the door for them, the *santwarja*."

"A true door, Mother? A gateway to a higher existence?" Vez remembered his heart racing with elation. What marvelous creatures these *Intalus* must be, how powerful, how able to help others, to improve the status of all elves. Perhaps even powerful enough to chase the humans far away and return the mountains to their earliest, rustic nature.

"A true door, indeed. When they purge themselves of limitations and doubts, they will be able to pass through. They would then be filled with the knowledge of the ages, and have at their disposal grand, sweeping powers. They would be ignored no longer."

As he crossed over the icy lip overhanging a still-running stream, Vez thought about his mother's face as she spoke. Looking back on the conversation, which took place some ten years ago, as the humans reckoned, he was in his mid-teens. The possibility of greatness, and the chance to help others, made him starry-eyed. Now looking back, he realized even then that his mother had her own plans.

She was waiting for this, for him and his chance to shine.

He believed that right up until they left the clan, until he led Grigor into the human trap, and let him die. Once he was reunited with his mother full-time, he noticed a difference in her. She was not nearly as focused on him as she was previously, in those brief moments they stole together over the past years. Veraena was preoccupied, anxious, and driven by a fixation with Bartolomey.

What did this lost king have on her?

The mystery brought him away from the comfortable bower where the others rested and dined, letting their attention stray from their greater purpose, satisfied to be warm, fed and happy. Veraena left some twenty minutes earlier without telling them where she was going. Vez intended to find out what she was up to.

Vez gave her a few minutes' head start before stepping outside, concentrating on his ability to hide himself, both mind and body, and blend into the landscape around them. The snow was knee-deep, and the wind stole away any scents that lingered on the air.

Veraena walked in the direction of the sun's setting, lightly padding atop the snow, checking behind her every so often to see if she was being followed. Vez hung back, allowing trees and large, fallen chunks of granite to hide him from her view when he could, but confident in his abilities. She did not seem to notice him, and she continued on, even as a light snow began to fall.

Vez tilted his face to the sky, letting the snowflakes land on his cheeks and eyes like feather touches. He began making an effort to connect with nature, perhaps in preparation for his own potential transformation into a mage. Anything for a jump start.

Perhaps he would have the best chance of all. Veraena did not answer him when he asked whether Bartolomey was his father, but surely the fact that she spirited him away from the clan meant something important. She did not leave him behind, as she did with Astan. She had not revealed herself to the son of Daven Talvi.

Wasn't that a grand joke? The sainted Astan Hawk, paramour of the false queen, shared a mother with Vez, the Insignificant?

Well, Vez did not intend to be irrelevant much longer. He would find out what was going on. His mother brought them all up here for some reason. What more likely than to introduce them to Bartolomey, especially Vez himself? Vez would meet his father at last.

A stick snapped ahead of him and he ducked behind a thick pine tree trunk, waiting, holding his breath in anticipation. He peered out carefully, finding Veraena standing in the center of an open space some twenty yards across. Her silver hair blew loose in the wind, her long jacket and pants a dark mahogany brown. She moved to the center of the clearing, making the traditional obeisance to the Lady, bowing deeply, touching her fingers first to her lips, and then to the soil, in each direction of the wind. When she finished, the wind died down, as if commanded, and she began to speak. He could hear every word she said.

Maybe now I'll discover what she's hidden from me all these days.

"Master?" she called, her voice strong, imperious. "I have come as you asked."

She waited in the clearing, first standing straight and still with hands outstretched at her sides. As the time passed, her shoulders shifted. She turned to look into the forests on both sides. "Master? I have brought the children. They are ready to become your soldiers."

Still nothing. Vez inched forward until he had a clear view of the entire open space. The once-blue bowl of sky overhead began to be obscured by clouds. Soon the scene could be hidden in shadow. Dismayed, he strained his ears to hear, but there was no response. Only Veraena in the clearing. Nothing else.

"Master? Please?"

The desperation in his mother's voice struck a note of fear into him. Veraena always seemed strong and invulnerable. Despite her separation from the clan, she was able to provide for them here in the northlands, enchanting a bower that expanded to accept and shelter them all. He never asked how. He just believed in her.

In his opinion, they shared better times when he was very, very young. He and Veraena living together in the wild, moving between temporary bowers in the mountains, staying just long enough to get established before they moved again. Those times he remembered as being wildly exciting, an adventure every day. Back then, Veraena was charming, warm and devoted.

One day when Vez was about five, Veraena had told him she was taking him to stay with relatives. He had protested bitterly, wanting to stay with her, but she insisted that a growing boy needed a solid home and a semblance of family. Kassen had been a kind foster parent, but Vez lived for those infrequent times when Veraena would take him away for hours, sometimes days.

Once Veraena had been dark and mysterious, but the *neris* he saw before him now was like a child begging for approval. That shook him. He took a deep breath, waiting with her. Would Bartolomey show himself?

Minutes passed, but finally Veraena's posture shifted. She stood straighter and shoved her hands in her pockets. A few moments later, a small fire bloomed in front of her, as far away as the height of an average elf. She waited, not drawing back, even as the fire grew and thickened until it was nearly as tall and as wide as a man. Vez felt pride at her courage. She was amazing.

A deep voice rumbled from the center of the fire. "Why have you called me?"

"You bid me summon you when we returned from the clan lands." Her voice was strong, proud. "We have arrived."

The fire crackled and burned. "Where is Grigor?"

She took a deep breath as the wind blew her hair back from her face. It was her first falter. "He did not survive the undertaking."

"Tell me what happened."

She cleared her throat, her right hand coming out to punctuate her explanation. "He fell into a human bear trap. His leg was ruined. He bled to death before we could rescue him."

A long silence. "Is that so? I believed Grigor to be protected by the talisman you gave him. The one you were commanded to give him as a reward for serving us."

"I gave him the talisman, as you ordered! I used it, as you instructed, to control him, to mold his behavior in the paths you wanted. You wanted him to take Astan's child!"

The fire flared, went dark, re-appeared. "And did he?"

She turned away only briefly. When she turned back to face the fire, Vez saw a trace of fear in the quiver of her jaw. "He failed you."

"So? Did your other 'champions' succeed where Grigor failed?" Mockery shot through the voice, a dark underlying char of acrid smoke in the fire moved through the flickering flame.

Veraena did not answer.

Vez held his breath. Why did she not tell him that Vez, her son, won the day? That it was he who took the talisman, thereby punishing the weaker *nian*? His hand absently patted the pocket where the necklace rested. Now was her chance. He nearly stepped out from his hiding place, but hesitated, having felt the sharp edge of her anger on previous occasions. He would trust her to wait until the time was right.

"They failed!" The fire blazed up, dangerously high and wide, enveloping Veraena where she stood.

"Mother!" Vez gasped.

He leaped from behind the tree and moved in a dead run for the lost *neris*. As he broke some invisible barrier in the clearing, the fire vanished. His mother fell to the ground. A carrion bird flew low overhead, screaming in triumph.

"No! No!" he screamed. "You can't have her!"

He reached his mother's side and knelt on the cold ground next to her, ice and snow melted where the fire had been. He focused on the woman whose normally dark skin was now pale and clammy. Her fingers lay limp in his hand.

"Mother?"

Pain hit the side of his head like a boxer's punch. He remained upright by sheer force of will, but worse than the pain was the sudden certainty that inside his head he was no longer alone.

Quite right, my impetuous young one. I am here.

"Get out of my head!" Vez grabbed at his hair and yanked it, a gesture that was quite useless. The pain drove him to his knees.

So, you are the one who dispatched my tool, my weapon, my chosen one.

Vez felt his face flush with blood and for a moment thought he might die. "Grigor was a worm. You deserved a better weapon," he panted. The pressure inside his skull continued to grow, a swelling of heat so complete that Vez found it difficult to remember anything outside his body, even Veraena's inert figure on the ground in front of him.

That was not your decision.

Vez forced himself to breathe. In. Out. In. Out. Fight the presence within. His fingers reached for the cold ground, and closed on a thick pine twig, its needles still soft. He tightened his grip on the stick, focused on the rough bark, pushed the pointed needle tips into his fingers, causing transverse pain. There. He felt like himself once more. Teeth clenched, he concentrated on the effort to encapsulate the presence in him, hold it, control it.

"Get out of my head!" Vez cried.

The presence faltered a moment, wavered, and then was

wrenched away. The jolt knocked Vez to the ground, but he wasted no time crawling to his feet, placing himself between his mother and the last place he had sensed the presence he assumed was Bartolomey. "I thought you would have been something more than a human schoolyard bully."

Vez stood tall, as broad as he could make himself, grasping that feeling of singularity, alone in his own mind, glancing frantically around for evidence of Bartolomey, waiting for the next onslaught.

The wind picked up, blew itself into a column of air half again as tall as an elf male, sucking up snow from the ground as well as debris that it flung off with centrifugal force at anything in its way. Vez ducked down as he was littered with pieces of pinecone and small branches.

A disembodied voice howled from the cone of twisting wind. "I need a body!"

"Well, you cannot have mine." Vez covered his face with an arm as debris continued to fly.

The wind swirled closer to him. "Arrogant pup, I shall destroy you."

"Stop," Veraena whispered. She pushed herself up onto an elbow, her other hand extended toward the tunnel of wind. "You will not harm my son."

"You cannot command me, female." The wind blew harder, the coalesced vortex creating a dull roar that echoed off the surrounding trees.

"Do not fool yourself, Master. You have taught me well."

Veraena pushed herself upright, to her feet, her body taut with power. As Vez watched, she drew in energy, sucking it from the very earth, enough to spark from her fingertips, her hair flaring with static electricity. She stepped lightly in front of Vez, who protested that he did not need saving. But she did not slow down. She raised her hands toward the rotating cloud, sparks actually shooting from her fingers.

Vez stood transfixed, as this woman became a weapon worthy of the name Firefly, the name she gave upon meeting Grigor.

Fire ripped from Veraena's delicate hands to hit the snowy cloud midsection. The impact staggered the white, windy cone. Bits flew off in all directions, leaving an ethereal skeleton of the vortex that shimmered a moment, before vanishing with a mournful howl. Afterward was only silence.

More curious than afraid that Bartolomey would return, Vez remained where he was, behind Veraena, her back still to him. His mother vanquished a mage. No being could do that, save another who was an *Intalus*.

Why did she hide this from him?

Emotions rushed through Vez, first a delayed terror, and then a sense of awe that segued into a burn of suppressed anger. While she knew how he and Grigor struggled to plot the abduction of Jelani's child, she did not lift a finger, as far as Vez was concerned. He knew she played at the seduction of Grigor, just long enough to suck him in, to force his hand. *Intalus* could have engineered the entire event, and without the failure Vez and his companions endured. A mage could have destroyed the false queen, could have laid the road clear for Bartolomey.

"But why would I?" Veraena asked quietly.

She turned to face her son. "There is much you do not understand about me, about my life. You have no right to judge what I *should* have done."

She brushed snow and old crackly leaves from her jacket and pants, repairing the damage Bartolomey caused in the scuffle. But her eyes were clear, sharp, and penetrating. "You did well."

Her words made him feel like he was a child again, needing approval and love. A flush of resentment skimmed his cheeks. "I would not let him hurt you, Mother."

"Admirable." She stepped closer, studying his face a moment before laying her bare hand on the top of his head. "Hush," she said when he started to speak.

She closed her eyes, and for a moment he felt her in his thoughts with him, separate, not mingled, but no less an invasion. He fought every urge in his body not to pull away, but his tongue would not hold still.

"You're no better than he is! Get out!"

As soon as he spoke, she released him. "I needed to make sure he left nothing there, my son. I meant no harm."

Annoyed, Vez paced around the clearing, imaginary crawlers moving under his skin. An awful feeling, being displaced, supplanted inside one's own head. Apparently a skill any mage could wield. Yet she thought Bartolomey might have left something.

"Does that have to do with what he said about a body?" Vez asked.

Veraena nodded slowly. "Bartolomey found a way to escape the vessel in which Lorenz trapped him. He found a place of power in the forest. But he has not yet found a host in which to place his consciousness. Natural things, trees, animals, they do not provide him a host with sufficient intelligence through which he can expand and challenge his environment."

The concept floored him, both in Bartolomey's sufficient strength to break some of the old magic and that he apparently tried merging with other animals.

Thank the Lady I was strong enough to resist him!

But if he and Bartolomey became one, would Vez become *Intalus*?

"No!" his mother said sharply. "Don't you think that. Ever. If Bartolomey took you, you would be no longer, Vez. You would be Bartolomey. His dark mind would swallow yours completely!"

"Oh." A much less attractive alternative. Vez frowned. "So where does he plan to get a body? Will he steal a human? He could easily take one of the queen's laggards. Not like one less of those slugs will be missed."

She just looked at him, her eyes troubled.

"He means to take an elf?" Vez gasped. "One of the *Lelan*? Against their will?"

Veraena took a step back and half-turned to gaze at the horizon. "Bartolomey grows weaker as the days pass. When he musters his power for a display like what you just saw, it saps him for some time. He has taught me much. I have a debt to repay him. But he risks my loyalty if he believes he will harm you in any way."

She shook her head as if sorting out what was important, as she walked over to take Vez's hand. "You have sacrificed much over our years apart. You should have had a mother to raise you and a father to teach you. But this was not what the fates brought for you. It is time that I fulfill my obligation."

A harsh thought threaded through Vez's mind. "Do you mean all your motherly duties? To all your children?"

Veraena's eyes widened. "You speak of Astan." A silvery laugh accompanied her quick reach as she laid a fond hand on his cheek. "Astan has his father and the Circle. He has no need of me. But you and I, we have much to do to show them that we will not be ignored."

Her voice grew stronger with each word, more defined, more drenched with emotion. Vez could swear the last phrase was fired by hate.

What was there in the life Daven Talvi and my mother shared that that drove her away, that made her such a victim? And what will happen when that survivor finds the strength to strike back for all the pain she endured?

CHAPTER 9

OWLS hooted outside the cave entrance. Was it night? If so, which night?

Daven remained far inside the cave, deep in meditation, in penitent thought for some time. Many times he took the rune stones into his hands. He knew them by blind feel now. Each of the twenty-four stones, assorted colors with a symbol carved into one side, had a special meaning.

No matter how many times he dipped his hand into the bag and chose new stones, the message was the same.

Salvation might have been within his grasp, but he had let it slip away. Betrayal was the result.

The picture of that empty crib haunted him, awake and asleep. Did the child deserve less consideration and care because it was male and therefore not the future queen the Circle had wanted? Of course not. Daven even balanced his disappointment with pride as he considered Jelani's coming of age, as she had faced the crisis at hand. Even if it had cost him a roaring headache.

Surely, Jelani was the queen the clan needed to bring them forward into a changing world, even as they drew farther back into the forests to avoid a growing human intrusion into their space. If the elf clan was to become strong and stable once again, it would have to find a way to co-exist with humans.

Who better to help with this monumental task than their half-human queen and her elf consort, both raised in the human world?

Daven listened to the owl a moment longer, before pushing to his feet. His stance wavered. With one hand on the cave wall, he made his way forward, following the sound of the bird to the mouth of the cave. The air was warmer than when he had entered. Melting ice dripped from tree branches. The sun's entry point was different as it began to pierce the dawn horizon. Gone was mid-winter season. Lost in his madness and rumination, how many days had passed? Perhaps seven? Or more?

Leaning against the hard rock of the cave wall, Daven assessed what his trek to this solitary refuge had brought him. The voices of the others faded from his head. His mind was clear and concrete in its thoughts. He held out a hand to catch some water as it trickled from the roof of the cave. His fingers were thin, almost bony, and his hand trembled the longer he held it extended from him. When his hand was full of water, he pulled it back and drank quickly. The crisp brightness of the water stimulated him. He stepped under the trickle at the entrance of the cave and let water fall into his open mouth, gulping the clear liquid.

With his thirst quenched, his body needed sustenance as well. The few winterberries and roots he had collected on his way here were gone. He needed a fresh source of food. The sun spiked orange rays of light as it shone across the lands, inviting a veritable chorus of birds to greet the day. So many birds. Time was passing. So much time.

Questions filled his mind. Was Jelani recovered? Had they found the baby yet? Were those responsible being dealt with appropriately?

The answer came to him from a quiet inner voice that was also outside him, audible to him through his connection to the soil. It was the Lady of the Forest.

Not yet. The balance is not restored.

The balance. The basic foundation of the clan's well-being, an equilibrium of six strengths, each element embodied in a living entity, mages who channeled energy among each other for the benefit of the *Lelan*. The elements paired in opposites: fire and water, air and earth, light and dark. A corresponding rune for each was in the set of polished stones he possessed. For many months the rune for 'light' was absent in his readings, even after Jelani joined the clan. It was as if the mage was missing. Without a balance force, the dark would spread, hence the increased number of evil occurrences that descended upon the clan

His old master Lantin spoke to him in the twilight sleep, reminding him of old lessons, teaching him the words, the feelings of magic once again. There was much to relearn before he could continue. But if he hoped to become the light, he would have to sustain himself until his training was complete.

Daven walked away from the cave, fighting the shudder in his knees. He had let himself become weak. If he encountered the enemies of the clan now, he would be ended where he stood.

He entered a small copse, thick with weather-sturdy plants, and knelt down, digging at their stems. He pulled out several of the bitter roots and ate them, choking them down and welcoming the sting it gave him. For too long he lived on the comforts of the clan, thinking no more was required of him than to support the Circle's reign until Jelani was ready to rule. He was so wrong. Sidetracked by the crisis from a quarter-century before and the premature loss of Queen Linnea, he did not fulfill his destiny.

As a young *nian*, he had set out to learn the deep magics of the soil, to tap into the energies of the earth itself to protect and defend those around him. If he was to join the inevitable battle between the clan and the evil which challenged them, he needed to return to those studies. He must train and open himself to the true nature of his calling.

The roots did not satisfy his hunger. Daven continued on, seeking more food.

Snow lay in varying depths between the trees, mostly in direct proportion to the amount of branches overhead. The early morning wind sent a chill along his spine. But Elves did not get cold, not like humans. Even though he was on his own here, the separation from the clan was not long enough to cause him a loss to the benefits of the clan. But those benefits would not keep his stomach full.

Several small animals cut across his path, but Daven let them pass unmolested. His nutrition did not require him to take the life of another creature. He should connect with the world around him, be part of it. This he remembered from one of his earliest lessons, a lesson learned along with other young elves of his age, including Linnea, Randle, Jense, and several warriors who had joined Daven in his long sleep. And, of course, Daven's then future mate, Veraena.

Veraena's talent had been evident even before they had begun to train. His attention at that time had been focused on Linnea, the dark-haired princess of the clan. Even so, he noticed Veraena. She set off his innate sense of competition. More than once Veraena had made a sexual play for him, but his hopes had been aimed elsewhere. Although Veraena hid her hurt, he had been aware of it through empathy.

When Linnea chose Vincent, Djana had urged Daven to wait before choosing a mate.

"Linnea will be the queen, my son," Djana had said so long ago. *"She knows her duty to the clan. She will reconsider."*

"Have you seen the way she looks at him?" Daven remembered complaining, his ego still bruised. *"She will never give him up."*

"Nonsense," Djana had scolded him. *"The purpose of mating is to create the next generation. And in this particular case the neris who will rule our next generation. Ele and Lorenz will instruct Linnea on what to do. You must be patient."*

Patience, however, had not been a worthy investment. Linnea had sealed her union to Vincent. Devastated, Daven took up residence in the cave, nursing his wounds and reconnecting with his pursuit of magic. When he had returned to the clan, Veraena made her interest clear again. That time, Daven accepted Veraena, trying to put aside his dreams of Linnea. A few weeks later Veraena had announced her pregnancy.

"Pregnant?" Daven had asked, his heart skipping inside his chest. *"With our baby?"*

"I should hope so," Veraena had replied a little tartly. *"Certainly no one else's."*

Realizing his poor choice of words, he caught her in his arms. *"We will have the best child, the smartest child, the perfect blend of you and me."*

Veraena appeared happy. Even after Astan was born, she seemed devoted to both of them.

Then Linnea became pregnant with Vincent's child, and the

entire clan was caught up in that drama as Bartolomey's rebellion grew. Daven had felt ripped in half, wanting to be a good mate and father while at the same time drawn to rally behind Linnea and the traditions. When Bartolomey's final treachery had left Linnea's life bleeding away, Vincent took Jelani to the human world. Then the Lady of the Forest sealed Linnea's essence in a tree and the clan waited.

After that, Veraena continued her magical studies, ignoring their son. Djana had stepped in to keep an eye on Astan, encouraging Daven to involve himself in clan politics as everyone tried to decide the best way to handle the situation. Bartolomey challenged the clan again and again, insisting he was the rightful ruler in Linnea's stead. Then the Elders devised a plan. They would hide and wait out Bartolomey, sending a cadre of trained warriors into an enchanted Sleep.

"You can't go," Veraena had said, when Daven volunteered. *"What about your child? What about me?"*

"What about the clan?" he had asked her. *"We can't put our own happiness above the success of the whole group."*

"Why not?" Veraena had countered, her violet eyes narrowing in pain. *"You don't know."*

At the time, Daven had been preoccupied with thinking about all that must be done to prepare himself for his task, for the Sleep. He had not paid attention to his mate. Veraena looked like she had something to tell him. But what?

A few days after that conversation, Daven had been summoned to the Circle's chamber. There he joined his brothers in the enchanted state. Not until he was resuscitated many years later had he learned that Veraena was gone, leaving Astan an orphan.

I failed her. After I promised her so much. I failed Astan, too.

"I have not been what I should," Daven confessed in a whisper. He knew in his heart that he deserved to be outcast, at least until he could make amends. "I wish to earn their forgiveness. Every one of those I have failed."

He stopped walking, pausing on a small hill to survey the trees below. Something blue caught his eye, something that jarred against the natural brown and white of the landscape. Curious, he made his way down the trail to find an abandoned backpack. He looked around. There were no footprints in the snow. Whoever left it was long gone.

The pack was heavy. He ignored the fact that it must have been left by humans. It was time to be practical. To him, it was a gift left there by the Lady. It was meant for him.

Unzipping the front, he found two six-packs of water in plastic bottles, several boxes of energy bars, and what looked like homemade beef jerky.

This will sustain me for days to come.

Making an obeisance of thanks to the Lady of the Forest, Daven slung the pack over his shoulder and returned to the cave. Just knowing that he now possessed supplies gave him a bit of confidence.

Soon he would be ready to find his mentor and resume his training. The world was in flux. When he learned how to right it again, all would be well.

CHAPTER 10

INDOORS was so small.

Six months back in the forest had adjusted Astan's tolerance level for enclosed spaces and processed air. Adjusted it right out of his system.

He often found himself pacing any space he could find in Lane's tiny apartment, which was not much. Even the dank hallway at the top of the stairs, with its musty odors, rodent droppings, and spider's nest, offered a few moments where he could clear his thoughts.

They could not remain here long.

He was not the only one affected by the close quarters, either.

It had been three days since their arrival at the tiny apartment, and already Crispy was beginning to regress. Iris tried to get him outside into fresh air on a regular basis, but Crispy preferred to spend time in the bedroom with the door closed. Astan, Jelani, and Elliun had taken over the half of the living room that did not house the computer Cave. Jelani slept on the couch. Astan tried to get some rest on the floor, when he could sleep. The baby seemed to nap anywhere, anytime, mostly oblivious to the chaos around him, despite the fact he was the centerpiece of their world.

Truly his son was an amazing creature. Astan could swear Elliun understood what was said to him by any of them, precocious in the extreme for a young one of six weeks old. Jelani constantly remarked that Elliun excelled beyond any expectation in the books she read on child development. Perhaps his mixed heritage shook the gene pool toward improvement.

Perhaps every father thought his son was wondrous.

Focus.

They could not stay here. Finding a safe alternative became

his most pressing priority. Once Lane visited the clan and they acquired information about the situation, they could decide whether to remain in the hard city or return to the forest.

Astan had no illusions about returning to clan lands. As long as those responsible for the invasion of Jelani's tree house were unaccounted for, they would not be safe there. The cabin might make a good refuge, as long as the magic that charmed the door protected them from outsiders.

Five steps toward the stairs, five steps back.

The door at the far end of the short hall opened. An old man peered out, his thin torso clothed in triple-layered blue flannel shirts, holes worn in the elbows down to bare skin. Rumpled gray hair hung into his face, half-hiding pale blue eyes.

"What do you want?" the old man asked, the words delivered soft and indistinct through a mouth with only half its teeth.

Astan froze. "Nothing. I did not contact you."

"You don't belong here," the old man said, eyes narrowed. He took a couple of steps toward Astan and then retreated, hands clenched into fists at his side.

"Believe me, I know it," Astan said, fighting the impulse to laugh. He pointed to Lane's door. "We're staying with Lane and Crispy."

The old man cocked his head, listening. Elliun's cry pierced the aging walls of the apartment building. "I thought he took that bird back to the woods." He continued to eye Astan. "But it doesn't sound like a bird."

Astan sighed. The old man did not look dangerous, despite his stance. Unlikely, too, that he was part of any conspiracy against the elf clan. "No, sir, not a bird. It is my son."

The man stared, weaved a little. Astan read pain in his eyes, but not a pain that was new and hurtful. More like pain from a blister worn by a tattered, ragged place in a shoe worn over many miles, a familiar discomfort that could not be relieved.

"I had a son, once," the old man said. "Lost him. Lost him years ago. When I started living in the bottom of a bottle."

Astan studied the man. "It is painful to lose a son. I lost mine for a brief time. If not for our friends, he might have been gone forever. We were lucky."

The man rocked his weight from one foot to the other, his pain radiating onto Astan's personal radar so intensely that he started to internalize it. So sad to lose a son.

Astan walked across the small space, took the old man's hand, and placed his other hand on the man's chest. "What's past is past. Release these walls that hold you trapped. Face your future free of this pain, my friend."

"Friend?" the old man whispered. The tension lines in his face began to relax.

Astan let him sense the relief he experienced when he first saw Elliun in Iris' arms. "Friends understand what other friends have gone through. Let go of this pain. See your way clearly once again." Astan pulled his hands away slowly and stepped back.

The apartment door cracked open and Lane's head popped out.

"Is he bugging you?" Lane asked Astan. "Don't pay any attention to crazy old Grandpa. Just come back in, okay?"

"Stuff it, Sonny," the old man said to Lane. But he offered a half-toothed smile to Astan before retreating into his own apartment.

Astan felt good about the encounter. He did not interfere with the condition of most humans. He found they tended to resent it. But this man's shoulders seemed too fragile for the heavy weight he bore. "He means no harm, Lane."

"Maybe not, but who needs the grousing?" Lane held open the door for Astan.

"You should be more patient," Astan scolded, slipping back into the apartment. "I would think as much damage as you have lived through, you would be sympathetic to his loss as well."

"Right, right," Lane muttered, as he closed the door after them. "Crisp thinks he's a saint, too. I think he's an old, dried up crab."

Astan retrieved a cup of herbal tea that he had brewed before stepping out.

With Crispy hiding in the back room and Kevin gone back to run his store, only Astan, Lane, Jelani, and Elliun remained in the front of the apartment. Even Iris had left for a bit, returning to her office to request personal leave.

If Daven could be found, Iris intended to move to the forest with him.

"Now, anything else you want me to find out for you up in the big woods?" Lane asked.

Astan sighed and looked over the list of suggested topics already determined worthwhile to discuss. Who remained on clan soil? Who was missing? Was Daven there? Was anyone else harmed? And what were the intentions of the Circle at this juncture?

All good questions, of course, but the truths Astan desired were not so easily discovered. Like who could be trusted? Would the Circle unite behind Jelani instead of trying to undermine her? Was Bartolomey still alive and ready to engage in further warfare against the clan? Astan doubted Lane would be able to find the answer to these particular questions.

"Well?" Lane prodded.

"You humans have a term for the correct method," Astan said. "I believe it's something like 'think outside the box'."

"Pal, I don't even fit in the box," Lane said, shoving a sleeve of cupcakes into his backpack. "Trust me on that."

"Don't go by yourself, Lane," Jelani piped up from her perch on the end of the living room sofa.

Elliun slept on a blanket beside her. Since their arrival, she had kept the child within an arm's length from her. Astan approved.

"Not like Crisp's going in his current state." Lane's face twisted into a frown. "He's about ready for someone to stick a fork in him."

The muscles of Astan's scalp knotted with tension. He rolled his head loosely from shoulder to shoulder, stretching his neck. "Jelani's advice is wise. In case the danger still exists, a companion would add a measure of safety."

"So that leaves who? Neither of you, apparently. Iris is having a blonde moment. I can't get a straight answer out of her, either."

"What about Captain America downstairs?" Jelani asked. "At

least he knows which end of a gun to hold."

"Funny," Lane growled. "Shooting off guns *for real* isn't my idea of fun."

Lane shuddered and kept shoving things into his backpack. Astan began to wonder whether it was a bottomless pit created by magic, each item folding in on itself to create more room.

"Yeah, you're probably right," Lane muttered and then heaved a great sigh. "Kevin's already volunteered to go. He just isn't so keen with this elf-and-pony show." Lane pinned Astan and Jelani with a look of purpose. "Looks like today's the best day to go. Roads are supposed to be clear and no snow 'til Saturday."

Lane walked to the sofa and bent over, not being able to hunker, as he admired the sleeping baby. "He sure is beautiful like this, Jelly Bean. Despite all the shenanigans, you done good."

Jelani beamed. "Thanks, hon. He was a group effort in more ways than one." She reached up and gave Lane a hug. "You be careful up there. If it gets dicey, don't hesitate to cut and run."

"Preaching to the choir, sista," Lane said, letting her go and raising his right hand. "Testify. Oh yeah."

"If you are not back by dark…." Astan wished the tentative note would leave his voice.

"Release the hounds. You bet." Lane's smile faded. "I'm serious, dude. If I don't come back, you come get me."

"You have my word." Astan offered a smile, hoping to boost Lane's confidence. He thought he should be the one going, but the group had nixed that idea.

Lane hesitated, scuffing a foot on the floor, fidgeting as if he did not know what to do with his hands. Finally, he took a deep breath and blew it out slowly, rattling his lips. "Guess I won't get there if I don't get started." He glanced toward the bedroom door. "Make sure he eats something, all right?"

"Of course we will," Jelani promised. "Our thoughts are with you."

Lane gave a half-smile that showed his insecurity and then shouldered the overstuffed backpack. "Fate protects fools, small children, and ships named Enterprise," he said. "Or at least Riker thought so. Stay cool, homies."

With a little wave, Lane swung himself out the door.

"You think he'll be all right?" Jelani asked.

Astan nodded. "The Circle will not harm him, not while they are in chaos. He will refuse to tell them where we are, and that is something they want to know. They will treat him well, hoping he lets his guard down."

"And Lane never met a cake he didn't like."

* * *

JELANI found it all too easy to fall back into what seemed now a luxurious lifestyle.

Running water, real walls, and a refrigerator stocked with cold drinks on demand and all the chopped ice she wanted. Television was another novelty. When she had lived in her apartment there was never enough time to watch it due to long hours at work and volunteering at the wildlife rehabilitation center. But with Elliun up at all hours of the night, she could always find something on the television to keep her awake until he finished eating, even if none of the programs particularly fed her soul.

With Lane gone, she and Astan were essentially alone and safe for the first time since leaving the clan soil in headlong flight. She longed to curl up in bed with Astan, pull the blankets up to their ears and feel his arms around her until passion sprouted to fill them with warmth. But this was no time for such behavior.

Astan spent a great deal of time staring out the window at the gray skies and the mountains in the distance. Jelani knew what that meant. "You're ready to go back, aren't you?"

"I don't feel we belong here."

"I belonged here for a long time!" Bristling, she let the panic that sent her fleeing from the clan govern her alternatives. "We could live in the city. Hell, we could live anywhere. We could go to San Francisco. San Andreas. Santa Fe. Out of the reach of Bartolomey and all the others who don't want us here." Tears burned her eyes. "Who doesn't want *me* here?"

He turned to stare at her, arms crossed in unyielding rigidity. His face held no expression, his coy way of showing disapproval.

"You would abandon your people?"

Outrage drove her to her feet, though she kept a tight voice low to avoid disturbing her son's sleep. "Let's get something straight, Astan. They abandoned me first. The Circle never took me seriously. Daven 'handled' me for them. Grooming me to become his."

Astan winced and drew back from her.

Okay, Jelani thought, maybe that was not fair. Astan was not responsible for his father's behavior.

"The bottom line is they have fought me every step of the way," Jelani said. "How long do I have to keep up the illusion that I'm in charge of anything?"

Astan grabbed her arms, his fingers digging into her skin. His eyes seemed lit with inner fire, a passion that had nothing to do with sex and everything to do with love. He focused in on her until she could see nothing else but his troubled face.

"They do need you, Jelani," Astan said. "More than they know. You are the queen they have needed all along. If they lose you now, the clan will die." Releasing her, he stepped back. "Think about this. If the clan does not survive, if the families are scattered to the winds, it's not just Rashia and the Circle who will perish. I am elf, Jelani. Your son is elf." His dark eyes held hers. "You, too, are now of the clan. We will fade away as surely as the evening sun."

Alarm snaked through her gut. "We could die?" She looked over her shoulder at the sleeping babe. Astan appeared serious enough, but that hardly sounded real. It wouldn't be the first time an elf tried to baffle her with bullshit to get her to comply. "You mean that?"

"Not in an immediate sense, *denami*. But we will lose strength and abilities and…."

"And become human." She studied him, seeing how much that thought troubled him. "It's not so bad."

"It's not what we want."

Hearing the anguish in his tone, Jelani relented. She reached out to caress his cheek. "If we can go back, love, we will. I'll try to keep an open mind, all right? For all of us."

Astan pulled her into his arms. "I'll find a way to keep you safe, Jelani. Both of you. I swear we'll make it through this."

She held onto him as though he were a life raft in a flood. His touch brought her calm, and healed her wounded heart as well. In the time they embraced each other, her mind came around to his way of thinking, as the hurt faded, just a little. Maybe she could truly serve the Bitterroot clan. All her life she had searched for a home and family. Could she really throw this new family away without giving it every possible chance? Especially considering the stakes for them all?

Of course not. Her stubborn streak would pursue that hope a little longer. She would try again.

But her patience would not last forever.

CHAPTER 11

"HERE I was, all ready to avoid making this journey again for the rest of my life."

Lane hemmed and hawed. He adjusted the seat in the ancient red pickup truck, and then heaved his bulk into it, still grumbling. "I never thought Jelani should have gone to her little house in the big woods. Nothing good could come of it."

Kevin eyed him from the passenger seat. "Is that so? Just like the Great Karnak, you saw the world of the elves tumbling down in the event she moved there?" He eased his leg, still in its brace, into a more comfortable position.

"It sounds stupid when you say it like that." Lane shifted the truck into gear and headed west on Broadway.

"Hmm." Kevin hunched his back against the seat, an unsatisfied look on his face.

"Besides, I wasn't so worried about the elves. I was worried about Jelly Bean."

Lane concentrated on the task of navigating, pleased that the roads were temporarily clear of snow in the middle of February. This wouldn't last. In Missoula, it often snowed right through Easter and sometimes until the end of May. A small blessing for today. Lane would not go so far as to designate it an omen.

Kevin leaned back against the worn seat, looking out the windshield toward the gray horizon and the snow-topped mountains above them. "What if the elves are the ones who matter, Lane?"

Lane held back a blatant scoff. "Seriously, man? They left Zooville to retreat into their forest glade. They don't want any truck with us lowly humans."

"But Crispy said your hypothesis is that man isn't ascended from apes. That he's descended from elves. That's phenomenal."

Was that it? Lane had not actually determined direction of evolution. The ultimate impact of his theory that elves and humans were of the same genetic stuff, combined with Astan's input about the effects on an elf of being outcast from the clan, made him wonder. "That does kinda throw a wrench in traditional Darwinian theory, doesn't it?"

"That shakes the whole scientific view of the world, pal. You could be some famous new geneticist and—"

"Whoa!" It was all Lane could do not to slam on the brakes. "No. No. No. I have no intention of becoming the latest guru. At least not for this. I like my little house and my few friends and my online life. I don't need all that crap."

"But what happens if the elf clan fails? Look at the change in the forests and natural resources over the last twenty-some years while they've been in turmoil. Pollution, logging, mass fish kills. Even that round of bighorn sheep deaths might tie in."

"All that stuff could be explained a lot of different ways. Viruses. The intrusion of men into the forest. Global warming."

Kevin coughed, picking at a muddy clump on the hem of his black polyester jacket. "Crispy says your friend Jelani can heal the forest. Trees, plants, even the birds and animals, just with her touch. And she's only half elf, right?"

Lane sighed and took the turn to the north on Highway 93. "Crispy says a lot."

"In fact, he doesn't. So when he does, I tend to listen. He's pretty serious about this."

Irritated that even Kevin seemed to be taking the side of the damned elves, Lane weaved in and out of traffic, his foot heavy on the accelerator to power away his frustration. "So what are you saying? Save the Elf Clan, Save the World? With Jelani scribbled in as guest cheerleader?"

Kevin finally grabbed the dashboard after one particularly jerky lane change. "Why don't you let me out here, pal?"

"Hmm? No. No, I'm sorry." Lane pulled his foot back, regretful. "Kevin, I'm just one guy, you know? I just want my life to continue on its semi-abnormal path from day to day."

"All I'm saying is maybe if the clan is restored to health, the human world—even your tiny corner—will benefit, too." Kevin shrugged. "Never mind. Let's talk about something else."

"Right." Lane chewed over the silence that followed between them. When it dragged too long, he retreated into a discussion of the online game they played together. That was an area of fantasy where he felt comfortable, not this land of elves and magic. "So, what do you think our chances are to actually slay Nefarian and Onyxia at the raid next week?"

Kevin snorted. "Not happening in one night. I would guess it'll take a couple of weeks to get the job done, even with the team we have. I mean, I think the warriors are up to it, if we've got enough healers to keep them going. But those dragons are a bitch."

Kevin and Lane had pulled together twenty-five of the best players on the Lane server to make a stab at the Blackwing Descent, one of the most challenging of the latest versions of the game. In his element now, Lane warmed to the discussion of the details of the game. He read online guides and researched 'cheats', making it a better experience for himself and his team. He spent as much time each day thinking about his WoW world, as he did his actual world.

Now if he could play in the real world as his character Xiomar, a bulky green orc with huge hands, fangs and the powers of a level eighty-five warlock. Well, then old Black Bart would get what was coming to him, wouldn't he?

The thought amused him.

Their animated debate continued all the way along Highway 93, until Lane pulled off at a familiar marker. His stomach slowly clenched into a knot as he remembered the last time he was here. Nausea boiled somewhere between his gut and his throat, chasing away even the promise of a cupcake, something that usually solved his problems. Memories of his past, the same ones he worked hard to bury deep, were threatening to overtake him. He had 'rescued' Jelani's baby from the ghost of his own history. As it turned out, it had probably been serendipity that saved the child's life.

He parked the truck at the end of the path, but made no

move to get out.

"Are we here?" Kevin asked, peering out the window.

Rocks were piled across the path, blocking motorized vehicles from going further up the trail.

"We're here." Unsure what faced them, Lane gave a big shuddering sigh. His reluctance to venture up to see the clan grew by the second. Then he gathered his courage. "Best get moving, or I'll probably just turn around and skip the whole thing."

The old truck door creaked as Lane clambered out. Nervous, he eyed the trees around them.

We could get whammied from any side up here. Idiotic to volunteer for a mission like this.

As Kevin came around the back bumper of the truck, Lane noticed the glint of a metal gun barrel inside Kevin's unzipped coat.

Lane felt both of his eyebrows pulled upward of their own accord. "Seriously?"

Kevin shrugged and zipped the bottom six inches of his jacket. "You all made it sound like it was worse than Kandahar. Just wanted to cover my ass."

"If Daven was here to whammy you," Lane warned, "that wouldn't do a bit of good."

Kevin hesitated. "But he's the one who's gone, right?"

"Right."

"Then we're good." Kevin stiffened, his attention focused on something behind Lane's shoulder. "Incoming!"

With a strong arm, Kevin yanked Lane to one side, pulling him down by the front left tire.

Lane hit his shoulder on the fender and yelped. "What? A bomb? Are you kidding?" He tried to sneak a peek over the hood, but Kevin had a death-grip on his jacket.

Something large glided overhead and touched down about ten feet to the east.

Kevin struggled to get upright, reaching for his weapon, his leg brace catching on the hem of his jacket.

"Whoa, man! Don't shoot!" Lane grabbed Kevin's hand,

pointing the gun at the ground as he used Kevin's counterbalance to pull himself upright.

Before them stood what Lane knew to be a small but full-grown male elf. Max's snow-white hair blew loose in the wind, and a warm smile dominated his impish face.

"It is The Lane! I knew you would come." Max bowed with reverence.

"The Lane?" Kevin asked, confusion scribbled on his face.

"Long story." Lane chuckled. "How are you, Max? Max, this is Kevin. Kevin, Max."

Max inched closer. He reached out one long pale finger and touched the dark skin of Kevin's hand, as though he had never seen a black man, which he probably had not. "Kevin, friend of The Lane, is a friend of the clan as well."

"At least an acquaintance," Lane agreed. "And how exactly did you know I would come?"

Max smiled and his eyes sparkled with mischief. "It is foretold."

Lane snorted. "Right. Nostradamus was all about some fat computer geek climbing the mountain to bring peace to the elf world."

The slim albino elf shook his head. "You will see. Come. I will take you to Djana. She will want to speak to you." Max held out a hand. "You bring news of the queen, do you not?"

Lane bit his lip a moment before he took the elf's hand. "I do not." He felt Kevin stiffen beside him. The deception troubled Lane. Some clan members legitimately cared for his Jelly Bean.

But he and Astan had agreed that the less the Circle knew, the safer Jelani remained. At least for now.

Max's face fell. "Nor of the child?"

"Perhaps you should take me to Djana, Max. We'll see whether we can sort out what's happened. Shall we?"

Max nodded and then started up the trail at a pace Lane would have normally found impossible to match, especially carrying a full pack. But Max somehow pulled him along, bearing part of Lane's weight as his own. Lane felt no more effort than walking across a level sidewalk.

Kevin grabbed the other pack, the one with duct tape, assorted tools, binoculars, first-aid kit, a couple of MREs—Meal-Ready-to-Eat packs—and several lengths of rope, before following behind them.

As they approached the thicker part of the forest, small faces peered around the tree trunks. Soon other elves fell in behind them. By the time they reached the ethereal rooms where Djana and the ruling members of the Circle gathered, they were leading quite the parade.

"All we need is tickertape confetti," Lane muttered to Kevin.

"These are all elves?" Kevin asked with wide-eyes.

"Straight out of the fairy books, pal."

Elves had gathered all around. Some wore elven green and brown clothing. A few wore human-style jackets and heavy boots.

Lane still held Max's hand, but he could feel his footsteps begin to drag the closer they got to the chamber where he had interviewed the Circle a few months before. He could not help but remember how they snookered him at his earlier interview. At least that was what they thought.

"Wait," Kevin said, seemingly as fascinated with the elves around them as they seemed to be with him. "So we're going to see all those elves you talked to, the ones we found on my computer?"

"I expect. Didn't bother to bring any wormwood this time. We'll have to hope they're not on the warpath."

Max stopped just before the door to the chamber. "War will come to the clan, but they intend you no harm. Not now." He raised a hand and waved it along an unseen surface in a semi-circle.

War will come to the clan. Lane did not like the sound of that. He hoped it was part of the big misunderstanding that caused Jelani and Astan to land at his apartment. If this was all the work of a few bad eggs, catching them and rendering them harmless might be an easy solution.

But if old Bart was truly behind all this, then Max might well be right.

As the door opened to the elven room with its opaque walls, Kevin's amazement took on a slight flavor of panic.

"Suck up," Lane whispered, leaning closer. "They really like sucking up. Like someone's rich grandmother. Pretend you want to be in the will."

Kevin frowned, looking confused, as the crush behind them pushed Max and the two humans inside, where two dozen female elves waited there for them.

Lane immediately noted a difference in the group since the last time he had been there. A fetid odor filled the chamber. Not a mouth among them held a smile. In fact, he noticed deep grooves in their faces and dark circles under their eyes. Lane remembered Astan's grandmother, Djana as one of the more distinguished and beautiful of the elf women, but when she turned to him heavy streaks of gray cut through her hair. She looked as worn as a weathered totem pole.

Max stopped a respectful distance from the elf woman. "I bring The Lane and his friend Kevin."

Djana eyed the humans, as if she could not decide whether to welcome them or slap them. "Is she with you?"

Djana's raspy voice grated on Lane's nerves. He just shook his head, holding his tongue in case she tried to pry the truth from him.

"Then why did you come? What would bring you here? Do you have news of her? Of the child?" Djana's voice broke. "Are they dead?"

Kevin stood at parade rest behind him, and Lane wished he could feel as comfortable in the face of this interrogation. What the hell was he thinking when he had agreed to come here? They would turn him into a newt for sure.

A singular sense of desperation was etched on the faces surrounding them. When Lane did not reply immediately, a murmur spread through the crowd.

"Speak! I command you!" Djana's tone snapped and crackled, and her bony finger came up from her side to point at Lane with ominous import.

As Lane fought the impulse to open his mouth, Kevin

smacked him in the middle of the back with a closed fist. It was enough distraction to allow him to resist Djana's command.

"Ma'am," Kevin began, his tone too polite, almost artificial in its formality, "Iris, the friend of the queen, came to the city with a wild tale. She said the queen and her consort left the clan and that the child was taken by those intending them harm. She also stated her lover, Daven, did escape from the clan, but for what reason she did not know. Has someone threatened vengeance against him?"

Djana took a step back, her knees nearly buckling. One of the other elves caught her arm and held her upright. "Vengeance? Against my son? Why would they? Who would say such a thing? Why does the woman not come herself?"

Lane winced as Djana glared at him, but let Kevin continue, figuring he was on a roll.

"You tell me, ma'am," Kevin said. "Iris was pretty shaken up by what happened here. You say no one knows where these people are. How many others are missing?"

A long silence interposed itself among them, each side equally distrustful of the other.

Finally, a big brawny big elf ducked through the doorway. "At least seventy-five, likely more," he said, casting a disgusted look at the old ladies.

"Beckley, hush!" someone scolded.

Beckley's expression hardened and his gray eyes turned cold as rock. "I won't hush. If someone had spoken up sooner, we might have been able to save the queen and her son. But all you worried about were your little political intrigues and your favorite pets."

Gasps echoed, and Djana's lips pressed together as if carved of stone.

"Astan warned you all this would happen," Beckley continued. "Daven knew Grigor still lived in the forests. He wouldn't let Astan put an end to Grigor's miserable life. So Grigor got the chance to steal away nearly half the Youngers. Some left before this. Some left since. He's the one who's seen as powerful now. Not you. Look at yourselves!" He waved a hand in the direction of the female elves, who cowered. "You've already lost the battle."

Djana's gaze fell to the ground. Those behind her wore shame on their faces, in their very frames.

"Just what you deserved," Lane said, their hold on him slipping enough to let him speak. "All of you. What you put her through. You tricked her. You drugged her. You didn't deserve her."

Djana, Astan's grandmother, straightened in what could only be interpreted as an attempt to pull together her shredded dignity. "We loved her."

The obvious gambit ticked off Lane. "Oh, bullshit. You used her. You wanted to gather in the troops, to regain the personal power you held back in the day when the elves lived high on the hog and each of you were little wanna-be queens in your own circles. Before you were all tainted by us humans." Lane's words bubbled up like a fountain in his throat, ranting not only for his dear friend but for all those who were pawns of others, used and tossed aside when they were no longer useful or loved. "Your son Daven was the worst of all. When he didn't win Linnea, he settled for second best. Until Jelani came along. Then he got greedy again, even when she chose someone else."

The stricken expression on Djana's face proved his comment had definitely hit home.

"You knew it, too," Lane accused. "You wanted him to be king. That would make you special again." He stared at her, the realization sinking in as he read it in her eyes. She had schemed to do exactly that and no one had called her on it. Until now.

A buzz went through the crowd. One by one, elves pulled away from Djana, leaving her an island in a sea of brown.

Lane turned to Beckley. "Do you know who else left the clan? Which Youngers?"

Beckley nodded. "Come," he said in gruff voice. "We won't find any truth here." He started out of the gossamer enclosure.

"Don't you leave us, Beckley!" a gray-haired old bat screeched after him. "I birthed that child. We'll find him. And we'll find the queen, too! If she's turned on us—"

"Watch your tongue, witch," Lane said, trembling with anger. "You're the midwife, right? Jelani told me about you and your plans to steal the baby from her. I'll do everything in my power to make sure you never ever see either of them again."

Kevin grabbed Lane's arm and then dragged him through the parting crowd and then outside to join the big elf.

With a look of shock on his pale face, Max followed close on their heels. "Take them to the rock," he urged. "We will be able to see who's coming from there."

Beckley grunted and started off in a new direction. Two others came behind them, both male, both young. The females retreated into the elven chamber, presumably to lick their wounds.

As though this were a military exercise, Kevin marched as best he could after Beckley, looking straight ahead, not seeming to heed the stress to his injured leg.

Lane, on the other hand, puffed along at the rate they traveled, faster than he was used to moving. A stitch in his side finally brought him to a halt. He groaned, bending over at the waist.

Max quickly came to his aid. "Stop!" he cried. "The Lane is troubled."

Beckley halted, turning back to them as he observed the trail they had traveled. "We are alone," he assured the others. "We may stop for a few minutes only. Better to pause at the rock."

"Sorry," Lane gasped. "I'm in crappy shape."

"Haven't I told you to get out more?" Kevin grumbled.

One of the two silent companions from the back of the pack placed one hand on each side of Lane's thick waist, where the pain was the worst. "Breathe," he said softly.

"I'm trying, man. I swear." Gasping as he tried to catch his breath, Lane found that as he continued, the in and out came easier. The stabbing pain faded to a steady ache, before disappearing altogether. "Hey, that's working. Good job, friend."

The young elf grinned. "Pieter. That's my name. I'm a cousin of Astan's." His face clouded over. "I wish I could see him again."

Lane felt for the kid. Family was hard to come by and painful to be separated from. "I think you will. Don't worry."

When he was able to continue, Lane followed the others up the mountain a little further to a large outcropping of granite marked by a deep indentation on its south side.

Beckley climbed on top of it, looking a little like an explorer studying the horizon's line. "We're good."

He jumped down, and the second Younger snapped his fingers, telekinetically rearranging several fallen tree trunks that were quite adequate as chairs. Beckley took the second tallest of them, gesturing Lane to the tallest one. Once Lane was seated, Beckley and the others focused on him like he was a slide under a microscope.

Beckley cleared his throat. "All right. Where are Astan and Jelani, and where did you take the baby?"

CHAPTER 12

DAVEN'S long mental journey took unmeasured time.

At last, he connected with the long abandoned part of his psyche that undertook the early training some forty human years before.

Communing with those places in his mind and heart, he began to feel a different vibration resonate through his body. Deep powers awaited him now, far beyond his ability to read minds once in physical contact with another.

He found the spirit of his mentor, Lantin. His mind was turned, shaken, stripped, and refitted to resume his quest for the magic within his reach. More than once, he had set it aside. First, it had been the hibernation. Next, he settled for his role as tutor and mentor to the young queen, who was so raw and unprepared.

No longer.

His mother and the Circle had distracted him from the development of his talent, an aptitude in which old Lantin had taken interest so long ago. That distraction led to his failure to protect his grandson, Elliun. He betrayed the blind trust Jelani placed in him. Even all those fine words he gave to Astan in the form of fatherly advice proved to be damaged seed wasted on good ground.

Daven sensed the touch of Elliun's mind, even here in his chilled retreat. As long as Elliun lived, there was time to save him. Daven could not risk returning to the world half-focused. He would have to see this quest through, all the way through. Only then would he be strong enough to combat the evil that plagued the clan.

He lay on the floor of the cave in a dry space, his eyes closed. Breathing slowly, much slower than normal even for an elf, he rested in a near meditative state, experiencing his contact with the soil. The spirit of Lantin led him through lessons in mindset and awareness, while the runes provided insight and gateways into magic.

Daven, where are you? I need to find you.

The voice was female, soft and whispery like a lover. His thoughts wrapped around the voice, just a mental touch. Whoever called was not with him in the cave. He knew it, even without opening his eyes. But she was persistent.

Daven, please!

Who could be calling? Linnea's spirit? Veraena? Djana? Who would seek him out?

I'm here, he replied with his thoughts.

I'm coming. The reply was tentative, unsure. *I need you.*

Daven considered the flavor of the voice, the tendrils of personality attached to it. The tone did not fit Veraena, who even in her younger days had been a force to reckon with. This contact seemed much less self-assured. It was not Djana, either.

Daven?

He sensed a soul traveling through the woods, feet heavy in thick-soled boots, leaning on a heavy stick to help her over the rough parts. Where was she? He could not see through her eyes, but he could feel her emotions. She was lost and afraid, far from home, and determined to find him. Then he knew.

Iris?

Yes, love, the voice replied. *They wouldn't tell me where you had gone. I thought it was north. You said the place of great magic was north. So I'm coming. You could help me. But you cannot stop me.*

Another distraction. With Iris present, how could he hope to concentrate, to bring his magic skills up to the needed level of strength? But he could not leave her in the woods alone.

Why would she risk herself this way? From the beginning, he had recognized her attraction to him. At first it seemed almost laughable, the kind of silly infatuation human females cultivated when they encountered a new male. But after she came to the forest to help with Jelani's final weeks of pregnancy, he had grown accustomed to her company. Iris' inner strength belied her frilly, superficial outer appearance that conformed to the

Hollywood standards of human beauty. She provided insights into Jelani, her human friends, and some of the elves as well.

It was possible she brought news of Astan and his family.

I'll come to you, he told her.

His promise made, he shook himself loose from meditation. A quick walk around the cave cleared his senses. He felt relief in the mental contact he shared with Iris and recognized his own growing excitement at their approaching reunion. He tried to shove her away and to redirect his focus toward the clan's best interests, but now he realized how much he missed her.

The sky outside the cave was a brilliant blue, as the sun made a valiant try to nudge spring into place. Daven sniffed the air, but found no hint of the soil in it. It was still frozen. Many nights would pass before the growing season came to these woods. He closed his eyes, letting his mind wander, scanning the forest around him.

He was much more in tune with the land now. His time spent alone, his solo rumination, returned him to the conduit to the deeper magic. How much longer would he need before reaching the level of access?

A mental cry of pain echoed inside his mind. Iris, in some great distress. He assessed her state and guessed from her wild, chaotic thoughts that she had fallen.

Irritated at his own torn emotions, he set off to the southwest, following her thoughts like a trail of shiny wet stones.

I'm coming, he reassured her.

I think I'm all right. Just twisted my ankle when I tripped over a fallen branch. Her mental tone echoed with self-recrimination. *I should have seen it.* A pause. *But I'm glad you're coming.*

Daven dashed over the terrain, maneuvering between thick tree trunks, his feet scarcely touching the ice-kissed earth. Iris was so human, with the vanities, the unpredictability, and the vulnerabilities humans seemed to share. He realized with a bit of shock that these qualities endeared Iris to him. Iris could never be a chilly self-sufficient *neris* like Veraena, whose ambition rivaled Daven's and whose maternal instincts fled when it suited her.

He understood at last Linnea's love for Vincent Marsh.

Human capacity for devotion, sheer doggedness, constant ability to surprise and be surprised, taking joy from either state, fascinated him. Bartolomey claimed adding human blood into the equation weakened the elves, but Daven was not so sure. The effervescent, ever-changing nature of humans might be all that saved the clan in the end.

Her mental voice patient with an underlay of suppressed worry, Iris reached out to him again. *Daven? Are you close?*

I feel you, Iris. I'll be there soon.

Daven turned southward toward the area the clan occupied. The forest floor lay thick with fallen pine twigs, which gave off a faintly pungent scent as he passed. Small bowers of downed branches hid little groups of animals sheltering in the proximity of their mates, winter coats thick and bellies pregnant. His burgeoning talents let him see that the amount of young would be less than last summer, thanks to the discord in the clan. He learned the queen's well-being held the key to the successful survival of this whole ecosystem. Despite the Circle's fine intentions, their efforts to govern the clan, to block Jelani's participation, had been the exact wrong course.

He swore to heed the lessons, to do better and not make their mistakes.

Surmounting a small ridge, Daven saw Iris. She was wearing her impossibly aqua jacket with a rainbow-toned scarf wrapped across the top of her head and tied under her chin. As he came down the hill toward her, he watched her wipe the remnants of salty tears from her wind-whipped cheeks. Seeing her in such misery tugged at his heart.

"Are you hurt?" Daven asked. He knelt in front of her, passing a hand over every part of her body in a healing scan.

Iris bit her lip as he touched the offending foot. "Just my ankle. My fault, like I said."

"Let me help you," he offered.

He wrapped his hand lightly around her boot, removing it with the gentlest of motion. He did not need to see the purpling and swollen flesh to know where she was hurt. His gift showed him her pain radiating like a heat source. He placed one hand on either side of her ankle and closed his eyes, willing the blood vessels to pump away the inflammation that beset her, calming nerve endings that wounded her, and channeling the light of the magic world into her system, to promote her well-being.

She reached out and laid her hand upon his arm, almost completing a circle of healing between them. Daven noticed Iris' innate ability to read the pain in others and to provide counsel, an unusual trait for a human. If Lane Donatelli was correct in his odd theories, perhaps she did have a vestigial power, left over from the days when humans were like elves. Perhaps she could even be trained to develop her talents into magic, despite her humanity.

His work complete, Daven released her leg, his mind afire at the thought of being able to share magic with Iris and Jelani's other friends. Not just any human would merit the honing of their gifts into something that could be truly dangerous. A selective cadre only, for now. But he could not hope to help them accomplish this until he acquired the full range of magic under his control.

"There," he said. "You will be able to make it to the cave."

Her faint smile conveyed no confidence or excitement. "Cave? As in a dirty, rocky hole in a mountain cave? No bed? Or food?"

"Ah, my sweet Iris, I've missed you." He pulled her to him for a warm kiss and exchange of their lovers' aura. "Come let me tell you what I've learned. And then you can tell me the news of the world."

He lifted her into his arms and headed back toward the cave, hearing for the first time the cry of a hawk overhead. If the birds were returning, surely the new season would not be far behind.

* * *

ONCE Daven brought Iris some fresh cold water, they shared a granola bar that she had brought in her pack.

He was hungrier than he had realized. The supplies he had found were nearly gone. His trip outside the cave and back let him know significant time had passed since his last venture out.

"Tell me of the clan," he said. "Has Elliun come home safely?"

Iris frowned. "You knew he was missing?"

Something in her eyes bothered Daven. "Astan and Jelani told me. Before they left. Have they returned to the clan?"

"I don't know. With everyone gone, I went back to the city. I thought you were searching for the child." Iris looked around, not meeting his gaze. "But instead you've been hiding in this cave?"

Her voice held the same tone of contempt Jelani had used to persuade Astan to leave the tree house.

"I am not hiding, Iris." Daven's words came out clipped and sharp-edged. The implication stung. "I'm preparing, studying, and learning."

"How does this solve the problem, especially if Bartolomey is waiting at the other end? He may be ready to attack. It doesn't sound like anyone's got time for school!"

A rush of almost human irritation overtook Daven at the way she seemed to be judging him. He reached out for her hand and caught it in his before she could pull away, long enough to read her thoughts and find the one answer he needed to know.

They are alive. And safe. Weak with relief, he dropped her hand.

"I'm sorry, Daven." Iris hesitated before laying her hand upon his knee. "We didn't know who to trust. You didn't go looking for Elliun. Jelani thought Grigor took him."

Daven stiffened. He had only searched her mind for basic confirmation of his family's existence. What else could have happened? "Then what?"

"Grigor's dead. Astan and Jelly found him in the woods, caught in a bear trap. Lane was the one who took the baby."

Daven's thoughts returned to that last day at the tree house. He had gone to meet with the Circle, barely registering the absence of Jelani's human friends. "So it was not Rashia, or Grigor. Instead it was the queen's friend that stole the prince."

Iris shrugged and moved closer. "Lane didn't steal Elliun. He thought he was saving him. Lane has, um, issues." She sighed. "They all have issues. But the point is they're fine now." Her clear blue eyes met his gaze. "How are you? Really."

"I'm well. Getting better." He sensed the breath entering his body and then leaving it. "Wait. You said Bartolomey. He's enchanted, contained in a vessel by Lorenz."

"When we were all together at Lane's apartment, Astan had a vision. One of those moments he has, you know, where he flashes on things? He has no explanation how Bartolomey could be alive. He just said it. Freaked Jelani out, for sure. Poor thing."

Daven's breath caught, as he considered that possibility. Uneasiness flooded him like a river drowned with snowmelt. He knew how accurate and painful flashes could be. If Bartolomey was in fact alive and free of the magic vessel, then the clan was in for a much greater challenge.

"I imagine she is," he muttered after a pause.

Iris wiped her hands on her denim jeans, before letting them rest on her thighs. "You said you were preparing. Preparing for what?"

Daven leaned his head against the wall of the cave. He took another deep breath and then released it. "The war that's coming."

CHAPTER 13

ASTAN Hawk knew no one could get into Vincent Marsh's cabin without Jelani's permission.

Still, he was leery of remaining there with his mate and their child. It was too close to the clan's territory and not easily defensible. Daven, who knew the cabin's location, could show up or even lead the Circle right to it.

So, of course, that was where Jelani wanted to go.

"We can't stay here any longer," she said, gesturing at apartment walls that hardly seemed wide enough to contain Crispy and the sprawling disaster of Lane's computer Cave. "It's too hard on Crisp. Poor guy." She glanced in the direction of the closed bedroom door, where Crispy had retreated to nap next to the sleeping baby. "We have a place. It's enchanted, if not enchanting. We could make it a little better." She sighed. "Get a real bed."

"How will you get a—"

"Lane will drive me," Jelani said.

She gave a flirty little smile, the kind he seldom saw from her these days. The expression reassured him. Maybe things were on the upswing.

"Lane isn't sworn to protect you," Astan reminded. "I am."

"Oh, here we go again." Her voice took on well-worn, mock-suffering tone. "'I'm your Guardian, which makes me second only to the gods of the forest in controlling your life, since you have no father or mother'. Blah, blah, blah." She moved close and slipped her arms around him. "Good thing I love you."

He took her in his arms and held her close. "That is a good thing, *denami*." He let himself feel her, deeply feel her, her thoughts, her emotions, her wants, right down to her heartbeat. His rhythm slowly synched with hers, even their breathing, and he opened himself to her. He let her sense his concern for their safety amid the many dangers that might await them in the forest.

"I know," she whispered. "But we have to trust that Lorenz and my father had the right idea. They were on the Good Guys' team back when the clan's break-up first happened. They were closest to it. They knew Bart. If anything's going to protect us, their spell will."

Nothing Astan said thereafter would convince her. He helped her pack their few belongings, and the clothes her human friends donated to them both. He did not mind hiking out into the forest, but looking at the stack of belongings Jelani intended to take, he was not sure they would be able to carry it all, and the baby, on their backs.

"We have no vehicle," Astan reminded her.

She reached into her pocket and dangled a set of keys at him. "Kevin said we could use his car if we needed to get diapers or anything. I think this counts as 'anything'. Besides, my nerves are about shot. Something is crawling under my skin." She fidgeted and put the keys back into her pocket.

"Are you ill?" Astan eyed her, not seeing any obvious signs of sickness.

"No. It's just a feeling. I don't want to wait. Lane can bring Kevin out to pick up the car later." She stacked up a couple more boxes. "Don't worry. I'll drive. Remember you stripped the gears on my car last time you tried it."

He grimaced. "That was an emergency."

"This could be, too."

She checked on the baby, and woke Crispy in the process.

Twisting his hands nervously, Crispy crossed the living room and then hung back behind the kitchen counter. "You're not waiting for Lane to come back? He's got the truck. You sent him there for intelligence."

"I can't imagine he's going to find anything intelligent from the Circle," Jelani retorted. "They're a bunch of liars and tricksters. I'll call and tell him to meet us at the cabin."

Crispy paced. "When will Iris come back?"

Jelani shook her head and checked the heavy diaper bag

again. "She's determined to find Daven. Wherever the hell he went."

"Let's hope she doesn't bring him back," Astan muttered. "We don't want to have to chase him away again."

"Iris does not love bad guys," Crispy insisted. He crossed his arms stubbornly.

Jelani looked at Astan and then at Crispy. "Of course, she doesn't. Daven probably isn't a bad guy. Well, maybe he isn't. He just has his priorities screwed up. Okay? Not everyone has the same plans for our little family."

Crispy frowned. "Why do you care about their plans? You're the queen, right? You should tell them how to behave. They should follow your royal commands."

Jelani laughed. "You'd think so, wouldn't you?"

"You should make them," Crispy said. "That's how it's supposed to be."

Astan considered Crispy's words. Indeed, Jelani was ordained to be queen by her birthright. The clan would not grow and become strong and healthy without its queen. The last twenty years proved that. His duty to the clan prodded him to reunite them. It seemed the only way to heal the land and the elves.

But could he reunite them? Jelani would never trust Djana and the others again. Not after the betrayals she suffered at their hands.

His thoughts came in bursts, flicked against his brain.

The clan without its queen continuing to decline, the individuals slowly decaying, losing their powers. The end of the clan soil, the humans overrunning it with their machines and development. The trees dying, murdered for the use of humans. Jelani herself fading, not as quickly, but deprived of the healing touch she brought to the plants of the clan soil, becoming mundane, self-centered again, perhaps losing her connection to their child. Leaving Elliun alone with the clan, as Astan was left by Veraena, leaving them both empty and lonely.

"Astan? *Denami?*" Jelani shook his arm, woke him from his dark vision. Desperation overcoming him, he grabbed her hand and squeezed it.

"We may have to deal with the Circle," Astan warned her.

"Your friend is right."

Jelani looked at him for a moment, only a hint of expression in her eyes.

The she gave Crispy a quick hug. "We'll see you soon, Crisp. Thanks so much for letting us stay here and eat your food and drink all your coffee." She shouldered the diaper bag. "Which reminds me, we need to stop at Butterfly Herbs for a chocolate hazelnut on the way out of town. A double."

* * *

HOURS later, as the sun neared the horizon at the end of the day's journey, Jelani surveyed her tiny domain with some small satisfaction.

While she had Kevin's car, she stocked up on food and supplies, even a stovetop coffeepot and some fresh-ground coffee funded by a cash gift Iris had left. A neatly stacked pile of cans and boxes sat in the northwest corner of the small cabin, rising nearly to the ceiling.

Alone in the cabin, Jelani watched the baby sleep in a blanket-lined cardboard box on the metal frame bed. She thought wistfully of the tree house nursery, stocked top to bottom with elven-made clothing, toys, blankets and a beautiful hand-carved cradle. The memory pained her. She returned to stacking diapers on the shelves of the rusty metal cupboard that once belonged to her father.

She choked with emotion. Grigor and his friends could have killed both Elliun and Jelani. And Rashia, who knew what that old midwife was capable of? Djana with her threatening dreams. Daven, who seemed so reasonable, his wishes gently shoved onto her without even her knowledge or permission.

No. Astan had to be wrong.

They did not need the clan. Her warning to Rashia might yet become reality. They could take Elliun and run. Far away, maybe to New Mexico, maybe even to Indiana. Surely her stepmother Carolyn would shelter them from those who had murdered Jelani's father.

The realization that even Carolyn was considered a possible

refuge demonstrated the extent of Jelani's desperation.

"Whoa. Now we're really out on a limb, hmm?" Jelani sighed. "Great. Now I'm talking to myself."

Astan was out in the forest scouting for the tenth time. She pulled the cloth curtain closed, hiding the contents of the cabinet. She stood in the middle of her fifteen-foot square kingdom that contained a small bed, a few folding chairs, a hotplate, a disaster cache of canned foods and juice, and two suitcases of borrowed clothing.

What would she do now that everything was put away? Elliun slept, well, like a baby, as Jelani finished off two cups of coffee she brought with her. She wished she would have brought some yarn or even a book to occupy her time. Astan warned her not to step outside until he was satisfied the area was safe.

She opened one of the folding chairs and sat in it, not knowing how much the day sucked from her until the ache set into her bones. Her eyes closed almost of their own accord, and she found herself reciting one of the elven relaxation mantras that Daven taught her. She just had to be in this place, at this moment. She was safe. Her child was safe. Astan would be safe if he ever brought himself back to the cabin where the old magic would protect him. All would be well. She let herself go, floating in a calm place until she could feel grounded once more.

Voices.

The sound was coming from outside. Panic pulled her to her feet. She cast about for something to use as a weapon. The gun had been left at the tree house. All she had here was, at best, a heavy can of beans.

She folded one of the chairs and gripped it tightly, ready to swing.

"*Denami*? Open the door."

"Astan?" She took a step closer to the door, still hesitant. "Who's with you?"

"Jelani," Astan's voice was ripe with exasperation. "Please."

"All right, all right." She set down the chair and opened the door.

Astan waited on the stone outside the door, accompanied by

several Youngers from the clan: Beckley, Pieter, and Merripen. Her first instinct was to close the door in the face of anyone with ties to the Circle, but her deep trust in Astan halted her hand. Also the fact that when they saw her, the Youngers immediately took a respectful knee in the snow, with a murmured: "My queen."

"What are they doing here?" she asked.

"They're about to get caught in a snow down drift, if you don't let them inside," Astan said, a faint smile lighting on his lips. He stepped across the threshold, slipped an arm around her, and kissed her cheek. "It's all right, *denami*. They come to help."

He moved her aside with a light touch and the three Youngers entered, filling up the small cabin, especially broad-shouldered Beckley. Their eyes went immediately to the bed, to Elliun.

Without thinking, Jelani stepped between them and her child.

"The prince is well?" Pieter asked. He had a slight build with hair the color of dried straw and eyes the pale blue of an early morning sky. Jelani remembered him as one devoted to mischief, always scolded by the Elders for some caper or another.

"He is well," Astan assured. He glanced out the door behind them. "Where's Max?"

"Why are they here, Astan? How can they help?" Jelani shivered against the rising sense of fear centered like a chunk of ice in her midsection. Surely, Astan would not force the Circle on her. He knew her better than that. She would not let them get their hands on Elliun. Her hand went to the pocket where she kept the keys to Kevin's car. She could grab the baby and make a run for the car.

Astan laid a hand on her heart. "Stop this," he said, his other hand cupping her chin, making her look him in the eye. "Would I risk you after all we've survived? You know I would not."

Beckley remained at a deferential distance, but his expression was warm. "We practically twisted his arm to let us come. I swear to you, Jelani, we were not followed. I would have seen."

She nodded slowly. Beckley's long-sight was well known to her. "So you aren't sent by the Circle?"

Merripen shook his head. "Hardly. The Lane said you would be safe here. Although he said you were in the human city."

Jelani rolled her eyes at the title. "Right. So Lane hooked up with you out there?"

Astan moved aside and opened a couple of the folding chairs. "Beckley and these others apparently met with Lane and got the details from him before he drove back to town."

A thump overhead preceded a series of thuds and a loud crash outside the door. Jelani stiffened, alert for another attack.

Pieter peeked out the window. "It's just Max."

With an irritated sigh, Jelani opened the door and invited in the slight, white-haired elf who was Lane's favorite. The poor thing was covered in snow. He must have scraped off half of what was on the worn roof when he landed.

"Are you all right?" she asked.

Max bowed deeply. "I am well to be in your presence again, my lady."

Jelani found herself blushing. Feeling more generous toward her guests, she set a package of cookies on the table where the others gathered.

"It is our intention to work with the true leaders of the clan to restore the balance of power," Beckley said. He gestured the other two Youngers into chairs.

"You and Astan," Merripen clarified. His was a face that could have graced any holiday cartoon about jolly, holiday elves. Sandy-haired, fair-skinned, innocent, and angelic. Right down to the gap between his two front teeth. Jelani did not know Merripen's age, but his stocky build put him squarely on track to be as large as Beckley once he reached young adulthood.

"Thanks for pointing that out." Jelani smiled, and was gratified to see the Younger light up at her recognition of him.

"It's not all good news," Astan said. He paced in the vicinity of the third chair but didn't take it. Beckley stood behind him, as a good second should.

Jelani concentrated on the shelf above the tiny sink, studying the worn variety of mugs her father had collected over the years. Several from the University, one from Mount Rushmore, a pair of textured olive green glass mugs which looked as if they were from the 1970s. After all these years without him, anything that her father's hands touched was treasured. Think about good things, not bad news.

Astan cleared his throat. "At least half of the Youngers have left the clan to join Grigor's group."

She frowned at the thought of the loss in numbers. "Grigor's dead."

Beckley jammed hands into his jacket pockets. "That was news to us. We're not sure who they're following now. Astan said Grigor brought Vez with him when he came to take the baby. Vez may now be the leader of that separatist band."

"Vez always seemed quiet, withdrawn from the others," Jelani said. "Without a mother or father in the clan, no one seemed particularly interested in him."

Beckley snorted. "When you were around, perhaps. When it was the Youngers only, he displayed quite an arrogant attitude." He cleared his throat. "He also had a serious desire for Fontine."

"Grigor's *neris*?" Jelani raised an eyebrow. "What better motive to kill him?"

"Exactly," Beckley replied. "So now the Youngers who were with him, as well as a host of Youngers and some Elders, gather somewhere to the northeast. Whispers arose after they left, indicating they found a leader. Someone to center their hopes for survival, since the clan seemed to be disintegrating."

"Vez?" Jelani sat on the bed, settling gently so as not to disturb Elliun.

"No, not Vez," Beckley said. "They speak of a woman. Dark-skinned with silver hair. And...."

Jelani noticed the change in the timbre of Beckley's voice, a hint of fear. "And?"

"They speak of *Intalus* living in the forest," Beckley added with hesitation. "A disembodied mage who seeks to rule."

Astan took a deep breath, as if the oxygen alone could provide him with strength. "If the whispers are right, it could well be Bartolomey." Before Jelani could protest, he raised a hand. "I don't know how. I don't even know for sure that it is. But that's what's being said."

Jelani bit her lip. That battle she did not want to fight again under any circumstances. As if in direct response, the nerves in her hand burned with the memory of the needles with which Bartolomey had stabbed her, trying to torture her into telling him the truth about her mother.

When Astan first mentioned the possible existence of Bartolomey, back in Lane's apartment, Jelani discounted it as impossible. Astan thought big. His visions often came in wide swaths, and perhaps just the trail of Bartolomey's passing was still included. But if the clan members still spoke of it, still believed it, she must consider it a possibility.

Elliun stirred, and she busied herself by readjusting his blanket, not knowing how to respond. When she looked up, all of them watched her, hung on her unspoken words. They wanted something from her.

"What?" Jelani asked.

"You're the queen," Merripen stammered. "The Circle doesn't have any answers for us. We await your commands, my lady."

She looked to Pieter, who nodded in assent. Then Beckley, who inclined his head. Astan was the last. His eyes were shadowed, troubled. What did they expect her to say? She didn't have any more answers than they did. Maybe even less.

"*Denami*," Astan said. He took a deep breath and then slowly released it. "I wonder if the magic Lorenz held has begun to dissipate. Many years have passed since he walked on soil. If Bartolomey was able to escape from the enchanted vessel prepared by Lorenz and The Vincent, the same magic we rely on here to keep Elliun and ourselves safe, it is possible that the magic which charms this place will fade into mist as well. Our friends have joined us for the purpose of protecting this place. They have promised to watch and guard against intruders." His gaze flitted about the room, as if he sought direction, guidance. "But if this magic of the old era will not defend us, we are but five. Even with Lane and the others, less than ten. Against a hundred or more championed by a mage of the forest? We'll never stand."

No way, Jelani thought. Why did it always come back to this? "You're saying we need the Circle."

"Not at all, Jelani," Beckley said. "He's saying the Circle needs its queen. Once they realize this, too, you will be in a position to win any concessions from them you must."

"Even Djana will have to see that to survive, she needs you," Astan said, his shoulders slumping in release as he finally took the chair. "Without us, the entire clan will go down in defeat. It will be the end of the Bitterroot generations. The end of everything."

CHAPTER 14

VEZ sat brooding on the branches of a tree over the river near the elven bower his mother created.

The cool wind blew around him, caressing his face. Everything he intended seemed to be in motion. The others, the number growing daily as defectors from the clan arrived, spent their time training, sparring with each other, talking about what it was like back with the clan, dreaming about the new future before them. Now that Grigor was dead, even Fontine seemed to have moved on without regret, creating herself a new persona as Veraena's shadow.

Nevertheless, Vez remained unsatisfied. He found himself more troubled than before he was committed to leave the clan. Before they attacked the false queen in her tree and before they failed at their mission. Though the clan seemed to be in disarray, if those deserting its bosom spoke truly, the queen, her mate and their son remained alive and well, and still a potential force to be reckoned with.

Possibilities closer to home intrigued him more. Having confronted the altered Bartolomey, having seen his mother interact with the fallen mage, Vez's instincts told him this might be the greater power struggle. He could understand the deep respect one held for the mentor-teacher who taught one all the necessary skills, and it might be appropriate for his mother to be subservient to such a teacher.

But if Bartolomey, once the mage adept, remained ephemeral and disembodied, did he deserve to remain the master?

Veraena said Bartolomey weakened the longer he remained without a vessel in which to traverse the world. Did they not need a strong champion if they intended to challenge the Circle of the Bitterroot elf clan once and for all? Bartolomey had already been once defeated by Jelani Marsh, in the time when he was strong and of the soil. If Veraena did indeed have the skills of *Intalus*, she could be a formidable opponent, superior to the weak and withering old husk of the queen's uncle.

The tales of the refugees hinted, however, that the queen and her son might have left the forest, never to return. Daven Talvi had fled north, and the remnants of the ruling Circle were fading, losing their power and control. If this was so, who remained to challenge them?

Surely now was the time to strike, while the clan's forces were vulnerable and frail.

"Victory will be ours," Vez said to himself, climbing lightly down the thick tree trunk. Landing on the remains of the icy leaves below, his feet crunched into the soil. He made his way into the heart of the rebel camp, exchanging greetings with elves he passed. He stopped just outside the bower as he recognized a set of hunched shoulders and the graying head of his foster father Kassen. When had he arrived?

Vez marched over to Kassen, noting that he himself now stood taller than the *nian* who raised him in the clan. Vez held himself apart from Kassen, who was not his real father. He only took him in on sufferance. But even so, a rough bond developed between them. Look at him now, he thought. The old elf stank, his clothing worn and dirty. He looked up as Vez approached, squinting his dark eyes as if his vision were failing.

"Vez, my boy? I heard you escaped with your life." Kassen reached a bony hand to clap Vez on the shoulder. "Clever lad."

During his growing-up years, the old elf seemed thoroughly attached to the skirts of the Circle witches, following their edicts without question. "Kassen, what brings you so far from home?"

Kassen laughed, an empty, hollow sound that held no mirth. "My home? I have none. None unless you will now take me in, Vez. The Circle no longer has a place for me. I must beg you for food and shelter. The son must now become the father, the one responsible. What kind of world is this, downside up and roundabout?"

Veraena crossed the open space between the bower and the

forest, approaching the newcomer. Vez forced a hospitable smile. "Of course you may stay, Kassen. Come in, have something to eat. I'm sure we can find you warm clothing. Here there is plenty."

Veraena must have overheard the aging *nian*'s plaintive question. She reached for his hand, which she held in hers. "Indeed, my friend. What sort of world has the clan brought us to?" She turned her brilliant smile on Kassen, who seemed as bedazzled as all the elves when they first met her. Vez had to admit, she did shine. She was a born leader.

She should be their leader.

With a fluid stride, Veraena led Kassen into the group, making him feel welcome and greeting the other elves gathered there. Several of them expressed surprise to see him, but a couple of the older ones welcomed him and led him to the food supply.

Terzon, who had become tall and lean in their days in Bartolomey's retreat, came up behind Vez and nodded in Kassen's direction. "What's he doing here?"

Vez shrugged. "He says the Circle's tossed him out."

"Is that so?" Terzon's tone reeked of disbelief. "He was one of Rashia's favorites."

"I know. He could be a spy."

"He could. Should I end him?"

Vez heard a sharpening of pleasure in Terzon's voice. Terzon actually wanted to kill Kassen. Vez instinctively rejected the notion of deliberate harm to the *nian* who had raised him. "No. There's no proof." He fidgeted, shoving his hands in the pockets of his over-jacket. The thought of killing Kassen had occurred to him, as well. "He's not the only one the clan has discarded as unworthy. We all know that."

"Just the same, he can't be trusted. Not yet." Terzon crossed his arms. "I'll watch him."

"It's wise to watch all those who come from the clan now. We cannot be too careful." Vez studied his companion without blinking. "If it is the wish of the Lady of the Forest to send us converts to our cause, we should be grateful. Perhaps the growing numbers of those arriving demonstrate to us that we are on the right path at last."

"Perhaps." Terzon's gaze flicked away from Vez, and his tongue moistened his lips.

Vez saw that Terzon's attention had been pulled to the vision of Veraena, coming out of the bower, her arm around the shoulder of Hidal. The Younger looked up at her, face radiant, listening for all he was worth.

She's my mother! Vez wanted to scream.

It was no surprise that Veraena had been able to subvert Grigor into a frenzied follower. Now, the others gathered around Veraena, as if she were queen. Where exactly did his mother's ambitions lie?

As if she heard his unspoken question, Veraena beckoned him. "Vez, walk with me."

"Of course," Vez replied, as he made his way slowly over to her side, conscious of the eyes upon him. He must be restrained, calm. He could not be what they were, mesmerized by her light. "I'll be out to the training square before long, Terzon."

"I'll see you then," Terzon said with a stubborn set of his jaw. His shoulders straightened, and he walked a little taller.

When they were out of earshot, Vez noticed Veraena's small smirk. "What?"

"Vez, my son, you have no need to worry about your position with me. No longer will we be separated. This I promise you."

He ignored the rush of blood to his face. "I'm not worried. I just want to know."

"Know what?" Her head cocked slightly to the side. A fallen tree lay ahead of them. She took his hand and pulled him down beside her to sit on the trunk. Her eyes seemed to be even deeper blue than usual, her attention warm and intimate. "I sense your unhappiness, Vez. Your questions. I need your full support and attention if we are to win this battle for governance of the clan. Please. Tell me what worries you."

Here it was, the opportunity he was waiting for, but when he tried to make the words come out, he could not do it. They stuck in his throat like dry grass.

Veraena laid her hand over his on his knee. "I know we

haven't been as close as you would have wanted, over these past years. It took time to find my way, to find my magic. If I had stayed with the clan, the life chosen by the Circle would have sucked me dry. Djana knew somehow that I was destined to become *Intalus.* Just as—" Veraena paused, wincing. "Just as Daven."

"Daven Talvi is destined to become a mage?" Vez asked. Although renowned for his elven gifts, Talvi had never displayed anything close to what Vez had seen from Bartolomey or his mother. "But how?"

Veraena lips pressed together for a moment. "The Elders knew. Both of us studied, learned the beginning steps. His interest in Linnea was known to all, but the human Vincent stole her heart. Daven turned to me for comfort, someone familiar. Not because of any great love between us."

She pulled back and looked away. "I confess, I knew this even as Astan was born. We would never be true lovers. Daven sought solace for his broken dream. I hoped to gain some advantage with Djana and the Elders. But the old *neris* knew. I was not the royal match she hoped for." She smiled without mirth. "Astan was three seasons in age when Daven volunteered to be a sleeper. Once he was gone, the Circle closed in on itself, retreating to the human city. I tried to stay with them, but I couldn't live there. The soil was covered with cold, unfeeling rock."

Vez nodded, his sketchy memory of the city a season, maybe more, before Kassen retreated into the woods with a few others in a small enclave hidden from Bartolomey's part of the clan. They nearly perished before they found a balance between their time with the Circle and their time in the natural world, just enough to sustain their bond with the clan, just enough so they would not perish, as Grigor nearly did.

"I left you with the clan, knowing they would take you in, find you a home. I knew you would be stronger with them than with me alone." She sighed, her hands clasping in her lap. "The choice of Kassen as your foster was fortuitous as it turned out. We can use him to our advantage even now."

"What do you mean?"

"I've showed Kassen what he must do, what he must say, to be welcomed back into the fading Circle. He will listen and learn, and when he shares what he has heard, we will be the wiser. His help will bring us victory."

Vez thought about Terzon's threats. "The other Youngers do not trust Kassen. They believe he spies for the Circle."

Veraena smiled and leaned forward to pat his arm. "I shall speak to them. Kassen shall not be harmed. We will care for those who support our cause."

The brief moment of intimacy allowed the courage he sought to wash over him, and he grabbed it with both hands.

"Is Bartolomey my father?" Vez asked.

She snapped erect, her eyes flashing with irritation. "Why do you keep asking me? You're grown now, a strong young *nian*. You've matured without a father. You stand on your own."

Her words hit him like a fist to the stomach. "Why won't you tell me?"

"Because it doesn't matter. You have me now, and these others." Her warmth faded.

He shook his head. Veraena was wrong. He knew this information did matter. His future depended on it. "It matters to me, who I choose to support. If the mage is my father and you intend to remain subordinate to him, then I can follow him as well." Vez felt a rush of energy burst through him at being able to say these words aloud. They drove him to his feet. "But if he is not my father, then my loyalty is to you. I would follow you as the leader of our quest to declare our independence from those old women, and I would bring all these others with me." He gestured toward the bower where the elves rested, unaware of the controversy taking place so close to their comfortable new home. "They have no reason to trust either of you."

"But they listen well, they want to—"

Vez could not keep the note of cruelty from his voice, letting that jealous streak drench his words in petulance. He hated they way it made him sound pathetic, but he wanted to stop being the only one who hurt inside. "They want to bed you. That's all. You use your sex to draw them in. Mother, they need a leader, not a lover."

Her shocked eyes opened wide. Her mouth dropped open, too. She seemed to wilt under his continued scrutiny.

Finally, Vez felt he had the upper hand. "So I need to know. Is the *Intalus* my father?"

She stared at him for several long seconds that felt like an eternity and then she stood. "No. He is not."

CHAPTER 15

WHEN Daven returned to the cave, exhausted after another period of communing with the natural forces that would galvanize his budding mage-hood, he saw a weary patience on Iris' face.

It was the same expression she had worn since her arrival many days ago. The drawn look vanished when she spied him, as it did each time he returned, and was replaced by a welcoming smile.

"So, are you a wizard yet?" Iris asked, pushing herself up from the rock she was waiting on. The teasing tone reminded him that she knew very well his study of magic was quiet serious. The human sense of humor was so unique in each of them. An acquired appreciation, however, for the average elven brain.

She held out her arms and gathered him inside, holding him. A rush of emotion came from their touch, their bond, the loss of missing him and the joy of seeing him again. Daven did what he could to show her she was also important to him.

"Not yet. But closer." Daven felt her warmth recharge him after a time spent meditating with the cold soil. The more he opened himself to the possibilities of profound magic, the more was revealed to him about life around him. Not just his human companion, but the animals, the plants, the very air released their secrets. "I connected today with the deep energy, I believe. Lantin seemed pleased with my work. I moved the earth by my thoughts."

Her head rested on his chest. "Progress. I'm proud of you."

His hand on her mid-back, Daven assessed her state of being, careful to keep some mental distance between them not for his own protection but for hers. For all her protests about wanting to experience everything possible between a human female and an elven male, Daven was not sure she was strong enough for a full bond to run open between them. He closed his eyes and let his mental walls open a small bit, so his energy meshed with hers.

A hint of alarm went through him as he realized how depleted her energy was since the last time they were together. How long had he been gone? He did not think of his time seeking the *santwarja* in terms of the passage of hours or days, but merely to completion. Each lesson the earth shared with him brought him closer to finding that door to the knowledge of the ages. Because he was elf, his sense of time expanded or contracted with the task in his hands.

Not so for gentle Iris.

"You haven't eaten," he scolded.

She shrugged. "I could stand to lose a few pounds. I didn't know how long we would be here, or I would have brought more with me."

He read her time-sense. He had been away five days. No wonder she was starved, in more ways than one. Humans needed more interaction than this to thrive.

"Let me see what I can find," he said.

The supplies found in the abandoned pack were gone now, as was everything she had brought. He would have to scavenge in the wild.

He left her briefly to gather some roots and other edibles he knew how to find in the still-frozen landscape. Some seasons were warm by this date, the trees and leaves anxious to begin their time of growth, but not this year. With the queen in hiding and the clan still fractured, little motivation existed to proliferate. The change would impact the whole region. If only the spring would wait for him to gain full strength.

Then what?

He mulled over his options as he and Iris ate what he found. She did not complain, but he knew it was not her kind of food. Basic nourishment only. "I know I've said this before, Iris, but you don't have to stay here with me. You could go home and be comfortable. Wear your slippers. Eat fried food." He smiled and caressed her cheek, knowing his words should release her from any obligation she felt and set her free. "I'm not one of your broken humans, love. I've finally seen the direction I need to go. I can get there without someone holding my hand."

Her face fell, and then she pulled away.

He sensed her dismay thick in the air around them, like a fall mist. He did not understand. "What? I thought this would please you. You do so much for those you serve. One less man demanding your time. I was sure that would be a relief."

"Daven!" Her voice choked. Iris stumbled to her feet and hurried out of the cave into the cold air.

Stunned, he stared after her a moment, and then followed. He was doing her a favor, thinking only of her well-being. What had he said to cause her such hurt?

When he stepped out of the cave she was nowhere in sight, but her trail was easy to find. He could hear her footsteps leading away from the cave into the trees, a jumble of dragging boots and tripping. Her disappointment also trailed behind, leaving a tangible vibration that painfully settled into his bones. Her thoughts were clear to him. He was a fool.

"Iris! Wait!" he called, hurrying after her.

At first he thought she would not stop. Finally, she slowed and came to a halt. When she turned to him, tears streamed down her cheeks. He looked into her azure eyes and read her pain.

Her expression struck at his heart. He grabbed her hands, pulled her to him. "*Denami,* I did not mean to hurt you in any way. I apologize from my depths. Please forgive me."

She sighed, a shuddering sound that thoroughly shook her. "If you were one of my young clients, I could understand how you might misconstrue my feelings. But I know you have gifts, even more magnified now. There's no excuse for you not knowing what I'm thinking, except that you don't care enough to pay attention."

He began to explain why it was so important that he concentrate on his study, but she laid a hand softly over his lips.

"I know," she said. "I know you must do what you're doing for the sake of the clan. I support you wholeheartedly, not only for Jelani, but for the others as well. I don't mind. Much." She smiled, a faint shadow of her usual sunny regard, before looking away. "I can be patient. I am trying very hard, Daven, because I want all of you to be safe, and happy."

"I know you are. That's why I suggested you return to the city, where you can wait in comfort." Daven tipped her chin up so he could see her beautiful eyes again. "I want you to be safe and happy, too. And not cold and hungry." He added a mental push, wanting her to understand his deep concern for her well-being. "Whatever is being taught to me is something I must learn to serve the greater cause, and this is my time. As much as I care for you, I cannot veer from this path. I have already postponed it too long."

Iris nodded. "I understand. I would never ask that of you, Daven."

"Of course you wouldn't. That's why you are so special." He let warmth flow through him to wash over her. But she was smart, too.

"For a human. Yes." Iris chuckled and grabbed his hand to squeeze it. "Even if I'm from the wrong side of the tracks, I still love you, Daven Talvi."

"Tracks?" He looked at the ground, seeing no trail of animal prints anywhere around them.

"Railroad tracks. It's a human saying. Never mind." She took a deep breath and let it out in a frozen swirl of mist. "Maybe you're right. I'm not doing you any good, not really. Distracting you, probably." She studied his face, seemed to read agreement there although he tried not to allow any feeling to show.

He did not want to be responsible for negative perception on her part. What would reassure her? "You have braced my resolve to live through what is to come, Iris. When I left the clan to come here, my only thought was that I must put aside everything I was. I had to protect them, even if it meant sacrificing my life for Elliun's. Your being here has shown me that I matter to someone beyond just what magic I can do." Even as the words came out, he realized they were true. Iris cared for him, not because of what he could do for her, or what the clan expected, his duty, but just because she loved him. Him. Just because. "Thank you for your confidence in me."

"You're worthy of it," she said. Sincerity shone through her words, and he thought for a few moments it was her professional tone, the same one he heard her use on Crispy many times. He knew, though, she never looked at Jelani's poor damaged friend the way she now looked at him.

"Shall I conduct you back to the city?" he asked.

She looked south over her shoulder, in the general direction of Missoula, and sighed deeply. "No, you have to finish this transformation of yours, as quickly as possible. No telling when the evil elves will attack again. Or Bart. Or whoever." She gave a small shrug. "Hopefully my car is still parked at the end of the road. I'll head back to town." She half-turned, and then hesitated. "Any message you want me to pass on?"

Was there? Daven considered how Astan and Jelani left him, bleeding, on the floor of the home he created for them. He thought about them hiding in the city, the queen abandoning her own people. Iris meant to keep from him any knowledge of Elliun and his whereabouts, with the agreement of all the others. What could he say to any of them that made sense now?

But in reality, he cared very much about them. He had nearly given his life to save the queen, the clan, their way of life. His future and theirs were entwined. The boy was his blood.

"Tell them for me, please, I look forward to seeing them all again, safe and healthy. I'll do that as soon as I become what I need to be."

"All right. I'll tell them." She hugged him tightly. "Come home soon."

"I will," Daven said, letting go and retreating a couple of steps.

"Soon," Iris admonished, her eyes wet with tears. Then she hurried off.

When he could not see her anymore, Daven made his way back to the cave. No time to rest now. He must grow even stronger. He needed to be able to cast his magic for attack purposes as well as defense, and to be ready to use his skills for the benefit of his family and clan.

Only then would he be able to return to Iris' side.

* * *

TIME passed. Without the distraction of Iris' presence, Daven lost himself in the pursuit of his goal.

Alone in the cave, he tried to school his mind to locate the door that would open, taking him into the *santwarja*. It seemed the harder he worked at finding it, the farther it slipped from him. Frustrated at the end of a particularly difficult cycle, he stormed from the hollowed rock, venting his disappointment on the thick trunk of a fir tree, beating it with his hands until they were bloody.

"Lady of the Forest, how can I save my people if you do not let me in?" he cried. "They need my help. Chaos is upon us. We will be lost to the evil ones if I cannot defend them!"

He fell to his knees, hardly noticing that they sank into mud, not ice. He wanted an answer. He waited.

After the initial silence that followed his outburst, the air gradually filled with the sound of tentative birdsong, the ruffle of fluttered wings overhead, even a hint of wind passing through the pine needles. A shaft of sunlight split the glade that lay three elf-lengths before him, cutting through the broad greenery of the trees above. Daven watched the beam illuminate the ground and all that sat around it, a brilliant burst of life and light. Time stood still as he stared, entranced. Surely this was a sign!

Something moved in the light, indefinable, shining so brightly that it hurt his eyes. But he did not look away, willing himself to connect with it. "Teach me, Lady," he whispered.

The ray of light slowly moved toward him, as if called. He held his breath. Surely he was about to be given the tools of understanding, perhaps even the keys to the door he sought. He closed his eyes, ready to receive his lesson.

The faint warmth of the beam surrounded him, the intensity of the light radiated along his skin. Inside the beam, the sound from outside stopped as if he were in some locked human chamber. Only silence. He waited.

Tell me what you expect of me, Lady. I am ready to defeat those who threaten us.

No answer came.

Am I not your champion? Is this not what you sent me into the forest to learn?

Again, nothing.

He waited, his patience wearing as thin as his body. He brought himself to the place where the deep magic could be found. He applied himself, reconnecting to the energies of the earth, working through the mental exercises. He left his family, friends, even Iris, to pursue this course because it would redeem him. Had he failed?

This was the only sign he had received, so far. He could not ignore it. He must wait. He must. With eyes closed, he listened not only with his ears but with his whole being.

My champion, are you? It was a gentle female voice that resonated within his bones. *The savior of your people? Have you learned nothing?*

Daven's eyes snapped open, his body feeling as though lightning had jolted it. This was not the answer he had expected. He controlled the instinct to stand and confront her.

"Lady, I do not understand."

Still.

What was she trying to show him? Daven rushed through the sum of knowledge he had gathered since coming to the cave, considering the access to energy of the soil he found and the magic he was able to perform. His gaze flicked from plant to tree to rock, trying to decipher her riddle. Apparently, he still needed to master some point of necessity in order to reveal the door to the deep magic. What could it be?

I thought perhaps you might have learned when you first came to me. But you have forgotten already. You bring tears to my soul.

He thought back to the first day and his headlong rush away from the clan, away from those he had disappointed. He knew he had failed Jelani and Astan. And he allowed the evil to touch his grandson, Elliun, though subsequent events now revealed the child had been saved.

But not by you.

That brought him up short. Of course, he had not saved the child. This was his failing. He was responsible. He began to let his ego run free once again. "You humble me, Lady. I must learn I am but part in life's story, perhaps an insignificant part. I am no hero."

A delicate wave of amusement ribboned through the light around him. *Your part in the story will be anything but insignificant, my child. But the story is not about you. The story is about all life, the grand scheme including all beings, those of the soil and those of the hard rock cities. All are worthy. All are champions in their own lives, but they serve me best when serving others.*

He nodded, absorbing the sting of her words. Was there more to them than just a warning about his sense of self? She specifically included a reference to the humans. Did they hold some position of importance in the elves' conflict?

All understanding will come in time. Now, find your way.

The light flickered around him, and then faded. Momentarily blinded by the sudden darkness, Daven looked around, surprised that dusk had set in while in conversation with the spirit. The birds were singing once again and the breeze held the fresh smell of spring. His knees were wet, his clothing soaked through. Stiff from the long kneeling spell, he stood and leaned on the trunk of the tree nearest him, the one that had borne the punishment of his earlier wrath.

"Forgive me, my brother."

He laid his hand on the trunk, letting energy come through his feet from the soil to run through him into the tree, allowing any damage to the tree trunk to fade. The pain in his knuckles would take a lot longer to restore to health. Another good lesson.

Wryly amused as he mocked himself, he returned in the direction of the cave. Before he reached it, though, he was met by another light, a golden light shining before him, revealing a portal hanging in the air. The doorway was ethereal, a shadowy wispy barrier that stood between him and the enlightenment that awaited.

"*Santwarja*," he whispered in disbelief.

Half-believing the apparition was a trick, a last barb from the spirit, he determined he would at least make the attempt. He took a deep breath and cleared his mind, the very last thought a reminder to keep himself humble. Then he approached the portal and stepped through.

The sensation flowed over him of passing through an icy waterfall. He shivered as his eyes adjusted to the filtered light on the other side. Heightened perceptions crowded into his mind like children huddled by a fire. He walked forward, this space separate from the world he had just been in. This was a place populated by 'Others'. Beings that were few and far between, but powerful enough to broadcast their presence over great distances. Even those in the distant parts of this place he could sense, a place that seemed to stretch as far as the mind could reach in an odd half-light.

As he took in the nuances of the new plane of existence, his heart was tugged by a familiar vibration. Curious, he followed the sense-memory, moving deeper into the enchanted place. He perceived movement in his direction, a feeling of curiosity as strong as his own, and it spurred him to move a little faster. The other quickened pace as well, moving across the filmy floor of this plane, not over rocks and hills of the real world. He could feel the approach, radiating a sense of power, something the likes of which he had not felt before. When he thought that surely sparks between them would draw together and explode into showers of fire, he stopped, his skin crawling with electricity. The other stopped, too, and as he turned his regard to identify the one who stood before him, his jaw fell slack and his eyes widened in disbelief.

"How is this possible?" he gasped. "You, alive and *Intalus*?"

The *neris* he had not seen for twenty-five years crossed her arms, her eyes defiant. "Did you think without you I would curl up and die? That I could not survive and become strong on my own?"

"Veraena." He could only stare.

Her silver hair floated around her, soft like milkweed puffs, her figure much like it was when they were together. Her eyes were different, now hard as granite and full of spite. Her voice was edged, too, like a dagger. He imagined her slicing him with it, blood running down his skin.

"Yes, Veraena. You did not expect to find me here, certainly not before you."

"I—didn't know." His tongue, usually nimble with words, seemed to be tripping over itself. "I'm glad to see you well."

"I'm more than well, *denami.*" She spit out the endearment with venom. "I grow more capable by the day. I no longer need you or your servile clan witches to care for me and mine. I control my destiny now. I'll be the one who destroys everything you hold dear, as you tore apart my world all those years ago!" She raised a hand high, and let her arm fall, her long fingers pointing in his direction. Energy crackled toward him, the whole plane shifting to knock him from his feet, and then the flat floor tipped up, scooped itself into angled hills and valleys. He slid toward the portal and passed through it with a thump onto the ground before it vanished.

"No! Veraena?" He grabbed for the faded doorway, desperate not to lose his chance. How did she arrive at the status of *Intalus* before he? Who was her mentor? He was afraid to follow that line of thought, suspecting the worst.

"Veraena!"

On his feet again, he searched for the entrance to the *santwarja* once more, but could not find it. Reduced to the level of the soil once again, Daven was lost.

CHAPTER 16

LANE shoved aside piles of stuff on the counter surface of the Cave to add his laptop to the mess. Not because he needed more computers there. Four were usually enough, even for him. But the laptop had acted funny since Max screwed with it in woods and announced it was now 'of the clan'.

First, Lane could open files on the computer by simply thinking about them. The computer seemed almost linked to his thoughts. The night before he had been able to manipulate the computer browser, switching windows by the sheer power of his mind.

Crispy watched in silence from the sofa for a bit and then came to peer over Lane's shoulder. After fifteen minutes of Lane's experimentation, Crispy returned to his seat and pulled the hand-crocheted blue afghan over his lap. He picked up whatever conspiracy theory book he was reading that week, but did not open it. Instead he just stared at his knees.

Lane eyed his roommate. "What?"

Crispy looked at him.

"What?" Lane asked again. "I know it's weird. Okay? I don't understand it. I don't know what the hell Max did to it. But—"

"Alien?" The little man's fingers were white where they held onto the book.

"No. Not alien, Crisp." Lane turned off the machine and closed the lid. "I can't explain it. I've opened it up, looked inside, tried to figure out what happened, but I can't find anything that looks out of place." He sighed. "I hate to say it, but I think it's magic."

"Magic?" Crispy's face brightened and a smile twitched at his lips. "That's great! Too bad it doesn't do any real tricks." He settled back into the chair and opened his book, apparently relieved.

Lane raised an eyebrow. "You're weird, bro. You think it's dangerous if it's caused by aliens, but elf magic is cool? Really?"

Crispy shrugged. "Elves I know. Astan healed my hawk, remember? Daven gave me help. Magic isn't so bad." His lips pursed. "Aliens are scary. We never invite them for dinner."

"Not that we know of." Lane tried to keep a note of irony from his voice. "You can never tell."

Crispy stiffened again, and Lane smacked himself in the forehead. "Damn it, Crisp, I don't mean that aliens are around here. Well, maybe the people down at the Oxford."

"They're not aliens," Crispy said in an infinitely patient voice. "They're zombies. They eat brains."

Lane just shook his head and waved a hand in Crispy's direction to dismiss any need for further discussion. The Oxford was indeed known for its brains and eggs entrée. He was referring to the odd combination of hippies, bikers, and cowboys that congregated at the bar, but zombies would do.

Twenty-four hours later, Lane prepared for whatever new revelations he might discover. Crispy hitched a ride with a park ranger out to the wildlife rehabilitation station for the evening. With any luck, Lane could have his whole experiment finished before his roommate came home to start his obsessive worrying. "Lions and tigers and bears, oh my," he whispered, booting up the laptop. "Let's see what's going to happen to this baby now."

Lane usually played his WoW game on his second computer, because of its superior video card and the speed he could wield with its selected DSL line. The laptop was much slower, difficult to mount any significant kind of raid. He mainly used it for brief runs, gathering objects he needed, background work for his serious play when he was away from the Cave. The changes in the laptop, however, made him wonder what else he could make it do.

He took a moment to attach a crossover cable, linking the network cards between the laptop and computer number two. He hoped that whatever 'magic' that was attached to the laptop was transferable.

Just a matter of minutes now....

He signed into his game on his main computer, and then on the laptop, watching as the monitor lit up on the big computer much faster. A minute or two later, the laptop screen caught up, and he signed in there as well. Now, for the trial.

Lane focused on the monitor of the desktop computer, willing it to open a window. Nothing happened. He furiously thought at it, choosing several tasks it could easily do, but it clearly did not want to.

Scowling, he turned to the laptop. "So, what about you? Can I get on the web?"

Sure enough, the browser clicked a new window open to his home page.

He looked from one screen to the other. What was the difference? Wired together, if it were any other program, it would have worked on both computers. The electronic data would have easily transferred through the cable.

"Just runs programs," he muttered. "Apparently it only runs programs driven by magic. Now who's crazy?"

He continued to test the laptop, moving beyond parlor tricks with browser windows, which the computer seemed to have mastered. Though the game was slower and more cumbersome on the laptop, as he worked through some basic farming exercises, the action seemed to run faster and more smoothly. The machine actually appeared to learn as he pushed it. He found the items he needed to collect as they became available at the online trading posts, even items never before carried.

That made him chuckle. "Something to this magic bit, hmm? Let's see what else we can do."

He tapped in commands for his large green orc character, a cartoon representation of one of the Horde's most talented warriors, a level eighty-five warlock who mastered the Curse of Exhaustion, the Soul Siphon and the Demonic Embrace, among other bits of evil. He had several Imps at his beck and call, and a host of minions who looked to him for direction. Xiomar the orc controlled a stellar amount of power, in opposite proportion to Lane's real-life control of just about nothing. Xiomar was awesome, in Lane's eyes. He kicked serious ass, too.

He maneuvered Xiomar into the Tanaris Desert area, ready to have him take on some other players one-on-one or PvP, as the game lingo termed it, when the appearance of one of his pet Imps made him stop typing. Previously the Imp was a skinny little reptilian creature with a pointed chin and large horns like a devil on his head. But now he had acquired a shock of white hair and a very familiar grin.

"Max?" Lane whispered, astonished.

The Imp did not respond to his verbal question, but when he typed the same comment into the computer keyboard, the imp gave Xiomar a cheeky salute.

"No way." The shock pulled Lane out of gaming mode, and he leaned back in the chair, a little overwhelmed. As other toons moved around his, lost in missions of their own, Lane took a few deep breaths and contemplated how it was possible that Max could have made himself a character on Lane's team.

This mystery definitely called for a Creamy Cupcake. Maybe two.

He pushed himself out of the chair and lumbered for the kitchen, practically on autopilot as he made a fresh cup of Earl Grey and grabbed a double-pack of cupcakes. What did this mean? If Max could put himself into the game, could he take himself out? If he could take himself out, what else could he take out? If he could take characters out of the game, could he manifest them in the real world? The thought froze Lane on his way back to his chair. He remembered thinking about the possibility of having Xiomar fight Bart, when he and Kevin had driven up to the clan lands. Might this truly be possible?

"Maybe old Max could show me how he does it," Lane said aloud, the sound echoing in the apartment, releasing his feet to return to his chair. Max might be able to direct the orc, but Lane found himself reluctant to think about letting someone else use his toon, even someone like Max. Xiomar was his own creation. Lane should be the guy controlling him.

He eyed the white-haired imp. Impulse drove his fingers to type in his regrets. "He's all mine. No offense, Max."

None taken. The Lane is wise.

Lane blinked as the reply message appeared in the dialogue box. "What the hell?"

An imp was an NPC, a non-player character. The game generated any actions or comments the imp might make. It wasn't controllable. Until now. And if an NPC could take on a personality, what could a player-controlled character do?

Lane's eyes narrowed and he sank his teeth into his first cupcake as he pulled the laptop toward him with his other hand. He focused on the image of Xiomar. "Go left, down the path," he mumbled past the creamy goodness.

Nothing.

Lane cleared his mind. He was going about it wrong. He did not need to hold on tight to 'drive' Xiomar. He just needed to be him, and do what he did. Xiomar was a hunk of thick, ugly skin, standing on legs like stumps. Pig-like bristles covered his body. He openly carried several weapons and held a host more inside his head in the form of spells and curses. He was big and bad. At a level eighty-five, he had acquired enough skills that not too many characters could stand against him. All Lane really needed was to feel him enough to be inside him.

Lane let his mind wrap around that concept. What would it feel like? Not just watching the big guy from the outside, applauding his skill level, but being him, getting what he wanted, using his hands to rip people apart. For most of his life, it seemed he had been someone's pawn, but this new concept was heady.

A couple of NPCs moved into range on the screen, scruffy little guys in peasant clothing. They ogled Xiomar and his imp. Were they plotting something? Were they crazy? Xiomar could take them out in a heartbeat.

And did. Without Lane lifting a finger.

He laughed in triumph as the spell shot out from his character's hands to devastate the pair, racking up his kill points. Max seemed pleased as well.

And so it begins.

Idly wondering how it would feel to add 'Evil Overlord' to his resume, Lane chuckled and practiced some more, finding his ability to manage the online characters improving as he let himself go and let the magic take over. His imp, the one who looked like Max, stayed with him, communicating in chat dialogue when prodded, though the imp did not initiate any conversation. It was as though Max's personality was injected just so far as to come through as reaction. Curiosity at the method burned into Lane's consciousness, but he tried not to let it distract him from the wonders he found in learning to manipulate his orc with his mind. Used to employing the course-setting protocols of the game that smoothly moved a character from one segment of the layout to another, he found Xiomar clumsily tripped over obstacles. A lot.

"Sorry, I'm still learning to drive," he moaned, as if an abject apology would save himself from Xiomar's huge dual-bladed butcher's axe. Xiomar would have no patience with that, for sure.

He continued to experiment until Crispy came home a couple of hours later, at which point he was glad for the interruption. Lane's eyes burned from staring at the smaller screen of the laptop, and he seriously needed something to drink. And a bathroom break. And maybe another cupcake.

"Hey, Crisp," he said, after he tended to his needs and he could join his roommate on the sofa. "How's the world of wildlife?"

Crispy's lips twisted into an uncharacteristic smile. "You won't believe it."

Uh-oh. Something good was coming. Not aliens, because the little man was fairly calm and un-twitchy, but something else. Lane wondered if Crispy found magic, too. "Probably not. Lay it on me."

"The hawk came back."

"The hawk?" Not what Lane expected, not at all. "The dead one you and Astan resurrected a couple of months ago? That hawk?"

"That's the one." Crispy practically wriggled with glee. "He found me up at the rehab."

Lane's brow tickled into a furrow. "The same one? You're sure? How could you tell up in the sky? How far away was it?"

Crispy made an annoyed face. "About three feet. He wasn't up in the sky. He came down and landed on a tree right next to me."

Disbelief. "Really."

"Yes, really. He looked me right in the eye."

Lane decided to humor him. "Well, that's cool. What's he been up to?"

Crispy just eyed him.

"What?" Lane asked. "I thought maybe he came by to set up a play date or something!"

Lane tried to keep a straight face but finally burst out laughing. The hurt in Crispy's expression was hard to take, but Lane needed an emotional release from his adventure with the laptop and Xiomar. So he laughed until his ribs ached. His thin roommate just stared, his arms crossed tight, lips pressed together hard, as if a clothespin held them tight.

After his hysteria played out, Lane choked up an apology. "Sorry, Crisp. Sorry. I swear. It's been a wild evening here."

"Oh, yes. I'm sure you and Mr. Laptop spent an evening sweating over naked girls together. At least I was in the real world." Crispy got up, shoving the couch back. He stomped off to the bedroom. His absence left Lane smarting a little.

Lane scowled. "No naked girls, thank you." He raised his voice as he turned toward the bedroom. "There were more important things for me to do!"

No response came.

"Damn it, Crisp." With a heavy sigh, Lane shoved himself up off the couch, half intending to go to bed. "Something awesome happens to me and you'd think you could be a little excited." He wandered back to the Cave, staring at the screensavers in active motion. "Never did care about the game, though." As he continued to study the movement, he suddenly realized who would be fascinated by this latest development. "Oooh. Kevin."

He plopped down into his chair and wheeled it into position to open his web-chat program, tapping in the words that would bring up Kevin's connection. Nothing.

"What?" Lane groaned. "It's Wednesday night. Where the

heck are you when I need you? It's not like there are any time lords on TV tonight. Not with it being a Wednesday. Damn it!"

He left an email message for Kevin to contact him at his earliest convenience. The sound of the shower running made him glance up. It would be at least a half an hour as paranoid Crispy scrubbed and scrubbed himself to remove any potential contaminant from the wildlife rehab. Thanks to Daven Talvi's gift, at least Crispy was healed enough to consider leaving the house to go as far away as the center. Lane could not complain.

It gave him thirty free minutes.

He could make it up to Crispy later. Maybe even take him a cup of hot cocoa for bedtime. Meanwhile, his fingers itched toward the keyboard of the laptop once again. He, and Xiomar, could do a lot of damage in thirty minutes. He opened his game browser and cackled, as the orc appeared in full green ghastliness, ready to slaughter anything in his path.

"Mine is an evil laugh. Now die!"

And the game was on.

CHAPTER 17

"YOU know, I'm actually getting used to living here," Jelani said to Astan, as their second week in her father's cabin came to a conclusion.

She injected as much of a smile into her statement as she could, trying to cheer him. The words did not constitute a lie. It was not like she hated the place, but she did not prefer it, either. It served its purpose as a convenient limbo.

Astan, sitting at the small table that normally was folded behind the door in a storage space, looked up, studying her. Dark circles lay under his brown eyes, and his expression was drawn. She knew he was not sleeping well, consumed with their safety. Even with help from his allies of the Bitterroot clan, Jelani knew Astan worried they would be attacked again. "I'm glad."

She smirked, knowing his words were even more untrue than hers. "Right. Let's watch out for flying pigs, shall we?"

Her glance flicked, as it did so many times over the course of a day, to check on Elliun. This afternoon, he lay sleeping on the cabin's small bed, already too big for the cardboard box that had served as his bed since they left the city. His maturation was phenomenal, much quicker than expected. She hoped he would not continue to grow at an accelerated rate or soon they would have nothing for him to wear. One of the Youngers with the ability to teleport objects had 'lifted' some things from the nursery at their tree house, so they had been fairly comfortable until now. But it would not be so much longer.

Elliun was not the only one who was growing, and not necessarily in a good way. The remains of a pack of store-bought chocolate chip cookies lay open on the small counter next to the stove. She slowly demolished it over the course of the morning. Her system, which at first rebelled at the onslaught of prepared and pre-packaged foods, with their concomitant loads of chemicals and preservatives, adapted much too well to eating junk.

Her whole world was concentrated in this small space. Two-hundred and twenty-five square feet, give or take an inch, did not allow her much room for exercise. Astan preferred that she remain inside. They never knew when an enemy might lay in wait for her. Worse, they didn't know for sure who their enemies were.

She picked up a cookie and examined it a moment before taking the package over to Astan. "Here, you eat these. I'm going to be Lane's size before long if I keep this up."

His gaze dropped to her midsection. "I have seen you fat before. It does not diminish your beauty."

She bit her lip. "I wasn't fat. I was pregnant. I don't ever intend to be fat, thank you." She swallowed back the remainder of her words. What she needed was to get out into the forest and walk, like all those months ago when she first moved out to the forest with the clan. As long as she opposed the clan, she could not be sure of a safe haven. So to an extent, she was a victim of her own success.

She leaned down and kissed his cheek. "It's sweet of you to say so."

He caught her hand and held it close to his chest, without a word. The gesture tugged at her heartstrings. Over the last year she had caused quite a few changes in Astan's existence. Some for the better. Some not. Guilt gnawed at her.

"I'm sorry, Astan. I know you never expected this kind of fight."

He shrugged. "I should have expected exactly this kind of fight. I should have double-checked everything. I should have made sure Bartolomey was dead. I should have found out what Fontine did in the forest. I should have forced Daven to choose our cause, not that of the Circle."

She sat on the other chair at the table, careful not to overbalance its rickety front leg. "And when you were done with that, you could have changed winter to summer and dawn to dusk." A fond sigh escaped her, and she held on tightly to his hand. "I know you are my appointed guardian, *denami*, but you are also my partner and the one I love. We are making our way through this mess the best we can. Surely we'll see the light at the end of the tunnel sometime soon."

The knock was not one of Crispy's elaborate paranoia-defeating rhythms that their human guests used or the usual tap accompanied by a birdcall that signified one of the Youngers. A stranger waited outside the door.

Jelani stiffened. "The light's on the front of a train, isn't it?"

Astan rose to his feet, changing from tired mate to stalwart defender. "The child, Jelani."

She nodded and slipped over to the bed, positioning herself between the door and her son, careful not to wake him as she sat down. Awake, he could be a handful. Better to keep him quiet until she knew how far the line of fire would extend.

Astan waited until she hunkered down, before stepping to the door. He closed his eyes for a moment, and she guessed he was trying to project his perception to the other side of the door in his usual flash-flick study. His eyes flew open.

He reached for the handle and opened the door.

"Djana?" Astan said in a startled voice.

Jelani's gut cried to keep the old *neris* out of their safe haven, but as Astan stepped aside to let her in, the change in the elf woman spoke volumes about the change in the situation.

Djana's hair, now entirely gray, hung limp and her body was reed-thin. The skin on her face, only a year ago tight and smooth when she and Jelani had met at the coffee shop in the city, now had the texture of aged vinyl, cracked and worn. Her dirty clothing reeked of old closets and mildewed curtains. Her eyes were not altered one whit from their former brilliance, though. As soon as she was over the threshold, those sharp raven orbs scanned the room for Jelani, and for Elliun. When she saw them both, her shoulders drooped with relief.

"Thank the Lady," Djana whispered. "It is true."

She stumbled and would have fallen, but Astan caught her. He kicked the door closed with his foot, so no one else could enter, before helping his grandmother to the chair he just vacated.

"Would you get her a glass of water, *denami?*" he asked.

Still stunned by Djana's decline, Jelani rose slowly, not taking her eyes from the woman, and made her way to the jug Astan brought in earlier from the spring outside the cabin. With shaking hands, she poured the water into a glass and then offered it to the elderly woman.

Djana took a sip, holding the wet glass against her lips for a moment. A ragged, shuddering breath escaped her. "It is good to see you well," she finally said.

So many sharp retorts boiled up in Jelani, but she choked them all into silence, determined this time not to let her emotion rule her actions. She thought back to her conversation with the Youngers. The clan needed her. Needed a queen. She needed to act like one.

"Thank you for your concern," Jelani replied. "We are surviving, as we must." She crossed her arms and stepped back, angling herself to be poised for action if Astan's grandmother lunged for the baby. *Maybe those extra pounds will give me better blocking skills if nothing else.*

Recovering from his surprise, Astan walked around the table to stand with Jelani. "What brings you here?" he asked his grandmother. "Who told you where to find us?"

The elf woman studied them both, her hands folded in the lap of her worn skirt. "It doesn't matter who told me, Astan. I mean you no harm."

"Who came with you?" he demanded.

"No one," Djana swore. "I came alone."

Jelani had several acid retorts poised on the tip of her tongue, but resisted the temptation to spew them. Djana had been surrounded by a coterie of hangers-on since the moment they had returned to the forest, almost as if *she* were the queen and not Jelani.

Casting a quick look out the single window, Jelani saw no spies or lurkers. "What do you want? You've seen we're alive."

"Who will you tell that Jelani and the prince are alive?" Astan asked.

Jelani could only imagine how Astan was wrestling with his emotions as his expression, so fluid, went from boyish surprise to a determined hard jaw line. She could tell he was prepared to strike down even his own grandmother to protect them. She hoped it would not be necessary. Making the choice between them would harm her own bond with Astan. She was grown-up enough to know better.

"I am no spy." The old woman sat up a little taller, as if to retrieve shreds of her former dignity. "I come on behalf of no one but the clan. Such as it is." The tart tone to those last few words sounded more like the old Djana that Jelani had known.

The baby stirred, snatching their attention like a brass fanfare. All three of them stared at the child for a moment, until he found his thumb again, letting it lie half in, half out of his mouth as he drifted back to sleep.

"He is well?" Djana asked softly.

"He's fine, grandmother." Astan's tone was laced with irritation. "All your predictions about Jelani's parenting were mistaken. She is a wonderful mother, even under conditions such as these you have forced us into." He glared, his fingers twitching. "Did Daven send you?"

Djana took another sip of water. She shook her head and then looked at the baby. "He has not returned. I hoped...."

Jelani frowned, but her fixation could be a natural thing. Most grandparents were obsessed with their grandchildren. Clearly, the clan had a greater stake in this child, even if he was altered by her human chemistry and coffee addiction to become male instead of female. He was still of their royal line. A sigh escaped her like air leaving a balloon. "You're as worried about your son as I am about mine."

The elf woman nodded. "No one has seen him. He disappeared into the woods the day you did. We thought perhaps he was with you. But your companion, the one called Lane, said Daven was evil. They said someone was hunting him. Likely the same ones hunting you." She looked into Jelani's eyes. "The only way we, as a clan, will survive this is to join together once again.

You know this."

Astan and Jelani exchanged glances, Jelani's heart picking up an extra beat when anxiety gripped her. Was this a legitimate offer, or a trick to get her to let down her defenses? What were Djana's intentions? She chewed her lip, reluctant to commit to an unknown path.

Her mate finally spoke up, his voice slowly rising, gripped by tension. "How can you expect us to agree to return to a place where we were unsafe and not supported? Where our queen was actively challenged by your Circle and threatened? Where neither side trusted the other? How could we even have 'sides' if we are supposed to be united?"

The noise woke the baby, who let out a squeak and then rolled over to study the three adults with great interest.

"Now look what you did," Jelani complained.

She went over and scooped the child into her arms. The boy stared at Djana. That annoyed Jelani even more.

"I think it's time for her to go," Jelani said.

* * *

FROM the moment Astan saw his grandmother looking so pathetic at the door, he had suspected she was there to invite them back on 'her' terms.

He and Beckley discussed the possibility while patrolling the area around the cabin in the days and nights since returning to the forest. Dangerously close to conspiracy, especially where Jelani was concerned, the two engineered a plan to force the Circle's hand, to make them surrender to Jelani's rule. He never expected Djana to come herself, though.

The only ambassador who might have been worse received would be Rashia, the midwife. He and Beckley agreed on this point, even though Rashia was Beckley's mother. Or maybe, because Rashia was Beckley's mother.

But even when they poked and prodded the Circle into making the first move, now they were about to lose the opportunity. If Jelani threw his grandmother out of her cabin, how would they ever get this movement started again?

When Jelani made the comment about Djana leaving, the elf woman stood up, clearly ready to provide some dramatic, martyred exit. Seeing the only realistic solution to their life issues about to fade away like campfire smoke, Astan jumped into the middle of it with both feet.

"I think we haven't finished this conversation." He stood between Djana and the door.

"It certainly sounds as though your minds are closed to any possibility of reunification," Djana said. "You sentence us all to death." She sighed, and her whole body drooped. "I will return to the clan and inform them."

"Drama queen," Jelani muttered. She turned away and laid the baby on the bed to change him, teasing and tickling him while she got him dressed again.

"Have you really learned nothing?" Astan asked his grandmother. "You come here to ask Jelani to return to you, but you intend to change nothing in your approach or manner. She will not return on those terms. I will not let her."

Jelani smiled, a gentle expression, as she settled their squirming boy on her lap to feed him. At first, Djana eyed her with suspicion, but gradually the worries in her face smoothed away. Jelani, totally absorbed in the mother-son bond, smiled down at her boy's dark eyes.

"This pleases me," Djana said. A sigh escaped her. "I could have trusted you. I should have."

"Damn skippy," Jelani murmured.

Astan heard an under-layer of tight tolerance, almost amusement in Jelani's voice, though he expected that Djana likely missed it. Good. Jelani was easier to get along with when she was pleased. Any agreement Astan could broker would have to be accepted by her as well. "We are prepared to discuss the queen's return to the clan, with a few 'caveats', as the humans say."

Djana raised an eyebrow. "Terms? You will dictate to the Circle?"

Jelani's voice cut cold across the conversation. "The queen will dictate to the Circle. That is her role. The role you selected her for. Remember, when you dragged her out of her old life with that glass slipper?"

She shifted on the bed, a tight sound in her voice. Astan could see the resentment in her eyes, and knew she could let loose a deluge of condemnation. He had heard it already. Even if she was right, this was not the time. They needed to mend fences, as the humans said, but they also needed to keep communication open to the clan. Any victory from this meeting must travel all the way back to the Bitterroot glade if they were going to succeed. Beckley and the Youngers agreed to push whatever friends that were left to support the queen, even if it meant choosing against their parents. He caught Jelani's eye, shaking his head just a little. She rolled her eyes, but she clamped down on whatever else she might have said.

Chewing her bottom lip, Djana looked away from Astan and slipped her hands into her jacket pockets. "I remember, Jelani. I may be old and nearly wasted away, but my memory is still good. The queen's duty to her people is well known and understood by those of us in the Circle."

"And what of the Circle's duty to the queen?" Jelani placed the baby against her shoulder, patting his back. Her tone had lost its hard edge, but that was probably just for the child's comfort. "Before we can return, I need to know we'll be safe. And that we have the support of the Circle. And the rest of the clan." She shifted her weight, sitting a little straighter. "We have a vicious enemy, perhaps more than one. We need to pool our strength for all of us to survive." Her lips fumbled with a smirk. "As you said."

How could Djana argue with her own words? Astan forced himself not to grin. His beloved was learning.

Djana nodded. "I shall speak to the Circle."

"And?" Jelani asked.

The old *neris* eyed the queen. "And?"

"And what will you tell them?"

Djana gave a sigh. It was dramatic and deep, but a concession nonetheless. "That the queen's terms shall be met."

Jelani looked at Astan, a question in her eyes, as if she were begging him to let her off the hook. But he knew he could not and he nodded slightly. She, too, sighed.

"When we are notified that the clan accepts, we shall return. Much to do to rebuild our strength before the war comes." Jelani bit her lip a moment. "What about Daven?"

Djana frowned. "What of him?"

"I don't want his interference, either. You can make sure that doesn't happen."

Astan studied his grandmother's face, saw her wrestle with her emotions. *She does not know where he is.* The realization sent a chill through him. Did Grigor's batch of fools capture him? If so, or even if not, where was he?

"When is he due back?" he asked.

She took a deep breath and blew it out like a soft spring breeze, reluctant with an underlying chill. "I have no idea where he is. Or even if he will return at all."

Jelani frowned, setting Elliun in her lap facing the other two. The baby alternately waved to his father and stuffed fingers in his own mouth. "Where else would he go?"

"I don't know. But if he is alone too long, he might begin to lose the protection of the clan's magic."

"But Iris went—"

"Iris isn't one of the *Lelan*," Djana snapped. "Did Daven teach you nothing?"

Jelani growled and Astan stepped between them. This was no time to return to petty bickering.

"Both of you, stop," Astan said. "Daven is fully mature. He is responsible for his own well-being."

A buzz of shock and realization zipped through Astan. The advent of the queen changed his responsibilities. In times past, he was responsible for guarding Daven, especially after the Sleepers rejoined the clan. Since Jelani came to the clan, he no longer needed to look after his father. His duties and priorities were now different. He was right to choose his mate and son when they left the clan.

Djana got to her feet again. "You may have rejected him, Astan, but he's still my son."

Astan twitched at how easily she read him. "Once the clan is restored to harmony, we may be able to spare a party to hunt him down."

She stared as if he had turned into some sort of poisonous snake. "Your father would never have put himself before another member of the clan. He sacrificed so much."

He had heard this song before, and Astan was not inclined to join in on the chorus. He opened the door. "Let us know what the Circle decides."

"May I at least say goodbye to my great-grandson?" Djana asked.

To Astan's surprise, Jelani gathered up the squirming baby and placed the child in Djana's arms. The movement apparently surprised Djana as well, because she just held the baby close, rocking him slightly, not moving from the spot where she stood. She watched Jelani's eyes, the two of them locked in some unspoken communication Astan didn't share.

After a few moments, Djana kissed the top of Elliun's head and returned him to his mother. "Farewell," she said, stopping only a moment to caress Astan's cheek before she disappeared through the door.

"Close it," Jelani said as soon as Djana was out. She sank down onto the bed as if her legs would give out.

Astan did as she asked. When he was sure she was gone, he came over to sit next to Jelani on the small bed, slipping an arm around her. She was trembling. "What is it, *denami*? I believe we have won. They will give us what we want."

She laid her head on his shoulder. "I agree. I just hope we're making the right choice."

"But we said—"

"I know what we said. But didn't you feel the waves of creepy coming off her?"

Astan felt drenched in a wash of confusion. "Jelani, you gave her our child to hold. I thought you came to terms with her."

"I thought so, too. I just don't trust her, though. I don't."

Astan sighed and pulled her close. "We'll get through this."

He smiled down at his son, who reached up with both hands toward his father's face. When the tiny hands touched his cheeks,

Astan felt a little spark run through him. Something in the boy's eyes let Astan know he recognized that electric connection.

No matter what he thought he could control in this world, there would always be the unexpected. What did Fate have in store for them next?

CHAPTER 18

THE scream from the forest grabbed Vez and propelled him in the direction of the trees.

Dagger in hand, he ran toward the sound, the anger and agony in his mother's voice driving him to rescue her. Who dared to harm Veraena? He would end them so decisively they would not know what hit them.

Vez practically flew past the strong firs and pines, his small talent allowing him to move swiftly before coming to a stop on the edge of a group of four trees.

He found his mother alone, pacing back and forth across the open space. Tears ran from her eyes and her shoulders hunched as she hugged herself, her fingers white where they held her arms. She muttered under her breath in the elven tongue.

Vez arrived first, but before he could speak a dozen of the others crashed through the brush. All held a weapon, some just a broken tree branch, ready to come to Veraena's defense. He hung back, curious what had happened but not wanting to share his concern with Veraena's followers.

The commotion startled Veraena enough that she stopped pacing. A smile snapped into place and she wiped her cheeks clear of moisture. "I'm so sorry, my friends. I disturbed a wolf sleeping in a cubby near here and he surprised me. That is all. Please, return to your studies."

The others did not leave. She went to them, one at a time, looking into the eyes of each, reassuring them she was fine. Gradually they accepted her words and one by one, faded back into the trees.

Veraena took a deep breath and seemed to relax, her eyes closing for a moment and then snapping open again. "You might as well come out, Vez. I know you're here."

He shrugged and stepped from his place behind a thick tree trunk. "And it seems I'm worried for nothing, is that it, Mother? A wolf? Really?" Mild derision undercut his voice as he approached, taking a stand a few feet from her, just out of arm's reach. "I have seen you play and run with wolves all these years. Perhaps those fools would believe you, but I know better. What frightened you? Your crumbling mage?"

He studied her face, seeing more than the trace of tears in her eyes. Something had hurt her. He fingered the handle of the dagger in his hand. "Tell me, so I may take action, Mother. I will not allow this."

When she finally met his eyes, the hint of amused pride on her face stung him. It was not what he expected, or wanted.

"I do not require your defense, brave Vez. Your effort warms my heart, however. I am pleased that should I ever need your help, I can count on it."

He shoved the dagger back into his boot. "Foolish woman. I would defend you to the death, as long as you tell me the truth." Furious, he crossed his arms and glared at her. "If you do not trust me, then we cannot help each other."

Vez still burned over his mother's failure to name his father. While she did at last reveal Bartolomey was not him, she still did not confess the true one. She put him off, saying it was not the right time. Once circumstances were right, she would be free to say. Was it better for him to consider her a slut? That she coupled with so many she could not name one, than for her to be straightforward? Surely that was not possible.

Now she lied to him again. He could read it in the way she held her shoulders, tentative in a way her practiced expression was not. His gaze locked on her, unforgiving. "I have heard you in many modes, mother. What I heard just now was your reaction to something that you didn't expect. Not a wolf at all. Something that hurt you. The tears prove it."

She watched him, affecting patience, waiting for him to back down. But this time he was determined not to. He was not without manipulative tools of his own.

"Fine. Then I will assume your mage did it. I will call him out and challenge him for the leadership of this little band. If he doesn't know how to treat you—" He turned his back on her and started to walk away, toward their small camp.

"Vez, no!" Veraena called before he was out of range and then hurried after him. "You're not ready for that. I don't want to lose you."

She threw her arms around him in what was for her an uncharacteristic show of open emotion, at least as far as he was concerned. Caught in her embrace, Vez tried not to struggle in his impatience to know what was going on. Definitely something out of the normal. When she did not let go, he gently disentangled himself.

"Tell me, mother. Don't play the games of the Circle witches. They lost the queen by deceiving her and keeping things from her. Do you want to lose me in the same way?"

Veraena's expression changed. He had used the right stick. He filed away that bit of success for future reference.

With a sigh, she drew him back into the open space, her eyes narrowing as she took a long look around at the trees surrounding the area.

"We are alone," she said. She hunkered down in the center of the space, a place where the snow was melted, exposing the soil beneath their feet. "I will show you something."

Afraid to speak lest the sound of his voice change her resolve, he merely squatted next to her.

She closed her eyes a moment, placing her hand on the bare soil, speaking words of entreaty to the forest's Lady. She laid her other hand on his arm, and he felt a little sizzle of energy pass through him that grew as her hand slid down his arm to the skin of his ungloved hand.

Vez held his breath, sure something of great magic was about to happen.

A few moments later, a light floated down through the tree branches above them. It embodied itself in a vaguely shaped beam twice his height and shot through with golden highlights. In its center was a shadowy oval that Vez recognized as a doorway.

"*Santwarja*," he whispered in awe.

"Yes, my son," she replied in a soft tone. "*Santwarja*. The gateway to the place where an *Intalus* gains his greatest power."

Finally. His mother saw fit to grant his wish of power. "Thank you, mother. I am ready." Prepared for the trial awaiting him, Vez stood, breaking their physical connection. At that moment, the doorway and the light vanished. His brow crunched tight with consternation.

"What? But what is this trickery?" He turned on her, yanking her to her feet. "Why do you play with me? Do you mock me with this teasing?"

She pulled her wrist from his grasp and eyed him as though he were something mildly distasteful, not quite worthy of hatred. "I do not mock you, my son. Your arrogance and impatience both show you are not ready for this journey, even if I offered it to you. You wanted the truth. I thought you were man enough to hear it."

Confused, he stepped back, wanting to seize her and shake her until she brought back the opportunity, his eyes searching for the portal once more. He was ready. He was young and strong and ambitious. He could learn. How could she take this from him? Did she care nothing for him at all?

"I do not understand!" Vez yelled and then looked away.

"What I was about to tell you was the story of my encounter in the *santwarja* with another." Veraena faltered over the words. "The shock overwhelmed me. That was the cry you heard."

He looked back at his mother, incredulous over the softening of her voice. "Someone in the *santwarja*? Who was it? Another mage? Not Bartolomey?"

"Not Bartolomey," she confirmed.

"Then who?"

"Daven Talvi," Veraena confessed with a sigh that seemed to swallow her.

A chill ran through Vez's body. "Talvi is now *Intalus*?" The implications of this news burned through him, hot like molten steel. "How is this possible? He abandoned the clan. He vanished."

Veraena gave a slow nod. Her hands came together in front

of her, delicate fingers that trembled until she interlocked them. "He's gone to prepare himself for the transition."

Vez channeled the overpowering disappointment and resentment that washed over him to consider the new possibilities this information brought. If Talvi became a mage, it still would not save him from the destruction which would surely rain down upon him and the rest of the pitiful clan. Bartolomey and Veraena were two. Two mages, particularly two practiced mages, would vanquish a neophyte playing with magic. Why was Veraena so worried?

"So, we will destroy him, *Intalus* or not, along with the rest of his followers, and the cursed queen. Your master is restored to power and we will start a new regime. Right? Is that not the plan?" An idea occurred to him and he suddenly grinned. "Here is the perfect solution to Bartolomey's problem. He needs a body. Why not one already trained as *Intalus*? He could just slip between his bones like a river filling a crack in the earth and—"

"No!" Her hand shot out and slapped his mouth closed.

The sting stole his breath. Rage bubbled up so quickly, he nearly knocked her to the ground. Catching himself just in time, he turned away and counted several deep breaths, shoving his hands in his pockets before he used them against her. She might be his mother, but she could not treat him like a wayward pet. Especially when he only said what he thought she believed, that they would vanquish their enemy. Unless....

He whirled to face her again. *Yes. There it is.* Her true feelings were written on her face like the scrawl on the queen's message board. "You care for him. After all he's done to you."

"I hate him!" Veraena's eyes flashed hot, and he wondered if she would hit him again.

Vez made sure he was out of reach this time. "Then why do you care if he is destroyed?"

She hugged herself again and walked to the other side of the small clearing. A crow called loudly from a branch overhead, but she did not look up.

"Yes," a deep voice sounded from between the trees behind Vez. "Answer the boy's question. Why do you care?"

Vez recognized the voice of Bartolomey and moved back into the clearing to place himself between the mage and his mother. He did not interrupt, though. He wanted that answer.

"Master, you should not concern yourself with Talvi. We must focus on our own goals." Veraena coughed as if the words choked her. She walked closer to Vez and stood shoulder to shoulder with him. "The young elves are nearly ready to lead the attack on the clan lands, as we discussed."

"Talvi," Bartolomey's eerie voice emanated from a hidden place in the trees.

Veraena shook herself and stood a little taller. "Master, he does not matter."

"So your words say," Bartolomey countered. "Your heart deceives even itself."

A small opaque cloud of snow dust swirled into being on the edge of the cleared spot, and then moved lightning-fast to surround her. The circulation in the cloud sent wind spinning off its edges, knocking Vez to the ground before he could intervene, keeping him there. She shuddered in the center of the maelstrom, her hair flying up, her arms flailing. The assault went on for many breaths before the cloud dissipated as quickly as it had appeared.

Suddenly released, Veraena stumbled but did not fall, a defeated look on her face.

"So," Bartolomey spoke again, his oily voice still coming from a place unseen, "you haven't told him."

Veraena's gaze flicked to Vez and then away again. "Master, please."

"Haven't told me what?" Vez pushed himself upright, brushing bits of ice from his pants.

"Not you, pup." The deep voice filled with amusement. "Your father."

Veraena paled. "We have so much to do, Master, we should be spending our energies in preparation. The team is nearly ready, we have been training as you've taught me, and the Youngers have demonstrated fledgling talents worthy of further exploration. Only yesterday…."

Veraena kept talking, a verbal diarrhea even Vez knew was

designed to distract him from Bartolomey's words. But it was too late. He had heard.

Your father.

There was no mistake about whom Bartolomey could be referring. His mother virtually radiated thoughts of Talvi.

Daven Talvi, his father?

The corollaries clicked through. If Daven was his father and Veraena his mother, then that made Astan Hawk his full brother. Astan had been raised within the bosom of the Circle as Djana's treasured grandson, while Vez struggled to exist in a makeshift home with Kassen a last-minute foster substitute. Astan became the mate of the new queen by virtue of that same heritage. A heritage stolen from Vez.

As the implications of the expanse of the loss he suffered sank in, Vez struggled to be angry. Anger empowered. Anger gave impetus. Anger meant action and strength and righteous direction. But all he felt was a drowning, suffocating heartache that soaked through to his bones.

They had taken everything from him in a conspiracy that robbed him of any possibility to become what he was meant to be. Clearly, Bartolomey knew. Veraena, too, knew exactly what she was doing. Did Talvi know? He never showed Vez any particular favoritism or enmity. He treated him like any other Younger. Astan Hawk could not find an acorn directly in his path, so Vez expected he was oblivious. Djana and witches for the most part ignored him, but they seemed to court Kassen's subservient blather. Did Kassen know? Who else cheated him out of his birthright?

His stomach seemed to hold a crawling nest of hungry spiders, and he could no longer even look at Veraena's face without being sick.

She knew it, too. She stopped talking and reached her hand in his direction. "Vez, listen. You don't understand what happened. You don't know the timing of it. Please, Vez. Hear me out."

"I don't hear you." Vez raised a hand in front of him, blocking her from his sight. "I don't hear you."

Swallowing emotion that threatened to choke him, he turned

and ran, blindly trusting he would not crash into anything, at least not in her sight. Or Bartolomey's. He ignored her anxious calling of his name. He was done being their little jester to kick around for a few laughs. He needed time to think, to plan. And when he figured out who was at fault for stripping him of the life that should have been his, he would punish them all.

He ran far from the glade. Ran until his breath burned in his lungs and his legs ached, before he could bring himself to stop. Leaning against a tall tree with thick rough bark on the trunk, he stripped off his outerwear and his shirt, pressing his bare back into the bark, feeling its rough edges, the pinpricks of pain a manifestation of the ache flooding his insides.

Was there nothing within his control?

His childhood was a series of rejections, transfers of affection, to the point that he wondered if he really knew what love was, or if he would be able to love anyone at all. All this, seemingly without anyone's concern for his part, for how he felt or what he needed. Daven Talvi, his father? Vez struggled to wrap his mind around that concept. Those months with the clan after the return of the queen, he spoke to Talvi many times, why did he not reveal the truth? Did he only want the one son, the sainted Astan?

Pain shot through Vez's interior once more, twisting like the slow entry of a sharp dagger. He jerked against the tree trunk, letting the bark tear his skin, pain for pain.

Talvi seemed the sort to gather in the lost, however. He was always friendly, even jolly with the Youngers of the clan. Surely if he knew, he would have....

If he had known.

Stung again by the effects of his mother's lies, Vez writhed against the tree, the pain he caused was at least caused by his own volition, not the deceits of others. He turned to face the tree and dragged both his forearms along its rough surface, feeling somehow justified as he saw the blood bead up before trickling down his skin. Tears burned his eyes and he let them come, here, when he was alone and far from the ridicule of the others. They saw his mother and envied him. If they only knew the truth, they would not be so jealous.

The pain threatened to swallow him whole, drown him, and he nearly allowed it. Only the deep voice echoing through the trees around him grabbed his attention and made him stop.

"Poor Vez. Trapped in the plots of a weak female, no one to save him."

Now this was a fine thing. Bartolomey here to watch Vez's self-punishment and humiliation.

Vez straightened and wiped his face with a non-bloody part of his arm. "I don't need you."

"On the contrary, my boy, I think you do." The voice condensed from a vague surrounding echo to a point much closer.

Vez spun to face him, realizing belatedly his vulnerability away from the others, but nothing was there. Just a voice, warm with intimacy.

"Relax, Vez. I have no more designs on your body. No, indeed. With your bloodlines, I could find a much better use for you than as a vessel to cart around my mind. You're destined for great things, I can see that. Do you feel it, too?"

Vez refrained from the easy retort that he did not feel particularly great or special, scrambling to hold together the shreds of his self-respect. "What do you want?" he snapped.

"I want you, Vez. I imagine you feel betrayed by everyone else, the clan, the father who never loved you, the mother who didn't raise you and won't even tell you the truth. Even the other Youngers set you apart from themselves. They exclude you, did you know that? They whisper about you when you're not around."

Vez stiffened. "What do they say?"

The voice took on a sad but sympathetic tone. "They wonder about Grigor. They say you're not worthy to lead them."

Anger flashed though the young elf. "I have brought them through tragedy and will take them through triumph."

"Of course, you will. We will."

Intrigued, Vez wiped blood from his arm with his shirttail. "We? You and I together?"

"I have much to offer you, Vez. I understand how you feel, manipulated by a female for the sake of love without regard for the well-being of those who depend on her. If we act together, we may just be able to achieve this objective, despite the petty lies and trivial duplicity."

The old mage sounded so reasonable. Vez found himself nodding. "The goal is what's important."

"Of course, it is. We must stand united. It is the only way that we can take down the false queen and her witches. Then you will receive the training your mother would deny you. We shall build you strong, so no one can hurt you again."

"Yes. I need to be strong. Invincible." Vez took a shuddering breath, trying to stop the trembling that ran through his body like an electrical current.

"We shall make it so." A swirl of wind surrounded him, brushed across his torn skin and healed it. "Get dressed now. Clean yourself. Say nothing of this to anyone." The voice backed away and once again echoed all around Vez. "We shall speak of it again, when we are ready."

Vez's mind filled with the picture of his mother's pretty face and the way it would change when he could turn the tables on her and use his very own power. With Bartolomey's help, he could do it.

"That you will, my boy. Now go home and pretend that all is happy and bright. Your day will come."

An emptiness around Vez let him know Bartolomey had moved on. He followed the directives the mage gave him and returned to the bower, his mind whizzing in a thousand directions. Punishment would not come today, but at least now he knew it would come.

And they would be sorry.

CHAPTER 19

STUNNED as Daven was, ejection from the *santwarja* did not stop him.

Over the next days, he made multiple efforts to re-enter that hallowed space. He was entitled. He knew it. The Lady of the Forest had shown him the way.

He waited on that spot where the portal had opened, casting different phrases on the blank air, willing each of them to reveal the entrance to the place where he could complete his training. He refrained from food and drink. He slept on the ground, not wanting to miss an opportunity now that he had found the place.

As the sun's light on his face tickled him awake, the answer came to him. It was no failing on his part. Veraena had blocked the doorway from the inside. What he needed to do was hide his intent to enter. Once inside, her magic should not be able to harm him. The *santwarja* was a sacred place of learning. While the mages could affect each other physically on the plane, they could not kill each other. Only in the real world could that happen.

And I have no intention of allowing her to do so.

Daven took a deep breath, as if to seal the promise to himself. Moving closer to the entrance he knew was there, he focused on the pine branch above his head. The dawn light reflected off melting ice, droplets of water shimmering like jewels. Over the last few days the temperature had risen several degrees. How long ago had he left the clan? Elliun must be growing like a young spring sapling, bathed in the fierce love of his mother and protected by the strong determination of his father. Pondering the child's round face and bright dark eyes, he slowly backed in the direction of the portal. Was Elliun smiling yet? Did he enjoy eating apples? Could he be walking by now? He imagined the baby toddling around the interior of the tree house with a smile.

If he was anything like his mother, Elliun would be a handful. Daven was certain of that.

Two more steps.

Then he whirled and pushed through an unseen barrier, one he could barely sense, but it did not matter. He was inside.

The feeling of altered reality was even stronger this time, extending as far as the walls that surrounded the chamber, which faded into the distance in a faint mist. The air was the same tinge of yellow as the sunrise. At first, he thought the air was dead, but as he moved farther into the first chamber, he gradually smelled something like the indistinct scent of beargrass flowers. Sweet it was, though impossible in this season. Magic at work.

Once again he sensed the presence of others on the plane, as indistinct as the scent of beargrass, but individual. He scanned quickly for Veraena's ghostly aura, but there was no impression of her being near him. He was safe, for now. She would not eject him so easily from his destiny this time. She caught him off guard before. Never would he have imagined she was here.

Clear her from your mind, lest you summon her.

Lantin spoke to him, an echo inside his head. Good advice.

Daven set his attention instead to discovering the parameters of this new place. As his senses adjusted, he noticed sounds in the distance, eerie voices wafting in from far away. Were those of the other mages, those who kept the secondary plane in balance? Perhaps they would be his teachers. He moved on.

The floor dipped, as a gentle slope lead to a shadowed corridor an arm-span wide, the air shot through with gray bands of light as the passageway wound left, and then right deeper into the plane. Daven followed the path down into the interior until it split into two parts.

Which path to take?

He tried to sense ahead along each trail, testing its atmosphere. The fork to the right seemed to have a dark edge to it, something he could not quite put his finger on, so he took the other. The ground lost its misty feel and hardened into substance as he continued in, first the consistency of soft dirt, then becoming more like the terrain of the outer world. Rock lined both sides of the path, as if he were in the mountains of the Bitterroot. The path darkened behind him as he moved forward, as if he was being guided in. The mystery of what awaited him at the corridor's end tugged at his mind, but he resolutely put his doubts square ahead of him, ready to push through them when he needed to, not before.

Worry to the point of becoming frozen was a human trait he could not understand. Like Jelani's friend Crispy. For such a long time he was trapped in his past, damaged and afraid to leave the confines of his home. Daven was able to melt some of those terror-built walls, opening the little man to new possibilities. To Crispy's credit, he enlarged on the bits of healing Daven provided. It was more than Daven expected from a human. Most of them wasted what was good and true. Even though he found them appealing, he certainly did not see humans as equals.

Focus.

A noise like claws scraping across rock startled him. He halted for a moment to ascertain the direction from which it came. He inched forward, listening, sensing a presence but nothing solid. He paused for a moment, before stepping around a corner. A blast of hot, white light passed before his eyes, burning a hole in the rock behind him, singing his eyebrows. He jerked back, breathing hard, too shocked to be afraid or even angry.

"Who's there?" he called.

His first thought was that Veraena had somehow trailed him to this place, but even as he opened his mind, he did not sense her. The feeling was familiar, now. He knew his attacker.

"Who is not important. The lesson is what you must learn."

Daven felt a rush of fondness. "Lantin." The essence of his old master still existed on this plane. "I find you again at last. Are you sent to teach me?"

Another flash of bright light, and an impact on the rocks above his head. A shower of broken granite fell, some of the chunks large enough that they hurt as they landed on him. "And as always, you choose to talk instead of listen."

Stung by the derision in the well-known voice, Daven leaned forward to cast a blast of power in the direction where he believed Lantin to be. The old elf's soft laugh showed that he guessed incorrectly. Instead, a return shot sent more rocks tumbling, one shard scraping flesh along Daven's cheek.

Lantin's voice, almost a whisper, echoed along the rocks, insinuating itself into Daven's very bones. "You come seeking great power, something you have pursued since the earliest days. Do you even understand the battle ahead?"

"We must stop those who would destroy the clan."

"And who would that be?"

Those of Grigor's old group, surely, stood against a united clan. "The rebellious Youngers who tried to steal the prince."

"Is that all you sense, Daven Talvi?"

Daven thought again of Veraena, wondering where she figured into this fight. Where had she been all this time? And how did she complete her training? "Did you teach Veraena?"

"No. She went outside the boundaries of the clan to gain her knowledge. She is tainted."

Daven thought over everything Iris shared with him, including Astan's suspicion that Bartolomey might still be alive. How was it possible? He was not there when Lorenz sent Bartolomey away in the enchanted vessel, but the magic should have held the traitor safe from outside influences. If Bartolomey led the rebellious elves, things could be very bad indeed.

Tainted, Lantin said.

He needed no talent like Astan's to understand this flash of intuition. When Daven gave up his own future and training for the queen, Veraena went on to finish hers. With the remaining of the queen's followers in hiding, there was only one she could have turned to in order to gain the knowledge she needed.

Bartolomey.

Very bad.

Daven closed off that train of thought for a moment, as he regained his focus. Studying the two craters in the rocks above him, he considered the angle from which the damage came from, about forty-five degrees off where the voice originated. He took a deep breath and readied his cast, not looking for immediate destruction, but a hit to weaken the rock, setting a trap for the unwary. He leaned forward, falling to his knees to propel the power blast up into the shadows above and to the left, watching as the rock absorbed the glow of light just where he intended. Satisfied with his achievement, he let his momentum carry him on, rolling across the exposed area of the path to a safe spot behind the rock on the far side.

Warming to the test of his newly-discovered abilities, Daven sent out mental echoes, discerning the limitations of the rock faces around him. The cavern that grew from the empty spaces of the *santwarja* seemed to live all around him, several times the height of an elf and just as wide. The stacked boulders were solid enough, but something within them did not ring true. As if the magnetic qualities of earth were different in this place. He would have to adjust his attack.

Still no comment from Lantin. Did that mean he took a hit or that he was using the moment to sneak up on Daven's position? Daven froze, listening with all his senses. No movement. He frowned. Perhaps he had been more accurate than he intended. He stood up slowly, silently, prepared to climb to the top of the rock to check.

Before Daven could blink, a black-clad Lantin appeared out of the stone next to him and placed a hand on his chest, a hand trembling with an electric charge that stopped his heart for a moment. The moment seemed to drag on for an interminable time, during which Daven was bathed in the twinkling amusement in Lantin's eye. Then Lantin stepped away, leaving Daven shaken and gasping for breath.

The familiar contours of Lantin's face appeared not to have aged, not a single wrinkle more than the last time they were together, more than a quarter century before. He wore a faded black robe and dark boots, gray hair loose about his shoulders. Eyes the blue of a twilight sky studied Daven critically.

"What were you thinking just then?" Lantin asked.

Daven shuddered, leaning back against the rock for support. He knew already the lesson that was coming. He would have taught it himself to any of the Youngers.

"I was worried I might have harmed you," Daven confessed,

cursing himself for being a fool.

Lantin nodded. "And so you lost focus on the enemy. You cannot afford to do this. Not against Bartolomey."

"So it's true. Bartolomey lives." Daven's heart sank. For his entire youth, everything seemed assured. Elves did not survive if they lived alone. The Queen had absolute rule over the clan. The magic of the Circle was more powerful than any other force in the region. Since he returned from his years asleep, everything he knew had been turned on its head. And with a half-breed queen, not much was likely to revert to the old days.

"He lives, but in an altered state. Only a matter of time until he gathers the energy to return to his full strength. Our clan is in dire straits, my son. Without *Intalus* to guide them, they will fail."

"But the queen—"

Lantin cocked his gray head. "Yes, the queen is the key. If she unites the clan and the mages who follow the light, then the clan may be strong enough to fight the evil."

Daven considered the young woman who held his clan and prayed she was capable of the task. Surely her character was built up after the troubles they had experienced over the last few months. He knew Jelani as well as he knew any of the other elves, except for Astan. He would wager on her side.

"The other mages? Where can I find them?"

"Six there should be, if the balance of the *Idellan* is to hold, and the clan is to prosper. When the mages are in balance, their strength is imparted, shared with the clan in equal measure." Lantin tucked his hands into the pockets of his robe. "You must understand the stakes of this contest. The mages are now out of balance, which means the clan cannot hold its own energy. The elves will waste away as their power is siphoned off to serve the needs of those who do not deserve it."

"What changed the balance? When?" No need to ask who. The answer was all too obvious.

The spirit of Lantin paced, his feet brushing the ground, leaving no mark as they passed. "Bartolomey was no dull student. He realized the strength of his bloodline, the balance held during the reign of his mother Ele. That, and the clan traditions would serve to keep him from the power he craved. The only way he could hope to challenge and lead the clan would be to weaken every individual. He used his time in the *santwarja* to identify *Intalus* in the clan."

Horror rising in him, Daven considered the depth of Bartolomey's evil. "He killed them?"

"Not all of them." Lantin stopped his constant movement, raising one hand, one finger pointed upward as he made his point. "One, only. The mage of light. Her death, along with the murder of Linnea, would have been enough to channel the clan's energy into whoever was strong enough to take it. And he was."

"But Linnea didn't die."

"No." Lantin nodded. "Her essence was preserved, which didn't stop him from taking the throne, but prevented the imbalance from becoming irreparable."

Daven's mind clicked forward, as implications fit together like puzzle pieces. "So when the clan fractured, left the forests, became Sleepers, Bartolomey could not hold them. Or their life energy. His power faded."

"Yes."

Thoughts moving faster, now. "Because Jelani has claimed the throne, the clan has gathered again, consolidating their strength."

"Yes."

"If Bartolomey and his followers can keep the *Idellan* out of balance and bring down the queen, then all that power will once again be his for the taking."

"Exactly."

"Unless."

"Unless?"

The lesson landed on Daven like a branch heavy with wet snow. "Unless there is a new mage of light to reinforce the balance."

Lantin's sharp eyes studied him. "We will see if you succeed in your challenge."

Reeling from the revelations, Daven grasped for something he could use for inspiration. "What of the other mages, those who have survived?"

"You may encounter any or all on this plane, as well as in the real world. Two reside with the clan, but they have withdrawn, worn away by the crisis. They are ancient, even by elven standards. Kalinda, who rules the air. Rudra, who rules the water. Though they might not openly stand to fight at your side, their support behind you will unite the cause of good."

Who else? Including himself, that was three, Veraena and Bartolomey made five. Daven ticked off the elements, the *Idan*, on his fingers. Air, water, fire, dark, light. Earth. Of course. The Lady of the Forest.

Lantin seemed to sense his response. "Good. Your feelings tell you truth. The Lady mirrors the queen. As one rises or falls, so does the other."

"Do they come here? How will I enlist their aid?"

The elf-elder shook his head. "While you are on this plane, you control only yourself. The clan, the queen, any other concerns must be set aside. You will command warriors and hunters, fighters and healers, once you leave here. But now you must focus on the essence of your study." He tapped Daven's chest. "You must be prepared to face evil. If you cannot stand up to it, none of these others will matter. You will perish, and so will everyone you love."

* * *

DAVEN trained with Lantin for many days, or so it seemed.

In the *santwarja*, he could work without food, without water. The atmosphere itself seemed to sustain him. He cast spells, he learned to manipulate the building blocks of nature, and most importantly, he learned to recognize the darkness.

He became aware of a gradual presence, the light with a certain cast that he recognized as Veraena. He did not know why. She left him alone after that disastrous first encounter, but his inclination was to suspect her motives. Her response was visceral and reactionary. She had not forgiven him. He understood her attitude at their earlier meeting was fueled by pain. He remembered how anxious he was to save Linnea all those years ago, that he hardly paused to listen when she gave her cursory consent for him to become a Sleeper. For twenty-five years that poison simmered.

Daven also knew an apology, however heartfelt, would be futile. Once the clan was reunited, perhaps he could make Veraena see reason. Until then, they would be enemies.

He steeled himself for the encounter, knowing he was stronger now. All the same, he was stunned at his first vision of her, tall and proud, silver hair flying loose around her shoulders, dressed in a dark blue jerkin the color of her eyes and tight gray leggings under black boots. She did not speak when she saw him, but stopped three elf-lengths from him, digging her toes into the ground. Her eyes burned with hatred. Her hands came up in front of her to waist-height, her fingers sizzling with a voltaic charge. The air snapped with a smoky edge.

He reacted with a charm to protect himself, but the murmured words came too late. An invisible jolt hit him, knocking him sideways. He stumbled into the rocks, but did not fall, shoving off the rough surface with his hands to face her again. He quickly completed the charm that would deflect the sort of attacks he expected, watching her face. Her jaw line was like steel. Every nuance of her stance challenged him to retaliate.

"I'm not going to hurt you, Veraena. I've done enough of that."

"Are you saying I'm not worth the fight?" She leveled another blast, this time at the rocks above his head, and they rained down on him.

He ducked aside, the rocks scraping and bruising him as they fell. But thanks to his defenses, he was still standing. And still determined not to harm her. "Can we talk? The way we used to?" He limped away from the rocks toward her.

She hesitated, her hands dropping to her side. "What would that prove?"

Daven stopped his approach well outside her reach, studying her shoulders, her knees, anticipating movement, hoping she did not challenge him. "I've learned more than just magic skills over these last months, Veraena. Too many mistakes to heal, but I'm willing to try. You should hear me out before you decide which action to take."

"Maybe I should." She did not smile, did not move. Nor did she attack.

Daven wondered if there might actually be a chance to persuade her back into the light. "Why didn't you tell us you were still alive?"

She crossed her arms, shifting her weight to her left hip. "What did you care? You wanted Linnea."

He nodded. "I was misguided. Too consumed with grand causes, and blind to what really mattered to my life." He took one step closer. "Our son. Our life together."

"I see. And what brought you to this great revelation?"

"Veraena, I want to talk about you. If I'd known you were alive, I would have come to find you. I would have taken you home to the clan. We could have lived as a family."

Her harsh laugh echoed off the hollow cave behind him. "Djana would never have allowed it. She didn't want me there. Especially without you." Her hands fell loose and hung at her sides. "She always thought she was better with Astan than I. She criticized me relentlessly."

She chewed her lip, unable to meet his eyes. He was reminded of Djana's behavior toward Jelani, always unhappy with the new mother's attempts to parent. He could imagine, especially when Djana was younger and more energetic, that she could have made life miserable.

"That's why you left Astan and went?"

"Astan was better off." She bit off her words and stared at the ground.

"Have you seen him? Have you met Jelani?"

"Do you think he'd like that?" she asked, her voice trembling a little.

Were those tears in her eyes? Surprised at her attitude, he reached a hand in her direction. "Veraena, *denami*, there's no reason we should be enemies."

"Daven." She sighed, and a smile inched onto her lips as she reached for his hand. When she held his left hand in her grip, she latched on and dug her long fingernails into his skin so he could not pull away. Her smile widened at his astonishment, and her free hand whipped up into the air, and then came down on his upper arm. Her eyes lighting with an almost mischievous pleasure, she clenched her teeth and sent waves of paralyzing power through his body. At first her touch burned and his muscles screamed, before they overloaded and the feeling drained away, his arms and his chest, his back and into his legs, before his head filled with blackness and he faded away.

He woke up later. How much later he did not know. He was lying on his back, the open air sweeping across his face. Above him, a stand of tall pines and a blue sky. She had managed to remove him from the *santwarja* again.

What had he been thinking? He knew how she felt. By the Lady, he even told her she was justified in feeling angry and vengeful! And yet he walked right into her trap. What a fool he was. His head and muscles aching, he pushed himself upright. He did not have to look to find the portal. After living inside the *santwarja* he was now part of it, giving him the ability to summons it to him the next time he needed it. But right now he took into consideration that if the enemy hunted him down on the inside one of the most sacred place of the elf clan, that they would be after Jelani and her family on the outside as well. It was time for him to return. He had learned enough to begin. Most of the other lessons, he could incorporate on his own. The queen was what was important now.

He hesitated, thinking he should return to the cave, but a moment's pondering reminded him he had nothing there he needed. He wanted home, and family, and all that meant something to him. Now.

A noise behind him made him whirl, wondering whether the revenge-bent Veraena had followed him. Prepared to strike out at her, he found instead a ghostly apparition of Lantin. His old master seemed much more solid and stronger inside the *santwarja*. His face was drawn in lines of disappointment.

"She is powerful," Lantin said. "Twice now, she has ejected you from the sacred space."

Daven's heart pounded, and his breaths came fast and shallow. "I tried—"

"And failed."

Lantin's calm assessment of the situation stung him. "But you said the danger already exists! I must return to the clan as soon as possible."

"If you must." The cool tone of Lantin's vaporous voice implied it was not a good choice.

Daven reconsidered, wishing for a moment he could have Astan's ability to piece together the answers to a problem. "You don't think I should go." He took in a deep breath and let it out. "You believe I need more study."

"Do you feel prepared to encounter Veraena or her twisted Master in the real world? If she can affect you so severely here in the sacred plane, you are not ready. Can you risk the life of the Queen and her child, your family and companions, on this half-accomplished task?"

Daven sighed, torn between the need to help now, and the wisdom of solidifying his powers before he put himself in a position to confront the other side. "Hard to know which course to take, Master."

An ethereal laughter filled the glade where Daven stood. "Now the student begins to learn. Come back to the *santwarja*, my son, and we will prepare you for the battle ahead."

Daven acquiesced. More training would not hurt him. He needed to be the best he could be. With a longing look toward the south, he summoned the doorway and entered.

CHAPTER 20

"WHAT do you mean, the garlic bread is gone?"

Lane's cry of dismay made Astan look up from his dinner plate.

"Right," Jelani said with a laugh. "That's what happens when you eat half the loaf all by yourself."

Astan glanced over at the tired blue couch in Lane's apartment. Crispy had claimed one end of it in order to cuddle the newest royal in the elf clan. Over the weeks since they had left the clan, Astan had come to see the devotion of Crispy and Lane to the welfare of his son, and he had very few worries about them being together.

A good thing, considering the proposal he was prepared to make when dinner finished.

The room filled with the sound of conversation, the group enthusiastic to be reunited.

Iris Pallaton, minus her usual sunny smile, looked a bit haggard. She had been working ten-hour days since returning to the city. "That's what I do, right? Serve broken humans?"

Her words held a self-mocking condemnation Astan did not understand. His cocked eyebrow only won him a quick peck on the cheek, and then Iris turned away to speak to Lane's wounded warrior friend Kevin, who sat at the table with a pad and pen, prepared to take notes.

Jelani had asked for one more evening with her friends in Missoula before they returned to the clan soil. She held back the news, wanting to tell everyone in person. Once they set foot in elven territory, the war could break out at any time. More than six weeks had passed since the incident at the tree house with Bartolomey's people, which meant they were likely well prepared. Max, who begged a visit to the city with Astan and Jelani, told them the Bitterroot clan counted over a hundred who had defected to the other side.

The diminutive white-haired elf good-naturedly tried every sort of food that Lane put in front of him, though he clearly was not prepared for meat ravioli and Lane's generous helping of Italian dressing on his greens. His expressions as he encountered the spicy dishes made Astan smile. Nothing seemed to dim Max's spirits.

"Djana says Bartolomey stole away the best and the brightest." Max smiled, his face lit from within by a bright radiance. "But I don't believe her. We have Beckley, Pieter, Gansen, and the Circle. Daven Talvi when he returns. We have Astan and the queen. And The Lane."

From the couch, Crispy snickered.

"And The Lane needs more garlic bread!" Lane proclaimed. He left the table to hunt for more food in the kitchen.

Astan satisfied himself with some greens and a chilled summer ale. His senses were on overload by the noise in such a cramped space. But it was the last time. The next afternoon, they would be back to the clan. For now, he could manage.

Jelani put down her fork, a sigh indicating to Astan that she was ready. He was adept at reading her. A guardian must master many tricks, even the ability to manage a volatile mate. He grinned at his own prowess, self-serving as it might be. No matter how she tried his patience, each day he found himself wrapped closer around and within her. Whether she would admit it or not, he knew she felt the same. They needed each other's strength to stand against the forces prepared to battle them.

Lane returned to the table.

Astan clinked a spoon against his ale bottle. "We should get to business."

"Spoilsport," Lane mumbled through a mouth packed with bread, but he turned his attention to the elf queen's mate, as did the others at the table.

Astan acknowledged him, before gesturing to Max. "What Max says is verified by the other Youngers. Many of them don't remember Bartolomey and the troubles of succession that started this war. What they remember is the division between the Queen and the Circle and how the division brought down the clan." He pursed his lips, pausing for effect. "When they see the deceit and the dark schemes going on behind the scenes, they rightfully reject such behavior."

"It makes sense, Astan," Iris interjected. "Most people will try one mode of response until it becomes clear that it won't work. And then they may take the complete opposite tack, instead of trying a more moderate compromise."

"But they really believe they're better off with Bart?" Jelani frowned, leaving the table to join Crispy and Elliun on the couch. The baby gurgled and reached for his mother, climbing into her arms. "Didn't they learn anything?"

"One might well wonder." Astan slipped from his chair and leaned back against the kitchen counter. "Word from those on the fringes is an attack is massing. The clan must stand united. Jelani and I return tomorrow to the clan soil."

Iris gasped, Crispy looked as though he might snatch the child from Jelani, and Lane's thick brow furrowed with worry. "You can't take our boy into a war, Jelly Bean! That's irresponsible!"

Jelani shook her head. "We're not going to, exactly. We have a favor to ask."

"You want us to keep him?" Crispy asked, with a dawning light of realization on his face. Kevin and Lane exchanged looks that were less enthusiastic.

"We don't want him to be far from us. But I do agree, we will be occupied with whatever comes to pass, and I do not want to be distracted with Elliun's safety," Jelani said. "Kirill has enchanted the immediate vicinity of the cabin for us. Elliun will be much safer there."

"At the cabin?" Lane stumbled over the words. "You think we should move to the woods? With no electricity? With no Internet? Are you crazy?"

Kevin's expression was nonplussed. "I know this is serious, Astan, but I'm not sure Lane can survive without an Internet connection. Over in the sandbox, we could only sign on few and far between. And for some of us it was worse hell than it was out in the field."

Astan, annoyed at such trivialities compared to what he and the clan faced, started to speak, but Max jumped up, his white hair flying about his shoulders.

"Your far-sender will work in the queen's cabin," Max said. "It is enchanted soil. Part of the clan. Like your machine."

Lane eyed the young elf. "Bullshit."

"It is truth!" Max insisted. "You will see. Did I not send you a message from there?"

Lane growled as he shifted his bulk in the chair, making the legs screech in protest. "And then what? Assuming Crisp and I play babysitter for a week or two, what happens next? You and Bart's Baddies go at each other?"

Astan shrugged at the simplification of what he expected to be something much worse. "It is not our choice, Lane, but theirs."

Lane wasn't finished. "What about that whole prohibition against killing? Didn't you say that Grigor lost his elf powers by killing an elf and poor old Richard? Wasn't that a rule? X leads to Y?"

"Maybe it depends on their level of power," Iris said. "Maybe if they're very strong, they won't lose as much."

"You mean Daven," Crispy interjected in a soft voice.

Iris fidgeted. "Surely the time he's spending up in the woods has to pay off somehow. Besides the fact he'll be able to cast spells and create better protection for the clan."

Uncomfortable, Astan contemplated Daven's return to the clan, especially stronger and more influential. Iris had shared with Astan and Jelani what little she understood about Daven's activities at the cave. No doubt he would seek the *santwarja*. Perhaps Daven was pure enough of heart to find it, but Astan doubted it.

"Actually, it's a matter of balance," Astan said, jumping back into the conversation. "If we kill for our own profit, then we lose our powers. If we kill in self-defense, we do not. The soil accepts our need."

"Are you kidding me?" Lane scoffed. "Who decides if you're acting in self-defense? A lot of people claim they were just protecting themselves when they take out someone jerking their chain."

Max's lips twitched into a frown. "The heart knows."

Kevin listened, arms crossed, only an occasional tremor showing his concern. Jelani rocked the baby, now curled with his head on her shoulder, and Crispy picked at imaginary lint on his pants.

"It's a subjective call?" Iris asked. "No outside authority sets it?"

Astan guessed she was thinking again of Daven's choice to abandon the clan to live alone. Or maybe what he might do if he somehow succeeded at his quest and became a mage. Surely, he would be in the forefront of the elven battle. Without Astan to protect him this time.

"The Lady of the Forest reads the hearts of the *Lelan*," Astan explained the best he could. "She is the one who determines intent."

Crispy glanced at Jelani. "I thought *she* was the Lady of the Forest."

Astan shook his head. "No, The Lady of the Forest is something deeper, a presence intangible. The world of the elf clan has six members with advanced skills, the *Idellan*, only six at any given time. The Lady of the Forest is essentially the Earth Goddess, if you looked at it from a human viewpoint. Other mages rule the air and water, and they teach the Circle. But someone else controls the magic of the fire. Someone not in the clan."

"Elves of the clan can't hold these powers?" Kevin asked. He shifted on the rickety kitchen chair, keeping his bad leg straight. He was not wearing the brace he often used when the weather was cold.

"Elves can advance to the exalted level through training and study," Astan said. "Apparently my father believes he can become *Intalus*. If he succeeds, he will hold the fifth place. Bartolomey—"

"Bart's the evil genius balancing the equation?" Lane practically cackled with glee. When the others failed to react, he groaned. "Come on, you guys. Earth, Wind, and Fire?" He counted on his fingers. "Water, too. They balance each other out. The others need to be two opposites, that's the way it is in all the literature. This is why everything's slanted toward the Bad now, because Bart has no opposite on the scale. For every evil Lord of Mordor, there's a Gandalf or an Aragorn. Light and Dark Jedi? Hell, even ordinary God and the Devil? We all got fed that at Sunday school. Light and Dark, Fire and Water, Air and Earth. So Daven needs to become this sainted wizard to combat Bart. Good for him, I say. It restores balance."

Max, finished with his plate of food, slipped away from the table and into the back rooms of the apartment. The sound of a toilet flushing followed, another, and then another, accompanied by Max's delighted laugh. Lane dispatched Crispy to curb the young elf's enthusiasm for modern plumbing.

Longing to be back in open air, Astan surveyed the group. He did not have Daven's talent for reading people through a simple touch, but he did have some skills with empathy. Lane remained self-involved, finishing food on his plate as he spouted fantasy platitudes. Jelani and Iris focused on the baby, one as devoted mother, the other as someone longing to be. When Crispy drew Max back into the main room, Max retreated to the Cave, studying the machinery, while Crispy hovered along the edges of the group, the crowd obviously making him uncomfortable as well.

Kevin's dark eyes were troubled. He watched Astan closely. Astan could tell he knew something was in the wind. His warrior nature, no doubt.

"So why are you bringing this to us?" Kevin finally asked. "Not just for a bit of intelligence-sharing. You want something."

Astan glanced at Jelani, this being her crowd and her news to share. He watched with pride as she embraced the idea of returning to the clan, seeming to grow and expand into her role as leader. They discussed options and made their plans. They were ready. She should make her own announcement.

She got to her feet, their son sleeping on her shoulder, and joined him. "Since I'm going back to the woods at a time when war is inevitable, we do want your help," she confessed. "The individual clan members each have a talent to use, and Astan will be in charge of coordinating them when the attacks come. But I know nothing about war. Heck, I hardly read the papers about your war, Kevin, not because I didn't care, but because I didn't feel there was anything I could do. But here, I'm going to be right in the middle of it. Whatever you can tell me about how to conduct a winning campaign would be a blessing."

"Don't you worry, Jelly Bean," Lane said. "We've done about a zillion raids."

"She doesn't mean your silly game!" Crispy frowned and got to his feet, nervously collecting the plates to carry them to the kitchen. "When those bad guys come for her, she's not going to have the magic singing sword of Poobah World or the Magic Crunchy-edged axe of Gelderland. She's going to have evil right in her face." He dropped the dishes in the sink and turned to face them, his face drawn with worry. "She needs something real."

"I've got something," Lane blurted and then snapped his jaws shut. Red-faced, energy almost burst from him. He looked excited to share something, but his jaws were clenched as if to prevent the words from escaping.

Kevin watched Lane a moment, and then turned his attention back to Jelani and Astan. "I would be glad to help however I can. We gathered info when we were up at the clan lands about the layout of the place, and I'm sure the guys will give us whatever else we need. We can find strong points, what's easy to defend, where we can set ambushes, that kind of thing."

"Thanks, Kevin," Jelani said, but her gaze remained on Lane.

Astan noted the puzzlement on her face. He considered pushing Lane for an answer, but let it go for the moment. Human interference in an elven battle would be contentious enough as far as the Circle was concerned. He would watch and wait.

Iris still radiated questions, uncertainties attached to her like pendant earrings, silent, but dangling to catch attention. Her hands lay in her lap as she sat on the couch, fingers rubbing against each other every so often as if they needed to make sure they were still there. Despite her attachment to his father, Iris was a trustworthy ally. Her feelings for Jelani and the rest of them were genuine, and Astan noted her ability to cut through false layers of pretension to true emotion. When Jelani had been pregnant and in need, Iris had no problem giving attitude back to the Circle on many occasions. If she was worried, it would be wise to find out what upset her.

"What are your concerns, Iris?" Astan asked at the next pause in the conversation.

A slight shrug twitched her shoulders. "You're expecting a lot, leaving Lane and Crispy in charge of Elliun, stranded out there in the woods." As Lane started to protest, Iris cut him off. "Not that you guys didn't do fine with him, but he was only with you for a few days. And it was here in town where you have access to electricity, medical care, a grocery store, and everything else. What Astan and Jelani are suggesting is that you take him out there where the fight will take place. And that you cope not only with the care of a child but an entirely new and deprived environment. Remember, it was less than a year ago that Crispy wouldn't even leave this apartment. A condition that existed for years."

"He's better now," Lane added with a *harrumph.*

Iris nodded. "He is better now." She turned to look over her shoulder at Crispy who fidgeted with the dishes, idly stacking them. "I'm very grateful for that, and glad to see him come so far out of the shell that held him back. He's well on the road to recovery. The last thing I want is to put him in a position where we'll see him regress or even retreat entirely."

"We don't want to see that either, Iris," Jelani interjected. "The elves have seen to the enchantment of the cabin and its immediate vicinity. And in reality, we expect the attention of Bartolomey and the others will be focused elsewhere, where we are conducting the battle."

"And I'll be there, too!" Max piped up from inside the Cave.

Lane bolted upright, his head swiveling toward the sound of Max's voice. "Hey, what are you doing?"

Max giggled. "I have never seen elves like this. Where can we find this clan? I would like to meet them."

With a frown, Lane lumbered over to the Cave. "Max, what are you—Holy shit-on-a-shingle, man." He stared slack-jawed.

Curious, Astan moved until he could see into the pile of boxes and computer set-ups where Lane spent most of his days. Max sat in the chair with wheels, spinning in a complete circle every so often, but his attention remained engaged by battle scenes on each of the computer screens. The action seemed to be between characters that were cartoon-like in nature. The characters whirled and jumped and quivered at the touch of Max's fingers on the keys.

"How can he hold an axe of that size?" Max wondered. "He is so slender. Surely, an axe like that would break his arm. And this one?" He tapped on one of the screens. "Look at this, a blizzard of magic? Will Daven Talvi be able to do this?"

Crispy muttered from his safe harbor in the kitchen, but Astan could not hear what he said.

Kevin joined Lane, staring in amazement at Max. "Man," he said, "it took me months to master that Instance."

"I hear you, pal." Lane scratched his backside and stepped closer. "Max, tell me how you got into that. Through my passwords."

Max opened his mouth, prepared no doubt to launch into a series of explanations.

Astan cleared his throat. "Jelani and I have much to do. We'll take Elliun home to the cabin and wait for you to come tomorrow. You will still do this?"

Both Lane and Crispy nodded, though Crispy's nervous gestures seemed to increase.

"I can help them out," Kevin volunteered.

Iris, her expression still one of disapproval, walked over to Crispy and slipped an arm around his shoulders. "I'll be available, if you need anything."

"And I'll be there," Max said again.

"We'll make sure they have protection," Astan assured Iris. "Even you have to agree they are more to be trusted than those of the Circle, whatever truce we have entered."

Iris relented. "Of course. You all will need to concentrate on what you need to do. I just don't see why he can't stay here with the Boys."

"We cannot protect Elliun here," Astan said. "The city, all concrete and steel, not a natural place. Not part of the clan lands. The cabin has The Vincent's initial charm as well as what Kirill has just provided, an enchantment to repel those who would enter. At present, all of those in this room have access. Kirill has keyed entry to the vibrations of each of us, not an easy task where humans are concerned. No one else can enter unless they are in direct physical contact with one of us."

Lane dragged his awareness from his fascination with the computers for a moment. "You mean we have to hold their hand to let them in?"

"Something like that. I think that leaves out most everyone we don't want."

"I guess!" Lane shrugged, before his focus was sucked back to the game.

Annoyed by the short attention span of the human, Astan took Elliun from Jelani while she gathered up the things they brought with them for the day.

Iris came over to give the baby a sweet kiss on the forehead. "I'm not sure how I can help, but you know I will. Just ask."

"I know." Astan offered a smile and touched Iris' shoulder in reassurance.

"You need to make things right with your father," Iris said. "No matter what has happened during this time of difficulty, believe that he loves you very much. He would give his life for any of the three of you."

"He'll have to prove himself to me before I'll trust him."

"He'll give you the chance, Astan. Give him one, too. Please."

Astan, unconvinced, turned away.

Jelani hugged Iris, holding her a long time before release. She sighed. "I'll miss you."

"I'll miss you too, hon. Give 'em hell. Don't forget you're the queen."

"I'll try." Jelani's voice quivered and her eyes filled with tears. Her gaze met Astan's worried look and she shook her head. "I'm fine. Just human, hmm?"

"How I know," Astan teased with a long-suffering tone.

"Shut up." Jelani chuckled and bid Crispy farewell. "See you tomorrow. Don't forget to bring your supplies. And cupcakes. And some of your chai tea, 'cause I'm all out."

"I will." Crispy hung back in the kitchen, emotions wrestling across his face.

Astan eyed the group clustered in the Cave. "Max, we need to go."

Max started to get up, but Lane stopped him. "Can Max stay? Kevin can drive him to the clan lands later. Or he can even come with us tomorrow. Do you mind?"

Now what did Lane have up his sleeve? "Max, do you want to stay?"

"Yes! I'll stay in The Lane's domain. I want to learn more about the elves of the Blood clan." His face lit up, delighted.

"Very well," Astan stated, handing the baby to Jelani, so that she could place him in the baby-pack she wore in front of her. He finished packing the supplies they had obtained earlier in the day into a backpack and slipped it over his shoulder. "Ready?"

"Sure you don't want a ride?" Iris asked.

"I need to get in shape. See you." Jelani gave Iris another quick hug and then hurried out the door.

Kevin, at least, had the presence of mind to give a little salute as they went out the door,

The last thing Astan saw before pulling the door closed behind him was Lane and Max enthralled in the make-believe world on the computer screens. It did not instill confidence.

CHAPTER 21

LANE looked up at the sound of the front door closing.

It was only then that he realized Iris had left. So had Astan, Jelani, and the baby.

Even Crispy had retreated to a hot bath laced with Epsom salts to clear his body of the mental and physical overload of being with so many people in such a small space.

That left Lane and Kevin to drag chairs in front of the computer screens, so they could watch what little Max, a novice, did with the WoW game, a game that both of them had played for years.

Lane was stunned at the extent of Max's natural affinity for machinery, especially computers that were certainly more advanced than anything the young elf must have ever seen. Max managed minor game quests on at least two fronts with two of Lane's toon characters. He seemed to learn through his fingertips how to acquire objects and win battle points. With each new accomplishment, Max wriggled in his chair, his glee almost tangible.

"Okay, wait," Kevin said. "I want to see something. Lane, boot up your laptop. I'm going down to get mine. I want to try him at PvP."

On an adrenaline high, Lane grinned and dragged the small dining table over to the edge of the Cave, placing it where he and Kevin would both be able to look over Max's shoulder at the same time they ran their own screens. He plugged in his computer, not wanting the battery to die halfway through combat, and then ducked into the kitchen for a cup of tea and a box of cupcakes. No sense in having to forage for provision halfway through.

Kevin was back in a few minutes, pulling his computer from

the case even before he could sit down. The case fell to the floor beside him, as he set the laptop on the table and pushed the power button. He moved his chair where he could see both Lane's screen and the ones in the Cave. "So what's the plan, Stan?"

Lane, totally jazzed by this development, the possibilities sending him near the bursting point, tried to decide where to begin. "What about Arathi Basin? That would have the skills we need to capture the base and defend the resource after we take it?"

Kevin appeared to consider the suggestion for a few seconds, and then nodded. "Might be a good dry run. We need fifteen. You want to call in anyone else?"

"Are Chraist and Ritaron on?"

Kevin pulled up the guild roster. "Why am I even looking? They're always on."

Five was a good number to work together on this end to attempt this battleground. The game would pull in enough others to giving them a fighting chance. They were ready to go.

"All right," Lane said, eying the Cave's main screen. "Max, get your headphones on. No. No not like that. Over your ears. Yeah. Right. Okay, can you call up my warrior Jonah? Go to the log-in screen and pick that name. It'll load right up." He watched as Max instinctively entered the right commands to make it so. "Yeah, that one. Okay, so we have Jonah, and Kevin's shaman, Chraist and Ritaron. And we only need one more thing to kick some real ass. Xiomar."

"What is a Xiomar?" Max asked, still poking at the keyboard, making his men move around.

"Xiomar, my friend, is a warlock of the kind that would make Bartolomey shit his pants." Lane chuckled. "He's big, green, bad, lots of teeth. Here, let me show you." He punched up the code for Xiomar and grabbed his headphones. "Everyone hear me okay?"

He received a chorus of replies, felt Kevin's anticipation from right next to him.

"All right," Lane said. "Let's be bad guys."

Kevin gestured to Max's screen. "Accept that invite."

Max cocked his head, studying the pop-up box curiously. "This is invite?"

"Just click on it," Kevin instructed, already studying the stats of the others appointed to their team from outside.

Max did as he was told. Immediately, four other small pictures appeared in the corner of his screen. "Who are these people?"

"That's the rest of your team," Lane explained. "That's Kevin's guy, and Chraist's druid. Ritaron's the paladin. And that one is Xiomar."

Max looked at the Xiomar icon, his eyes growing wide. "It is a monster."

"Wait 'til you see what he can do."

Moments later, they were in the battlefield, and Kevin urged Max to be ready once the fence opened. The gathered players then sent their toons down the hill through what looked like fields of worn dried grasses, or perhaps fields of wheat down toward the farm.

"Okay, guys, we'll take LM." Lane turned to Max. "That's the lumber mill," he said off-mike. "Across that stone bridge, ahead and to the left. Yeah, that one."

Lane tried to keep an eye on all his little band, as they rushed along the paths on varied mounts from a raptor to his own flaming horse, all moving in unison. Other members of the Horde team, those who were queued and waiting, headed off to attack the Stables, the Blacksmith, and the Gold Mine. Their team as a whole would have to control each of these targets in order to win the round.

He debated trying to drive Xiomar with his mind as he had the other night, but that was practice. The way his friends played, this was deadly serious and he needed to play his very best. What he wanted to show them could wait until this battle was finished.

As they crested the ridge, they came upon three Alliance players, already dismounted, the first trying to secure possession of the mill, while the other two rallied in front of him in defense. The flag was gray, signifying that no one owned the site yet, but in a few seconds, it changed to blue. The Alliance scored.

"Our first combat," Lane blurted with glee. "You ready, Max?"

The white-haired elf gave a merry laugh and pressed the keys. "I follow The Lane to battle!"

"Wish they were all this enthusiastic," Lane muttered.

He took a deep breath, before calling out a series of targets, one for each team member. The screen lit up as the parties exchanged fire in streaks of red and blue, but the dark hand of the Horde eventually made short work of the Alliance defenders. Lane decided he would let Max take the prize, since it was his first game.

"Max," Lane instructed, "right-click on the flagpole! The blue one right by the edge of the cliff."

Max maneuvered his toon into place, and clicked on the pole, which turned gray and then a minute later turned red. "What do I do with it?"

"Nothing. We just have to keep control of it 'til all the teams win one." Lane kept typing, involved in a heavy swordfight with an Alliance warrior. "You just needed to get it."

Max eyed him. "That does not seem like much of a goal."

"In about a minute, someone will try to stab you for it, so keep an eye out. Chraist, watch out for Max! He's a noob!"

"Oh. I am a noob? I thought I was a warrior." Max chewed his lip, staring at the screen as though the creatures circling around on it would jump off the monitor and grab him.

Lane chuckled. "A noob is a newbie. A new player. It's not something bad. Well, not much, anyway. Never mind. Just hold that flag!"

The lumber mill situated on top of a hill proved to be an excellent training ground for teaching players how to defend an outpost. Alliance players would come from any side of the hill, trying to come up and recapture the flagpole, but Lane's team fought hard to maintain their control. Several times one of the team fell, wounded, but Ritaron moved among them, healing their injuries and rebuilding their strength to fight again.

Kevin snickered. "I've got one. Max'll love this. I feel a

Typhoon coming on."

His teammate muttered over the headphones, and Lane laughed, too. "Good idea. Let's show Max what we can do."

They watched as their friend's druid character mustered a spell called Typhoon aimed at the Alliance attackers, which allowed her to conjure a wave of water that blew the attackers off the side of the cliff where the flagpole stood.

Max gasped, and clapped his hands. "Do it again!"

Lane nearly encouraged her to try again but another group of Alliance ran up while they were engaged with the first, and they were not in a very good mood. "Can't now. More killing to do."

The battleground continued until the Horde players gathered sufficient resources and time held to set off the counter total needed to complete the mission, and then trumpets sounded and the Horde was rewarded with a report of how well they had done in battle.

Kevin groaned at his stats. "Oh, man, ten HKs and only one kill."

Lane reviewed the chart. Honor Kills were not bad, just not as sexy as credit for a killing blow that you made yourself. "I got six, but look at the DPS. Nineteen K."

Still poking at his keyboard, Max made his toon turn in circles. "What does it mean when you have two flags?"

Lane jotted down notes on a pad next to him for future reference. "That means you captured the target twice." He set the box of cupcakes out on the table.

"Twice?" Kevin said. "When did that happen?"

"Remember, he got it back from that rogue, when you were fighting the Alliance paladin?"

Kevin grinned. "Wasn't watching. True enough."

Max reached for one of the cupcakes. "Can we play again?"

"Not right now." Lane went back to debriefing the other team members for a few minutes, taking their suggestions for future joint ventures.

Max licked filling off his fingers. "You have shown me that your conjuring can make powerful magic. Your hero killed many of the enemy and also protected the rest of his clan. Too bad that we can't have Xiomar to help us fight Bartolomey."

Lane froze for moment. "Well, I may have something to share with you about that." He took a long drink of his tea. "I'm thinking we might be able to."

"Bull," Kevin said. His eyes radiated disbelief. "What? You're gonna haul Black Bart into the game?"

Lane shook his head. "No, my brother. I think I can haul Xiomar out into the real world."

Kevin dropped a cupcake. "Get the hell out of Dodge."

"Haven't tried it yet, but I have been able to control Xiomar without using the keyboard." Lane tried not to sound conceited, but he could not help bursting with pride. "Want to see?"

Of course they did. Lane traded places with Max. The three of them crowded together for a good view of the screen, as Lane began to show them. Punctuated with exclamations from Kevin and knowing nods from Max, the session satisfied Lane's need to prove himself.

"Truly The Lane is wise in the ways of war," Max said.

"Well, I wouldn't go that far," Lane protested. "But if I can do this, there must be some way to control it. I don't know. Bigger than that." With his left hand resting on the keyboard, Lane pointed to the computer screen, before waving his hand toward the room beyond the Cave. "I wish that Xiomar could live in the real world so we could use him to help Jelly Bean and Astan."

After a beat of silence, all three stared at the screen where the figure of Xiomar vanished. A low roar came from the other side of the carton-and-crate wall.

"What the hell?" Kevin said, his hand tight on the back of Lane's chair. "Where did it go?"

Max just smiled and dashed around the end of the Cave wall. "Here he is!"

Kevin and Lane exchanged looks of horror.

"Crispy," Lane gasped.

They were on their feet in a moment and followed Max into the living room.

There in the center of the small space stood a seven-foot tall

green orc with every one of those teeth he had warned Max
about.

"Sweet Jesus," Lane muttered.

Just then, the bathroom door opened and Crispy walked out,
wrapped in his thick blue terry bathrobe that covered him from
throat to ankles. When he saw what was between him and Lane,
he stared, his eyebrow snaking up in annoyance.

"Don't worry, Crisp," Lane said, but the words did not come
out in his voice or from his mouth. Instead, they came from
Xiomar in a deep booming voice that reverberated off the walls.

"Really? Smelly green monsters? I'm not cleaning it up when
he poops on the floor." Crispy turned and walked to the
bedroom. The door closed behind him and then locked with a
snick.

"Hellfire." Lane started for the bedroom, but stopped as he
came even with Xiomar.

The toon rocked slightly from foot to foot, breathed with a
rough, raspy magic, and the stench? Worse than a locker room of
teenage males after a championship game. Xiomar's solid black
eyes studied him without mercy or any sort of emotion within
them. Simply a killing machine, one Lane knew all too well was
smart and ruthless.

Fascinating to stand eye to eye after all these months of playing with him.

"So who are you really?" Lane asked, but got no answer.

He glanced back to Kevin, who stared first at the monster,
who seemed oblivious to his surroundings, and then at Max, who
seemed perfectly pleased that the magic worked.

"I'll be right back," Lane said. He slipped past Xiomar and
knocked on the bedroom door. "Crisp? Open up. It's just me. I
promise."

"Go away," Crispy replied after a short pause, his voice
sounding very far away.

"Crisp, come on." Lane leaned his forehead against the door.
"He's not going to hurt you. He's going after Bart. That's the
only thing." He peered out to see what was happening. Max
stood near Xiomar, studying him like a shiny new object. Xiomar
made no move that showed threat or even intention toward the

slight elf. Lane supposed he wouldn't. Not until Lane directed him to. If he was really just a magical extension of the toon from the game.

What the hell had he done?

He knocked again for Crispy and his gaze moved to the door handle. "Don't make me get the ice pick, bro."

As he waited, he replayed in his mind the steps he had taken. He wished for Xiomar to be alive, and to help in the war. His hand was on the enchanted computer when he made his wish.

Holy crap.

"I've got control of the thing, Crisp, through the computer keyboard," he promised, hoping it was true. "Just think how great this will be in the battle. Xiomar's a cold ass killer. He'll take out all the baddies before any of our people can be hurt. That's a good thing!"

Another long pause, but at its end, he heard the rattling of the lock as Crispy turned it, releasing the catch.

With a sigh of relief, Lane opened the door. "Crisp, he won't hurt you."

"It's a horrible green monster. I know what it can do. You showed me. Remember when you made me watch? That stupid game is taking over your life."

Lane sighed. What could he say? It wasn't stupid? That it meant something? That, yeah, maybe it did consume way too much of his time? Of course it did! But in there, Lane felt powerful, as if he could control his existence, something that he lacked in the 'real' world since he was a child. Sure, it was escapism, but why shouldn't he escape from the detritus of his ruined life?

"I'm doing it for Jelly Bean," Lane swore. "Just think if we have him to protect us out there at the cabin. Let them come after us. I'll turn Xiomar loose on them and they'll wet themselves before they run away, screaming like little girls."

"What if it gets loose?"

"Come on. I'll show you I can make it disappear." After the words left his lips, Lane realized he did not really know if he could.

Several more minutes of coaxing finally brought Crispy to the doorway. Lane got him to promise to wait there. He inched around Xiomar, who seemed to take up a disproportionate amount of the living room space, and also around Kevin, who had not moved from his spot of disbelief.

Returning to the Cave, Lane reached for his keyboard. "Go away, my friend. We'll call you when we need you." Tapping the keys, he logged out of that character and held his breath.

Xiomar disappeared.

Max peered around the edge of the Cave, his face a mask of disappointment. "You sent him away."

Lane blew out a long sigh of relief. "Yeah. We don't need him now, and he was pissing off Crispy."

"You'll make him come back?" Max asked.

"Yep," Lane replied. "When Bart's Bad Boys come after us."

Max grinned and then vanished around the corner. The bathroom door closed.

Crispy appeared in Lane's line of sight, heading for the kitchen where he put on the teakettle.

Lane pushed away from the desk and stood up to stretch. He caught Kevin's eye.

"So," Lane said, rather pleased with himself, "magic."

Kevin turned slowly and then took a couple of steps toward the Cave. "You did see—I mean. Orc. There." He pointed toward the living room. "Big, smelly fighting orc. Here. There." He blinked. "With a sword."

"And not the singing sword of Grand Poobah, either," Lane said, a little louder, his words underlined with an edge directed at his roommate.

"I'm not listening." Crispy set a cup on the counter and dropped a tea bag in it.

"I've never seen anything like that, man. I don't know." Kevin stumbled and Lane shoved his wheeled office chair quickly in Kevin's direction so he had somewhere to sit before he fell.

"Pretty awesome, huh?" Lane eyed the empty space where Xiomar had lived and breathed, reliving those moments, congratulating himself for solving the problems their little band faced. Just let Bartolomey and his group show their sorry faces. Xiomar, and Lane Donatelli, would take care of that threat in no time at all. Then old Daven and the witches of the Circle could look down on humans and their world forever. But they could not do it without remembering it was a human that saved them all.

That thought alone improved Lane's outlook immensely, and he headed over to the kitchen to scour for something to eat. A real man needed sustenance after a demonstration like that.

"Hey, Crisp, you have enough tea for everyone? I think we could all use a little celebration. Then we better get packed."

CHAPTER 22

SPARRING with the other Youngers over several seven-days, Vez came to see they now constituted a formidable fighting force.

Terzon could move the earth, what the humans would call geokinesis, changing rock to dirt and back again, causing it to pile high or fall down on unsuspecting victims.

Fontine used her gifts to bring forth fire and augmented them with Veraena's help. Now she could grow a flower of fire in her hand and use it as a projectile weapon.

Veraena was also able to help several of the others boost their immature talents into dangerous abilities.

Yadin, whose prior aptitude was to be unnoticed in a crowd, learned to make himself invisible to humans. Even most elves would not notice him if they were just passing by, but if actively seeking him they could hone in on his location.

Lokni, one of their most recent acquisitions, had learned control of the winds from Circle member and clan elder Kalinda.

Try as Vez might, he could not seem to teach himself much more than his original ability, transmigration. As he had shown Grigor months before, Vez could travel in seconds to any point he could see, as if the distance between the two points simply vanished. While this had advantages, Vez saw mostly the detriments. Even if he could arrive somewhere before anyone else, he still lacked any advanced combat skills or other trickery with which to engage an enemy. Despite the time his mother grudgingly took from training with the others to work with him, she was not able to enhance his proficiency in any major way.

Which is why I need the mage, Vez thought.

He also needed the chance to prove himself as a leader. So far, other than a few small spying parties, the group had left the queen and her family alone. Yadin reported that they moved into the cabin once frequented by The Vincent, but it was common knowledge the cabin was enchanted against entry by outsiders. In recent weeks several of their group had tried to approach the place, but had been rebuffed by some new magic protecting the rickety-looking shack.

A strike against the false queen or her child would certainly improve his standing in the eyes of Bartolomey. He likely could not pull it off alone, but with himself and a few chosen companions, he could certainly make a run at it. So he began to plan.

His plan bloomed into opportunity in the next few days as Veraena took a group of the Youngers to raid the clan's supplies. Along with her went Yadin, who could help her to sneak onto the clan's soil without detection. Once his mother and her little band left camp, Vez hunted down his own choices. There was Hidal, now a master of shadow control who was able to create an area of darkness around himself at will, and Gianina, a pretty dark-haired *neris* whose skill entailed projecting her voice in a sharp piercing cry that could shatter glass or render another unconscious. He asked them to accompany him on a walk.

"Where are we going?" Gianina asked, traveling lightly despite the heavy human boots she liked to wear.

"Thought we'd see if we might be lucky enough to surprise the queen," Vez said.

Hidal's eyes widened as he ran alongside Vez. "Does Veraena know this? She did not mention it to anyone."

Vez tried not to bite his tongue. "Veraena will be told when she needs to know. The raid she has set forth this day is enough for her to worry about at this point. Besides, if we fail—" That thought nearly made him trip over a large log. He coughed. "If we should fail, just as well no one knows. If we succeed, all the better for the surprise of it."

Hidal nodded. "We dare not fail after Grigor's attempt. His sacrifice must not be repeated."

Vez contemplated Grigor's 'failure' and his fate, and agreed silently he did not intend to end up the same way. "We shall be careful. Once we are close to the place we can decide if it's worth the effort."

"Of course," Hidal stated, as he moved a little faster, trying to keep up with Gianina. But they both kept their distance behind Vez.

Vez's first reaction was paranoia. Why were they hanging him out in front? Waiting for something to eat him up? Setting a trap for him? He considered the way he handled Grigor, feeling certain parallels. Should he stop, let them pass him?

They were not bright enough to make up such a plot on the fly.

If he was going to lead this pack, then the front of the line was the proper place for him. He would do the best he could.

Veraena picked a location for Bartolomey's troops to train that was quite far from the clan soil, for obvious reasons. That made traveling back a time-consuming proposition, but the three elves had honed themselves through Veraena's teachings, sharpening themselves against each other, and they were tough now. They ran on through the forest, their passing silent.

Vez noticed the first signs of spring all around them. While the leaves on the deciduous trees would not return for another month, as the humans reckoned it, the sun shone for several days, and the air felt less chilled. Ice melted off the pine branches, leaving some damp and muddy places on the ground. The three elves never got their feet wet, thanks to their innate abilities. They made good time as they covered the distance, arriving in the vicinity of the cabin at approximately midday, when the sun was at its highest. The spies among them described the location and the exterior of The Vincent's cabin, a broken-down hovel of splintering pieces of wood, topped with a roof of torn and dilapidated shingles. A home fit for a Queen? Hardly. Just further proof, as far as Vez was concerned, that Jelani Marsh did not deserve that title.

Once Vez spotted the roof of the cabin, he held out a hand and stopped the others. They inched up behind him on the ridge overlooking the place, the same expression on their faces.

"This is the home of the queen? Not an elven bower? Not

even a solid building? Has she fallen so low?" Gianina asked.

"She is finally living at the level fit for a human imposter," Vez said. "Hidal, can you shade us from their view?"

Hidal stepped apart from them. Closing his eyes, he raised his hands from where they hung at his sides. As they came up, a faint shadow grew around the three elves reaching to the trunks of the trees on either side of them, not particularly dark, where it would be noticeable, but just in a natural way under the trees, an extra bit of shielding from curious eyes below.

Once they were better concealed, Vez and his team moved to the very edge of the ridge. After several minutes of study, he determined that the windows on the back side of the cabin were only partially covered by some sort of blue cloth.

Movement inside drew his eye. There were a couple of Jelani's human friends, the small sickly one and the fat sloppy one. The baby lay in a basket on a table. Vez did not know who else might be there. Better to find out before making a mistake.

"Gia, take the north side, Hidal, the south. I'll come up to the back. Then we can meet in front. When we are gathered there, we will together take the child. The humans cannot stop us."

"What about the enchantments of the door?" Gianina asked, head cocked and her small fists on her hips. "We cannot get through those without an enchanter of our own."

Vez had considered that obstacle in the time of their traveling, but he wrote it off as a non-issue. "I don't think we'll have to break the portal to enter. The egos of the humans will be their undoing. They will come out to meet us. When they do, Gia, you will have your chance to render them helpless. Once the door is open, we should be able to walk in."

His co-conspirators nodded in agreement. Hidal murmured a charm that would allow each of them to carry a faint trace of the shade protection. They split up, the other two moving to the sides, and taking the rocky paths downward toward the cabin. Winter apparently had been harsh to the hillside. Trees lay on their sides like fallen warriors amid piles of rocks lost to mudslides. A pair of black crows cawed from the branches above. Vez waited until they were most of the way down the hill, before envisioning a spot near the covered part of the window, and set his mind to be there.

The sound of off-key singing came from inside, making him wince. He visually checked on the other two elves, and noticed they were at their appointed places. He joined them in making thorough checks of the trees, rocks and other visible points around them. He saw no one.

Continuing around the cabin in Hidal's direction, away from the exposed window, and keeping an elf-lengths distance from the cabin wall, he continued to listen. He did not know the individual voices of the humans, but he detected at least three inside. This threw him a little. An unknown quantity. Should they call this off?

Not when we've come this close.

He and Hidal continued around the front, finding no other windows uncovered. No way to discover who might be inside. He dashed across the front of the cabin to a spot behind a thick trunk where he could keep a clear view of the door. The others joined him, each breathing quickly with anticipation.

He opened his mouth to call out the humans when a racket overhead grabbed his attention. A flash of red feathers blazed across the space between them, accompanied by a piercing screech of challenge. The hawk landed on the roof of the cabin right over the ramshackle door, his bright eyes fixed on Vez and his companions.

A few seconds later, another body glided down from the trees, but this one was much heavier, topped by a shock of white hair.

"Max!" Gia gasped, pulling back further behind the tree.

Vez growled. The little mutant was going to spoil his fine plan. He lit his mind on fire, searching for possible ways to save this.

Max landed on the ground just in front of the door, and cocked his head up at the hawk before turning slowly to stare out into the trees. He must have caught a flicker of motion, because he reached for the door and was inside in one smooth move, leaving the bird to sit guard.

"What now?" Hidal grumbled.

Vez juggled possibilities. Just because there was an elf working with Jelani's friends did not mean their mission was blown. Vez always thought of Max as the runt of the clan litter. He was not big enough to hurt anyone and his fascination with human machinery was nothing more than a waste of time. He presented no real threat. They could continue.

Discovered now, there was no point in hiding behind the tree. He stepped out boldly into the small clearing before the cabin. "Come out, humans, and face the true members of the clan. You do not belong here."

He waited for the usual prickly human response to an ego challenge, which often involved launching themselves at the speaker in blinding anger. His companions stood arms-length away and behind him, one to each side. Seconds passed, and he wondered if he misjudged these people after all. Not wanting to move closer, to give himself plenty of room to fight, he waited, considering what else he could say that would be of a provocative nature.

The rickety wooden door burst open, but did not fly off its hinges.

Out came a huge green being, thick-bodied with rippling muscles and a sword in each hammy hand. Black clothing covered most of its body, and its chest was covered with chunky leather armor. The thing dripped slobber from an impressive row of sharp teeth, and when it stepped forward the ground shook. It stopped two elf-lengths in front of him, leaned its head back, and roared. The sound it made vibrated the branches overhead and rattled Vez's bones.

"I am Xiomar the Mighty!" the creature proclaimed in a bold, deep voice. "I fight to protect the elf prince. Prepare to die!"

CHAPTER 23

JELANI did not expect a tickertape parade when she returned to her tree house on clan soil, but she at least thought someone would be there to meet her.

Astan, Beckley, and a few others were helping to carry up things Kevin had dropped off at the cut below. In her hands she carried a heavy box of supplies, while the backpack with her clothing weighed down her shoulders. If any were to challenge her at this very second, she would have been hard-pressed to put up a fight. But it seemed not to be an issue, despite all her earlier angst about it. Not one of the elves was in sight as they entered the clan's preserve.

"Just as well," she muttered, trudging on despite a twinge of annoyance.

She was a queen, damn it. The image of Queen Elizabeth came to mind with that stiff upper lip and the way Princess Diana had always faced attack from the press.

Before meeting the elves, Jelani had been totally self-involved and unable to finish anything she started. But since Daven had materialized in the alley behind the Butterfly Herbs coffee shop, her world had expanded to include marvelous gifts. Like her ability to heal the forest. Even more special was the gift she and Astan shared, their son. After these past weeks of taking care of Elliun in the cabin, leaving him with Lane and Crispy was tearing out her heart.

No, she did not want to return to her old life. She was learning to feel and that was what she needed to do.

Damn them for not being here to meet her.

She groaned as she balanced the box on one knee to place her fingers in the small hollows on the tree trunk. The door swung open. Standing on the threshold, she was overcome by a wave of nostalgia for this place. There was the bentwood rocker the elf Elders had made for her. Was the nursery still be filled with Elliun's gifts? Then there was the bedroom where she and Astan had spent many happy hours.

Blinking away tears, she pushed her way inside and set the box on the table. She shrugged out of the straps and let the backpack drop on the floor. With her foot, she nudged the pack under the table with her foot.

Then she noticed the chaos in the room. Furniture still lay topsy-turvy. Baskets had been emptied, their contents scattered in Jelani and Astan's mad rush to leave in order to search for their missing son.

It seemed so long ago.

The elves followed her inside, talking strategies and comparing talents. Astan piled up what he and the others brought in a corner of the living room, where he stood for a long moment, just looking. Jelani could feel his emotions tug at the thought of being back among the clan, and particularly here in this place that was made for only them.

Through the open door barreled a yowling black ball of fur that scrambled right up onto the table, clawing at Jelani in a needy way.

"Azrael!" Jelani cried, snatching the cat up in her arms.

His claws picked and pulled as he reacquainted himself with her, and his purring was so loud it resonated through the tree house.

Astan grinned. "Someone's glad to see you."

"I've missed him."

Delighted, Jelani scratched behind the cat's ears, rubbing her cheek in his thick fur. He must have been spending quite a bit of time outdoors. His coat was thick as an Eskimo's. He encouraged and tolerated her ministrations for a few minutes before having enough. He jumped down, disappearing into the nursery.

Awkward, Beckley stood off to the side, leaning heavily on his left leg, hands in his pockets. "So, Astan, we'll want you to see the damage the Others did in their raid."

"Fine. I'll be along," Astan said, before entering the bedroom.

A moment later he reappeared and began straightening the mess.

Jelani, feeling a need to connect with her mate, did the same. It was important that they re-establish themselves in this space and make it theirs once more.

"Do you want help?" Merripen asked. He waved a hand and the fallen chairs sat themselves upright.

"I think we better do it," Jelani said with a gentle smile to take any sting from the rebuff. "Could you please tell Djana and the Circle that I will meet them in their space in twenty minutes?"

Beckley raised an eyebrow, a little smirk playing across his lips. "Starting early, are we?"

"I'm the queen. I have to make that my own. So I'd better start from the beginning, right?"

Jelani ignored the little feelings of panic screaming way down inside her. Those old elf women may have frightened and bullied her before, when she wasn't well, when she was still trying to learn her way. But she didn't dare let them do it now. Not if she was going to be strong enough to save them all.

He grinned and gave her a little bow. "Yes, my queen." He herded the other Youngers out the door, to leave the queen and her mate in peace.

Astan disappeared into the bedroom. Jelani continued to pick up the detritus of that last dramatic night, disposing of the spoiled food and tossing most everything else into a large basket to be sorted later. No sound came from the bedroom, no echoing clutter removal, nothing. Finally her curiosity got the better of her. What exactly was he doing in there? "Astan?"

"Mmm," came from the bedroom.

She frowned. What did that mean? "Astan, come on." She crossed the room to the bedroom door and stopped to stare at her mate, lying naked in the bed. "What? What are you doing?"

Astan's smile was that of a mischievous little boy. "You said we had fifteen minutes."

"How can you think of that at a time like this?" Exasperated, she still found herself drawn toward the bed, only half against her will. Astan's ability to compel others was not particularly strong, but he scarcely used it. In short bursts, he could be quite hard to dispute.

"How can I not think of that when I finally have time alone in a safe place with you, *denami*?" He reached out a hand to her. "Come join me."

She brushed her hair back with one hand, feeling him pull her gently toward him. "I look like hell." She managed to kick her shoes off before she landed in the bed among the tumbled sheets and the thick, multi-colored quilts they were given when they first moved into the tree house.

"You look beautiful," he said with a smile that showed he knew how trite it sounded. But the next ten minutes unfolded in a soft radiance, familiarity giving them instant recognition, knowing where to touch, how to be intimate, time constraints driving the rhythm of their coupling at a frantic pace. The sweet contact, the give and take, and the final explosion and release made Jelani feel strong and vibrant again.

She lingered, kissing him in the afterglow. "Now I don't want to leave," she whispered.

Astan's eyes burned with passion. "I don't want you to. Now I know we're home again." He clasped her hand, holding as much of the surface of his palm and his fingers against hers as he could.

When she closed her eyes, she could feel his presence all around her, protecting her and sharing his strength.

"But—" She sighed, squeezed his hand, and then let go. "The Circle awaits."

He lay on the bed and watched her as she dressed in black slacks and a black sweater from her backpack. "Isn't black clothing considered evil in the human culture?"

"You mean the black hat?" She laughed. "Maybe. It means you're the biggest, meanest guy on the block, the one no one messes with."

"Well. It sounds appropriate."

She ran a brush through her hair and pinned it up, before pulling on her boots. She checked herself in the mirror, making sure she stood straight, with a confident light in her eyes. She was ready, and she was going alone. Glancing back at Astan, she saw the expression which always came to him after they made love, the one that looked like he was satisfied with the life choices he made.

"I love you," she said.

"I'm glad, Jelani. Very glad." His smile was so enticing, she nearly got distracted again.

"Astan! I've got to go." She threw a blanket over him and ran for the door, grabbing her jacket on the way out.

* * *

JELANI walked toward the bower where the *neris* of the Circle waited for her.

The familiar path, the snow melted from it, if only briefly, brought back dozens of memories. When she glanced up, she saw faces looking back, young and old. Smiling faces. Some of the younger elves waved at her. Delighted to connect with her people again, she waved back, feeling her steps grow lighter.

Until she got to the entrance to the bower. The last several steps dragged.

Standing outside the gossamer sheen separating the private room of the Circle from the rest of the world, she silently studied the Elders with trepidation. It was Djana who tried controlling Jelani's life, pushing her toward an alliance with Daven instead of Astan. Rashia was the midwife who threatened to steal Elliun from her. Uralia, the mistress of herblore, was the one who argued supplies with her, insisting Jelani prioritize herbs for her already overstuffed jars and over the healing of damaged trees and other tragedies. She glanced around at the other faces, some had been more supportive of her during her time there, some less supportive.

Jelani was not the only one who had changed during their time apart. The aging she had seen in Djana was rampant through the rest of the Elders. Their hair was gray and matted. Clothing hung in dirty layers on their frail bodies. Thin fingers curled like claws, as they nattered at each other. They were a pitiful bunch. Coming in on her cloud of vitality, Jelani felt superior for the first time. She took a deep breath and stepped inside, her head held high.

The immediate silence that greeted her arrival was a little eerie, as were the stares of the Circle Elders as she entered. In the back there were some seats open on the tree trunks they used as chairs. Before she would have gladly taken one of those, but that was when she was insecure and timid about her place in the clan. No longer. She marched up front, standing where she could pin each one of them with a glance.

No more Mr. Nice Guy.

The cliché rocked around inside her head and made her smile. She had no intention of being mean. She just was not willing to be the doormat any longer. The old bats were not so sure of their role, however. She waited, back straight, chilled hands in her pockets, her bravado not entirely serving to keep her warm, as they silently debated which way to play things. A small counter ticked off the seconds in her head, reaching almost a hundred before Djana cleared her throat and stood up.

"My Lady, we are grateful you have returned to us." Djana's voice quivered at first and then firmed up along with the line of her jaw.

A wave of warmth rippled through those gathered. Jelani noted several of the Elders began to relax, even allow a few smiles. Djana, however, seemed to have to force the words through her teeth. They stared at each other for a moment, silently battling for superiority.

"Thank you, Djana," Jelani said after a cold moment, reminding herself that she could handle this. "I am grateful to be reunited with my elven family, and hope our continued association will bring peace and security to us all." She took her hands out of her pockets, thinking she sounded entirely too pompous. Better to let her manner of speaking break down any remaining walls between them. "Seriously, we have a lot to deal with here and we need each other. All of us." She eyed Rashia, sitting off to the side and picking at the hem of her worn brown dress. "I've never felt as much a part of a community as I did here. This community is worth saving. We can't waste time bickering among ourselves, when Bartolomey and his…."

She stopped at the collective gasp that passed among the group, followed by whispers.

"No one has told you that Bartolomey lives?" Jelani frowned, studying their concerned faces. "We don't know how, after my grandfather enchanted him into the vessel. But it is clear he controls the opposing group. It is the only explanation."

"Other evil forces exist in this plane other than Bartolomey," said a dark-haired Elder from behind Djana's shoulder. Jelani could not remember the elf-woman's name, but thought it started with an M.

"Kassen says," another broke in, "that the group is only a band of disaffected Youngers. They are no threat to us."

Jelani's eyebrow rose, her surprise creating a small pinch at the top of her face. "Must I remind you they tried to take the prince? If my friends had not saved him—"

"You mean the humans stole him," Djana said in a dry voice. "Hardly more laudable." She made a business of arranging her clothing as she sat down on the trunk behind her, soft deer-hide boots peeking out from under her skirt. They, at least, looked new, unlike the rest of what she wore.

Irritation crept into Jelani's mood. "They saved him for me, unlike what Grigor and the others would have done."

"And now Grigor is dead," Rashia pointed out. "The others are milling about aimlessly up by the Hungry Horse. We need them back."

"Exactly," Jelani said, trying not to lose control of this discussion. She had hoped Djana's performance at the cabin meant she would help facilitate this meeting. But without Daven or Astan here to show off for, apparently there was no percentage in Djana's effort.

"Didn't you pay attention when we took in those who followed Bart the first time? How many of them just gave us lip service and then as soon as the door was open again, split to go serve the Dark Lord? We do need them back, but not in their current deluded state. They attacked me when none of you were watching. They would have taken my son. I'm not asking them back as if they simply stayed out to late to play. If they want to join us, there will be changes made. Permanent ones."

"Of course," Djana said. She looked at Jelani with a speculative eye, yet there was something approving there, too. "We would expect no less. Surely, a thorough study of exactly what is going on out there will be useful. We have elves who will scout the territory, now that there is a central authority to command them."

A rabble of comments behind her were quickly smothered as Djana stood and turned to face her sisters. "You have all complained bitterly about the queen's absence. You blamed it on Daven. You blamed it on Astan. You blamed the queen herself, and her immaturity."

Jelani, standing behind her as she addressed the group, stiffened as Djana carefully parceled out the fault for what happened to everyone else but her precious Circle. Rebellious words tumbled around on the back of Jelani's tongue, jockeying for position as they prepared to set Djana straight, but she did not get the chance. Doing her best to count to ten first, in her new determination to cooperate, Jelani stared out through the walls of the bower, less opaque than usual. Apparently, the Circle's power to do basic magic was also failing. They needed her.

What she said about the Youngers who defected applied as well to Djana and her people. They needed to prove themselves to her. The sad thing was that might have to be an on-the-job training event. The clan did not have enough time to unlearn all this useless rhetoric.

"You asked for the queen," Djana continued. "We all did. We weren't sure she would ever return to us, or that we would have an alternative we could live with if she didn't."

Djana's eyes flicked a little sideways, and Jelani wondered for a moment just what Plan B might entail. Was there a spare princess hiding in the woodwork? This might be a little awkward.

"She has satisfied me she is serious about her duties," Djana added. "And I can assure you she has become an excellent mother to little Elliun."

Another little buzz of speculative approval echoed.

"Our business now is survival," Djana declared. "We must take this gift given to us by the Lady of the Forest and turn it to our advantage. Bartolomey has sent the foundation of the elf clan spinning out of balance. Only when we are united will we be able to help restore it. We have the...."

Djana stopped, and her face went white. A rush of disbelieving whispers spread through the small group.

Movement from the entrance caught Jelani's eye. "No way in hell," she said.

Daven Talvi stood by the door, his once-broad shoulders now of more humble size, as was the rest of him. He was at least forty pounds thinner. His hair had grayed, but his eyes were those same twin hazel embers. He scanned the older *neris*. Then his gaze fixed on Jelani, who stood behind his mother, Djana.

Crossing the space between them, Daven knelt before Jelani, his eyes downcast. "Blessed be the clan. Grateful am I to find you here, safe and whole, my queen. I appear, ready to serve."

For a moment, all Jelani could do was stare at him. She remembered their last meeting, when she and Astan left Daven for dead. Now her heart went out to him. He looked like a different man, one who had suffered much, one who might have gained knowledge.

The only one more surprised by Daven's actions was Djana, if her face was any indication. Her dark eyes glittered with emotion and the expression on her face was unreadable.

Daven did not move, apparently waiting for Jelani to say something. What was there to say? It wasn't like she carried a silver sword that she could knight him with.

Jelani took a deep breath and scoured her mind for the right words. "Thank you, Daven Talvi. I accept your service."

Rising to his feet, Daven gave a smile reminiscent of the first time Jelani had seen him at the coffee shop. "You have grown into quite a queen." He held her eyes for a long moment, before turning to Djana. "Mother."

After a short hesitation, Djana held out her arms and embraced her son.

Jelani took the opportunity to study the reactions around the room. The others seemed to be watching her with more respect now. A warm feeling came to her midsection and her knees. She had won. It had taken the help of both Djana and Daven, but she was now where she wanted—no, needed to be.

Jelani took a moment to offer her own small prayer to the Lady of the Forest.

After Daven finished greeting his mother and the other members of the Circle, he settled Djana back in her seat and came back to stand near Jelani. Though he did not touch her as he would have done in the past, Jelani felt as if he could read her thoughts even at a distance. He paced a little, his gaze distracted and his breathing rapid. She did not have to be telepathic to pick up his agitation.

"Daven, you've come back at a real turning point," Jelani said. "I'm glad you're here."

He dragged the back of his hand across his lips as if unsealing them. "You have no idea what the clan is up against. The *Idellan* is out of balance."

"We know that," Djana snapped. "The individuals have begun to lose their magic. We have lost our complex protections. The Others intrude on our very space and steal our supplies. Even the soil fades in the failing light."

"Bartolomey is alive," Jelani said. "He has recruited Youngers and others who are disaffected with the—" She bit her tongue. The Circle had been civil since she had entered their room. She should show them the same courtesy. "With the situation."

Daven shook his head. "Bartolomey is not your worst enemy." His gaze fixed on his mother. "Veraena has become a mage. She follows Bartolomey. And she holds the *Idan* of fire."

CHAPTER 24

THE pull of the clan soil, although weakened, had guided Daven home.

The elven power of the clan had waned, its strength drained by the dissension among its members. Moving through the clan encampment only moments before, he had noted tattered bowers, the lack of bustling industry among the inhabitants, even the lack of childish laughter.

Had he stayed away too long?

After his return last year from the twenty-five years of Sleep, waiting to save the previous queen, Daven had noticed changes in Djana. But nothing like this. In only a few short months, she had become an old woman.

I have learned much, Mother, Daven communicated to her telepathically. *If we are to survive, we must return to the old ways.*

What have I been saying for these many months? Djana's mental voice was pointed, even a bit jagged. *She's the one who has stirred things into a maelstrom.*

No, Mother, this isn't her fault. I'm talking about something older. Our duty is to the queen and the queen alone. When the queen rules, there is no need for a Circle or for other individual glories.

Djana's jaw set, and her eyes flashed with resentment. *This is what your communing with frozen nature has revealed to you? That we must abase ourselves, despite all we have done to hold the clan together?*

Such was the belief you had as well, before the teachings of the santwarja opened your eyes.

Daven broke mental contact with Djana and then privately considered the scope of the task at hand. Not only would they be fighting the malevolent brother of the dead queen, in whatever form he might be, and an embittered and much empowered Veraena and her followers, but it seemed the Circle would have to confront their own traditions as well.

Jelani tapped Daven on the shoulder. "Wait a minute. Did you say Veraena?"

"I did."

"That's Astan's mother, right?" Jelani's brow furrowed with puzzlement. "I thought she was dead. Or lost. Or something."

"Better she'd have stayed away," Djana retorted in a cold tone. "She will find nothing for her here."

"Her son is here," Jelani reminded, her voice dropping to a low growl. "Maybe that will mean something to her."

"She could have had her son all these years. She abandoned him. She left him to me." Djana glared at Jelani. "Don't tell me you think I've neglected Astan in any way."

Daven was about to interject, but Jelani stepped in front of him, actually shoving him aside.

"I didn't say that at all," Jelani pinned Djana with a hot stare. "I just wonder how you treated her. I've seen how you deal with people who don't follow your every whim."

Djana opened her mouth and then shut it. At first Daven thought it was because of his strong-willed impulse to silence her, but he was amazed to realize his mother had actually learned a little discretion.

Jelani turned to Daven, her face melting into earnest concern. "Does she know? About Astan? Does she want to see him? What about Elliun?"

Daven cleared his throat. Jelani was asking the same questions he wished Veraena would have asked. But Veraena had not given him a chance to discuss their broken family and never once mentioned their son. Surely she knew about her grandson. An unnatural mother indeed.

"She did not ask," Daven admitted with a lame shrug.

A beat passed as Jelani assimilated the information, and then shook her head. "Her loss," she said. Her expression was troubled. He wondered what she was thinking, but withheld the scan which would have answered his question. The queen deserved her privacy.

The other Elders returned to their seats, watching Daven

eagerly. Djana's expression was more guarded. "So what shall we do to protect ourselves?" she asked him.

Daven hesitated, looking to Jelani. "With your permission?"

The young queen appeared startled by his respectful request, but quickly covered it. "Please. We need to hear this."

Straightening his shoulders, Daven turned to face the group and laid out the possibilities as Lantin had discussed them with him. "We are likely going to fight a battle on many fronts, and in several layers. It appears Bartolomey remains ephemeral for now, but if he can muster his power from a physical body, we will be pitted against two full mages, as well as those who have joined their followers. We have some support here in the clan, and I will be able to defend to some extent, as I have passed through the *santwarja*, but I am only one.

"The remaining battle will be fought hand-to-hand. Astan is well versed in the arts of personal combat. He and Beckley will be able to lead the ground troops. I will speak to him. We have much to heal between us, but I am confident he will be ready when the battle comes."

He studied them, feeling their positive outlook fade. "We'll need a miracle."

* * *

LANE tapped furiously on his laptop keyboard, guiding Xiomar in full physical presence outside of the cabin.

Max, who had hunkered down just inside the doorway, held a look of amazement.

Concentrating on *becoming* Xiomar, Lane let the magic Max had instilled in the small machine pass through his fingers and into his own body. Xiomar's pig-like black eyes gradually became of use to him, and he watched fear cross the faces of the three elves waiting in front of the cabin.

He issued his challenge and then leaned his head back and roared.

Baby Elliun, who was sitting in his infant seat on the table, dropped his bottle and glared at Lane. But, amazingly, he did not cry. Elliun's expression was a perfect mirror of the look Jelani often gave when annoyed.

Lane nearly laughed, but stopped himself. He had to focus on maintaining the illusion of Xiomar. At least until he frightened away those jerks outside.

"Leave this place!" Xiomar/Lane yelled, gesturing with the sword in his right hand.

It was just the sort of weapon Crispy was mocking the other day, the magical sword with a beautifully carved hilt and a blade of shining steel that probably weighed twenty pounds. The light flashing off its blade caused the elves behind the leader to withdraw back into the trees.

The elf in front, a stocky blond dressed in a heavy jacket and mud-flecked pants, stepped forward, his eyes narrowed as he stared at Xiomar. "What sort of enchantment are you?" he demanded.

"I am a level eighty-five Orc Warlock of the Lane clan!" Lane bellowed through Xiomar. He swung the sword in a wide arc. "You shall not pass!"

The blond took another step, his head cocked as he studied Xiomar from all angles.

Max, moving along the wall to the window, clapped his hands and laughed. "Vez doesn't know what to do!"

Kevin watched out the window from behind the sash, keeping his taut body perpendicular to the intruder, creating less of a target. "Can't say I blame him. I'm pretty sure if that popped out at me, I'd need a new pair of pants."

Frustrated, Lane flexed, creating a side-to-side movement in Xiomar. What was this elf's problem? The girl had already slipped from sight. The average guy on the street should take one look at the giant green toon character and do one of two things: film it for the Internet or run away screaming. Lane had a feeling this elf was not a regular Internet user, which left the latter.

Why was he still standing there?

Punctuating his effort with a tight growl, he assessed his strength in Xiomar's body. He had taken Xiomar for several trial runs with Kevin and Max supervising. They knew what Xiomar could do, having watched him demonstrate his power and prowess in the online game, and cheered Lane on as he slashed his way through the forest, hacking tree trunks and cursing up a storm, just because it sounded so much cooler in Xiomar's gravelly roar. He was ready.

The elf outside was not behaving as expected. He retreated a few steps, but just enough to confer with another one while gesturing toward the door. The elf looked into the woods and called for his female companion, but she did not return.

One down, two to go.

"Watch that second one, Lane," Kevin cautioned. "The fool's going to make a run for the door." He ducked over to the stove and grabbed the rifle he had brought. At Lane's pained look, Kevin opened his hand in a half-gesture of apology. "Just in case," he promised.

Lane returned his attention to the view through Xiomar's eyes and decided to go for it. "You were warned!" he rumbled and then charged the two elves.

"Now they'll be sorry." Max peeked out and winced, waiting for a collision.

Nothing happened.

Xiomar lumbered toward the elves, the sword in his left hand cutting the air with a mighty whistle as he reached them, prepared to slice them in two. They cowered down into hunched over piles of quivering elf-flesh with nothing to defend themselves in hand. But when Xiomar's sword actually came even with them, it passed through them harmlessly.

"What the—" Lane's heart skipped a beat or two, before he swung the other sword at the elves as they started to stand. Nothing.

The one Max called Vez frowned and straightened. "It's a trick. Nothing but illusion. Only smoke."

"No!" Lane cried out, as he tried to figure out what was wrong. Xiomar could do physical damage. He, Kevin, and Max had seen him cut down trees with his sword. What was different now? Something was terribly off.

"Here they come!" Kevin yelled. "Crispy, get that baby somewhere safe. Now!"

From the corner of his eye, Lane saw Crispy grab Elliun out of his infant seat and duck under the table, covering them both with a blanket. Max ran for the door, shoving his way outside. Lane reacquired control of Xiomar and forced him to turn toward the cabin, propelling him forward. He thought Max intended to confront the two, each outweighing him almost double, but instead he shot upward, landing in a tree and sending out a heart-wrenching screech, almost painful in its intensity.

The sound reverberated off the surrounding trees, causing the windows to rattle violently. The two elves were nearly shaken from their feet, but Xiomar was not affected. He passed them and Lane careened him back into the house, yanking the door closed behind him.

"What are we going to do?" Crispy asked.

Kevin unlocked the window and opened it just a crack. "I'm taking a few self-defense shots, that's what I'm doing," he said. He aimed out the window and fired four shots. A cry of pain came from outside.

Xiomar wheezed by the door. Lane's fingers remained on the keyboard, as his mind struggled to understand the debacle they just witnessed. The green warlock seemed to take up an insanely large amount of space inside the small cabin, but he could not decide what to do next. He had thought this all out, counted on it, and yet it failed. He had failed.

"Whoa!" Kevin said, leaning closer to the window. "Where did all of them come from?"

"All of who?" Crispy crawled out from under the table.

"All those old women from the clan. They're out here in a line right across the front of the house."

Crispy gulped with a little squeak. "Are they after the baby?"

"Doesn't look like it." Kevin coughed. "Lane?"

Lane studied the information on his screen. Had he done something differently this time?

"Lane!" Kevin bellowed. "Front and center, soldier. We've got witches!"

"Witches?" Lane murmured. The term got his attention, and he tapped on the keyboard to close his browser. Xiomar vanished in a flurry of shadowy particles. Lane shoved himself up from the table, crossing to stand next to them at the window.

Sure enough, there were a dozen or so scary old gray elf ladies blocking the access of Vez and his buddy. Rather more effectively than Xiomar, if the expression on the Youngers' faces counted for anything. The witches did not speak, just faced away from the cabin, as if standing vigil.

Crispy cuddled the infant close as he came to look.

Elliun seemed to be as fascinated with this new development as the rest of them, his bright dark eyes focused out the window on their new friends.

"Max must have called them," Crispy surmised.

"I can't believe they came." Lane studied the scene, noting a red flower of blood on the shoulder of Vez's companion. "You winged one of the intruders."

"Looks like it." Kevin propped the rifle against the wall. "Wasn't really aiming to hit, just stall them. It worked, I guess. They're leaving." He cocked his head, eyeing something outside near the door. "Who's that?"

Lane leaned closer to the window, craning his neck to see what Kevin was looking at. A tall man with graying hair, lines etched on his face, and a familiar bearing raised his hand to knock.

"Holy mother of warlock's hemorrhoids," Lane muttered. "That's Daven Talvi. What the hell is he doing?"

"Knocking," Crispy said in a droll tone. "Should I let him in?"

Lane checked to make sure the other two elves were gone. "I don't know. Jelly Bean was pretty hot about—"

"Never mind," Crispy muttered. "He's here. Hi, Daven."

Lane followed the finger his roommate pointed toward the door.

Daven stood inside the enchanted portal.

"Now just wait a minute, pal," Lane warned.

Daven remained just inside the door. He raised a hand in a non-threatening way. "It is good to see you again, Crispy, and so far from your apartment. Congratulations." He paused, turning toward Lane. "I come in peace."

"Yeah, I remember the last guys that said that. They blew up half the planet." Lane scowled.

How had Daven gotten in? What was happening to the world of magic? Nothing was going right!

"We were alerted that the prince was in danger. The *neris* of the Circle wished to show their goodwill by coming to his aid." Daven's warm gaze, the only thing which had not changed about him, went to the baby who gurgled and waved.

Lane stepped in front of Crispy. "Jelly Bean said you weren't to be trusted. I can't just go behind her back."

"I assure you, Lane Donatelli, that the queen would have no objection to us being here to protect her son. She is even now on clan soil, planning our defenses."

Daven offered his usual politician's grin, but something was different about it. He seemed less slimy and more genuine, but not because of any artifice Lane could detect. The essence of the man had changed. He seemed older, wiser, and less interested in how he was perceived than how he could help.

Or maybe that was just what Daven wanted them to think. Lane remembered full well how Daven had whammied him once before.

Lane remained standing in front of the child, perhaps eight feet distance between him and Daven. His heart pumped fast, too fast, his world still not back on an even keel after the fiasco with Xiomar. *Think, damn it, think.*

"Why didn't she come with you, if she's so cool with you interfering?" Lane demanded.

Daven studied him for a moment. "She trusts you to care for her child. There was no need for her to come. We came at Max's bidding to deal with the Others." The edges of his mouth curled into a smile. "And what was this I heard about a large fire-breathing warlock?"

"Yeah." Lane sighed. "About that." He turned to Kevin. "I don't know what happened. I did just what I did the other day when Xiomar hacked down that tree outside." He glanced out the window to see the broken stump still standing there.

"Those elves sure went right through him like he was tissue, though." Kevin frowned.

Crispy tried in vain to keep hold of Elliun, now a squirming ball of baby. "All right, all right," he said, bending down to set the child on the floor. Elliun took off crawling toward Daven as soon as his knees hit the ground.

"Yesterday he was substantial. You know what he can do." Confusion set in, giving Lane a headache. Then he noticed Daven swing the baby up into his arms. "Put him down!"

Lane launched himself at the elf, but froze mid-stride.

I swear to you, Lane, I will not hurt this child. I will not take this child from you. I have learned much in my time away. I serve only the queen now.

All the time, Daven looked into Lane's eyes, an arms-length away, before releasing him. "Elliun knows we are blood. Look at him. Does he seem worried?"

A little disoriented, Lane had to admit the baby looked fine. "If you do, I'll hunt you down myself."

Daven nodded. "Agreed." He smiled at the baby and bounced him up and down, causing peals of laughter. "You don't understand why your machine-generated creature failed to attack Vez and Hidal."

Lane muttered a warning about Daven getting into his head again, sliding back into his chair. "It should have worked. Kevin and Max watched every day this last week. Xiomar was a killing machine. He could do everything here that he did on the screen." He shook his head.

"If I am welcome, Lane, you might introduce me to your friend."

"Hmm? Oh. Sorry. Kevin, Daven. Daven, Kevin." Distracted, he booted up the program again, prepared to activate Xiomar and find out what went wrong.

Kevin glanced away and shifted his weight to the other leg, fingers twitching as he halfheartedly held out a hand to Daven. "I've heard a lot about you, sir."

Daven laughed, a warm, round sound as he shook Kevin's hand. "And none of it good, I take it. That's all right. Before I went into the mountains, I'll be the first to admit my priorities were not in a proper order."

"What's in the mountains?" Crispy asked. He went to the small stove, setting a pan of water on the fire to boil.

"The *santwarja*, a training ground for those who wish to become mages." Daven appeared relaxed as the baby pulled on his lips and ears, as if they were rubber toys.

Lane eyed him from behind the laptop. "Really? You just walked into Mages-R-Us and walked out with your sorcerer's diploma?"

"What is Mages-R-Us?" Daven asked.

Satisfied he had made his mocking point, Lane did not answer.

Daven chewed his lip a moment. "Of course not. Nothing worth having is so easy. I have been many months in training on the plane of the *santwarja*, instructed by the essence of my old master on points of magic." He gestured to the door. "My magic is more powerful now than even that of Lorenz."

Daven had come right through that door. It was true. Maybe there was something to what he was saying.

"So who are you as good as then?" Lane asked. "Old Black Bart?"

Crispy gasped at the name and turned away, the teacups in his hands clicking together as his hands trembled.

"I am on a level with Bartolomey," Daven said. He took a deep breath, falling into a silent introspection. For the first time, the baby burst into tears. Lane was on his feet in a moment, but Daven waved him off. He held the baby close, rocking his body from side to side to comfort him. "I should not have let the dark one creep into my mind. He is frightening on any level, certainly for a child." He gestured to the computer. "Show me your monster."

Lane's first instinct was to pout and refuse, but what would be the point? Daven would just make him do it some other way. Who knew? Maybe he would even be able to explain what happened, since he was now officially a mage. Whatever that was. Sure sounded cool. A mage. Better than a magician. Almost official.

Lane eyed the computer. Now that he generated a toon, life-size, into the real world and controlled it with magic, what did that make Lane? A cyberpath? A technomage? He would have to think about the proper term for that. He punched up the code for Xiomar and wished him into existence. The large orc appeared just where he had vanished, and Lane didn't bother to hide his smirk at Daven's startled expression.

The tall elf handed the child to Crispy and approached Xiomar. Tempted to make the toon roar and swipe at Daven, Lane fought with his conscience and subdued it, making his fingers play nice. "What did you say this does?" Daven asked.

"He's a level eighty-five warlock for the Horde," Kevin offered and then continued with a litany of the awesome abilities of this particular game character. "Lane and Max managed to make it alive somehow. It should have mowed those old boys down."

Daven walked closer, passing his hand through the orc's body. "Yet it is insubstantial."

"He threw me into the brush yesterday!" Kevin protested. "I still have bruises on my ass!"

"Curious." Daven walked all around the toon. "Show me what it does on your machine."

Now Daven was going to diagnose his game? *Fabulous.*

"Sure," Lane said, rolling his eyes. "Why not?"

He concentrated on the screen, wishing Xiomar back inside the game, and the green orc appeared on the monitor a few moments later. As Kevin and Daven watched with expressions of fascination, Lane ran Xiomar through about three minutes of his worst mayhem, demonstrating just what he could do. Crispy also peeked over Lane's shoulder as he passed out tea for everyone.

"He is quite dangerous, if ephemeral," Daven observed. "You said he caused damage on this plane."

"Yes, that's what I said," Lane snapped. Finishing his demonstration, he decided to bring the warlock back to life. It was not a lot of magic, but it was all the magic that he could do. *So there, Daven.* Lane tapped the keys, and made his wish, compelling the toon back into this world. This time, he gave in to the impulse to roar, and the sound shook the rafters.

Daven sat down his steaming cup and walked over to Xiomar, this time more cautious. Lane smirked again, his mischievous tendencies bubbling up inside. He waved Xiomar's empty left hand in Daven's direction, just for fun, and was stunned when his thick arm caught Daven in his midsection, knocking him into the table.

A moment of shocked silence followed, and then Elliun started to giggle. Crispy hurried over to help Daven up, asking if he was all right.

Even more confused, Lane stared at the computer. "What the hell happened? I just did that and it was nothing."

Kevin crossed his arms. "You know, something was different. This time Daven 'saw' what Xiomar could do. Once he understood his capabilities, he became real."

"I agree," Daven said. He straightened his long shirt, checking to make sure he was uninjured before retrieving Elliun from Xiomar's vicinity. "Somehow Max has combined the magic with the purpose of the machine. When the purpose of the creature is to be dangerous and protective, the magic will make it so."

"But only when the person on the pointy end of the sword knows it." Lane sighed. There always had to be a catch. "So how is that useful?"

They stared at each other, fidgeting for a few minutes.

"Hey," Crispy said. "Maybe Kevin has a spare laptop we can send up to the woods. Do you think Bartolomey wants to play a game?"

CHAPTER 25

ASTAN was sitting on the same rock where he had sat six months before.

The only difference was that his father had been there and they had talked about their family history. At that time he thought he understood their world. But now everything was turned around.

Maybe everything had turned around again. Since Daven's return from the forest, he stood firmly behind Jelani, even when she contradicted the Circle. He even went out of his way to be available for Astan, not to dictate to him as before. Instead, he asked for Astan's advice and input. He acknowledged Astan's role in the clan. It did not feel as though it was just an act. Iris was right. Daven's attitude was genuine. He was now part of the team, for what it was worth.

In the clearing below there were forty-two Youngers and a dozen of the older elves working on their battle form. Each of them brought what Jelani would call their 'game face', their best possible effort. Several approached Astan's ability to alter his relation to the gravity of the soil below him, allowing him to be light enough to jump high in the air or heavy enough to land hard and break bones. Elron, son of Windthorn, sent his calls to the birds of the air, directing them to targets selected of his will. Others practiced dagger play or archery or even enchanted slingshots. Daven's words spurred them to intense preparation, even more urgent after the attack on the cabin. Daven and the Circle defused the attempt, along with Lane and some odd sort of computer magic Astan did not understand.

The healers among them, Pieter, Elorra and the others, worked with the herb-mistress and other members of the Circle getting ready.

Astan did not want to think about what they were practicing for. While they had been separated from the clan, he felt as though each day he was dying just a little. Now he was finally reunited with his elven brothers and sisters, just in time to watch them be torn apart by a war that began a generation before.

His leg cramped where it lay against the rock. He jumped down, stretching it out. Daven's words did more than excite the multitude. The news about Veraena, his mother, caused a host of old wounds to open. Where was she all those years when he was trapped in the human city with Djana? Free in the forests, apparently. Even though she knew where he was. Knowing that Daven entered into the Sleep, she had still abandoned him.

Now Veraena was back, but as an enemy.

Over the years, Astan often envisioned what he might say to her if they would have met, perhaps something engaging. Or maybe something along the line to make her realize back then he had needed her and that she should have taken him with her. He would have been good and done whatever she would have asked of him. This time, he would not do 'whatever' it was he did before to make her leave.

Jelani's friends might be amused that Astan shared their feelings about a mother's betrayal. While Veraena never abused him, Astan believed neglect and rejection caused as much pain. He hid it while growing up, since Djana and her Circle did not indulge much self-pity among the Youngers. Daven's return started melting the ice in Astan's heart. His love for Jelani further exposed the pain. Learning that Veraena did not come for him, even just to see if he remained alive, ripped apart the last of his reserve.

Enough.

He headed down the hill, emotions stirring in him like a boiling stew-pot. As Astan approached, Beckley looked up, distracted just long enough in the hand-to-hand combat with telekinetic Merripen to take a heavy thwack to the left shoulder, making him stagger.

"Time!" Astan called, a little late but still with good humor. "Everyone rest a moment. Then move on to a new partner."

While the others scattered, Beckley came to Astan, whose agitation transformed into pacing. "Walk with me," Beckley said, starting up the incline. "I need no gift of farsight to see you are unhappy, my friend. There are many reasons to be out of sorts in the current situation." He studied Astan with a sidewise glance. "The queen seems content. Your son remains safe."

"True. Jelani has finally come into her potential." Astan smiled, pleased at the thought of his beloved in the role of the queen as she was meant to be. "I can't believe Djana still has a tongue, as she must bite it so often."

Beckley chuckled. "All of them. Not just Djana."

Astan drew in a deep breath and let it out slowly. "It's not the battle that's coming, either. I'm not happy about that, but it is necessary. They will not allow us to co-exist. Bartolomey and his minions have upset the balance of power in the clan's energy. Daven says." He growled. Was he back to parroting his father's words so soon? He thought he was done with that.

"Daven says that unless the balance is restored, peace will not come to the clan." Beckley shrugged. "It's no less true just because your father said it."

Astan grunted. "I know I said we needed everyone, but—"

"Astan, he's worked to learn his skills, just as we have. Let him do what needs doing. You can work out your problems later. After."

They walked on, coming to the top of the ridge. Looking over the valley, Astan saw patches of snow on the mountaintops, but much less so than the past months. As the queen's heart thawed and warmed toward the clan, so did the terrain around them. It would be an early spring. The human weather forecasters would never be able to explain it.

Beckley stood less than an arm's length away, waiting, silent. It was a companionable silence, one that two *nian* could share, each thinking his own thoughts without a need to explain. During Iris' time at the tree house, Astan noticed the way human women dissected every sentence, every thought until there was nearly nothing left. Elven females were more reticent, for the most part, preferring to keep their own counsel. Unless of course, they were of the Circle, in which case they had plenty—for everyone else.

The thought raised Astan's spirits just a little. The last thing he wanted to do was to share his feelings of worthlessness with Beckley. He was no weak human, emotions running amok, blaming everyone else for his problems. He was the mate of the elf queen, facing a civil war against his own people. Beckley was right. His personal issues could wait.

Beckley shifted his weight, as his gaze studied the land below. "You know, I am thinking of pursuing Elorra. Once this is finished."

Astan turned to him, surprised. "Elorra? You and Elorra." He tried to imagine the two of them together, quiet, broad-hipped Elorra, whose talent was to heal forest animals, and quiet, broad-shouldered Beckley. With a start, he realized the two were likely very complimentary. He grinned. "I wish you well with your pursuit, brother."

"We will all be fine, once this is past." Beckley clapped Astan on the shoulder with a matching grin. "Now come on, let's get back to our preparations. You need to show Kalin that little move you've got, the shoulder roll. It'll make a difference someday, I'm sure of it."

Feeling more centered, Astan accompanied his friend down the slope to where their companions awaited. They were almost ready.

* * *

VEZ and Hidal skulked back to the bower after their failure to snatch the prince. The blood on Hidal's shoulder had darkened to a dull brown. Gia was nowhere in sight.

Vez looked at his cohort with narrowed eyes. "We're not going to say anything about this."

Hidal snorted. "Why would I tell anyone? Not like it was any great triumph."

Vez felt his anger and frustration bubble up inside, and he grabbed Hidal by the front of the shirt, slamming him into the trunk of a nearby tree. "We knew it was a long shot. We took a risk, all right? Sometimes the big risks don't pay off."

"And now the Circle knows what we're after." Hidal cursed and shoved him away, checking his injured arm. "We're wasting our time out here, just playing at things. We need to get back to clan soil and show them who's in command. If this Bartolomey is so powerful, why aren't we already there?"

"Yeah, well it's because—" Vez dropped his hands to his sides, losing his impetus. Hidal was right. They were in limbo. They needed to quit preparing to go to war and just do it. "I need to talk to Veraena."

"You do that." Hidal gave him a dirty look and then slouched away to find some of the others.

Vez glanced around to see if anyone noted their arrival, but none paid them any particular notice. A quick look inside his mother's bower showed she was not there. Vez's first instinct was to search the places where the other Youngers slept to discover in which of their beds he might find her.

You can't think like that. We must unite in pursuit of victory. Bartolomey said so.

He closed his eyes for a moment, sensing the vague connection he now shared with Veraena, one that he had cultivated so she could not separate herself from him again. She was in her clearing, the one where she practiced her spells. His quick-speed brought him to the trees outside the clearing in three jumps. Peering from behind a tree trunk, Vez scanned the open area and saw only Veraena, her silver hair streaming out behind her, as she practiced with a long sword. She slashed and parried and twirled, breathing hard, working herself into exhaustion. He lost track of time in the ebb and flow of her movement. She was so beautiful. How Talvi could have left her was beyond Vez's understanding.

When she finally stopped, sinking to one knee, leaning on the hilt of her silver sword, he nearly came out. He stopped when she started talking to herself.

"I cannot be weak. I cannot. I must last through this 'til the end." Her head bent until it rested on her hand, still holding the sword. "The imbalance must be preserved. It is the only way."

Vez wondered what she meant, desiring the preservation of

the imbalance. The Circle—nay, all his teachers, had always stressed the importance of balance in all things, including nature. Why would she choose an imbalance? He shifted his weight, finding a more comfortable position in the hard mud. He needed to wait a little longer.

"Each must fall," she muttered. "One by one. Air. Water. Soil. L-Light." She stumbled over the word and caught her breath.

She rose to her feet. "Vez can vie with those old *neris*, even the ancient *Intalus* who remain with the Circle. They will swear alliance to us or perish." The sword vanished into the leather scabbard that was tied to her hip. She went for a gourd of water she left on a nearby boulder. Pausing for a long drink, the fingers of her free hand fidgeted with the edges of her tan jerkin and her foot tapped out an uneven rhythm on the soil.

Meanwhile, Vez tried to assimilate the implication of his mother's words. She could have been speaking another language, for all that they made sense to him. *Intalus?* In the Circle? He made a quick mental count, could not think of a one he would consider strong enough to be a mage. Certainly, he could vanquish any of them individually. His mother was certainly right about that. He shuddered with the effort to understand.

Veraena paced, arms crossed, hugging herself. "Five of six. We must keep the balance uneven. As the Master has said, the only reason he did not perish was because of the lack of balance. The Dark remains ascendant. For now." She stopped, pensive in the middle of the clearing. "A guarantee if the Light falls."

The Dark? The Light? What in the Lady's name was she talking about? Certainly she equated the Master, Bartolomey, with the Dark. So who was his opposition? His mother represented the *Idan* of Fire, of that Vez was sure. Fire was not the same as Light, he could tell this by the way she phrased it. And when she said 'light', she barely got the word between her lips.

It was not difficult to guess which mage still held ties to his mother's heart, regardless of what she admitted to Vez. *Daven Talvi.*

So he must die.

Vez heard enough. He made his way out into the clearing, stopping in front of his startled mother. He straightened the bottom of his jacket with a jerk and brushed away pine needles. "I shall dispatch the faithless bastard," he said.

Her hand went to the hilt of her sword quickly, as if prompted by instinct alone. "Those who eavesdrop on others often hear what they shouldn't." Expression troubled, she kept looking over his shoulder as if she expected someone to appear.

"I thought we agreed to work together," he said, studying her for subtle signs that she was holding up her part of that agreement. He did not see any. She seemed more secretive than ever.

Perhaps she was protecting herself from Bartolomey.

Perhaps.

"You could not hope to challenge Daven now," she scolded. "He is not weak like those hiding amongst the clan. He remains young and strong." She relaxed, releasing her sword, the maternal smile returning to her face. "I will face him myself."

Vez eyed her, the feeling of betrayal flooding him like acid from his heart. Would she really kill Talvi? Or would she use her power to convince him of the mistake he made? Was this her way to get back into his life? He could not believe it.

If she and Talvi reunited, then what? Astan Hawk would once again be the first son? Where did that leave Vez? On the outside again.

The thought chilled his voice as he spoke to her again. "And once Light is gone? Will you remain a slave to Bartolomey? Or will you bring me to the top of the mountain with you?" He fought a petulant bottom lip that threatened to pout, like that of a small boy thwarted in his wishes. After all, he and Bartolomey had an understanding. Knowing his mother's intentions gave him information he could use as leverage to better his position, whichever way turned out to work in his favor.

"Vez, my darling, of course I will." She stepped close to embrace him. Her scent, so spicy sweet, so reminiscent of the old grandmothers' baking ovens, surrounded him. "We're together now, you and I. We each have our part to do in this. As long as the mages are out of balance, the power and energy of the clan is released, free for recapture."

"The energy of the clan, Mother? What are you talking about?"

"This is why Bartolomey has brought us to this point, my son." She hunkered down, drawing him down with her, so they remained eye-to-eye. She lowered her voice just above a whisper. "He discovered that when all is in balance, as it was when Lorenz was king, when Ele was queen, the six points contain the power of the clan. The energy goes into the well-being of the clan itself. Prosperity is theirs, and the mages share their power equally to contribute to that well-being."

She paused, studying him. "Do you understand so far?"

"Yes, Mother." Vez had learned this teaching many years before. This was nothing new or surprising.

Veraena's eyes danced with delighted ambition. "What do you think happens to that power if the clan doesn't steal it?"

Vez frowned. "How should I know? I'm no magician."

"This is not a matter to be treated lightly. Listen, and learn." She leaned closer. "If the clan does not claim the power, then it belongs to the mages, to increase their strength."

Dawning realization finally kicked in and the pieces began to fall into place. "Which is why Bartolomey could defeat Lorenz's magic."

"Exactly."

"So we must defeat one or more of the *Intalus* to make this happen? Then we will be strong?"

"Yes, Vez." She looked at him with approval, even love. He could tell she believed he would follow her every command. He almost dreaded asking the next question, but something deep within him drove the words from his mouth.

"And what shall we do when they're all gone? When you, Bartolomey, and I are all that's left? What then?"

She looked away, up, into the trees, a faraway stare. Her lips pursed before curving into a soft smile. "Even the Dark cannot withstand the power of Fire."

CHAPTER 26

SEATED at the heavy wooden table in his mother's bower, Daven mulled over the implications of Lane's computer-generated monster.

The creature created through the enchanted machine carried real possibilities. The hitch, as it turned out, was that the person seeing the monster must believe in its existence in order to be affected by it in the physical world.

Daven's mage training gave him the ability to project 'belief' onto a host of others. Using this skill, he theorized he could convince their enemies that Xiomar the warlock was indeed real. But he did not tell this to Lane. Daven had been very careful while at the cabin not to use or suggest anything Lane might consider a 'whammy', because it was necessary to build trust with Jelani's human allies.

Lane possessed a huge heart with a bundle of skills and hidden passions. Before, Daven had been guilty of overlooking this, as he had with so many traits in the humans he had encountered. Now his eyes were opened. He knew not to get himself mired in Lane's computer addictions. But if what Daven suspected was true about the upcoming battle, Lane could be very valuable to the future of the Bitterroot clan.

Daven fumbled at his waist for the cloth bag of runes. He held them mindfully for several long moments and then reached in, choosing three. He laid them carefully on the wooden surface before him and studied the black markings on the stones.

Les. The Great Battle. Since Jelani and Astan left the clan back in the frozen season, this one rune consistently appeared. It seemed inevitable. Daven sighed and moved on.

Nith. Sacrifice. The depth of meaning in this rune, explained by his teacher Lantin, went beyond a loss or a giving up of even personal treasures. Nith implied sacrifice of a life, or something one held dearer than life. A vision of Iris' face passed before him, and a sinking, icy sensation passed through his gut as he realized he could lose her. He might have to choose between Iris and the clan. He had faced a similar decision once before and had made the wrong choice.

Esa. Reversed, the stone meant transformation, a revolutionary change of sorts in thought or action. This one did not speak to his core as the other two did. Many possibilities existed. Did this mean change in the leadership? Was Bartolomey destined to dethrone the queen and the Circle, and subvert the clan for evil? Did this mean the humans would overrun the elven lands and wipe them from the soil? Would the queen indeed leave them, as she had once threatened to do?

All these potential outcomes saddened him. He would think more on them. Perhaps the worst of it could be averted. Perhaps.

"Any words of wisdom?" Djana's tone held the sour tang of early crabapples.

Daven glanced up, forcing a smile. "Why can you not trust that all will develop as it must?"

"You don't trust," Djana shot back. "You read those stones like they give you breath. Over and over. You don't like what they're telling you."

Daven swept the runes into their bag. "No. I don't." He leaned back in the chair, studying the *neris* who had given him birth, offered counsel when he needed it, and opened her home when he returned from the *santwarja*. Since the return of Jelani and Astan, the clan's health had improved. Even the eldest among the Circle looked a little less gray with more spryness in their steps. From his time in the other plane, he now recognized which among them were the mages who controlled air and water. All these years they had quietly practiced their arts and kept their end of the balance stable without calling attention to themselves.

"How do we alter it?" Djana asked. She fussed with cups, stacking them on a corner cupboard. "All these years we have taken steps, we've looked ahead, always trying to avoid the potential pitfalls. Bartolomey has crossed us at every turn, still holding on to the thought that he can change the way the clan survives."

"Sometimes the baby has to stumble, mother. You can't prevent every banged knee."

While Daven meant the clan, or the world, or some larger metaphor, what came to mind at that moment was holding little Elliun in his arms back at Jelani's cabin. In every sense of the word, the child had grown so much just in the time Daven had been gone.

He had concerns about the child staying so far from the clan with Jelani's human friends, but he agreed with the queen that Lane and Crispy only had the child's interest at heart. With a little help from the Circle Elders, the cabin would remain safe. They did not dare risk the child's well-being. Daven's enhanced reading skills gave him some clues as to what Elliun would become. He came of two strong lines in the elf clan. Even with his human blood, the future was bright for the boy. If there was a future.

I've got to make sure there is. Whatever it takes.

"Banged knee? What are you talking about, Daven?" Djana's face screwed up into a puzzled frown. "I'm talking about being wise and taking control of the situation before it's completely out of hand. That's the only way we've preserved the clan, ever since Bartolomey indulged his delusions of grandeur."

Djana droned on about how she and the other Circle members had sacrificed their own desires and wishes to save the clan during the hard years, waiting for the queen's return. After the first few sentences, Daven just quit listening. He had heard it all before. By the Lady, even he had spoken similar words in the past.

He would rather concentrate on positive actions, like the turnaround Jelani had made over the last few months, going from a confused and frantic young woman to a being of truly regal stature. She handled him and Djana beautifully in front of the Elders. This was definitely a step in the right direction.

Lantin had said the queen was important. Daven had never felt it until now. The queen focused the balance that held the magic together. There was no other way.

* * *

AFTER Vez and his little band had staged their assault, Kevin remained at the cabin with Lane and Crispy. After two days, nothing else had happened.

"I've got to check the store, Lane," Kevin said. "I mean, yeah, I put up a sign about a family emergency. But if anybody in my family stops by, they're going to wonder what emergency I'm talking about!"

"I know, I know," Lane grumbled. He was a little claustrophobic at the moment himself, with the three of them and the baby in the small space, computer or no. His back hurt from sleeping on a worn sleeping bag on the floor. He was out of Earl Grey tea. He could not make his magic work against Bartolomey. What was the point of all this anyway?

"Don't forget to look in on Grandpa Tom for me, would you?" Crispy asked in a low voice. "He hasn't been feeling so well."

"Sure thing, Crisp." Kevin packed his few things into a black canvas knapsack and slung it onto his back.

"Really, Crisp? We're babysitting stray alcoholics now?" Lane heard the edge of irritation in his voice and regretted it immediately. He didn't have anything against the crabby old guy, not really.

"Tom is part of the interdependent web of life," Crispy announced with great authority. "He's not any less important than you or me or one of the elves or one of these trees or my hawk. Nature needs all its parts to function in balance."

Lane rose from his chair. What he wouldn't give for a real toilet. "Yeah, it would be nice if a lot of things functioned the way they were supposed to."

"I hear that, man." Kevin laughed. "Anything I can bring when I come back?"

"Got a spare army?"

Kevin did a double take. "A what?"

Lane gave an awkward laugh. "Nothing. Just a thought." What was he saying? What good would an army be against magic anyway?

Kevin stared at him with an expression Lane could only describe as amazed. "An army. I never thought...."

"Dude, you have an army?"

"Well, yeah. Bunch of guys are back from my unit, the 230th. Might be they're interested in a little weekend warrior action." Kevin glanced over his shoulder at Crispy, who was mixing some cereal with pureed fruit for Elliun's breakfast. "Guess they're more likely to want to shoot than negotiate, though."

"Doesn't bother me," Lane said.

"Interdependent web," Crispy reminded.

Lane scowled. "What do you think is gonna happen here, Crisp? We're all going to get together and have a bakeoff or something? I think this'll get a whole lot worse before it gets any better. People are going to die. Elves are going to die. Hell, maybe half the forest is going to die. I don't know."

Crispy sat at the table where Elliun waited for his food, waving his little hands in the air. "But Jelani's powers are meant to build up things, not tear them down. War doesn't make sense."

Kevin stared at the floor. "War isn't always about making sense, Crispy. Sometimes it's about restoring order."

"Yeah, Crisp," Lane piled on. "Things here are in a serious SNAFU. Until someone rides herd on old Bart's ass and gets rid of him once and for all, none of the elves will be safe. Thought it was going to be me and Xiomar, but I guess that's screwed."

Kevin was quick to give him an encouraging pat on the shoulder. "Don't count out the warlock yet. I think we just need some fine-tuning. Remember what happened to Daven."

Lane was not convinced. "Yeah. Whatever."

"Meantime, I'll ask around. We all can. I bet you can pull together a dozen people or more who love the forest and don't want to see it destroyed. Who knows?" Kevin shrugged. "All right, I'm out of here. Call if you need something. Otherwise I'll be up next weekend."

"You got it, my friend." Lane walked with Kevin to the door and outside, careful to survey the area for intruders. The witches were gone, but Daven said they would return if needed. Despite his rant at Crispy, Lane would be just as happy if they were never needed again.

Kevin marched over to his car. After loading his backpack and rifle into the passenger side, he circled to the driver's side and climbed in. He rolled down the window long enough to give Lane a confident wave, and then drove away.

Lane watched Kevin go and could not help but feel a little lost. He slouched back inside the cabin, at odds with his world.

Plopping into a chair, Lane felt both the chair and the world wobble beneath him. "What the hell are we doing in the middle of this, Crisp? I thought I knew. I thought Xiomar was supposed to help. Now that's crapped out. What's left for us to do here?"

Crispy handed the baby some rubber toys and put the empty cereal dish in the small plastic dishpan. "We do what Jelani and Astan asked us to do. We take care of Elliun."

His roommate's calm delivery frustrated Lane even more. "But then what? What if Bart and the boys overrun the place? What if the whole clan is wiped out? What if they bomb the queen's tree?"

"Then we take care of Elliun." Drying his hands on a towel, Crispy turned to look at Lane. "We know all about bad foster care, and we would never be like that. If we have to raise him, we will. But we'll do it, because it's what we said we would do."

Lane read the sincerity in Crispy's voice and saw it on his face. Poor, damaged Crispy meant what he said one hundred percent. Crispy viewed things in black and white. Lane, on the other hand, lived in a forest of grays. Now that he had committed to helping the elves, Lane wanted to help, but his expertise did not involve talents like flying or spell-casting. Not in the real world, anyway. His talents lay with technology.

If he could not make his technology affect the elf world, then what could he do that would even help? Short of getting his oversized cupcake-fed carcass in the way, that is.

Okay, he had a gun. And not some little popgun like Jelani had shot in the tree house, setting off Lane's childhood phobias. This was a substantial weapon, a Mark XIX Desert Eagle 44-magnum with a ten-inch barrel. He had purchased it back when he and Crispy first moved in together fresh from foster care, in case any of the old ghosts from his past showed up. He and Iris had joked about it being home defense for cave dwellers, but he had only fired it a couple of times at a shooting range. A soldier he was not.

But he could learn, if it would help end this thing.

Real-world solutions were not as fancy as his online designs, but maybe Crispy was right. Lane needed to stop counting on the computer world to save him.

"You know, I think those eco-terrorists guys are done with the clan," Lane said. "But what about your buddies up at the animal rehab? They like the forests, right? They want to see everything healthy again."

A curious look crossed Crispy's face. "Of course."

"Maybe we can raise our own little fighting force to help out. Let's take a run down to the convenience store and make some calls."

CHAPTER 27

ALONE in the forest on his way to a rendezvous with Fontine, Vez encountered a violent wind.

It swirled down from the trees, forming an airy cage that trapped him on a small circle of soil in the middle of the roaring funnel.

Startled and frightened, Vez would have stumbled but for the power of the wind. The maelstrom was deafening. Dirt and dead leaves and sharp pine needles spun around him, scouring his face.

A rumbling voice penetrated the vortex, and Vez's very bones and sinews left him no doubt who was causing the event.

"What did you think you were doing, pup? You could have set off the war before we were prepared to prosecute it!"

The wind buffeted him, shoving him from side to side. Vez started to answer, but a gust stole the breath from his mouth.

"I thought I could trust you to be smart. I thought you were different from that incompetent worm Grigor. I thought, as Veraena's spawn, you would have enough wits to make choices that wouldn't damage our cause."

A long howl echoed up through the funnel, rattling Vez's spine. He struggled to free himself, but his boots slipped on the shifting ground.

"Instead," the voice continued, "you alert the humans to our intentions. Awake their defenses, provoking them into magic. What were you thinking?"

The air stream condensed and coiled around like a constrictor snake, starting at Vez's ankles and slithering up his body. Arms trapped at his side and pine needles scratching every inch of exposed skin, the slow compression prevented him from taking a full breath. Then it stopped at his neck, leaving just his face and the top of his head free. He looked up into the sky and wondered whether it would be for the last time.

As he struggled to breathe, the tempest moved upward a quarter of an inch at a time, slowly covering his chin and then his lips. Battered and bleeding, he strained to secure clear air just as the wind wrapped around his nose and eyes as well.

Can't breathe. Can't breathe.

Desperate, Vez could only suck oxygen from that last breath for so long before he saw spots on the inside of his closed eyelids. Then he saw only black.

When he awoke, he was lying on the cold ground in a pile of crumbled brown leaves and small branches. Every muscle ached. He kept his eyes closed, terrified that Bartolomey was waiting to dole out more punishment.

Along with that fear ran deep self-loathing that he would allow someone like Bartolomey to bully him at all. Vez was not one of the untagged Youngers, floating from moment to moment in their little elf lives. He had a purpose.

Did his mother know about this? Had she allowed it? He stiffened at the thought.

Clearing the dirt from his throat, he pushed himself up to a sitting position and opened his eyes. He surveyed the area around him. He was alone.

Out of the corner of one eye, Vez caught a flicker of movement in the trees.

He scrambled to his feet. "I'm ready for you, old man!"

For a long moment, all was silent. Then the vortex closed around him again, stealing his breath.

"You're not ready for me, pup." The disembodied words seemed to emanate from the ground. "Let me tell you this. Until you show me that you are worthy of my notice and support, you will be nothing in our eyes. You may not sleep in our bowers. You may not share our food. You may not mate with any *neris* under our protection. You have one last chance."

How dare he? Bartolomey was no better than the old spellbinders of the Circle, obsessed only with power.

Heart pounding and ready to scream out in rebellion, Vez spied Fontine watching from behind a tree, her eyes wide with fear. She had witnessed Bartolomey's rebuke.

One last chance.

Vez's own words echoed in his head and his heart. Along with the sound of Fontine's footsteps as she ran away, weeping.

* * *

TWO days later, the night air was cold, a damp wind chilling even the stoutest of the elf Youngers as they moved through the woods toward the clan soil.

Vez heard every snapped twig, every harsh breath along the trail behind him and willed the six others to move in silence.

Veraena's earlier raid on the clan's supplies showed a considerable weakness in the clan defenses. Large parts of the perimeter remained unguarded, whether because of the lack of elves available to watch it, or their sheer arrogance, expecting no one would dare attack them. Vez leaned toward the latter, finding the leadership of the Circle to work very much in that mode. The new queen was not factored into the equation. She never impressed him as a serious threat, except to the peace of the clan, which should be ruled by its rightful leader.

We'll be there soon enough.

Vez would prove himself tonight. Somehow Master Bartolomey had known the whole story behind the botched strike on the queen's cabin.

Now he led the attack his mother had conceived, preparing to incapacitate one or more of the mages concealed within the clan. Lokti came along to lure the mage with power over the air, Kalinda, into the open. Rudra, the mage who controlled water, for a time had mentored Grigor and, according to Kassen, was a recluse who seldom left her bower due to extreme age and failing health brought on by the clan's decline. The third mage, Lady of the Forest with power over earth itself, possessed an unknown mirror image which was either a kindred spirit among the elves or possibly the queen.

Before leaving the camp, Veraena had pulled Vez aside, speaking in a warm low voice that practically sounded like a purr. *"I'm counting on you, my son. Remember, the Master and I will look out for you. As long as the Idellan remains unbalanced, we have the power to keep your elven self strong. What you accomplish will set the course for the rest of our lives."* When Vez asked about the return of Daven Talvi, Veraena's temper had flared. *"Leave Talvi for me,"* she had hissed and then offered a forced smile.

Walking through the forest, Vez could not rid himself of the image of that false smile or of the memory Bartolomey's attack. He felt a stab of sympathy for Grigor Biren, who had been torn between loyalty to Bartolomey and love for the beautiful Fontine. It was the exact place Vez now found himself. He wondered which of those traveling with him thirsted to take his place in the same way he had lusted after Grigor's position.

What was it the humans said? *Be careful what you wish for.*

Had he come too far to change directions? If he could not stay with his mother and Bartolomey's troop, he would have nowhere to sleep.

Were the bridges to Talvi and the Circle not burnt behind him? Neither had been kind to him in the past. Now they would likely kill him on sight.

The small cadre of elves with him manifested a number of different talents. Yadin could vanish from the sight of others. Contanel could make metal white hot with just a thought. Lokti had some mastery of the wind. Shanson was skilled in healing. And two young twin elves who tagged along were physically agile and fast. Was it enough to make this mission a success?

Vez prayed silently that it was.

The past two days had been wretched. Fontine was kept from him, as Bartolomey promised. Fear that they would take her from him permanently ate at Vez's gut. It could be done, he was sure of that. Veraena and Bartolomey were both capable of such cruelty.

Soon Vez and his little troop had positioned themselves just outside the section of the clan soil where Rudra's isolated bower was located. She seemed the best target of the three mages, in the event they could only take one.

Vez eyed the tree line and saw nothing amiss. He took a deep breath and turned to Yadin. "All right. Like we rehearsed it. You go first, to see how far you can get without alerting any of the others. When you make it to her door, signal us, and the twins and I will join you."

Next Vez turned to Lokti and Shanson. "Wait here. When we have taken care of the target, we will return and prepare for the next entry."

All nodded in understanding.

Yadin sprinted off toward the perimeter. He slowed near the edge of the soil and then faded from view.

Vez sighed with relief and leaned his back against a tree.

"Vez?" Lokti asked from behind the tree, as if ashamed to show her face.

Watching for Yadin's beckon, Vez did not turn around. "What is it?"

"Fontine is sad about the way things have developed," Lokti said. "She doesn't feel safe with Bartolomey, not like last time. The situation is out of control, she said, and she worries for the sanity of the Master. She told me what happened to you." Lokti cleared her throat. "She wanted me to tell you this."

Vez turned and looked Lokti in the eye. She was a pretty girl with red lips and a generous smile that he had not seen of late. None of them smiled much anymore, now that he thought of it. "Thank you for telling me. I've worried about her as well."

Lokti's brown eyes looked troubled. "Vez, I don't want to hurt Kalinda. She was like my mother. Why do we do this? It feels like the cold governance of the Circle all over again."

Vez hesitated. How could he explain a quest for personal power at the expense of everyone else in the clan? Months ago he would have been able to ignore the moral cost. Without seeing a genuine goal ahead of him, a cause worth serving, he found it increasingly difficult to focus on the end.

"Lokti, I—" Vez began, but was cut off when a hard fist punched him in the back.

"The signal, Vez!"

He turned at the summons of the twin who had hit him. A quick glance across the distance between them showed that Yadin had indeed arrived.

Vez looked back at Lokti, regret churning in him. "All right. Let's go."

He steeled himself and set the distance in his mind. Closing his eyes, Vez moved to a space beside Yadin, arriving almost immediately. He cocked his head, but did not hear an alarm. He stepped behind a tree trunk, keeping himself concealed until the other two caught up.

In a moment all four stood on the threshold.

Yadin elbowed Vez him in the ribs. The avaricious fire in Yadin's eyes warned Vez that this one could be the next elf sucked in by the promises of Bartolomey and Veraena.

Trapped, Vez ducked inside the shaded bower.

The smell of Rudra's old rags was overpowering. His eyes watering, he made a fast pass through a living area littered with the detritus of the old mage's life. How could she live in such a mess? Only a dim light came in through the thin walls. There were no small glowlights in the main room, magic-powered or otherwise, to illuminate the space deep in shadows.

"We should have brought someone who could generate light," Vez muttered.

Slowed down by the obstacle course, he searched for the elder *neris*, the others on his heels. In the farthest room from the door a faint light shone beside the bed. On the bed was a thick pile of tattered blankets, covering a sleeping form.

Vez fingered the hilt of the dagger tucked into the sheath attached to his belt. One swift plunge of the dagger would end the old mage's life, and set his mother and her Master on the road to the power they wanted so dearly. It was all he had to do.

The twins breathed loudly behind him, their trembling presence testament to the adrenaline rushing through their veins. "Do it," one of them whispered.

Yadin moved around to the other side of the bed, a challenge in his eyes.

Vez thought about how his mother had taken Yadin on her last raid instead of him. What had she whispered to Yadin during the course of that adventure?

Vez's hand closed on the hilt and he pulled out the dagger,

holding it in front of him. He imagined raising it and thrusting it into the center of Yadin's chest.

No. That's not what you're doing here.

He looked down at the huddled old female on the bed. So easy. But what would it cost him? Although Vez had stolen the talisman from him, Grigor had died because of the injury from a human's trap. If Vez stabbed Rudra and took her life, he would suffer the most painful consequences to come to an elf, the loss of his powers and exile.

Veraena promised they would not let that happen.

But how could he know for sure?

In his mind, he heard Lokti's plaintive question again. Why did they have to do this, to take all the risk, while Veraena and Bartolomey remained safely out of reach?

"Go on, Vez," Yadin hissed. "Before she wakes up."

The disdain in his companion's eyes made up his mind, and Vez hardened his resolve. He counted to three. No, he must do it. He closed his eyes and stabbed the blade into the heap on the bed.

The three *nians* gasped and then grinned with approval, but Vez knew something was wrong. The dagger went through the pile much too easily. With a mixture of dismay and relief, he re-sheathed the dagger and then pulled aside the blanket. No body lay there. Only a mound of cloth. The beginning of the end. His stomach did flip-flops as the implications sank in.

Vez looked into Yadin's eyes with the dark knowledge of the truth. "They knew we were coming."

Yadin was on the move for the door almost before Vez finished speaking. "We've got to get out of here!"

Vez took a final look around, making sure the twins followed Yadin. If they got caught now, Vez was finished. Bartolomey and Veraena had made that clear.

"Hurry!" Vez snapped, shoving them out the door.

He ran on foot instead of using his gifts, leaving no chance his people did not return safely. It was perhaps the only thing he would have to offer to save his own life.

CHAPTER 28

DAVEN sensed something in the wind.

The little intrusion at the cabin had been either a distraction or the efforts of an uninformed splinter. The ultimate goal was much larger, as Lantin taught. The balance of the *Idellan* was uneven until Daven was reborn as the mage of light. So it was inevitable that they would come after the other mages.

At first, Kalinda and Rudra objected to leaving their comfortable bowers, but the queen added her persuasion to Daven's. The two Elders found themselves ensconced with Djana, who hardly had time to object she was too busy to babysit before Daven left her doorway, bent on rooting down this trouble at its source.

As soon as he cleared the clan soil, Daven summoned the portal to the *santwarja* and hurried inside. The atmosphere on the alternate plane seemed hostile, a lingering scent of charred wood embers in the dry air. His feet made no sound on the dirt floor as he ran deeper, his mind tuned to search for one mental signature. He sensed her as a glow in the distance, a burning spot of fire that flickered in and out, avoiding him. Knowing she could exhaust him before he had the chance to confront her, he stopped running.

"Veraena! To what purpose do you play this game? Face me!"

Nothing. He waited, as time passed, noticing the rock walls around him seemed taller than the last time he was here, three or four times his own height, and their color was not the dusky cold granite of the Bitterroots but a much warmer, almost red stone, like the pictures he had once seen of the desert rock in the states of the southwest. What had changed? How?

The temperature inside was also warmer, like a desert. Was it possible for the plane to move? He did not believe so. Its nature was altered by something or someone. Two mages, working together, might exert enough power to effect such a change. Perhaps sending their underlings after the mages of the clan was only one battlefront. To make the *santwarja*, the place where a mage could retreat for rest and rejuvenation, into an unwelcoming and toxic space could serve the same purpose.

Daven practiced patience, keeping his breaths deep and slow, taking in the details of the moment around him. For the first time, the *santwarja* seemed a closed-in place, a trap, with its lack of sky, no trees and no animal sounds. Not even a hint of breeze moved within. It was an artificial place, set for an artificial purpose, over the centuries that passed serving only the few seeking magic. And some who seek more than their due.

He did not move, letting the silence echo through his bones. The *santwarja* was lifeless, a device through which to learn and discover magic, much like Lane Donatelli's computer, a gateway to other information, but not meaningful in and of itself. Those invited to share the knowledge could enter, an exclusive group of gifted ones who were handpicked by the Lady of the Forest because of their dedication to the clan and the soil.

How could that divination process go so wrong?

Daven sent out a sensory mental tendril, still searching for Veraena. He was careful to keep his mind blocked from any chance Bartolomey could pick him up. On this plane, he suspected Bartolomey was much stronger, not needing a physical body to evidence himself. Though they possessed the same skills, Daven knew Bartolomey's persuasion methods. Daven could be lost, and never escape the *santwarja* to alert the rest of the clan. This was a risk he did not need to take.

A soft scratch of earth behind him alerted him that someone was near, but they were too close for him to move out of reach. A sharp jolt of electric energy passed through his shoulder, numbing his arm all the way to his fingertips. He scrambled away, his shoulder burning, and turned to find Veraena watching him, her eyes dancing.

"Sloppy, Daven. Sloppy. Lantin should have taught you better."

He rubbed his arm, willing it back to full strength, and eyed her. "Veraena, you can't have changed so much that you would follow Bartolomey in this misguided scheme. Don't you realize the final impact?"

Her voice twisted with pity. "Do you think I'm such a fool that I don't see the benefits of what we're doing? It's quite intentional, I assure you."

The arrogance of her!

Daven thought about the young *neris* of long ago, back when Astan was born, back to when she began training to be a mage. Her temperament was one of the sweetest among the clan. She was much liked by the young males, even fought over. Her long braided hair hung to her waist, a very pleasant woman to look upon. He held that memory for a moment, before sending the image to her. She jerked as if he slapped her.

"Why did you do that? I'm not that girl any more. You can take credit. You ruined me!"

The words stung, but he bit back a sharp response. He may have hurt her, and he truly regretted that. But what she had let herself become in the years since could not be entirely his doing. "I've told you I'm sorry. I was wrong."

"You have no idea how wrong you were." She pointed to a tall pile of rock behind him and jerked her hand forward.

The rocks tumbled down, and Daven scrambled aside, the last of the falling rock catching his ankle, trapping his foot. He struggled to free it while she paced before him.

"Did you ever love me?" she asked.

"What?" The ragged bruise already purple on his leg, Daven winced as he tried to push aside the rocks. "Did I love you? Of course. You're the mother of my son."

"Ah, yes. The sainted Astan Hawk. The son you found so important you walked away and left him."

"I went into Sleep for the best interest of the clan!" Daven finally yanked his foot free with a muttered curse. "You said you understood." He limped away from her, considering what he could do to prevent her from hurting him. "I would have returned to you."

She laughed, an ugly sound. "You would have returned to Linnea. I'm not stupid. You left me when I was young and pretty. A young mother. One with talents that could have complemented yours. Left when—" She turned away, tapping her foot in staccato rhythm, and then looked back to him. "When I was pregnant with your son."

He replayed her words, thinking perhaps the pain was making him hallucinate. "My son? No. Astan was born."

"Not Astan." She walked close and looked him in the eye. "My son, Vez."

He stumbled back into the pile of fallen rock, stunned. "My son? Vez?"

Was this another of her deceptions? The words caught his attention, started his heart pounding, and sent his world spinning. He tried to picture the young man, but had no separate recollection of his own, only Jelani's borrowed memory of the attack at the tree house. That was a frightening jumble, and he knew he needed something better than that. If he could lay hands on Veraena, he could absorb her memories of Vez, but he could not do that safely. "How is that possible?"

She paced in front of him, looking down at him where he fell. "Are you asking me how baby elves are made? Really, Daven, I thought after the debacle of the queen's spawn, we all know how that happened. Your cursed Circle uses pregnancy to keep its subjects occupied, and to their own benefit." Her face twisted in a scowl. "Once your mother heard you intended to Sleep, she made doubly sure your genetic line would survive."

Daven grappled with the idea of a second son, one he never knew of. If this was true, no wonder such a child would be disaffected about him and the clan. And my mother, still weaving her tangled web. "Did you know before I left?"

Veraena shrugged. "It was about that time. But you'd already decided to leave me, leave us, to dedicate your life to saving Linnea. What would have been the point in telling you?" Her voice tightened and she extended her left hand toward him. "You didn't want me. That much was clear. Now it's your turn. I don't want you." She glanced at her hand, letting her fingers uncurl gracefully in his direction.

He thought for a moment it was a hand of friendship and forgiveness, but instead fire shot out from her palm, singeing his hair. He rolled aside and scrambled upright, his right hand held out in front of him, wielding a shielded magic. "Does he know?"

A cruel smile slipped onto her face. "He does now. He hates you for it."

Her words felt like a punch to his midsection. Disbelief gradually gave over to acknowledgement that this could be true. Another son. Two sons. And he had failed both of them in his selfish bid to save Linnea. But this time it was not his fault.

The injustice of the situation settled on him like a lead weight. Stirrings of anger spiraled through him, provoking the urge to hurt her. How did she dare to keep this from him? If he had known she was pregnant, perhaps he would not have taken the Sleep. Maybe.

Emotion filled his head and made it hard to think clearly. He must focus, reminding himself that once they shared a love for each other, and that time remained to make things right again. Already he had set a course to prove to Astan that he could be trusted. If the Lady smiled on him, he could find the strength and the words to win Vez back. He looked at Veraena as if she hadn't just torn out his heart, wanting to feel love for her, to see her as anything but a monster.

"Veraena, I don't want to hurt you again. I'm begging you, don't continue with this." He watched her warily, considering what he could do to incapacitate her without causing permanent damage. She was not the one who needed to be neutralized. If we could get her away from Bartolomey's influence, maybe she could be saved.

Her eyes flashed with golden fire. "Maybe she doesn't want to be!" She grabbed for him, ablaze with flame, totally engulfed. Despite his efforts to protect himself, he could feel the heat from her as the fire spread along her body onto him. She projected the flames onto his body, and he could smell the odor of the fibers in his clothing burning. He squirmed away trying to get out of her grip, but she held firm and came closer, closer until she knocked him off his feet again, landing on top of him. The inferno continued all around him, stealing his oxygen.

She was going to push this to the end.

Regret flooding through him, he summoned an icy blast like the heart of the winter from deep inside, and accelerated it through his skin, feeling the cold penetrate, and settle in, the heat receding. Once he was in control of it, he wrapped it around his former mate, cutting off the fire in a glaze of ice. Their faces just inches apart, he looked into her eyes and saw only fury. A fury that burned so hot it seared his soul.

He closed his eyes and grabbed her by the shoulders, tossing her away. She hit the ground hard, grunting at the impact as she rolled over a couple of times. She was slow to get back up, the lingering cold stiffening her limbs. Daven knew as soon as she was limber again, she would be on him. Her eyes still burned. He could not let her get in another shot.

Daven climbed to his feet, feeling his knees creak in the process. "Tell Bartolomey we won't allow him to steal what belongs to the clan."

"I'm not your message-boy!" Veraena snapped.

"You're the closest thing I've got."

Daven reached into his pocket for a dried powder of lupin and tossed it at her. He directed the particles to swirl into her face, covering her nose and her mouth. Then he ran toward the entry to the *santwarja*.

The poison would not kill her, but it would make her sick long enough for him to get away and regroup with the others. She was not going to be easy to kill.

But if he was lucky, she would not have to die.

CHAPTER 29

ASTAN stood off to the side in the clearing, where he and his fellow elves prepared for the battle.

He strapped on a leather jerkin and some protective gear brought to the forest by Lane's warrior friend, Kevin. As he checked his own buckles, Astan looked at the others gathered with him. The Youngers Astan had grown up with geared up the same way he did, making ready for what might well be their deaths. The sight rattled his already tense nerves.

This was real.

The last time they fought Bartolomey it had been just Astan and Jelani, aided by her grandfather's magic. This time the evil one had managed to recruit many to his side. The first couple of raids from the rebels had not caused any real damage, though the clan lost some valuable supplies. But the most recent incursion, watched from beginning to end by the Circle to see just how far the traitors would go, could not be ignored.

The only way to win this, to finish this, was all out battle.

"What troubles you, brother?" Beckley asked. "Each of us has trained for many long days in waiting for this moment. We are ready."

Astan took in a deep breath and blew it out slowly. While everything else might spin out of control, his breath was still his to command. For now. He chose to deflect Beckley's concern. "Not to hear the Sleepers speak of it. They are full of complaints and criticisms."

Beckley eyed the group. "And yet how many of them are here? Most of them are content to remain safe in the bosom of the clan, claiming to protect the women and children."

"Exactly." Astan looked across the clearing to the large rock that topped the hill.

Jelani waited there, also wearing leather over her soft green clothing, her hair braided and pinned securely on her head. She and Max carried on some intense conversation Astan could not hear, Max gesturing often toward the valley. Though Astan had tried to persuade her to remain with the Circle, she had insisted on coming, insisted on fighting with those who were willing to defend the clan.

They had left their son Elliun in the tree house with Crispy. The tree house had magically expanded to contain not only Crispy and Elliun, but Lane and even Iris, all of whom had come at Jelani's insistence to avoid any possible capture by Bartolomey and his minions. She had issued the order in her new tone of voice, the voice of royal command. There could be no discussion or complaint.

But, Astan realized with pride, she deferred to him on the battlefield.

Jelani caught his eye and broke into a smile, giving him a wave. Changes had occurred for each of them over the last few months, but during all that time, he loved her more.

He allowed himself a small smile in her direction. With Beckley watching, he did not feel right waving. It was just wasn't very *kingly*.

"Kevin and his army will join us?" Beckley asked. The warm note of amusement underlying his question let Astan know that he had seen the exchange with Jelani.

"Yes. But I remain reluctant to bring firearms into the battle."

"Why? We can then win easily. We will lose fewer of our own."

"Killing is not the elven way."

"It is not the elven way to become a traitor," Beckley growled. "Nor to poison other elves and suck the energy fields dry. But that is what we face!"

"I know, I know." Astan busied himself checking his buckles again. "I have asked them to use hand to hand combat. Fight to injure. Not take a life, whenever possible. We have to hold true to our beliefs, Beckley. If we don't, then we are no better than the enemy. And I believe we are better than the enemy."

"I don't mean that, Astan."

"I've been talking to Daven." At Beckley's expression of surprise, Astan rolled his eyes. "I know I said I'd never speak to him again, but he's changed. He has the best interest of Jelani and Elliun at heart now. I truly believe this." That realization came quietly, like a whisper of smoke on the night air, lingering on the edge of his mind. Daven did not push the words at him, as he always did before. Instead he was patient, waiting for Astan to accept him.

"Daven warned me even if this came to war, the clan could lose the integrity of the *Idellan* if we conducted ourselves as humans would. You remember those reports on the human communication channels, where they counted their successes by the numbers of other humans slain? We cannot conduct ourselves in the same way. We are the *Lelan*. We know deep in our core that each living thing has inherent worth, and we honor that. We honor the life energy of Bartolomey and the others no less because they don't use it for the good of the clan."

Beckley stretched his left shoulder and then his right. "This armor is heavy." He readjusted the straps before turning his attention back to Astan. "We may be the *Lelan*, but I warn you. Their arrows can kill as well as ours can, and they have no qualms about using them. I will not lie down and allow them to wipe us out to preserve any so-called 'integrity' of the clan."

Knowing what Beckley said was true, Astan nodded. "Agreed, brother, agreed."

"Someone's coming!" The cry went up from the western side of the clearing and the group immediately went into defensive mode, crouched down in lines facing the direction of the attack.

Astan glanced across to Jelani, who stood with a bow in her hand, arrow poised for flight. Several of the Youngers stood around her, a protective guard.

With all eyes on the forest to the west, they waited.

Astan used the tense moments to access his inner visions, hoping he would receive some clues on how to conduct the battle, but his sight was dark. Whatever information he needed to flick through to answers was not yet in his grasp.

Running footsteps approached the clearing, but the noise was not enough for a fighting force. Astan drew his dagger and moved quickly toward the front, Beckley following close behind.

"What do you see?" Astan whispered.

Beckley craned his head upward, scanning the woods. "Do not fire! It's Daven Talvi."

Daven stopped, eyes narrowed, as he saw the gathered fighting force. "Before you go, there is something I must tell you." He took Astan's arm and pulled him aside. He did not let go. "I have just come from an encounter with Veraena. She has shared some shocking information."

Astan pulled away. "I want nothing from her."

"She offers nothing," Daven said darkly. "I fear we may have to destroy her. Anger has consumed her."

Astan gaped. "She's angry? She disappears, leaving me an orphan for twenty-five years, and *she's* angry?"

"Not angry with you, Astan. With me, for abandoning her."

Astan sighed, his jaw working with emotion. He was equally infuriated with his father's career decision, especially after he learned the decision was aimed at his own self-serving ambition to be king. "What is so shocking about that?"

"Nothing." Daven glanced over to the others, several of them watching with obvious curiosity. Daven grabbed Astan's arm again, his grip tight and his eyes filled with pain. "Astan, I want you to deal with this before it is shared with the others. Veraena did not leave only you, she left your brother as well."

Astan's chest tightened, as though a rope was being pulled tight around it. "Brother? What brother?"

Jelani headed toward them at quick pace. Within seconds, she arrived at Astan's side.

"Vez is your brother," Daven answered.

"What?" Astan and Jelani spoke in unison, and then looked at each other, bewildered.

"That's not possible," Jelani said.

"I assure you it is. Veraena was pregnant when I went into Sleep. She says the Circle wanted her to be, in case I didn't return." Daven shifted his weight to the other leg, looking uncomfortable. "She told no one. Not even me. After she gave birth, she left the child with a foster and began her search for revenge."

Astan saw the shadow which crossed Jelani's face. She knew the capabilities of the Circle in regards to fertility. "But Djana must have known."

Daven looked him in the eye. "I imagine she did. After Veraena left the clan, the Circle lost control of them both, which Djana may have taken as an affront. But I don't understand why she wouldn't have explained or told you once Vez rejoined the clan in the fall."

Astan fell silent, trying to absorb yet another treachery perpetrated by the older generation, another pregnancy engineered to serve their purposes that went wrong. How could they live with a life built on lies and misery?

"So they knocked up Veraena for a little insurance?" Jelani's tone was sharp and accusing. "And then kicked her ass out. How like them. Does Djana know you discovered this? What did she say?"

Daven shook his head. "I came straight to Astan." He gestured to the group. "I wanted you to know before anything happened."

"Before what happened?" Jelani asked. "Before we killed the elf who tried to kill me? I'm not exactly forgiving on this point, Daven!"

"In all fairness, Jelani, he didn't know either," Daven answered. "Veraena kept the truth from Vez until very recently. I would guess she waited to inform him when she knew it would do the most harm."

Astan anchored his spinning thoughts and shook off the miasma of sorrow.

"When we come back," Astan said to Daven, "be sure to explain to me why we are fighting to save the old ways. I really don't see how they serve anyone." Bitterness seeped into his voice like a tea brewed too long. He turned to the others. "Let's go!"

Astan took Jelani's arm and walked away from his father. He

did not look back, afraid his grief and disappointment might simply explode.

* * *

THE group made rendezvous with Lane and Kevin at the top of the trail leading from the road. The humans were accompanied by two dozen men and women, dressed in camouflage jackets and pants and heavy boots. They all carried firearms, even Lane.

Jelani eyed him skeptically. "Really, Lane? After all the crap you gave me about guns? You actually brought Bertha along?"

"War is hell," Lane muttered, not meeting her eyes.

"Uh-huh."

Jelani studied the rest of them. Kevin was not the only one with a brace on his leg, there was one with an artificial hand. They had already experienced the hell of war and yet volunteered to fight in one that had nothing to do with them or their way of life.

"Thank you for joining us," Jelani said with a welcoming smile.

"Glad to get the lead out, ma'am," one young man said from under a camouflage-material baseball cap. His blond hair was shaved close, military style.

"Yeah, action's a good thing," another added. "Too quiet here at home sometimes."

A murmur of assent passed through the group.

Astan stepped up, his face grim. "I also appreciate your effort on our behalf, and thank you for your service. That being said, I want it to be clear that our intention is not to kill our brothers and sisters, even if they serve the dark master."

Mild confusion passed over the faces of the waiting soldiers. Kevin cleared his throat. "Let me get this straight. You want us to fight the war, but we can't win it?"

"Seriously, Astan." Lane's brow curled into a furrowed caterpillar. "After all these jerks have put you through, the earth would be better off without them."

"You have said as much of the Circle. We don't intend to kill them, either."

Jelani glanced at Astan to see if he was being ironic, but he appeared quite sincere. She jumped in before they both started listing people who would be better off dead. "Look, what Astan means is that there are few enough of us as it is. Don't kill anyone you don't have to. Those weapons will wound just as well as take lives. We need every member of the clan to keep us strong."

"Clan?" The blond boy studied her with questions in his eye. "You're Scottish?"

"Not exactly," Jelani replied, caught off guard. She had presumed Kevin would have told his army buddies they were dealing with something supernatural. Apparently not.

Lane snickered and Kevin looked sheepish. "Need to know basis," Kevin said.

"Of course," Astan said, nodding.

Then the tree branches wobbled overhead.

Max came floating down, his bright eyes fixed on the strangers. "Is this a real army? Where are the orcs and trolls?"

An awkward silence stretched among them, each one fixed on the elf as he landed on the ground in front of them.

"Sarge? Are we expecting orcs and trolls?" one woman in Kevin's group asked.

"My friends, you'll see some things today that'll knock your socks off," Kevin said, turning to his troops. "But don't worry. Nothing here is different than it has been for centuries. We're the ones who have changed."

A rumble of questions among the troops went unanswered.

Then Kevin turned and saluted Astan. "Orders?"

"Beckley says they're coming," Max informed, stepping up beside Astan.

Astan rubbed Max's white-haired head. "Then let's not keep them waiting. This way!" he called, heading into the forest to battle.

CHAPTER 30

VEZ did not lead the attack force that set out to confront the clan warriors.

He wanted to, but Bartolomey would not allow it. After two failed missions, Bartolomey found Vez wasn't worthy of much at all. The last two nights he was forced to sleep in the open air, the others forbidden to bring him food or any sort of comfort. Misery, cold, and hunger. Those were the things that made him fall to his knees and beg Veraena to let him come along on this attack.

She stared down at him, cold and implacable. "You've been such a disappointment, Vez. I had hopes for you. You promised so much, but you've delivered almost nothing."

"Mother, please. Please." He fought back tears that choked him, determined not to let her see how much he hurt.

Veraena watched him, arms crossed tight in front of her. "Maybe Astan's the one I should have taken back."

"He wouldn't have fallen for your tricks. He's too much of a hero." Really stung now, Vez tried to inject sufficient rancor to show his hatred for his brother, for them all, but instead it made his voice tremble. He was tired, too tired to be playing word games with her. He could have been more careful with what he said. *Should have.*

"Tricks?" Her eyes flashed with fury.

Realizing his mistake, he scrambled to recover. "Not tricks. He's just not susceptible to—" No. That wasn't any better. He should quit while he was behind, and stop digging his own grave.

"Susceptible to what? My womanly charms? Magic? The same thing all your young friends see in me?" As he waved, trying to put her off, she grabbed his face, her nails raking his cheek. "No, I want to know. How is Astan Hawk better than you, or any of your friends?"

Shaking, exhausted, he fell to the ground. "Please, just let me go. Just let me go. Please."

She stared down at him so long he almost thought she meant to fry him there. But she finally relented. "Fine. You go. But as a foot soldier. You have no command duties. Hidal and Yadin will lead the attack."

He could only nod. Choked up, he could not add anything. He was just grateful for the opportunity to redeem himself. If he was not being judged as a leader, perhaps he could find a way to shine, even make them look bad enough to pull himself into position to get back on top. He did not move until she was gone, then he retreated to a quiet spot in the forest where he could prepare. His sense of self rattled around inside him, lost in the changes of the past few weeks.

He always tried to keep the outer shell of his core strong, the part that protected him. It had served well when the other Youngers mocked him for having no father or mother, or for living with Kassen in his makeshift house, where they often subsisted on whatever the Circle parceled out in its so-called magnanimity. Vez grew up knowing he could count on no one but himself. He should have kept it that way. Once he let Bartolomey and Veraena see how much he wanted to be included, his whole world spiraled out of control.

Leaning against a tree, he hugged himself. He ached with the pain of betrayal. Vez thought that if he tried hard enough, they would care about him and that he would finally have the 'real' family he always wanted. But no matter how hard he tried, he was never able to please them. Instead, they played him between them, like the vindictive witches of the Circle. They were not any different than those they fought against.

The other Youngers passed by the place where he cowered, bows slung across their shoulders, laughing and talking each other up. He glanced at their number as Fontine passed by. She looked startled to spot him there in the shadows. After an anxious peek behind, she hurried out of the group to his side and slipped an arm around him.

"Come on, love," she whispered. "This will soon be over." She pulled him into line, half-supporting him. "Reach in my pocket."

Vez automatically started to reach, before quickly pulling his hand back. He was not sure if he could trust even Fontine. Looking up he noticed Hidal's gaze on them. "Why?" he asked.

She seemed reluctant to speak. "I brought food. In case I saw you," she whispered.

"You shouldn't have. You'll be punished." He pushed away from her, worried about the consequences, not to himself, but to her.

"Don't be stupid!" she hissed. She grabbed something from her pocket and shoved it into his hands, before running forward to walk with one of the other *neris*. Hidal eyed Vez for a moment and then turned his attention back to the front. Vez crammed the bread in his mouth and started chewing. *Thank the Lady for Fontine.* Now to finish off those who followed the false queen, so he could have his life back.

Vez used his ability to move from the end of the pack to a spot near the front, where he could hear what Hidal and Yadin were saying. Scouts reported back the location of Astan and his fighting force, as well as the information that humans had joined them, with guns. The news surprised the co-leaders, who immediately began to argue about the best way to combat firearms. Vez listened for a few minutes as they got nowhere, before his attention faded away, drawn to the conversations among the others.

"Waiting to see what we do," one finished.

"Why didn't the other Sleepers come with us?"

"Not like they want to get caught."

"Or lose their abilities. Who wants to live human?"

"Grigor survived."

"Only because Firefly saved him. Then he betrayed her, and she finished him good."

A longing sigh. "I'd never betray her."

"When she takes down the Master, she'll be the beautiful new queen of the clan, that's what Yadin said."

Vez marched along, pondering. So who had betrayed whom? She led Grigor along the path, Vez would bet on it. And when Grigor did not suit her, she began grooming Vez. Now she moved on to share her secrets with Yadin.

How long before Vez became the next corpse?

CHAPTER 31

TO say Lane was not prepared for full-scale combat in the real world was an understatement.

First, there was no comfortable chair in easy reach of Earl Grey tea and Creamy Cupcakes. Real combat was muddy and wet and cold and exhausting. Even with Pieter's healing help, Lane found himself struggling to keep moving forward, carrying the heavy gun and the protective vest across his chest and back.

"Guess Crisp knew what he was doing, staying behind with Iris and the baby," he grumbled as he fought to yank his booted foot out of a sucking hole filled with mud.

Max, walking beside him, his feet scarcely touching the ground, grinned up at the hefty human, hero worship clear in his eyes. "The Lane is brave to join our brothers and sisters at war."

"The Lane is crazy, you mean." Lane trudged along, trying to keep up. Why hadn't winter hung on? It was barely April, and usually the ground was frozen for weeks longer. Travel would have been so much easier.

A yell ahead of them alerted him something was about to happen. Then chaos broke out. An arrow flew past his head, just missing Max. Shouting and the sound of wood hitting metal filled the air.

"Here!" Max said.

Grabbing Lane's hand, Max pulled him aside onto a little rise where they could see all that was happening. Careful to conceal as much of his bulk as he could behind a tree until he caught his breath, Lane watched the battle unfold. In the forefront elf fought elf, a truly awesome sight as he saw the effect of the training Astan often spoke about, the magic abilities playing off one another. Astan was in the middle of the fray, his hand-to-hand amplified by his ability to alter his density. Often he would rise above the others as high as their head, either to escape a swipe by another or to allow him leverage to land on his opponent, to subdue them. Beckley fought by his side, a juggernaut of strength knocking enemies right and left.

To his surprise, Lane found that his Jelly Bean had an amazing arm for archery, hitting several of the enemy elves in non-vital areas. He recognized Merripen, who moved fallen tree trunks into the path of oncoming foes to block their forward movement, and Elron who called hawks and other raptors from the sky to confound attacks by Bartolomey's people. The scene looked like a melee right out of Lord of the Rings. He could swear he recognized Crispy's hawk among the combatants.

"I want to get in there," Max said, his lower lip protruding just a little.

"So what's keeping you?" Lane asked.

"The queen said I must keep an eye on you."

"She did?" Lane scowled. So Jelani thought he couldn't handle himself, did she? He would have to show her. Fake battles on a computer screen might not teach you how bad a conflict smells, but he knew something about parry and thrust, give and take. "Then you better watch this!"

Standing at the top of the ridge, he gave Xiomar's best war cry and ran down the hill, waving his gun, his pack flapping behind his back. "Look out, you mother pus buckets! The Lane has arrived!"

Max's delighted laugh followed him, and Lane caught a glimpse of the elf gliding down overhead into the middle of the fight. Lane had enough to do in trying to stay upright as he reached the bottom of the hill. He ended up in a small group of Kevin's friends who were slowly getting beaten back by a young blonde female elf who threw fireballs and a male who kept appearing and disappearing.

He appeared right in Lane's path as he came headlong down the hill, and Lane mowed him down like cardboard, tripping over the elf's feet and probably doing some serious damage to a couple of ribs. With the breath knocked out of him, Lane saw stars just like in the cartoons. The elf didn't get up.

"Yadin!" the female elf cried. She broke off her attack on the others and ducked in to grab the fallen elf. In a flash, she pulled him out of the line of fire.

Lane creaked to his feet once he could breathe again. He tucked his gun away and picked up a three-inch thick stick from the ground. He ought to be able to crack someone's head open with that.

He stood, feeling as solid as that stick, waiting for someone to come at him. He did not have to wait long.

A tall thin elf launched toward Lane with hands outspread. When he came close, he clapped his hands together and water exploded over both of them.

"What the crap?" Lane burbled through the deluge, trying not to drown.

The elf landed behind him. Instinctively, Lane turned on his thick legs, his stick already in motion, and caught the elf across the mid-section. The impact jarred Lane's arm all the way back through his shoulder.

"Ow!" Lane yelled. "Damn, that hurts."

The elf staggered sideways, but did not fall. Recovering, he studied Lane for a moment with eyes a piercing shade of apple green. "Your kind is not welcome here, human."

"Believe me, pal, I've got a whole list of other places I'd rather be. But you guys had to go and piss off my Jelly Bean. So here we are." Lane raised the stick again, breathing heavily at his effort. "You going to surrender now, or will I have to bruise my other arm, too?"

In answer, the elf pointed skyward and clapped his hands again, drenching Lane once more. As the elf ran away to the north, Lane sputtered, coughed, and wiped his face.

"Fine. I'll take that as a maybe!" Groaning, Lane limped aside, even colder as the wind bit against his wet clothing. What the hell was he doing here? Not much more use than the proverbial bump on a log. And there were way too many logs, for that matter.

Two of Kevin's buddies ran across his line of sight in pursuit of a pair of brown-dressed elves. Lane hoped they were bad guys.

Without uniforms, it might be hard for those of the Guard to tell who was fighting with them and who was not. Until they got whammied.

The noise of battle came from the direction the elf had gone. Lane started to follow them, coming into view of several of the others, including Kevin and one of his team, but stopped. All around him, birds started flapping their wings and lifting up from the trees into the sky, screaming like the world was coming to an end.

About the same time, the ground under his feet rumbled.

No way in hell.

Not that they didn't have earthquakes in Montana. They surely did. There was one huge kicker in 1959 out by Hebgen Dam. But this could not be a coincidence. Lane looked around for safer ground. He did not think any of Astan's buddies possessed geokinetic power, but he would definitely put money on this not being a natural event.

Must be one of Bart's guys.

The earth rumbled under his feet again, and then something shifted, knocking him to the ground. Rocks nearby tumbled down, crashing into pieces as they landed. Kevin yelled out something, but Lane couldn't hear it. A large chunk of gray rock, some two feet across, suddenly shot up in front of Lane, looming overhead. With a muttered curse, he ran.

"To the left, to the left!" Max called down, gliding lightly overhead.

Damn skippy.

Lane ran to the left.

The ground continued to shake. A huge tree broke in half, the top falling down behind him. The impact nearly knocked Lane from his feet again. He stumbled, but kept running, trying to stay clear of the rock formations. Around a large pile of granite, he came upon a dark-haired girl lying on the dirt, blood running from her forehead.

"Whoa, what's this?" Lane looked around. "I need a healer!"

He knelt next to the girl, who he realized was amazingly pretty, and ripped off a piece of his shirt to dab at her wound.

She didn't move. Was she already dead?

"Hey, you," he said, leaning forward to examine her wound. The ground shook again, sending a spray of small rocks from above onto Lane and the girl.

"Knock it off, you deathtard!" he yelled.

The new movement made her groan, which was a good sign.

"Can you sit up?" Lane asked. "We ought to get you someplace where crap can't fall on you."

She groaned again, but did not reply.

The sounds of fighting continued in all directions, an occasional arrow shooting past. As far as safe locations went, maybe being behind that big rock was not so bad.

"Hey, what's your name?" Lane asked, worried that she had suffered head trauma.

There was an awful lot of blood. Something jogged his memory from years ago in the foster home. Crispy, during one of his drug-induced rampages, fell into a window and cut his head, he could recall someone stating that head wounds tended to bleed a lot. Maybe that was all there it was to it. Maybe.

She mumbled something that sounded like 'Laura' and stirred. He helped her sit up. She moved closer and leaned her head on his shoulder.

"Beckley?" she asked.

"Haven't seen him for awhile, hon. Hang on, okay?" Lane leaned his head back. "Medic!"

CHAPTER 32

VEZ picked up his pace and arrived on the front line when the two groups met in a heavily-wooded area.

He carried a thick staff, which he wielded a little more easily, thanks to Fontine's gift of sustenance. The first one he knocked down was a skinny elf that was one of his boyhood friends. The thin elf halted, his hand raised to cast a dispersion wave, when he noticed whom he faced. Vez did not hesitate, smacking the elf on the side of the head, and the opposite knee, dropping him to the ground. Vez jumped over the fallen body and moved on, pinpointing a place he wanted to be and skimming himself there.

He worked through several clan Youngers, ones that used to mock him when he first came to the clan, using the stick to knock them down or out before they could use their given talents on him. His ability let him move around the area of the battle fluidly, so he was able to avoid many of the attacks aimed at him, while striking at other clan Youngers with whom he had butted heads. His stick was formidable, took elves off their feet, but what he needed was a real weapon.

Seeing what he needed, he moved to the east in a rush of wind, having no qualms bashing down two young females that had rejected him in the past, before he engaged one of the humans, knocking his gun loose. He picked the thing up and felt the cold metal in his hands. Comprehension came swift. He was now in a superior position to the other *nians* who came with him.

Let them challenge me now.

Vez climbed a nearby rise in the land, taking a moment to assess, trying to decide the direction of destruction he was prepared to enter next. He checked on Fontine's whereabouts, saw her narrowly avoid being mowed down by Jelani's fat human friend, while Yadin took it square in the chest. To his right, he saw Hidal set upon by two of the clan Youngers, one of whom had the power to turn Hidal's shadow-throwing ability into a frozen state. Vez knew the two. At one time, they were his friends. He held nothing against them.

Except that they were now enemies.

With an angry roar, he swung the gun around to fire, prepared to defend his companion. He had witnessed hunters shooting things. The small curved metal hook needed to be pulled in order for it to work. He sighted down the barrel, just as he had seen the humans do. His finger moved into place, ready.

But he could not pull it.

He dropped the barrel, letting the gun fall away from his face. Hidal went down hard. Vez let it happen. When Bartolomey ostracized him, Hidal did not help him. In fact, Hidal only looked out for himself. So why risk magic on him?

Belatedly, reality sank in. Did anyone see him hesitate? If Veraena found out about his lack of defense on Hidal's part, she would tell Bartolomey. And that would be the end of Vez. Bartolomey promised it, and there was no reason to believe it would not happen.

The battle raged all around him. Terzon climbed onto a ridge overlooking the copse and took the pose that preceded his implementation of a ground-moving spell. Vez knew he should seek safer ground. About to shift, he froze when a twig broke behind him. He whirled to see who approached. Astan Hawk, a smear of blood and dirt trailing down his left cheek, stood before him, a bloody dagger in hand.

Vez fumbled with the gun again, pointing it at Astan. Here was his chance to get rid of one of the biggest thorns in his side and at the same time rip the heart out of the queen, his mother's lost paramour and the Circle. All he had to do was squeeze.

Astan looked surprised to see Vez. Then his gaze shifted to the gun barrel. "I know the truth," he said.

"What truth is that?" Vez countered. "The witches' truth?"

Astan watched him intently. "The only truth. We are brothers."

Vez scoffed. "What's that worth? Neither of my parents

found it important enough to share the news until now."

"Daven didn't know until a few days ago. He only just told me. I thought I was alone in the world. Your—our mother hid you from us."

"That changes nothing."

"It changes everything." Astan flicked his dagger into the ground at his feet. "I will not kill you."

"Then you're a fool." Vez's finger tickled the metal hook. "I should end you now."

Astan nodded. "But think about this. We have much in common. Blood, history, and the need to find a place in our community not defined by parents and others."

Pretty words. They confused him. What was Astan doing? Setting a trap? Vez tried to guess the game, but he could not see it.

"Astan!"

The scream cut the air behind him, and the false queen herself came running through the trees in their direction, bow slung behind her. Vez did not move, something compelling in Astan's eyes drawing his attention. Astan had not made a move for his weapon even with Jelani in sight. His hands were open, palms toward Vez.

A tremor ran through the ground, and then a jerk-jolt, knocking them all from their feet. Vez's elbow hit the ground and the gun ejected from his hands, flying out of his reach. A loud rumble filled the air. He looked up toward where he had last seen Terzon. The elf stood atop the ridge, moving first one hand, and then the other, commanding the rocks to move. The ground continued to shake as Jelani crawled the rest of the way to Astan's feet. The two elves faced each other, now both of them disarmed.

"Stay out of this, Jelani," Astan warned.

Her dark eyes flashed with anger. Vez could see that she had not forgotten her encounter with him, Grigor's botched attempt to steal the prince. "After what he's done—"

"After what's been done to him." Astan continued to watch Vez.

"If you're not going to take care of him, then I will." The queen pulled a dagger from her boot and raised it.

Vez scrambled to his feet, stumbling as the ground took another shift, but Astan grabbed her wrist. "I said no!" He turned to her, his tone cold as the rocks. "He is my brother. I will not harm him. I will not allow you to, either. That is no different than letting him die by my hand." He retrieved the gun, slinging it over his shoulder. "There are two wars here. Both must end."

Several arrows flew overhead, and all three of them ducked. Vez's instinct was for flight but this behavior on Astan's part intrigued him so that he could not move his feet.

"Two wars?" she asked. "What are you talking about?"

He turned back to Vez. "You know, don't you? We fight each other, but not because we must. Because the Elders tell us to. Because they want to carry on the old ways. The world has changed."

"Power and supremacy haven't changed. Those who rule still control the balance of power."

"Do they?" Astan let go of Jelani, taking a step in front of her. "More importantly, should they? Look around you. We have humans who fight with us. Humans are a part of the new world in a way which was never true when Bartolomey reigned, when the Circle reigned. We need to adapt. We need to let go of the old ways, not to perpetuate them."

Astan sounded sincere. Considering his other options, Vez almost wanted to believe those flowery, lofty statements that sounded so right. Could he?

"If we—" Vez was cut short by a small avalanche of rock from the hill to their left.

Astan grabbed Jelani's wrist and yanked her aside as the rocks came down, turning his body into the shower of falling stones, some of them the breadth of an elf's hand. Then he reached for Vez, who was trapped behind a pile of rubble and stone shards.

"Too much the hero," Vez muttered, before taking Astan's hand.

An electric shock of recognition ran through them both as they stood, staring at each other. Vez felt like he could look into

Astan's soul. The expression on Astan's face indicated he was experiencing an equally shattering moment. The battlefield around them faded into a clouded, dull roar, even Jelani's urgent questions ignored in the magical seconds that passed as reconnection took place. Vez knew at that instant that Astan meant no deceit, that he was indeed sincere in his wish for brotherhood, and for peace. He thoroughly believed that they would all be stronger if their world came back into balance.

"I'm tired of the constant fighting, Vez. Tell your people to lay down their arms and I will do the same. Let's put this effort toward making the new world a place for all of us to live."

"They're not my p-people," Vez stammered. "Hidal and Yadin, they lead this group." He glanced around but saw neither of them. Hidal had not rejoined the fight. He did see others of his group, one with an arrow in his chest, others bleeding.

"Be the leader they need," Astan urged.

Could he do it? He would be dead either way. He took a deep breath, testing his resolve. "All right. Just so we can talk about it."

"Fine." Astan turned away to comfort Jelani and reassure her he had not taken any serious damage in the rockslide. Vez let out a cry like a falcon's, repeating it twice. Then Astan called his people off with an owl's deep hoot. They waited, hearing the sounds of combat wind down. When silence fell, Astan gestured to a natural cubby space under a nearby tree. "Let's talk."

CHAPTER 33

LANE heard two sets of footsteps, one from the left and one from behind them, both converging on his location.

The first to arrive was a tall, balding elf dressed in shades of dark green. He frowned at the blood and then reached into his pocket for a handful of leaves.

The other was one of Kevin's cohorts, a slight-built brunette with glasses and dressed all in camouflage, who jumped down into their little niche with a first aid kit in hand.

The elf, clearly feeling his territory invaded, came closer, eyeing the medic. "You won't need that," he said.

The woman, whose nametag identified her as Borens, adjusted the brimmed cap on her head and studied the girl. "She's hemorrhaging. Do you have a better plan?"

The elf looked at her, his lips pursed as though he just ate a raw lemon or lime. "I do." He laid a hand on top of the girl's head and closed his eyes. Lane felt weak, like when Daven healed Crispy. He noticed how the medic seemed to feel the effects as well. Within a moment, the feeling slowly passed and the cut on the girl's head stopped leaking body fluids.

The girl's eyelids fluttered open, and she looked around at them, her expression a little lost. "Where am I?"

"Elorra, where are you?" came a bellow from behind the rock.

"Here," she said. She stood, seemingly no worse for wear.

The elf healer smirked. The medic just tucked her bag under her arm with a little *hhmph*.

Lane pushed against the rock, shoving himself upright, and moved aside just as Beckley came crashing around the granite slab.

Beckley took one look at Elorra and the blood on her

clothing and the blood on Lane's shirt, and his face turned angry red. "What happened here?" he said through clenched teeth.

Lane's throat dried up and he could not make a word come out.

"I fell when Terzon shoved the rocks in our direction," Elorra said. "Janien was here." She gifted the healer with a smile. "I'm fine."

Beckley eyed each of them, still not mollified. Finally, he took her in his arms and held her close, whispering in her ear.

"How did you do that?" the woman in camouflage asked the healer. "It happened like magic."

The healer snorted and stepped back. "I am needed elsewhere." With a nod to Beckley, he quietly slipped away.

Embarrassed at the show of intimacy, Lane cleared his throat. The birds had settled back into the trees, and the sounds of combat were gone. Could one side have won already? He fidgeted, knowing Beckley would know, but hesitant to interrupt.

"Hey, man, I hate to ask, but what's going on the other side of the rock? Sounds like everyone quit. Are we done?"

Beckley's eyed hardened. "They're talking truce."

"Truce? What about 'we're going to wipe them out'?"

"Something between Astan and Vez. I'm not sure what it's about. But they came together, and then they called a halt to everything and went off." He shrugged.

"Weird." Lane took a step back. What the hell was going on? Vez and Astan? After what Vez did to Jelani? The only choice Lane could see was that Astan would put a fist right in Vez's face, break out a few teeth, maybe knock him out flat.

No one would treat my woman like that and survive.

Well, if I had a woman.

Curious, he inched past Beckley, laboring up the newly-created hill to survey the battle ground beyond.

Kevin's medic followed him. "Did you see that?" she asked, looking a bit shell-shocked.

"See what?"

She gestured back to the elves.

"Oh, yeah," Lane mumbled with a nod. "That. They're

interesting folk."

"They're not human," the medic said. "Are they?"

Lane chewed the inside of his cheek for a minute, looking down over the abandoned glade. They certainly were not standard-issue Afghanis or desert lords, that much was clear. Kevin should have seen this coming.

"You know," Lane answered, considering his words, "they probably don't want any of this to get out. I mean, because people are, well, you know the old saying about how a person is smart but people are stupid."

"So what are they?" Borens asked.

Should he tell her? Lane sighed. Kevin had not made the job easy. If he would have just explained it all to them before they signed up, Lane would have been off the hook. On the other hand, these people were out here risking their lives to help total strangers. That deserved some level of honesty.

"They're, um, elves."

"Elves." The look on Borens' face was one of complete disbelief.

"Yeah. Elves." Lane chuckled. "The queen even lives in a tree house."

"Sarge never said." Borens pulled the cap from her head, ran fingers through her hair, and shook out her curls. Then she glanced over Lane's shoulder. "Guess that explains the magic part." She cleared her throat and cocked her head. "So are we done here?"

"No idea." Lane reached in his pack and brought out a pair of binoculars. He surveyed the trails below them, looking for Astan. He did not see him anywhere. Or Max. He did spot Kevin and some of the other Guard personnel off to the right. He handed her the binoculars, pointing them out. "Your friends are down there."

"Thanks." She handed them back, tucked her kit into her pack, and then started down the path to join the others. After a couple of steps, she turned back to Lane. "Elves? For real?"

"Yep." Lane grinned, remembering his own absorption process. Did not come easy.

"Right." She continued down until she reached the others, pointing back up the hill to Lane after Kevin spoke to her. Kevin gave him a little salute, and Lane returned it.

Lane waited for Beckley or someone to come tell him what the new plan was, but minutes later none showed. He inched his way down to where he had last seen Beckley.

The elves were gone.

Torn between rejoining Kevin and wondering whether someone would shake his world again, Lane chose a third option. He ducked behind the rock and dug in his pack for something to sustain him through round two, a Creamy Cupcake. He peeled the cellophane off as quietly as he could, shoving it into his pocket, and slowly consumed the fluffy cake with the fluffy cream filling, the sugar hitting him like a drug fix. He closed his eyes and leaned back against the rock, letting the calm set in. Maybe they would get back to fighting in a few minutes, but for now, he could let himself escape from the world.

If only he had enough for everyone, maybe he could save the whole clan.

CHAPTER 34

THE battle had not felt right from the beginning.

Astan despised his hands, covered in the blood of former friends and comrades. He had wounded many, but killed none. No reason existed for them to be at each other's throats, other than the older generation, which sent them out to die, while they remained safe in their bowers at home.

Did this imbalance of power Daven spoke of, the one that allowed the mages to steal the power for themselves, have to exist? Not if they didn't let it. The clan's new queen, the circumstances of her birth changed the way the clan conducted business. Time for the rest of them to catch up.

Astan weaved between the trees, lending a hand when one of his people fought one of theirs, wondering how he could make them all disengage. Jelani was right. Their true opposition was not each other, but the Elders. As long as the goal was to return to the ways of old, none of them would make progress.

The revelation stopped him in his tracks. That was it. They would have to separate themselves from the past and enter the new age of the Bitterroot Clan. If the Elders chose to keep up this ridiculous conflict, let them. But there was no reason to sanction it with the blood of the Youngers.

He continued on, hoping to find one of the leaders of the other side. He had no idea who that might be, but he suspected Vez would be among the logical choices. Brother against brother, they led the fight. Perhaps as brothers, they could end it as well.

After crossing nearly the entire battlefield, he came from behind a clump of trees and happened on Vez, holding an automatic weapon, one that the humans must have dropped. Vez spun around in his direction and for a moment, Astan saw his own death.

But Vez did not fire.

Faced with the *nian* who attacked his beloved and left her for dead, Astan could have been vindictive and hateful. Surely those feelings swirled in his gut, and he could have turned them into action, the dagger in his hand finding a home in the body of the elf that stood before him. But the only way to affect the kind of change that needed to occur meant burying those old quarrels and moving forward.

When Astan saw his brother for the first time and Vez agreed to negotiate cessation of hostilities, the rush of relief was like the arrival of an unexpected miracle.

All the while, Jelani quivered beside him, angry because he was even speaking to Vez. Considering what the other elf had done, Astan could understand her feelings. "*Denami*, we must look to the future. When you first became queen, we said everyone must be re-integrated into the clan, but we let some slip away. Those have caused all this new trouble. Now we have a chance to make that right. We need everyone." He looked into her eyes, not letting her look away. "We'll have to start with the worst to set the example."

She chewed her lip. "I hear you, Astan. I know what you mean. I don't have to like it."

"No." He smiled and caressed her face.

"Go," she said, with a grudging shrug. "I'll make sure all our people survived."

"The queen is concerned for the welfare of her subjects. As it should be." Astan squeezed her hand and sent her on her way. Then he straightened his shoulders and steeled himself.

Vez paced in the small space under the trees, awaiting him. His smile bordered on the mocking, but his eyes were sincere. "So tell me, Astan, how will we save the world?"

Astan laughed. "I'm not shooting for the whole world. Just this corner of it."

Vez stared out at the copse, his eyes picking out his team members. "Even if you win over the Youngers, you'll still have Bartolomey standing in your way. He's going to hold on 'til the very end."

"I know. We're prepared for him."

"With what? That fake monster the human created?" Vez snorted. "That won't slow him down for a minute. And Mother will make mincemeat of a new mage. How do you think you can win this?"

Astan didn't want to consider those things, the negative side. His plan was just coming together, the flicks against his mind showing him pictures of the possibilities. Peace and prosperity could happen in his lifetime, if he stuck to the voices in his head. "Because this will serve most of us. The Youngers will survive, growing even stronger as a united force, and live to see their own children grow up. Without the nattering of the Elders over their shoulder every moment."

"What's your plan for removing Bartolomey?" Vez eyed him, ripe with doubt.

Astan held on to his own caution, not abandoning everything in the face of his new optimism. This sudden spirit of cooperation could in fact be a ruse to gather information. He wasn't a fool. "Still working on it," he said.

"It's important. You better come up with that plan, and before too long. The Master may not be whole, but he's gathered a great deal of strength."

"Good to know." Astan kept smiling, though he felt a slow drain of his happiness and energy sucking away at the memory of his earlier confrontation with Bartolomey at the tree where the previous Elf Queen was saved. Bartolomey's power was nearly legendary. He nearly killed both Jelani and Astan. He had killed Jelani's father, Vincent Marsh. Only the spirit of the old king, Lorenz, was powerful enough to vanquish him. Did the clan have a champion prepared to face him?

Astan sure hoped so.

"I think our mother and father need to make their own peace. We should let them handle their own dispute, don't you think?"

Vez raised an eyebrow. "She'll kill him."

Astan tried not to bristle. "We'll see." He knew Daven was new at his skills, but his father brought a lot of heart to his calling. They were not beaten yet. "What I need is to make sure the Youngers, all of us, will put a halt to the fighting initiated by the Elders. We aren't their puppets any more."

He studied his new-found brother, seeing a reluctance to meet eye-to-eye, a hunch to the shoulders, a lack of the confidence that he held earlier. Something must have happened to Vez, something he blocked from Astan when they clasped hands. If he slipped from the favor of those in control on the other side, perhaps he would not be able to sway the others to follow him. But surveying the field outside, the injured elves on both side, he guessed enough of a toll was taken. That night, his brothers and sisters of *Lelan* would have something to think about.

"I'll do what I can, Astan." Vez shuffled toward the entrance, his feet dragging. "But it may provoke some trouble. What happens if I show up on your doorstep?"

A fair question. After the incursions on clan soil, Astan knew Vez and his companions would not be welcome. "That would be trouble, wouldn't it?" He borrowed an apt phrase from Lane. "Time to put up or shut up, right?" Vez gave him an odd look, and he laughed. "Sorry. Humans have such odd ways of speaking." He nodded his head toward the trees outside. "I mean that if we are agreed and come together out there to covenant a cessation of the fighting, then my followers and I will guarantee your safe passage into clan soil."

He waited for some sort of light in Vez's eye, some indication that was waiting for such an offer to cement a chance to betray the clan, but he did not see it. Perhaps Vez believed this cause in earnest. They were truly brothers, for the first time.

"And the others?" Vez asked. "Fontine? Lokti? Cantanel? They are welcome, too? Those willing to come with me will be in danger from those still loyal to Bartolomey. You're telling me they will be safe?"

"I give you my word."

Vez paced another minute, deep in thought, before turning to Astan and nodding. "The situation has become deadly. If I am to be with Fontine—" He sighed, a sad breath that rattled his chest. "I have no choice."

What was the best way to accomplish this monumental task? Astan considered his options. His original intent to announce the cease-fire in the open seemed counterproductive, if the result would be a retaliatory strike on those who agreed to Astan's plan. But without some general declaration, the fighting would only continue.

The ground rumbled under their feet again. Time was up. "Gather those who would come with us, and meet us at the large rock at the head of the trail. We will conduct you safely home."

"I hope you know what you're doing," Vez said. His expression relaxed, his shoulders less tense.

"So do I."

Astan watched Vez disappear into the greenery outside, and then he stepped out, giving the bird's whistle that would call Beckley to him. It seemed the best course of action was to quietly collect his own people and withdraw, sending the humans home until the elven community could sort out their differences.

The thought of retreat felt cowardly.

The thought of retreat in the hope of saving lives, though, seemed more valiant.

Beckley and Elorra came through the trees on his right, she covered in blood and he ready to burst with aggravation. Astan held up a hand before Beckley could start. "Here's what we're going to do…."

CHAPTER 35

"IT'S not possible. Do you see this? Do you *see* this?"

Daven came to the doorway of Djana's bower, following the direction of her pointing, trembling finger to the central clearing of the clan soil. A group of bloodied elves marched toward the bower where the Circle normally met. His eyes picked out Beckley and Max easily.

"Where's Jelani?" he asked, a sickening wave passing over him.

"I don't see her," Djana muttered. "Why did you let her go out there?"

"Stop," Daven said without rancor. "No use protesting what's already done."

He walked out to meet them, Djana's complaints trailing behind him like baby ducks in a row. The group's momentum did not stop as he joined them. They kept walking until they entered the Circle's private space. He stood just inside the doorway, watching as they all crowded in, a silent multitude following one after the other in what seemed a never-ending line.

Jelani appeared in the middle of the pack with her arm around Vilen, one of Daven's fellow Sleepers whose left foot now dragged as he walked.

Other faces Daven had not seen in a while, belonging to those rumored to have crossed to the other side. His curiosity piqued, he counted at least fifteen strangers among those taking seats in the Circle chamber. Lane and his military friend, both with blood-spattered shirts came in toward the back of the pack, accompanied by Iris and Crispy, carrying baby Elliun.

The last two stopped in front of Daven. Astan and Vez.

Confronted by the son he had never formally met, Daven found himself speechless. He searched the young elf's face, seeing the cheekbones Vez shared with his mother, the strong chin Daven shared with Djana. With a wrench of his heart, he also saw the similarities between his sons, a strength in their eyes and a determination in their spirits. All these years they were kept apart because of his own selfish choices and their mother's stubbornness. He wanted to reach out to them, but a grim pall hung over them.

They were not ready to be family just yet.

Astan nodded a stiff greeting to his father, as he moved the end of the group inside. Merripen and some of the others rearranged the fallen tree trunks to provide seating for most of the nearly one hundred noisy souls who strained the normally sedate bower. Astan crossed to bend down near Crispy and Iris, checking on the welfare of his son, before he joined Jelani in the front, a purposeful look on his face. Jelani, too, appeared resolute. They had all grown up in the past weeks, faster than he would have expected, but they seemed content enough.

A noisy bickering approached from outside. Daven did not have to look to see who it was. He just stepped out of the way.

"How dare you?" Djana demanded before she cleared the doorway. Several of her cronies trailing, she eyed the group with hostility, red-faced, breathing hard. "This is a sacred space. The space belonging to the Circle! What gives you the right?"

Jelani stepped forward. "It's my right. Given to me by my mother. My father. My grandparents. I lead this clan."

The assemblage gave a rousing cheer in response.

Seeming confused at the answer, Djana rocked back on her heels, the old *neris* behind her holding her up. She reached a hand out to Daven in supplication.

He did not take it. Daven read her expression. She knew it was a futile gesture. He was not the Circle's man any longer.

Daven surveyed the elves and humans, healers moving among them, tending to those with wounds. "Why do you come here?"

Vez stood. "We ask for sanctuary." He waved a hand at those around him and some twenty elves stood with him. "We ask for the protection of the clan."

Djana was so agitated she actually spat. "We do not provide refuge to traitors!"

A murmur of assent went through the women with her.

"We do, if I say we do." Jelani came down to stand between the Elders and her troops. "Astan and I have given our word that these elves will not be harmed. And that they will be welcomed into the clan again." She pursed her lips as if wrestling with the words she wanted to come out. "Vez and his companions are welcome."

"Have you lost your mind?" Djana sputtered, pointing at Vez. "That one tried to kill you!"

"Do you think I've forgotten? That I will ever forget?" Tears came to the queen's eyes. "When I thought he had taken my child—" Her voice choked off.

Vez watched, stolid at first and then his composure broke. He pushed his way forward through the throng and knelt before the queen. "Forgive me," he begged, his eyes downcast. "I was wrong, my judgment clouded. Forgive me."

Jelani, her eyes wide with amazement, looked down at the penitent before her. Then her gaze met Daven's. His first impulse was to direct her, but he caught it in time. Instincts were within her. She would choose this for herself.

She hesitated, looking to Astan, then to those gathered around, before turning her attention to Vez. Her shoulders straightened as she wiped the tears from her face.

"I forgive you, Vez," Jelani said, laying a hand on his bowed head. "The brother of my mate is also my brother."

An enthusiastic murmur spread through those in the chamber. Vez took the queen's hand and let her raise him up, exchanging warm glances with her and with Astan before he returned to his place in the crowd.

Daven scanned the bower, taking the emotional temperature of the group. While most of them seemed pleased, Lane was not one of them. He and Kevin stood in the back of the room, arms crossed tightly, wearing matching frowns. Iris, too, seemed preoccupied, her normally smooth brow wrinkled with some worry. Since her return to the clan, she stayed with Jelani at the tree house, taking shifts watching Elliun with Jelani's other human friends. Daven did not push her to meet with him. But whenever he saw her, he ached for her companionship.

As a raw and untested mage, you have plenty to occupy you at this juncture. Iris will wait for you. Her eyes tell you as much.

Djana still steamed at the occupation of 'her' space by the Youngers and their companions, but it was clear Jelani and Astan had no intention of releasing it to the Circle.

Daven sidled closer to her. "Will you stay, or will you go, Mother?"

She shot him a look of disgust. "This new devotion you've found to the queen is quite touching. Do you still hope to displace your son as her choice?"

The room grew quiet as Djana's malicious tone caught the ears of those within. Astan stiffened but did not move. Across the room, Vez watched, Fontine holding his arm. Jelani flushed, and Daven could see she remembered the conversation the day Astan pieced together his father's history. Everyone waited for him to answer.

Daven licked his lips thoughtfully and then looked Djana in the eye. "I have many hopes, Mother. I hope the clan will live in peace. I hope the divisions among us will be healed. I hope Jelani and Astan can forgive my mistakes and welcome me as they have these others."

As his heart emptied of his dreams, he turned to Iris. "I hope I will earn the love of a woman who has waited, taking second, third or even lower place in my priorities as I've learned and become who I am meant to be."

He took a deep breath and let the remainder of his emotion flow with his words. "I hope most of all, that when these other wishes come together, I will have time at last to get to know my sons as I should have known them all along, and become the father they deserve to have."

The silence that followed his poignant declarations was so complete they could hear the spring winds whistle through the pine needles overhead. Long moments passed before Iris came to take Daven's hand, leaning close to give him a soft kiss on the cheek.

"What is meant to be will be," Iris said.

Daven smiled at her. "We can wait until the right moment speaks."

She squeezed his fingers and then turned to face the group. "For those of you who don't know, my name is Iris Pallaton. Before I became part-time nanny to your prince, I worked as a counselor, helping people build relationships and straighten their lives around. Many people encounter hard times. It doesn't always mean they're damaged, or broken. I'd be glad to help you get through this. It will be a small price to pay for all you've given me."

"We would be happy for your assistance, Iris," Astan said, watching Jelani wipe away tears.

In a huff, Djana turned to leave, her twitchy Circle-mates nattering in her ear. "Never in all my days…."

Beckley called out from the far side of the bower. "Never in all your days did you stick your neck out for us, Djana." He held Elorra's hand and gestured to the healing wound on her forehead. "Where were you when we were out fighting Bartolomey's underlings? Not risking your own precious selves, that's for sure."

"Djana, stop," Jelani said. "We need you here, too. Your whole Circle. All of the clan. If we're going to stand united, then we can no longer afford to break off in little irritated groups. Call them. Bring them here, so we can work together."

"There's not room in here for everyone," Djana complained in a tone meant to end the discussion.

Jelani fixed her in a pointed gaze. "Then make room."

Daven sensed Djana's rebellion at being given orders, and decided it would save time for him to now step in. He held out his hand, holding her in place. "You do it, or I'll do it, Mother. Don't you want to show your spirit of cooperation?"

Djana's eyes flashed and for a moment it appeared she would reject Daven's suggestion. Their wills battled until finally she surrendered. She reached for the hand of the *neris* next to her, who took the next in line until they formed a linked group. Then she murmured in elvish under her breath, the others chanting with her.

A few moments later, the bower doubled in size, though that meant some trees ended up inside the boundaries. Daven didn't think it detracted from its beauty at all, nor from the pleased smile on Jelani's face.

"Thank you," Jelani said. "Now, let's get started."

CHAPTER 36

THE negotiations went on for hours.

"This stuff gives me a headache," Lane confided to Max.

Kevin had bailed long before. Lane had hoped he and Crispy could sneak out with the baby, but no one had excused them. After Jelani's big whoop-ass speech, he was afraid to cross her.

"Can't you feel it?" Max said. The battle grime that was previously on his face was now gone, as he watched the goings-on with a sparkling joy that practically radiated from his body.

"Feel what? The need for a large cup of Earl Grey and some WoW time? Yep."

"No." Max's face fell, his gaze disappointed. "The connections grow."

"Connections?"

"Yes! Can you see them?" Max gestured at the large group before him.

"Uh, nope. No connections here."

Lane surveyed the group, most of whom had left here and there to change into clean clothes or to bring in food to share. Daven shared his knowledge of Bartolomey's true intention, and what a bastard he was. Astan actively recruited his team for the next battle, pleased that some new converts would be joining him. The space buzzed with the voices of many elves, punctuated every so often by the distraction of the small Youngers' needs, or Iris trying to get them to re-focus.

Now Iris, she was in her element. She was never happier than when she was helping someone, unless it was when someone was actually making progress. Seemed like both things were happening here. All she needed was a little elf-baby of her own, Lane thought, and she would probably be in heaven.

"Long as no one starts singing *Kumbaya*, I'll be all right," Lane groused.

"The Lane should see this," Max insisted. He reached for Lane's hands and held them tight in his. Their palms grew hot, almost scorching, but Max did not let Lane pull away. "I'll show you."

When the pain got too intense, Lane finally protested. "Max, dude, what are you doing? I'm going to lose my fortune-telling lines any minute now!"

"Look," Max said. "See them now?"

"See what?" Feeling put-upon, Lane looked up and caught his breath. He saw gossamer connections, ethereal strings flowing between the elves as they talked, shared, and bonded. Different colors seemed to indicate different levels of passion or intention, if he was reading facial expressions correctly. The more they talked, the more connections floated above them, linking them together. Lane could only stare in amazement. "That is unbelievable."

Max released Lane's hands and danced in a little circle, white hair spiking up and down. "It hums right through me."

"You're a strange little man, Max. But you're our kind of strange." Lane grinned and continued to watch the changing rainbow before him.

"I'm not a man, nor am I strange," Max said without a hint of resentment. "This is my world. I welcome you to it, as you welcomed me to the land of Azeroth. We each have our skills. That's why we make a good family."

"Family?"

That thought never occurred to Lane. For a long time now, that word was without meaning to him. From his drunken, mentally-ill mother, and all the other assorted nuts and fruits of extended relatives. Foster families, none which lasted long until his teen years, when he and Crispy stuck together for dear life. The loose association he created with Iris and Jelani, as the four of them supported and cared for each other. That felt more like the idea of "family" to him than anything else. But now there was an option to expand his horizons, to look outward, and build bridges to the larger community, from Kevin and his brave comrades, to Max, Daven, Astan, and the other elves.

It was frightening.

It was earthshaking.

It was exciting.

"I am proud to have The Lane as a brother in arms." Eyes sparkling, Max handed Lane some sweets from a tray one of the Elders brought. "It is not your cake, but it is tasty."

"Thanks, kid." Lane chuckled and ate the confection, vaguely maple-flavored, but definitely sweet.

As he savored it, he looked around the room, tracking the connections Max had showed him. He noticed an odd pattern forming, almost a net over the group, in a deep shade of green. The net began in the back of the room, where Daven held up one hand, a very intent look on his face, and continued up to the front, where Jelani stood, her hand up as well. The green strands encircled her hand and then flowed back out over the gathered crowd.

What the....

Lane looked back and forth between the two, seeing the net becoming wider, more stable and the weave closer together as they went on. Small tendrils of ephemeral gauze wafted up from the elves to link with the net in a spark of fusion. What were they doing?

Max dashed off, pushing his way into the group, darting out and in as the green strand chased him and caught him up. All the time, he laughed with delight. He burst out of the crowd and ran straight for Lane, the green strand following him.

Alarmed, Lane stepped backward. "Now you wait a minute, Max. You can't whammy me without my...."

Max circled behind him and then came to the front. The emerald filament wisped into a soft lasso around Lane, as Max waited, breathless.

"Permission," Lane finished. He blinked and reached for the strand that floated up toward his shoulders, connecting to him via a green curl of what looked like smoke. "Max, what have you done?"

Lane assessed himself for a moment. His mental state was

confused. His heart rate was too fast. And his goodwill toward the world perhaps compromised. But that could be his paranoia speaking. Nothing had changed. He still felt like himself.

But if he did magically change, would he realize the change? Or would they have brainwashed him into thinking he was something he wasn't before?

Or maybe it was a delayed-action thing. In the morning he would wake up and find that he was a giant cockroach. That thought made him shudder.

"Max?"

The diminutive elf laughed. "The Lane thinks too much. You're just one of us now. We all are. The queen has bound us all together."

Lane glanced up at Jelani, as she released the strands from her wrist and they all floated upward, dissolving slowly into nothingness. Astan joined her, Elliun in his arms. They embraced. Lane caught a look at her face, her expression blissfully happy. After all those two had been through, they certainly deserved it. He allowed himself a small window of joy, afraid to feel too much, just in case the magic took over and he changed into a sunflower, or a gleaming eagle or something.

Max's attention focused over Lane's shoulder, and he bobbed his head respectfully. "Daven Talvi," he said.

"Thank you for your help, Max. I wanted to talk to Lane about his protector, the one from his computer?"

"Xiomar?" Max jumped up and down and clapped his hands. "He is a wonderful champion."

Lane turned around, surprised. "What about him? You proved there wasn't much I could do with him as long as the other person didn't believe."

Daven slipped an arm around Lane's shoulder. "Now that's where I think I can help."

"Is that so?" Lane felt a blip of anticipation on his personal radar. The loss of Xiomar was a real downer. He had been so convinced he could win the war with his creation. Not that the joint war effort wasn't the most excitement Lane had experienced in years, but it was not where he felt his skills were best needed.

"It is." Daven watched the others for a moment, before suggesting they step outside. "We may prepare better without so many listening."

"Sure. It's too loud in here, anyway." Lane let Daven lead him from the bower, only afterward wondering if Daven whammied him as well. But it was all right.

As long as we are talking about Xiomar, then I'm willing to take a wham for the team.

Taking some fresh breaths of the cool spring air, Lane acknowledged, at least to himself, he was relieved to be out of that space. "Can't believe Crisp is still in there. A year ago he would have run screaming from an enclosed space like that."

"A year ago, he never would have come here," Daven reminded him.

"Oh, yeah." Lane allowed a grin. "So what can you do?"

Daven eyed him speculatively. "The plan I have in mind bears great risk, both for me personally and for you. In order to make your monster deadly to those on the other side, I must connect to them and implant the suggestion in their minds."

"Well that doesn't sound so bad." Lane gestured toward the bower. "Just get them all together and cast a bunch of funny string, right?"

Daven sighed. "No, not exactly. That method worked here because all these people share essentially the same goal. And they are not mages."

"Mages. Oh." Lane's stomach turned over. "You mean to say Bart."

"I mean to say. In order to fix the reality of Xiomar in his mind, I must link directly. He remains quite powerful, and until now, I have avoided him at all costs. If I reach him, and stay in contact with him long enough that he understands the message, it will also give him the chance to attack my being, either on the *santwarja* or on this plane."

"Oh, that sucks." Lane had heard enough about Bartolomey and his cruelty from Jelly Bean and the others that he knew any dealings with him were serious bad news. Black Bart was an elf to be avoided at all costs, especially when it came to something as precious as your mind. "Maybe that's not such a good idea."

"That was my original thought. I wouldn't have suggested it, other than the fact that so many of the Youngers returned with Vez."

"Vez. As if," Lane growled and then saw Daven's eyebrow raise. "Look, I know the kid's your son. And you just found out. And what a sad tale of woe and all. We all have our troubles, huh? But Jelly Bean's a bigger person than I am to be able to forgive what he did."

"Sometimes it is valuable to look at the long-term good, rather than the short-term desire for revenge." Daven eyed him for a long moment. "We have a much smaller fighting force to combat now."

"But you've got two active mages, right? I mean, scuttlebutt around here is that you've got a couple of mages too but they're dried up old bats, pardon my expression, and so they won't be much help."

Daven looked as though he was going to correct Lane, but finally just shook his head. "You are correct that the Elders who have held those *Idan* for many years are reaching their end of days. The young *neris* in training with Kalinda has rejoined us. We will now be able to persuade Rudra to choose an apprentice, now that she sees how precarious the situation might be. The Lady of the Forest, she who represents the soil of the clan, will not take either side. Hers is a point of balance only, as she weighs with the queen."

"So what flavor are you, anyway? I asked Astan and he didn't seem to know. If the old ladies are for air and water, and the Forest Lady, as you say, is for earth, then what's left? Fire. That's Vez's mother, right? That leaves you and Bart." Lane cocked his head. "Good and evil?"

Daven steepled his fingers in front of his chest, seeming to choose his words with great difficulty. "Not precisely. Elves don't see others in terms of inherent good or bad. One's actions define what one becomes. One who does good, will be good, no matter what their nature. One who does wicked things, will be bad, even if they came from the purest of hearts. No, the definition of my position would be more one who draws from the light." He nodded, satisfied with his phrase.

"Wait. Wait. Does that mean Bart comes from the dark side?" A mental picture of Darth Vader popped through Lane's mind, and he cackled. "Awesome."

Daven's brow scrunched with confusion.

Lane waved him off. "Never mind. Pop culture reference. So, now tell me how we're going to make this happen. You're going to sow Bart's mind with the fact that Xiomar has physical form and can inflict damage, so he really can. If Bart believes it, maybe the rest of the mindless batch that follows him will buy it, too." Lane wrestled with the stray thought that going head-to-head with Bart might be dangerous to him, but he had supreme confidence in Xiomar. Even Black Bart could not stand against his warlock.

At least he thought so.

"You sure I've got the *huevos* to pull this off?" Lane asked. "I mean, that's no time to choke, you know?"

Daven laid a hand on his shoulder. "Lane Donatelli, you have a gift. You will bring your champion to life, and he will fight with all the heart you have to share."

The sincerity in Daven's eyes reminded Lane of his grandfather, one of the few family members that was not a nut and who had been kind to him. Daven sounded proud. Despite every impulse to reject it, Lane felt those damnable warm fuzzies crawling around inside him. Feeling awkward, he cleared his throat.

"Okay, so I get to let Xiomar rain death on the baddies. Sounds copasetic. I'll get some practice in this afternoon. But like you said, there's more than one mage. What happens when Momma Bear comes flying in to the rescue?"

Daven took a deep breath. "It will be my task to make sure she doesn't."

CHAPTER 37

NOW to do what I have put off since I began this journey.

Daven debated whether to force the encounter with Bartolomey out in the open or in the *santwarja*. He would be easier to find in the *santwarja*, as there were a limited number of beings on that plane. But it would also be expected. That Bartolomey would come in person was less likely.

Also, just as they would be less obvious on the mortal plane, so would he. But how could he find Bartolomey and get close enough to gain physical contact with his essence? That was all he had to do.

If he could convince Bartolomey that Lane's monster was real, Lane could destroy him.

He worried for a moment he might be sending Lane to his death, but he did not believe that would be the outcome. Lane would not be alone. The other elves would engage the underlings, drawing Bartolomey's attention. Bartolomey still would not be able to take physical form, as far as Daven could learn, so an ephemeral form against an ephemeral form seemed to be a balanced match.

Besides, Daven gave Lane's natural abilities a little boost when he put his hands on him. Now that Daven saw what Lane was capable of, he was able to help him focus and empower that skill, as Daven was always able to do with his companions. He believed with his heart that it would be enough. He entreated the Lady, that Lane, a champion that never recognized his own nature, would rise to this occasion.

Out of habit, he reached into his bag of runes, searching for guidance with a single stone. He drew *okki*, the leader or shaman. That did not help in the least. To whom did it refer? Himself? Bartolomey? Even Veraena? He sighed. He must find another way.

Although he did not want to press his newfound relationship with Vez, he could not ignore the fact that out of all of them only Vez had recently been in Bartolomey's company, which made him the resident expert. To make Lane's project work, this must happen.

Once the group meeting broke up, Daven searched out Vez. He found him with Fontine, the two of them walking hand in hand through the trees in the center of the clan soil.

Fontine noticed Daven and pulled at Vez's sleeve. Vez's eyes narrowed as he looked up.

"Vez," Daven said. "May I have a moment?"

After Vez whispered something into her ear, Fontine tossed a curious look in Daven's direction. She kissed Vez on the cheek and slipped away into the woods.

"What do you want?" Vez asked.

"You know the war's not over."

Vez stopped just short of rolling his eyes. "That's brilliant. Good thing you're not the one in charge any more."

Daven tried not to bristle. "How committed are you to bringing the war to an end?"

"Me?" Vez shrugged. "It's no good for any of us. Astan's got it right. Too many of you telling us what to do. Letting us take the risk for you."

Daven's spirits sank. What he wanted to ask would put Vez square in the line of danger. It was not fair. "I know it's not fair. I wouldn't ask you if there was anyone else I thought could make it happen."

Shoving his hands in his pockets, Vez kicked at a small hillock of mud. "And if I don't help you?"

Daven shrugged. "Then I'll have to figure out how I can be smart enough to get close to Bartolomey."

The younger elf studied him. "If I don't help you, you'll go anyway?"

Should he tell Vez the truth? If Vez was planted here only to gather information, if he would return to Veraena and tell her what Daven had to say, it would ruin everything. He could touch-sense his son, but they were not so comfortable with their new relationship. He would have to trust him, or not. He went on his instincts.

"I don't have a choice," Daven said. "This plan must succeed if we are to end the war. I must get close enough to Bartolomey to place a suggestion in his mind."

"A suggestion? You're not going to kill him?" Vez stared at him, stunned.

Daven thought about that possibility a moment. "A frontal attack against both mages would be doomed to failure. We need to divide them to conquer, and strike each at the appropriate time."

Vez digested that. "So why do you need me?"

"You know where to find him."

"True enough." Vez sighed. "But he'll know once Hidal and Yadin return that I've come here. If he sees me, he'll kill me on the spot."

"Then we'll have to make sure he doesn't see you." Daven smiled, hoping to encourage the lad.

"And my mother?"

"Unless they are in physical proximity, we should be all right. By the time the battle begins, I hope to have her engaged elsewhere. Now, you have the ability to teleport, correct?"

"Not like some of the others. I can shoot myself to a place within my vision." Vez pointed to a point some two hundred feet away. "I could travel that far in a heartbeat."

"Can you carry someone with you?"

"I never have." A thoughtful, crafty look crossed Vez's face. "You want me to take you?"

"My talents allow me to show you how to extend your own." How could he do this? Daven did not know how familiar Vez was with his training or how his mage powers might differ from those of Veraena. "It may be possible to increase your range, to allow you to go to a place, not just within your direct sight, but one that you have seen before. One you are firmly familiar with. If this is so, we could travel, in that heartbeat you mentioned, to the place Bartolomey can be found. If we locate him quickly and

I accomplish my task. Then we may escape just as quickly."

Vez paced, the fingers of his left hand rubbing his chin as he pondered his choices. "And what suggestion you intend to inflict on him?"

"That Lane Donatelli's technologically-generated monster will kill him."

* * *

VEZ stood on a ridge watching a pair of hawks fly and glide, trying to catch updrafts as the air became warmer. Daven had instructed him to meet him here, a place where the general location of the other camp could be seen in the distance. But only one thought occupied Vez's mind.

The plan was insane.

Even after Daven explained how the big green orc could inflict physical harm after one saw it in action, Vez found it hard to believe. He had been able to pass through the thing as if it had been made of mist. Hidal had seen it, too.

"That is one of our greatest strengths," Daven replied, with a mysterious smile. "This tactic will be underestimated by the enemy. Precisely for that reason. And this will allow us to strike true and hard."

That part of the plan made a little sense. No one would believe a fat, clumsy human could kill Bartolomey. They would hardly give him credence on the battlefield at all. It would be one hell of a surprise.

Vez had gone back to Fontine, the only other he trusted. They talked over the request, trying to determine whether it was a trap, and examining the risks. She worried about the dangers in exposing himself to those who were now their enemies. In the end, she encouraged him.

"The only way you and I will have peace in the future is in knowing that Bartolomey can no longer harm us," Fontine had said. "Any of us. Now that we know he will continue his attacks on the clan, there is no other choice. This is your chance to show your true heart, Vez, to show all our brothers and sisters the Vez that I know." Then she had smiled and embraced him. "You will be a hero."

A hero. Right. Maybe a dead hero.

Ready to start pacing again, Vez turned at the sound of a faint footstep behind him.

It was Daven at last with no cloak or weapons, only himself in a simple elf-jacket, pants, and boots.

Vez took in a shaky breath, focused on firming it up. *Be a hero.* "So, we're ready?"

Daven nodded. "We are. We will be fine. He held out a hand. "Your courage makes me proud."

A little surprised, Vez hesitated, self-conscious, before reaching out and taking his father's hand, as he had seen humans do. Unusual, but it made him feel good. He guessed in that touch was also the exchange of power Daven promised him. He allowed one quick thought about his own chances for personal power, now that he was stronger, but sublimated it immediately. A little smile showed him Daven had not missed it, though.

"It is difficult to learn that one's own ambitions might not be the driving force that improves the world for everyone," Daven said. "Yet it is the most important lesson of all."

In that moment, Vez was gifted with a host of memories. Slices of Daven's own journey to humility and the searing cost of his previous beliefs, including the loss of his mate and his sons. As Vez absorbed them, he found himself staring into Daven's face, amazed at how alike they were, even after being separated all these years.

Daven squeezed his hand and then let go. "We will have many seasons to reconnect, Vez. Now, time is of the essence. Are you ready?"

Struggling to deal with this newfound knowledge, Vez nodded.

"Very well. Fix in your mind the place where Bartolomey may be found, every detail you can muster. Think about where you want to appear."

Vez had put some thought into this, and knew the most likely place they would find the Master was the clearing where his mother always spoke to him. "Yes, I have it. We'll land in the trees near it, so that we have some cover."

"Good. I do not intend for you to be discovered." He took hold of Vez's arm. "When you are ready, take us there."

Vez focused on the place he had hidden before, a hollow behind a large boulder, a place big enough to conceal the two of them at first. *This had better work.*

"Now," Vez said. He closed his eyes and wished them both there.

When he opened his eyes, he was at first disoriented from the movement, but pleased to see they were at the spot he chose.

"This is it," Vez confirmed. "Mother speaks to Bartolomey there in the open glade."

"Very well. Remain here. I shall try to engage him."

Daven walked out into the open, chanting some charm so softly Vez could not hear the words. He circled the clearing a dozen times, and then a dozen more. Nothing. He glanced back toward the place where Vez waited, and Vez guessed he wondered if it was a trap. Vez's heart raced. The longer they lingered, the more likely they would be discovered. That could be disaster.

One thing would catch Bartolomey's attention, insubordination from Vez.

Before his good sense could talk him out of it, Vez walked into the center of the clearing. "Master Bartolomey, I come to renounce my loyalty to you and I name you the evil villain that you are!"

Daven froze. "Vez, no!"

"Do you want him to come or not? Now get out of the way 'til you can get him!" Vez stared, until Daven moved out of the clearing.

Vez stood alone, calling the dark mage who had nearly killed him once.

Now who had the insane plan?

He tried to listen to his heartbeat, but it seemed to be skipping all around. His breath came fast, and his head started to spin. He tried to look in every direction at the same time, not knowing where the onslaught would come from, only that it would, and that he would have a limited window to distract Bartolomey so Daven could accomplish his goal.

He thought of his pretty Fontine for a moment, her face in a gentle smile. *This has to succeed, love, or what you say is true. We will never be able to live together in peace.*

With luck and perhaps intervention by the universe, they might get out alive.

His first warning was a crackle overhead, followed by an electric tremor that ran through his body. He leapt sideways, the only thing that saved him from the bright flash of lightning that struck from the sky, accompanied by an angry roar that shook the very bedrock around them.

"Have you learned nothing, pup? Do you beg for your own death?"

Wind swirled chunks of granite into a loose form of an elf, a jagged, bulbous thing that lunged toward Vez. The doppelganger waved its arm in his direction, sending the rocks of its arm flying at him. Vez moved as quickly as he could, but at least three of the missiles hit him, tearing open his flesh. He scrambled aside, the pain overwhelming, trying not to be distracted by the rough blotches of blood that appeared on his shoulder and thigh.

How much distraction did Daven need?

He said he needed to get close enough to root the idea in the dark mage's head, but did he need Bartolomey's actual body? Or would any manifestation do? Too late to ask now. Daven did not approach the rock monster, so he guessed that it was not enough.

Onward.

Groaning as he came upright, Vez faced the grotesque mockery of an elf, chest thumping as he tried to contain his fear. "I don't want to die at all. I want to live."

"Then you are more a fool than I believed," Bartolomey chided.

The thing whipped its other arm in his direction. A piece of gravel caught Vez on the side of the head, bringing stars before his eyes.

"Young *nian*s like you are so easy to tempt," Bartolomey continued. "You want to be adult, you want to be free, and you

think accumulating power without putting in the time for study
and practice and hard work means success. Pathetic."

Vez strained to remain conscious. Just a few seconds, that's
all it would take. *Don't you fail Fontine.*

"I was wrong," Vez said, shoving the words between his
teeth, the effort sapping his strength. "Besides, you aren't the one
with the power. You can't even show yourself. You send these
representations of stone, earth and air. Why would I hope to
learn anything from you?"

The earth shook again and the rock-man disassembled,
tumbling to the ground. Wind shot down from the sky, clearing
the rocks and everything else loose from the open space. Vez, his
teeth rattling in his head, remained by grabbing onto a securely
rooted sapling. An awful sound, like the shrieking of a thousand
hawks, filled the air. Vez would have covered his ears, but he
would have blown away. Instead, he held on and prayed.

At least he got Bartolomey's attention.

"Do you really want to see me, pup? Then feast your eyes,
and bid goodbye to this world!"

A flame burst up in the center of the clearing, and the form
of an elf walked out of it. Not totally solid, fire licked off its
exterior and with outstretched arms headed straight for Vez.

Vez wanted nothing more than to teleport away, now that he
knew he could take himself all the way back to the safety of the
clan lands. He could be with Fontine in a matter of seconds, safe
and sound. Instead, he waited for this hellion to tear him to bits.

Come on, Daven. Save us both. Do me this one service, as my father.

In a blur, Daven moved out from the trees.

Bartolomey grabbed Vez with one of those burning hands.
Vez screamed in pain.

Daven seized Vez's other arm. "Now, Vez, now!"

Something happened. Lost in his own anguish, Vez could not
discern what. A bright light filled his eyes and Bartolomey was
suddenly no longer attached to him. Daven twisted the arm he
held, bringing Vez's thoughts into focus, as he put his own body
between Vez and Bartolomey.

"Vez, my son," Daven's voice said in his ear, "you must send us home."

"Home, yes. Please." With a sigh of relief, Vez pictured the spot outside the bower he and Fontine had been given and wished them there.

A moment later, his arm still at fever heat, they appeared at the place he envisioned. He felt Daven's strong arm around him, heard Daven call for Astan, saw Fontine's shocked face, all before the pain overtook his consciousness and he faded into black.

CHAPTER 38

ASTAN arrived at the bower where Fontine waited, her face pale, hands twisting against each other.

"Where are they?" he demanded.

"Inside." She moved out of the way and Astan went in, finding Vez unconscious on the floor, bleeding in several places and his jacket burned away on his right arm, his skin blackened. Daven was at least upright, but he too had burn marks on his back and right shoulder. Astan approached his father first, but Daven waved him aside.

"Vez needs your help more than I do. He challenged Bartolomey, something I have not been brave enough to do myself. The effort cost him dearly." Daven gazed down upon his second son with a mixture of concern and amazement.

"Never said he was smart," Astan muttered. "Help me get his jacket off."

Handicapped by his own injuries, Daven lifted Vez so Fontine and Astan could pull off the ruined jacket.

Fontine gasped when she saw the blistered arm. "What did he do?"

"Don't worry, Fontine," Daven said. "He'll be fine."

Daven's usual platitudes grated on Astan, but he did not want to allow his response to cloud what he was doing.

"Did you succeed?" Astan asked Daven.

"Yes. Vez distracted Bartolomey long enough for me to get close and touch him."

Astan studied the wounds, estimating the amount of pain they caused. Was it sufficient payback for what Vez had dealt to Jelani? No one could have ordered him to do this. He did this of his own will, to help the clan. Perhaps it did not even out things. Whatever else, Vez had gone a long way toward making reparations for his transgressions.

Vez was an interesting muddle of contradictions. Astan looked forward to getting to know him better.

He knelt on the soil and then laid his hands on Vez, one just below the wound on the right shoulder, another at the solar plexus. The shock of the injuries Vez had received threatened to steal his life force, and his heart beat in a slow rhythm, his pulse weak. Concentrating on the energy all around him, the life force of the others in the room, and the power radiating from the earth below, Astan pulled it together and channeled it into the inert body before him. No fancy magic touches, no flashes of light or sparks, no bright colors, just his bare palms on Vez's body, giving his being the energy it needed to work through and heal itself. The moment slipped sideways and blurred, the seconds ticking by in distorted shapes during the energy transfer itself.

When the injured Vez absorbed enough of what he needed, the disorienting feeling faded, and Astan once again felt in synch with his own world.

"He will be fine," Astan said.

"Thank you, Astan." Weeping with relief, Fontine fell to her knees next to him. "You have been so kind when we were ungrateful to the clan for what they provided us. We will never be able to show enough gratitude."

Astan privately agreed with her, but forced a comforting smile as she embraced him. "Those misunderstandings are in the past. We must now look to the future."

"We'll never leave again," Fontine promised. "I swear it."

Daven reached for Astan's arm to help him up, shaking off protests about his own injuries. "You tend to Vez, Fontine. I want the two of you to remain here when we go to finish this. Vez has done his part."

Vez struggled to open his eyes and then tried to sit up. "No. I need to be there. I mean to see this through to the end."

Astan deferred to his father on this point, but had to be a realist. "We could use every bow and sword we have."

"Perhaps you are right. Vez, you and Fontine decide. We would be proud for you to join us."

"Thank you, Daven." Fontine embraced him and then set about taking care of Vez, who would still need time for his wounds to disappear.

Daven led Astan outside, supporting him at first, until Astan felt more stable.

"Hold up a minute," Astan said. "Let me help you."

"The hands of the king are powerful," Daven said, allowing Astan to tend him.

"Yeah. But I'm satisfied with a few gifts from the Lady. I need no crown on my head. Seems like so many of the mistakes the clan has made in the last century have to do with the pursuit of personal power. Me? I'd be satisfied if I knew Jelani and my son were safe, and that the Lelan would be in harmony with their environment instead of constantly at war with it."

Daven nodded in silence.

"If you've prepared Bartolomey," Astan said, "then we should move as soon as possible."

"Agreed. In the moments of confusion, he may not have realized my true purpose in being there. He may have believed I rushed in to save Vez, and missed the moment I implanted the message." Daven pursed his lips. "We can only hope. But in the event he ponders it at length, he is much more likely to guess what we truly intended."

Bartolomey was many things, but stupid was not one of them. Astan imagined that, given enough time, the dark mage would guess the nature of the contact made.

"The troops are ready," Astan informed. "Awaiting my orders."

"Then give them. We will go to battle. Hopefully for the last time."

* * *

LANE Donatelli marched at the front of the column, as Astan and the other elves made their way through the forest toward the stronghold of Bartolomey.

It was not only Astan's own crew of some seventy fighters. The majority of those who had returned also accompanied them, as did Daven and the Sleepers and several members of the Circle. All were armed with traditional elven weapons. Nearly three hundred marched to battle.

Astan said that none of them were as significant as Lane, who walked with Max and Beckley on each side.

And none of them *scared shitless.*

Since he and Daven agreed to pull off this stunt, Lane had run Xiomar through his paces. Whether practice made perfect or whether it was something else, Lane found he could control Xiomar without the keyboard. He moved as Lane moved, which was a stretch since some of Lane's muscles had not been used in years. Max helped with some scenarios, and Xiomar demolished three trees and half an abandoned bower. Several of the Elders had even come to watch the exercises, going away with dropped jaws. But he put forth his best effort, knowing the body worked, what an orc's capabilities were, and how the weaponry and magic worked.

Lane could be Xiomar.

Now, the game was loaded in his laptop and ready to go.

He had missed the last encounter with Bartolomey, when Jelani rescued her mother from her giant tree, having shown up at the end after all the excitement. He heard enough about the Evil One over the past year, though. Anyone who schemed to hurt his Jelly Bean or her family deserved every hack of an axe that they got. Preferably a lot of them.

He fixed up a carrier for the laptop and traveled with nothing else. Pieter bolstered his physical endurance, although it had improved since living with the elves because he actually went for a walk at least once a day. He even ate fewer Creamy Cupcakes, since the Grizzly Grocery was much too far away to visit on a regular basis. He was in far better condition than when he had visited here the first time.

Damn elves. Who asked them to make me healthy?

Lane marched along with Beckley, keeping up pretty well, trying to avoid stage fright. He was the linchpin of the whole operation, Astan had said. "A star at last," he muttered to himself.

"What was that?" Beckley asked with a sidewise look. He shifted his axe from his left shoulder to his right.

"Just giving myself a pep talk," Lane said. "It's not every day I get sent to kill a wizard."

"You are quite brave, for a human," Beckley said and then gave a wide grin. "Or maybe just more stupid."

"Oh, thanks," Lane grumbled under his breath and kept walking.

"The Lane will save the day," Max said with a chortle. The look on his pale face was one of delight. Astan originally had suggested that Max stay behind, but Lane insisted he did not travel without his trusty imp sidekick.

"The rest of us may contribute, too," Beckley said with a bit of annoyance.

"Friends, it takes a village," Lane said, leaving them both looking a little puzzled.

Astan sent word through the ranks that they had reached the compound. He divided the group into two teams, a semi-elite group of fifteen that would accompany Lane to the clearing in hopes of encountering Bartolomey, and the rest planned to overrun the remainder of the occupied space, certainly outnumbering those who remained, hopefully able to subdue them without excessive loss of life.

Lane had his eyes on only one prize, the destruction of Black Bart.

The groups split. Vez and Daven led their group to the place where Bartolomey could be found, Astan traveling close with them, a situation Lane found hard to believe. Elves carried a different sense of values, that much was true. Some magic ooga-booga stuff and the drop of a hat or two, and they seemed to be able to set aside hatred and history to be together as if they never parted. Lane would never have been able to do that with the mother he had grown to hate over the years. She was gone, and he was glad. But what an empty hole it left in his life.

No time for that now. Concentrate.

Daven dropped back to confer. "How far away can the machine be to be effective?"

"Dunno exactly. We've tried a hundred feet or so and it's worked fine." Still not in perfect condition, Lane breathed hard while the pace of their move through the woods caught up with him. "I'd guess we could even try half again or that much." He grinned. "Hell, Daven. It's magic. Guess as long as I believe it'll work, it will, right?"

Daven smiled back, clapping him on the shoulder again. "Exactly right. Please, set up the machine wherever you feel it will be protected. We couldn't afford to lose the projection."

"Sure thing," Lane said.

As Daven walked away, Lane had a nagging feeling that he had just been handled. Or helped. Possibly whammied.

"Damn it," he muttered.

It didn't matter, though. At this point, it was all in pursuit of the cause, and Lane needed all the help he could get.

Xiomar, on the other hand, just kicked ass. And anything else he could reach.

Lane and Max scouted around, finally locating a spot under a tree trunk that had started to pull out of the ground, leaving some bare soil exposed, but mostly under cover. Lane crouched down and dug out a space for the laptop, making sure the bottom of it was in full contact with the earth, a position Max assured him would make for the strongest magic transfer. Once the computer was secure, he called up the game frame to release Xiomar.

Seconds later, a collective gasp let Lane know his warlock alter ego had materialized. He chuckled, but heard the sound in Xiomar's deep baritone. Pushing himself upright, he studied the hulking green orc and raised his fist in the air, seeing his creation do the same.

"Victory!" he cried, and Xiomar's echo shook the trees around them.

"Victory indeed," Daven muttered, with a mysterious smile.

Astan stared, trepidation written on his face. Lane saw the same expression mirrored around the group. A wave of elation rushed through him.

Judge me by my size, do you? Well take that!

While his feelings ran hot, he decided it was best to forge

ahead. He reached out his mind to the form of Xiomar, planting himself firmly inside the monster's head. It changed his perception of the world, looking down on the others from probably a foot and a half higher, the strength in Xiomar's muscles that Lane had never owned, the sheer, sleek motion that was his as he lifted up one foot, set it down with a thump, and then the other.

Lane/Xiomar headed for the clearing, ready to do battle.

Six traveled forward with Xiomar, including Astan, Beckley and Max. Their task was to take care of any other elves who might try to interfere. The rest stayed in the woods to protect the computer and Lane himself from attack while he was engaged with Bartolomey. His companions took cover in the woods around the clearing, spreading out so they had access from all angles.

"I summon Bartolomey, the scum of the earth, the bane of the winds, the poisoner of the water, the false god of the fire!" Lane/Xiomar roared. "Show yourself and receive your just punishment!"

Damn, that sounded cool. Being a badass was seriously awesome.

Lane tried not to giggle. That would be such a break in character.

He waited for several minutes. Nothing happened. He stomped a little further into the open space. "Don't tell me the great Bartolomey is a coward. I thought I would have a worthy adversary at last. Is there no one who can face me?"

Movement at the far side of the clearing caught his eye.

A single elf emerged. Yadin, who had once been one of Astan's friends, carried a sword, only half the size of the one Xiomar waved defiantly in the air.

This was war. Lane tried to put himself into the mental mindset of the game. The goal was to take down the boss. If he needed to take down a couple of elves to get Bartolomey on the field he could do that. Whatever it took to score, he could do.

"Ha!" the elf cried. "I heard about you from Hidal. You're nothing but smoke and a lot of talk!" Yadin moved to the middle of the clearing and stopped.

"Is that so?" Xiomar bellowed. "See if that's what your dark Master tells you!" He moved forward, Lane almost feeling his breath expand and contract along with the barrel-chested orc. He knew the others watched, ready to intervene, but he would handle this one.

"I'm not afraid of you!" Yadin stood his ground, sword at the ready.

"Your error, friend."

This is it.

Lane sent Xiomar crashing forward, his huge sword in hand. The elf weighed maybe a third of what the orc did. He would make quick work of the skinny punk. Xiomar swung the sword at Yadin. Metal found metal with a loud clang.

At the first solid contact, Yadin's face registered shock and surprise. Lane did not slow down. Instinct took over. He beat Yadin back with his attack, their swords meeting in a symphony of sound that resonated through the nearby trees. Yadin broke off first, jumping back, breathing hard. Then he vanished.

"What the—"

Xiomar floundered a moment and took some empty swings into the air around him. Really? He had drawn the only elf who could be invisible? How was he going to defeat that?

Yadin would have to reveal himself. All Lane/Xiomar needed was a little patience.

Xiomar paced in the clearing, not letting down his guard. Every so often he would take a swing or a stab, hoping to connect with the invisible one. "Is there no one else, no other champion to face me?"

"Can't you find me?" Yadin asked off to Xiomar's right.

Xiomar went in that direction, hoping he would at least trip over the fool. But he found nothing. An eerie laugh came out of nowhere.

Frustrated, Xiomar returned to the center of the open space, setting his senses on high. Too bad he could not make the sky rain flour or something, so that he could catch a glimpse of the elf who taunted him. Or snow, so there would be footprints.

No, the elves were not heavy enough to leave prints, he

reminded himself. What else could Xiomar do? If his enemy was in stealth mode, he could what? Use Howl of Terror, but that would scare all his buddies, too. What else? Shadow Fury would stun everyone within thirty feet. That might do it. But he did not want to risk hurting his team. He could wait out Yadin if he must, or a dozen others if they came.

Why didn't others come? That was suspicious in itself.

Perhaps they fought those who attacked Bart's compound, battling tooth and nail for the right to choose their leader. But even Lane brought companions with him. Why would Yadin come alone?

"Bartolomey, I grow weary of these games," Xiomar roared. "Don't waste my time with minions. I know you're here. Show yourself."

Step-by-step, he turned and watched for a sign.

Suddenly the tip of a sword protruded from the front of Xiomar's abdomen. With a frown, he yanked the sword all the way through and out the front. The blade had no effect on his form, as he was only a projection. He tossed the sword aside and swung his left hand wide, releasing a bolt of black fire in the direction from which the attack had originated.

The spell hit Yadin, making him visible as he sailed halfway across the clearing. With a crunch, he landed in a heap, his neck twisted at an odd angle.

"You did it!" Max burst into the glade, running across to Xiomar. "I knew you'd find him. I can't believe you didn't see him. He was right there all the—" Max halted mid-sentence with his eyes now wide open.

"Max?" Xiomar shook his shoulder. "What's the matter?"

Max did not answer. Instead, he ran toward the far side of the clearing.

"Max?"

Still nothing. A pillar of fire appeared in Max's path, the flames shooting some twelve feet high. Max headed straight for it, walking as if he were in a dream.

"Max!" Xiomar's long steps easily intercepted the elf, placing himself between Max and the fire.

The motion seemed to break the spell. Max stopped and looked a little more like himself.

With a start Xiomar realized where the blaze was coming from. He was face to face with the essence of Bartolomey.

"Now you die, you bastard," he said, stepping toward the evil. Xiomar gathered his energy and winged a ball of black flame at the dark mage.

The energy collided with Bartolomey's essence. Fire splayed in all directions. Then errant flames were sucked upward into a shower of angry red sparks that swirled like the body of a fervid dust devil, singeing the branches overhead. The rotating cloud tore across the ground, pulling rocks from the crust. Stones flew inside the funnel, changing slowly from gray to violent orange.

Too late Lane realized what Bartolomey intended. The mage sent all those rocks flying in his direction.

Even though Xiomar might not feel the physical impact, the enchantment that infused the stones tore large holes in the magic manifestation of the orc's body, shaking Lane's ability to control him for several long seconds.

Unfortunately, Bartolomey noticed.

"What sort of deception is this?" Bartolomey purred. "Daven Talvi, you expose yourself as the novice I expected. For shame. You risk your hold on the clan for this petty ruse?"

"Petty, am I?" Xiomar roared, charging the dark mage, his sword drawn. He slashed at the cloud for all he was worth, wanting nothing more than to obliterate this son-of-a bitch. Where the blade penetrated the vortex, it pixilated, practically dissolving in Xiomar's hand.

"Petty and pathetic." Bartolomey's laugh deepened until it filled the clearing, echoing off the trees. "Daven, stop hiding behind these tricks. Face me like a mage."

Lane felt himself slip from behind Xiomar's eyes. He shook his laptop, trying to get the mojo restarted. When the two synched again, he geared up to send Xiomar after Bartolomey.

But little Max had returned to the open space. "This is not of Daven Talvi's doing. Only The Lane can project such magic." He crossed his arms in defiance. "You noob."

"Max, get the hell out of the way," Xiomar growled.

"What? Oh!" Max's wide-eyed stare showed that he finally realized the danger. He tried to run, but was too close. Bartolomey took hold of him again.

Lane struggled to hold Xiomar together, his mind whizzing at high speed, scrambling for options. If the battle continued much longer, Lane did not know if he could maintain the manifestation of the warlock in the face of Bartolomey's magic. For the first time he considered the real possibility of failure.

Cannot happen. Daven whammied me. I have the magic. I have the will. I will do this.

Bartolomey's shadowy form now held Max in its hands. Lane felt sick. He had let his attention slip, just when it was most important.

"The Lane, is it? One of my dear niece's human friends? I'm impressed. But you see, I can't let that stand. Magic doesn't belong in the hands of those inferior to the elves. They just don't know how to handle it." Bartolomey's appearance changed into something smoky, something vaguely elf-shaped, though taller, maybe some eight feet high.

"Oh, yeah? I can handle you, creep." Xiomar went to move forward, but Bart held up Max who struggled and tried to strike back at the ephemeral mage.

"This one is important to you?" Bartolomey rumbled.

Xiomar should have protected Max. "Put him down!"

"I think it only fair. What do you call these? Minions? A trade, yours for mine."

Bartolomey jolted Max through with some sort of electrical current that made him shake and jitter. Then Max went limp. The dark mage tossed him aside like garbage.

"No!" Xiomar roared.

He launched himself at Bartolomey's form, punching and swinging and dropping every form of darkness he could think of on the evil elf. Bartolomey fought back at first, but Xiomar did not let up. He pounded the mage, letting the frustration of being weak and helpless for all those years build up inside him and push right through his fists.

When he finally stopped, all that was left on the ground was a small pile of blood and ashes. Xiomar looked down at the ash, his expression dispassionate.

He turned away and rushed to Max's side. With bloody hands, he picked up the small elf as carefully as he could.

"Healer," Xiomar croaked.

Astan came out of the woods at a run, approaching Xiomar with some hesitation. "Put him down," he said.

Xiomar complied. Lane's control on the warlock flickered and he nearly pulled back into his human self. Until the others began to shout.

"Watch out, Astan! Behind you!"

Xiomar and Astan turned around, both of them fixated on Yadin, upright once again and going for the sword Xiomar had taken from him. He walked in an odd, jerky fashion. When he turned to face them, they could see dark glowing eyes.

"That's not Yadin," Vez called from the woods.

"No," Astan confirmed. "That isn't. I need time to work with Max." He bent down, at his healing once more, as the others came out of the woods, weapons in hand. Xiomar held his ground in front of them, keeping Bartolomey's zombie at bay.

"You're brave, Vez, when you're hiding with your tail between your legs," the zombie called. He tried to get around Xiomar, but constant movement of the orc frustrated his effort.

"Vez has served the clan well today," Daven said, stepping into the clearing, splitting Bartolomey's attention. "He has no need to expose himself to you."

"We have no need of you, Daven Talvi." The Yadin-thing tossed a sharpened metal wheel in Daven's direction. Xiomar lunged for it, trying to divert the weapon, but Daven beat him to it. The metal thing flew off at a sharp angle, sinking deep into a tree trunk.

"Watch Astan," Daven warned.

Xiomar, chastened, moved back to a protective position.

Yadin's attention wandered, and he took a step in Max's direction.

"You don't scare me any more, old man," Vez yelled out

from his hidden position.

Bartolomey marched Yadin's body in a little circle, ending with a jerky salute. "It should have been you, pup," the zombie said to Vez. "Your brain would have been no loss to the clan."

Vez stepped out of the woods, entering the edge of the clearing a good distance to Daven's right. "I'll let the clan be the judge of that."

Astan helped Max to his feet and handed him off to one of the Sleepers with them. "Get him out of here," Astan said. He turned to Bartolomey/Yadin. "Let's end this."

"End it? Let's see, one of me against what? Four and one fading apparition? I think that might be fair." Yadin swayed.

"Except you forget, Bartolomey," Daven warned. "When you take another's form, you take his vulnerabilities."

"Daven's right," Astan said. "Yadin is gone. That is only a monster. Finish it."

The rain of arrows and daggers that flew at what remained of Yadin was astounding. Each one made the body stagger just a little.

Daven stepped forward, filling the air with an elven chant of protection. No other body there would host the evil one.

Bleeding from a hundred places, Yadin's body tumbled to the ground, but soon the bleeding stopped.

Well, that was done. Relieved, Lane shut the laptop and entered the clearing, the weary looks on the faces of the others surely the same as his own.

"How's Max?" he asked Astan.

"He'll be all right," Astan replied. "Even Bartolomey can't shake a spirit so strong."

As if summoned, Max skittered out from the cover of the trees. "I knew The Lane could not be vanquished." His face was lit with fan-boy zeal.

Lane managed a tired smile. "Right."

"So is it time for the celebration of the cupcakes yet?" Max asked.

"Oh, hell yeah," Lane said, but his voice faltered as his eye caught movement over Daven's shoulder. A small cloud of gray particles rose from the body on the ground, vibrated in place as though trying to coalesce once again, hardly two yards away.

What the hell was wrong with this evil? What did it take to kill him?

Lane stood there a moment with his laptop, waiting for one of the others to do something. But he was closest. All that magic in his hands. What could he do?

It came to him almost without conscious thought. He opened the laptop, lunged for the cloud, and slammed the laptop closed on it. "BSOD!" he shouted.

He counted to seven, before opening the clamshell. The bits of mage hovered a second, before blowing apart in every direction. Then the world fell silent.

After a shocked moment, Daven turned to Lane. "BSOD?"

Lane grimaced. "Blue screen of death. It was the dirtiest thing I could think of."

"Blue screen of death." Daven just stared at him. "Right." His jaw shifted, his brow furrowed in thought. "But just for my own peace of mind, let me do this." He raised a hand to the sky. "Bartolomey, you have been permanently scattered to the winds. Neither the air, nor the water, nor the earth—" He glanced sidewise at Lane. "Or any device of man shall harbor your being again. Return no more!"

The words hung in the air as if written in neon letters, and then gradually faded. Daven turned to Lane. "Because you have destroyed Bartolomey, you have created another imbalance in the *Idellan.*"

"What? Are you kidding?" Lane sputtered. "Everything's messed up again?"

"Not at all. What is needed is balance. What better balance than the balance of elven mage and human technomage as an appropriate step into the new age?"

"Technomage?" Lane tucked the laptop under his arm again. His breaths coming hard and fast, emotion bubbling inside him, the fear he swallowed down, the tension, the thrill of success with Xiomar, so many feelings.

"Lane?" Astan approached him, tears in his eyes.

"Aren't we finished?" Lane asked.

"We are so finished." Astan's face flushed with satisfaction. "We couldn't have done it without you. Thank you." He held out his hand. "I welcome you to the clan."

Lane took Astan's hand almost automatically, feeling warm acceptance coming from the other elves around them. Even Max slipped in to hug him.

Shaken, Lane pulled away and stumbled to a nearby tree stump. His chest felt as if it would split open. Tears burned his eyes. He let them come, opened his heart and let himself release his long-held sorrow.

It was he who finally finished off the evil one who had hurt so many of the people he loved. And it was he who saved Max. After all these years, he found the family he always longed for.

There had been enough pain and enough pretending there wasn't. Now it was time for healing.

* * *

DAVEN knew it would not be long until Veraena showed up.

He was right.

She appeared in the middle of the clearing in a halo of fire, giving credence to the nickname the Youngers had given her, Firefly. Fueled by passion, hate for him, love of the fallen mage, he could not guess which, she glowed with the depth of her emotion. She surveyed the scene, prepared to let loose on any victim she could find.

Daven shed his cloak in a burst of white light.

When she saw him, she came straight for him, half suspended in the air, small flickers of flame trailing behind her. "What have you done?" she cried.

"What needed to be done, Veraena. We could no longer allow the balance to be in jeopardy." Daven adjusted his position, checking the landscape around him. He instructed the others to move to a safe location in the event it came down to a fight between himself and Veraena. Most of them complied. He caught a glimpse of Astan's anxious face on one side of the clearing.

Astan, this isn't your battle. Don't interfere.

Veraena's eyes burned with the same intensity he noticed in the *santwarja*. She would not hold back, not when there was a chance to have it all. For her it was now, or never.

"So you let the human finish off Bartolomey." There was mockery in her voice and her expression. "What a gutless jellyfish you are."

Daven did not take the bait. "Veraena, it's over."

"It's just beginning!" Her feet touched down and she walked around him in a circle. "The balance is off again, my love." A calculating look crossed her face. "I intended to end Bartolomey anyway and take his power for myself. It was also my intention for our son Vez to do the killing, gaining Bartolomey's strength for his own. But no, Astan managed to ruin that plan with all his cowardly 'heal the clan' garbage."

Her eyes searched the surrounding area until she pinpointed Astan's location. "He always was your son. After you decided to Sleep, he asked for you incessantly. Everything was 'Father, Father, Father'. It made me sick."

Daven took in the words, even though they were offered for the purpose of hurting him. He listened, and he owned the fact that he had inflicted pain on both of them, Veraena and Astan. He accepted this fact months ago in the cave. The words could not harm him any longer.

"Veraena, it's not too late for you to return. Your sons would welcome you."

"It's much too late!" Her eyes flashed, and she practically spat fire. Her hands came up from her sides and she showered him with a hot blast of sparks.

Daven tried to deflect them, still hoping he could get by without hurting her. After their last encounter, he suspected he would have no choice.

"Veraena." Daven lifted his hand and pushed her away from him, out of reach.

She slid across the ground into the dirt. When she stopped, she growled and leapt to her feet. "Don't you patronize me!"

She glanced up and circled her hand in the air, pointing to a set of branches on the pine tree overhead. They snapped off and crashed down on the spot where Daven stood.

Astan reached for his father and yanked him aside. Daven could sense the trained response to guard his father overwhelming even Astan's desire for self-preservation. The branches only hit Daven a glancing blow on the shoulder, but they still hurt. He remained upright, though he stumbled.

"Don't make this choice," Daven said.

He wound a bundle of energy in his right hand and then released it on Veraena. She jerked and twitched for a moment, her eyes unfocused. He wished he could send her miles away or even to another plane. Maybe she would decide she was better off and stay there.

But he wasn't that fortunate.

She stared at him a long minute, as time seemed suspended, the silence engulfing them both. His attention focused on those eyes, eyes that burned with passion. What was she doing?

A few seconds later, he realized his clothing was smoking.

"Anhelda!" Daven cried.

A shower of ice materialized above him, melting over him like a rain shower, the chill stopping the burn. He should have known better. She could not be trusted.

With a scream of frustration, Veraena threw herself on him, knocking him from his feet. They rolled together the length of an elf into a soft patch of wet ground. She grabbed his jacket and held him so close he could feel her breath on his cheek.

Her face close to his, she looked deep into his eyes, into his heart, her gaze hard to decipher. *You know, Daven, there is still a chance, but not the one you think. We could rule, you and I. While the balance is off, we could start again. Remember how it was?* She projected into his mind some of their first days in magic training, happy times when he almost thought he could love her instead of Linnea, when he almost allowed her in. *I could make you forget her now. We could be happy together.*

She pushed so hard that he almost succumbed. If they were together, he would not have to kill her. They could survive, and their sons could survive.

But the clan would die.

He read through her coquettish mental tone and into her heart, feeling there the absolute loathing she held for him. It was a trick. She never meant to love him again. He needed to confront her or surrender.

But he read something else there, the beginnings of doubt, of insecurity. She needed Bartolomey to make her strong. Could she continue without him? Daven did all he could to instill the answer to that question in the negative. He needed to deflect her ambition.

"No," Daven said aloud, pushing her away. "The balance is restored. The new world calls for a human presence in the mix."

She gave a blood-curdling screech that stabbed Daven to the core. "I'll kill you first!"

"Then kill me." He knelt in front of her. "If it takes my death to settle this, then so be it."

Her eyes widened, she seeming startled at his sudden capitulation. He looked up at her, hands at his sides. If one more death would bring peace to the clan, it would be a small price to pay. She reached for him, hesitant, suspicious, but he intended no resistance. When she realized this, she gathered her strength for a final blast.

"Mother, no!" Vez ran forward, still marked from his confrontation with Bartolomey. "Please, don't do this to us."

"So, you've decided to take your father's side in this?" Her voice dripped with disdain.

"No. No, not at all." Vez reached out to her. "We can't have sides any more. If we have 'sides', someone will have to win and someone will have to lose. The only way we all survive is to come together!"

"Vez is right," Astan said, walking up behind Daven. "Bartolomey is gone. For the first time since Ele and Lorenz ruled, the *Lelan* has a chance."

She looked from one to the other, to the faces of the others in the clearing. "But Daven ruined my chances! He ripped out my heart!"

Daven felt her drawing down power to end him, but he did not resist.

"He was wrong...Mother," Astan said, choking on the last word. "He can't bring back those years, but he can make up for it in other ways. If the clan is strong. Please." He held out his hand to her. "Put this chapter behind us. Be the clan's *Idan* of fire. Help us all live."

Daven sensed her hesitation and confusion. "The world has changed from those days, Veraena. Our greatest challenge is not each other, but the influx of human development around us, the pollution of the water and air. If our clan is whole, and balanced, we may make the world better. The balance for us is no longer marked by light and dark, but by those who share this new world, elf and human."

He gestured to Lane, who waited on the side with the others. "Here is our new brother mage, a wizard from the human community, who risked his life to bolster our world. A technomage, who brings his own gifts to the balance and opens the doors of communication with our brothers and sisters of the human persuasion."

Veraena looked at him as if he were speaking a foreign language, then her gaze moved to her sons before moving on to where the others stood. She drew her hands back from Daven and shoved them into the pockets of her feathery jacket.

"Don't fight us, Mother," Vez said. "We want to be a family. We need you."

"The alternative is to destroy you and send you where Bartolomey has gone," Astan added in a harsher tone. "You don't have to come home again. If you agree to a ceasefire, a truce, you will keep your status as the mage of fire and keep the balance."

Daven held his breath while Veraena wrestled with her conscience. No one spoke, everyone hanging on her decision.

"I can't fight you all," she said at last. "If this is what must be, then I will live with it."

"We will all live, and that is what matters," Daven said.

He stood and stepped aside, taking Lane and Max's hands in his. Max reached for Beckley's hand. The others circled around, Astan and Vez holding their mother's hand for the first time in years. Daven sent a little pulse of healing through his touch around the linked circle to the others.

"The war is over," Daven said.

CHAPTER 39

LANE studied his notes, finally satisfied that he covered everything.

He looked up with a smile. "That's it for today, folks."

Six people of assorted ages, military veterans gathered around the table in the back of Kevin's shop, sighed with relief and packed up their computers. Murmuring goodbyes, the beginning computer students shuffled out to enjoy the sunny July afternoon.

Kevin came into the back room, a stack of money in his hand. "Here's your half," he said, setting fifty dollars on the table next to Lane.

"Wow. I'm rich," Lane said. "Doesn't seem fair to take money from old people."

"You could give it back," Kevin said, holding out his hand.

"No, I don't think so." Lane pocketed the cash while he still had the chance. "Need before greed, my friend."

"I'm just glad you're teaching them. Nice to see you out of your place. You're almost human."

"Bite your tongue. It's much easier being a warlock." Lane packed his computer into its thick case, the one in which he had hidden little Elliun in six months before. "I kinda miss it."

A buzzer sounded in the shop part of his storefront, and Kevin peeked out. "Be with you in a minute," he said, before turning back to Lane. "You don't ever manifest Xiomar? Not even up in the woods?"

"No real need to, now that the elves are all huggy-feely again." Even as he spoke, he felt a pang of regret for the magic he had created. "Well, except for Max. He begs me every once in awhile. So, I have to. You know, just for Max." A sheepish grin crept onto his lips. "You hate to disappoint the kids."

"Right. The kids." Kevin laughed and stepped out to wait on his customer.

Lane tucked his bag strap onto his shoulder, giving Kevin a wave as he passed on his way to the front door. He took the stairs, hardly out of breath by the time he reached the top. He had almost gotten in the door when Grandpa Jerkface came out of his apartment, glaring at Lane.

"What's up, Tom?" Lane asked, hesitating on the doorstep.

"You didn't tell me it was your birthday last week." The old man inched forward, pulling a box about fifteen inches square from behind his back. The package was beautifully wrapped in blue foil, a layered white bow in the exact center of the lid, like a cake topper. "Here, take it."

Lane, stunned, reached for the box automatically as the old man jabbed it at him. "Tom, you didn't need to get me anything."

Tom's face split into a crooked and partly toothless grin. "You're like my sons, both of you hoodlums. Enjoy, all right?" Chuckling, he wandered back into his apartment and closed the door.

Lane stared at the box with disbelief as he continued inside. Sons? Who was he kidding? "Crisp, did you tell Grandpa Jerk— uh, Tom that it was my birthday?"

Crispy looked up from a map that covered the table. "I know what he got you, too," he said with a smug expression.

Lane set his case down in the Cave, and then rattled the box. The contents thumped heavily from side to side. "It better not be a dead thing."

Crispy rolled his eyes. "As if."

Lane listened to the box. "It's not ticking."

"Open it!"

"All right, all right." Lane tore the paper open, revealing a large shoe box. "Oh, no. Oh no, no, no."

"Oh, yes." Crispy clapped his hands.

"Holy mother of crunchy termites," Lane said. He opened the box to find a sturdy pair of hiking boots. "What are these for?"

"These boots are made for walking."

Lane shot him a look, but the smirk on Crispy's face didn't fade one bit. "Funny."

"Come on, Lane. You know you can't wear those old rotting tennis shoes out in the woods forever. These will be great."

Lane studied the boots, recognizing the brand name as an expensive one. "How could he afford these?"

"He said after he met Astan, he started feeling better. He actually got a job down at the department mart. I think he gets a big discount."

"Well, he really shouldn't have." Lane wanted to feel guilty, but somehow he just couldn't make himself. Crispy was right. He did need shoes that would hold up in the mountains of the Bitterroot. As the first and only technomage of the elf clan, he surely must evidence his magnanimity by visiting his people every so often. It was the least The Lane could do.

"All right," Lane conceded. "But we're buying him pizza next week."

"Get the Pompeii pizza from Biga's. It has spinach to make you strong." Crispy went back to his map.

"What are you looking at, anyway?" Lane peered over Crispy's shoulder. "That's Glacier."

"Yeah. I thought maybe we'd go camping."

Lane raised an eyebrow. "Out in the wild?"

"Sure. We've got to cut the cord some time."

Lane knew Crispy was referring to the high-speed Internet cable that ran into the Cave. With a twinge of dismay, he focused on the thought that the laptop still retained its magic. He should be able to access the Interwebz from the woods. Maybe even play the game. What else would you do, when you were out in nature? "I'll let Jelly Bean know we're coming her way."

Crispy gave an absent nod and continued his perusal of the map.

Lane smiled and sat down in the Cave, checking each of his screens as the screensavers flickered off. Nothing hot in the emails, everything calm at last. He leaned back in his chair and opened a package of Creamy Cupcakes.

Yep, everything was just as it was meant to be.

* * *

"ASTAN, Iris awaits."

Daven took a deep breath, trying to infuse himself with calm, while Jelani buzzed around her living area, gathering toys to put in her travel sack. He could not see what Astan was doing, but he had Elliun in the back room. Maybe changing his clothing. Again.

"He's only going to play with some of the other children. He doesn't need much, Jelani. He will be completely entertained without all those plastic baubles."

The mild scolding had no effect on her. "I just want to make sure he has it in case he needs it, Daven. Remember, you promised to quit telling me how to parent." She walked past him, turning just enough to the side that he could see the slightly rounded hump of her belly under the front of her flowing green dress.

She became pregnant of her own volition this time, shortly after the battle of the clearing. "We've got to grab the good times before they pass us by. I feel secure in this decision. I will set the example for the rest of the clan."

And she did just that. At her direction, his son Vez was welcomed into the clan, his sins against them forgiven. His heart cleansed by the fire they passed through. Vez set up a home with Fontine in a proper elven bower. And they also were expecting a child in the season to come.

"What's the rush, anyway?" Jelani asked. "Does Iris have somewhere to be?"

"She set counseling hours in her office this afternoon."

Daven appreciated the effort Iris made to balance her life. She spent half her time with him and the clan on the mountain, carrying through on her vow to help the clan work through the rough relationships left by the war and its aftermath.

And making me feel like the king of the world.

The rest of the time Iris helped her human clients in an office she opened for herself, giving up her work for the county agency that had brought her to Lane and Crispy in the beginning. Her financial needs were covered by her private clients. Her personal needs were met by her new family in the clan.

"She's so good," Jelani said, stopping her constant motion for just long enough to share a smile. "Where would we all be without her?"

"Precisely."

Daven felt his heart fill with warmth as Astan came in with Elliun in his arms. The baby, strong and ahead of the human growth curve, as befitted his elven genetics, squirmed to be set down. Once his feet hit the floor, he ran to Daven. The proud grandfather scooped him up and tossed him four feet into the air, and then allowed him to float slowly into Daven's waiting hands.

"No need to show off, Father," Astan rebuked him.

"Will you both relax?" Daven asked, stung by their need to correct him. Not like he had never had a child. "But keep hurrying."

Astan helped Jelani gather everything else she needed to take, his eyes always watchful to anticipate her. Astan was a wonderful guardian for this young queen. Both of them were growing into their roles admirably. Once again the clan was balanced together at last, with their leaders, mages, and queen.

Daven helped in healing the rift with each of his sons during the months since the war. At last he felt properly connected to the clan now that he was in his appropriate place. The path they had traveled was as rocky as any on the Monida Pass, but they kept working, along with Iris' careful tutelage and guidance, until they were reconciled.

The little family finally joined him on the doorstep, and then they left the tree house.

Daven offered to reduce it to the size it was before Lane, Crispy, and Iris had stayed with her, but Jelani insisted she liked the extra room. It stayed.

Elf children and others trailed along behind them as they made their way through the clan lands to the bower where Daven and Iris lived. It was an unpretentious spot between several strong Douglas firs, all of it firmly on the ground, at Iris' insistence. Daven charmed the walls to be opaque at all times, allowing the couple their privacy. Jelani and Astan both carried on conversations with their entourage, happy and smiling in a way Daven never noticed during all the months the queen resided with the clan.

He stepped aside to let them enter the bower, all of them following the queen inside, finding places to sit, friends to greet.

Delighted to see them, Iris moved through the gathered group, bringing them refreshments, the perfect hostess. "We'll start as soon as they get here," she said.

I am a lucky nian. Very lucky.

Some small sense of discord pulled at the corner of Daven's mind. The mental alert drew him aside, sent his gaze searching among the trees. Where was it, that hint of threat? The longer he looked, the bigger the knot of worry that clutched his stomach.

Then he saw her.

Veraena pulled back when he spied her. She watched from a tree branch on the edge of the clan lands, not moving, not threatening in any way. Her clothing blended into the natural colors of the forest. He would not have known she was there at all without that small vibration of magic that accompanied her. No doubt how she found him, as well.

Vez and Fontine walked up through the clan lands toward Daven, hand in hand. Daven touched Vez's shoulder in reassurance as they passed him, not giving him any sign of Veraena's presence. It was not the first time she had appeared, but each time was the same. She stayed until she was noticed, never coming in to actually speak with any of them. The healing Daven initiated among them had gone only so far, allowing Veraena to function as the clan's mage, loosely connected to them, taking strength from and contributing to the healthy energy of the balanced group.

Veraena avoided Daven. This was the only contact she allowed, entirely at her discretion and control. She would come, almost as though she only meant to check on them, to make sure everyone was all right.

Or to see if we've passed over, more likely.

The noise inside picked up as Beckley and Elorra joined the party. Daven looked up again and Veraena was gone. No matter.

She came around often enough to keep her pledge to support the clan as their mage. That was all he could expect from her. Maybe someday she would feel comfortable enough to join them, to take her place as their children's mother and Elliun's grandmother.

She and I missed our chance. I can regret that, without diminishing my love for Iris in the least. But she still has a family to share her life, if she would only reach out for them.

Daven straightened his shoulders. He must live now, not in some fantasy time in the future. He had come full circle, from an elf desperately desiring something he could never be to the status of *Intalus,* who with the queen kept the clan in balance and in tune with the cycle of life. Everything would be well now.

Taking one last look, he went inside to the party for Beckley and Elorra. It was what Iris called a 'shower'. He tried to understand how she would make the rain happen indoors, but finally decided to wait and see.

These humans had unusual ways of looking at things. He thought of Lane and smiled to himself. Unusual, but sometimes they turned out fine.

Just fine, all the way around.

THE END

About the Author

Lyndi Alexander dreamed for many years of being a spaceship captain, but settled instead for inspired excursions into fictional places with fascinating companions from her imagination that she likes to share with others. She has been a published writer for over thirty years, including seven years as a reporter and editor at a newspaper in Homestead, Florida. Her list of publications is eclectic, from science fiction to romance to horror, from tech reporting to television reviews. Lyndi is married to an absent-minded computer geek. Together, they have a dozen computers, seven children and a full house in northwestern Pennsylvania.

* * *